BODY COUNT

A THRILLER

CAROLYN RIDDER ASPENSON

SEVERN RIVER
PUBLISHING

BODY COUNT

Copyright © 2022 Carolyn Ridder Aspenson.

All rights reserved.

No part of this book may be reproduced in any form or by any electronic or mechanical means, including information storage and retrieval systems, without written permission from the author, except for the use of brief quotations in a book review.

Severn River Publishing
www.SevernRiverBooks.com

This is a work of fiction. Names, characters, businesses, places, events and incidents are either the products of the author's imagination or used in a fictitious manner. Any resemblance to actual persons, living or dead, or actual events is purely coincidental.

ISBN: 978-1-64875-438-8 (Paperback)

ALSO BY CAROLYN RIDDER ASPENSON

The Rachel Ryder Thriller Series

Damaging Secrets

Hunted Girl

Overkill

Countdown

Body Count

Fatal Silence

Deadly Means

Final Fix

To find out more about Carolyn Ridder Aspenson and her books, visit severnriverbooks.com

For Erika, Morgan, and Justin

PROLOGUE

His work was his art. He planned each individual judgment to reflect the severity of the sin, but the final act, the inescapable send-off to hell, was a choice.

He'd finished with the women, for the time being, but the men would bring him great pleasure, and then, if the job was not finished, he'd continue.

The calculated and detailed process was all integral to gain the justice he sought. He'd mastered the art. Each detail given careful attention, practiced repeatedly and then executed perfectly and with extreme caution. No mistakes would be tolerated. Justice was too important to serve with risk of failure.

The anticipation and expectation of reaching the goal, of serving justice on evil, was exhilarating. Each judgment was carefully planned and executed, and the sweet pleasure from the outcome...it was all immensely satisfying. He relished in how the sinners' eyes begged for forgiveness, how they pleaded for a chance to change. But it was too late. His triumph was made more enjoyable by the frantic terror that washed over their faces as they understood their end was imminent, their chance to repent had passed. The time had come. They must pay for their sins.

Years of researching, watching, planning... It all came to a heated finale where he was finally allowed to rejoice in his success.

He was the Mastermind.

1

The sagging hog wire fence and a broken locked gate with a rusted *Private Property/No Trespassing* sign dangling from it surrounded the abandoned property. Other than trees on the outline of the perimeter, the land still faintly resembled a horse farm. The grass near the fence, dormant and brown for the winter, was filled with law enforcement and fire personnel, giving no indication it was once a well-maintained equestrian farm stocked full of retired racehorses. In the distance, I spied the deserted and decaying stable, its once-vibrant wooden structure partially collapsed from years of neglect, burning in a red-and-yellow flaming inferno. For half a second, I stared at the stables and imagined what we'd find, then steeled myself to expect the unexpected. Because dead bodies always brought the unexpected.

I trotted back to my Jeep and slipped out of my boots as I unlatched and opened the back door. I'd just bought the pair of real-leather calf high heels, and the last thing I wanted was for them to get ruined from walking through a burned building and a crime scene. I stuffed each foot into a Doc Martens boot; more comfortable, and most certainly more durable than my heeled office-only boots. I preferred my standard work boots, but I'd been unable to find a decent quality pair anywhere in over a year.

My partner stepped up beside me and tapped my foot with his. "Why don't you just wear these all the time?"

"Because I can feel the judgment of half the department beating into my flesh when I wear less feminine attire." It was hard to not smile when I said that, even though it was true.

"You still think you're being judged? After all this time?"

I shrugged. "Judging is constant and continuous. Some just notice it more than others."

He smiled. "Maybe some are just more paranoid than others."

"Also, the work boots I normally buy are out of stock everywhere."

He rolled his eyes. "You could have led with that."

"But it's fun watching you get your undies all up in a bunch."

"You're spending far too much time with Savannah. Using Southern phrases with that Chicago accent sounds so wrong."

"But it's growing on you. Admit it," I said.

"Not in the least."

Rob Bishop and I had been partners for a few years running. In the beginning, we'd hit every bump in the road toward trust but it eventually came. Since then, we'd developed a routine, and part of that included how we handled death scenes.

There were three kinds of cops. The kind that showed no emotion at any crime scene, the kind that threw up at a murder scene, and the kind like Bishop and me, who joked and kept it light. If we didn't, the dark would creep into our souls, and we couldn't do our job.

Those who knew us understood, but some others thought we acted in poor taste. Those others hadn't seen what I'd seen, and they didn't know the dark places a mind could go. I did, and Bishop was just a few steps behind me. I knew from the call, the scene would require a whole lot of release; thus, snark.

I closed the Jeep's back and stared at my partner's feet. Noticing his shoes looked freshly shined, I pointed toward the burning stable and said, "You obviously haven't been up there yet."

He shook his head. "Figured I'd wait for you."

"Aw, you're scared. That's sweet."

"Yeah, that's it." He zipped up his heavy winter jacket. "I waited because

I'm freezing my ass off, and I knew you'd want to go over everything with me, so I decided to sit in my warm vehicle and prepare for our titillating repertoire that's always present as we hit a crime scene."

"Is that what we're calling it?"

"I thought it was witty." He shivered as he hugged himself. "Why is it so cold? It's never this cold in Georgia."

I laughed. I'd moved from Chicago a few years before and had been grateful for the warmer winters from the start. I held open the sides of my light black leather jacket. "Don't be a wuss. You can complain when your nose hairs freeze."

He leaned against the back of my Jeep. "Does that really happen?"

I nodded. "And it isn't fun." I squatted down and heaved my bag over my shoulder, groaning in the process.

"You don't need your purse at a crime scene."

"It's not a purse. It's my cop stuff."

He laughed. Patting his belt, he said, "This is all the cop stuff I need."

"Whatever," I said. "Let's go."

We walked up toward the stables as the sun set through the clouds in front of us.

"It's kind of pretty, the way the flames give the sky a golden-red hue," he said.

"Yes, I'm sure the firefighters stop and admire the beauty of the flaming destruction to decide whether it's okay to put out the fire."

He ignored my saltiness and pointed to the smoke rising toward the clouds. "Look at that." He eyed the flames engulfing the building next. "That thing went up like a dead tree." He shook his head in disbelief. "I just drove by here the other day. Can't believe the old stable is going out like this in a blaze of glory."

"I see what you did there."

"What did I do?" he asked.

"'Blaze of Glory'? The Kenny Rogers song? You used it on purpose."

"I'm surprised you know that song."

"My mother loves country music. I listened to Kenny Rogers under duress all the time," I said.

"Kenny's awesome, or was before he died. You don't like him?"

"If I'm going to listen to eighties country, which I do on occasion, it's stuff like Waylon and Willie," I said.

"Impressive. Back to the fire," he said. "It's just sad. The stable's been around forever. Hate to see it go in—"

"I know, a blaze of glory." The fire was tragic, and we were on the same page about that.

"What would you prefer, a bulldozer?"

"I'd prefer it was designated a historical building and be rehabbed."

"Looks like that's no longer an option," I said.

"How'd you guess?"

I shrugged. "Female intuition is incredible."

He looked at me and rolled his eyes. He did that a lot around me. "Yes, that's it."

I smiled. "We're here because there's a body on scene. I'm guessing the fire wasn't accidental."

"Safe assumption." He sighed. "It's almost Christmas. The victim's family will never be the same again, especially around the holiday."

Crimes usually increased during the holidays. Depression, loneliness, anxiety, lack of cash; all of that contributed to the rise, but Bishop knew that. He was just venting. He loved his town, and he hated to see anything bad happen. That always struck me as odd, given he was a cop and spent most of his time dealing with bad things. But when things happened around the holidays, especially finding a dead body at a fire, he was exceptionally frustrated. Bishop believed the world could be better and the simple things went a long way in getting it there. Like, say, not committing murder right before a big holiday.

I believed the opposite. I believed the world was only getting worse and all we could do was slow the pace to the inevitable complete demise of morals and ethics.

Fire Chief Hal Pickens walked over and removed his large red fighterfighter's hat and offered us a sad smile. "Looks like we've got a long night ahead of us."

"Merry frickin' Christmas," Bishop said.

"I feel ya," Pickens said. "But there isn't much we can do about it now."

"What've we got?" I asked. I zipped up my leather jacket. It was windy and cold, even with the fire burning nearby, but I didn't want my clothes getting covered in ash, and I definitely didn't want Bishop giving me a hard time for being chilled and therefore a hypocrite.

"It's good. Looks like someone took a skinner to the guy's neck." He shook his head. "Can't imagine that felt good."

My eyes widened. "Probably not."

Bishop groaned. "Guess I won't be eating dinner tonight."

I checked my watch. "It's already past five. We won't be out of here for another three, four hours."

"I mean because of the mental image I got from his description, not the time."

"Sorry about that," Pickens said. "Come on. I'll walk y'all over to the body. There's something y'all need to see."

I didn't bother asking what it was. If Pickens wanted to provide further details, he would have. "Appreciate it," I said.

He maneuvered us through the crowd of law enforcement and fire department personnel, stopping briefly to answer questions from his team.

The scene belonged to the fire department since they were called to the fire. We were required to assist, and happy to do so, but they were in charge, and we followed their lead. Since the department received a 911 call on the fire, they arrived two minutes prior to our closest patrol. When they arrived, as they had moved to put out the fire, they found the victim. They notified the officer on patrol, who notified dispatch, and it made its way to us.

Procedure required fire to handle the scene as long as necessary for them to do their job, but their job included more than just putting out the fire, and with the discovery of a deceased person, their job became more important. Investigate the cause of the fire, search the scene for evidence related to the cause, determine the starting point of the fire; their job was complicated and different from the police's, but often more important. Without their investigation, it was virtually impossible for us to find our mark. Our job was to work alongside them until they finished their job, and that could take days.

I hoped that wasn't the case. I glanced at Bishop. His skin looked a little green. "You all right?"

"I was planning on a venison steak tonight, but I'm not feeling it now."

The scene wasn't pretty.

"Well, hell," Bishop said. "At least he's not burnt to a crisp."

"Agreed," Pickens said. "Not the way I'd want to go, though, that's for sure. Stick me in my recliner, cold beer in my hand and a good movie on the tube, then let me fall asleep to my death. That's all I'm asking."

"Keep the dream alive," I said.

The body sat propped up against an old oak tree, and the tree immediately brought me back to my preteen years. Jenny and I would sit in her front room and listen to her grandfather's Tony Orlando and Dawn albums, thinking we were rocking out to some classic rock. Little did we know, classic rock for the mid-nineties was Led Zeppelin, not Tony Orlando and Dawn or Barry Manilow.

"No yellow ribbon?" I asked.

Pickens stared at me with a confused look on his face. "Excuse me?"

Bishop hummed the chorus to the song. "She's talking about that song, 'Tie a Yellow Ribbon'—great."

"What?" I asked.

"That's going to be stuck in my head all day."

I chuckled. "It's called an earworm, and you're welcome. Oh, and it's better than 'Blaze of Glory.'"

"I like that song," Pickens said. He laughed, but when he glanced down at the body, he stopped. "That's what I was talking about earlier," he said. He pointed to a plastic baggie stuffed in the man's hand.

I got on my radio and asked for immediate assistance from crime scene tech. "We need an assist with the camera, please."

Nikki responded, "Ten-four, Detective. ETA: five minutes."

"Ten-four," I responded. I grabbed a pair of powder-free gloves from my not-purse and slipped them on.

"Can I borrow a pair?" Bishop asked.

I glanced at his belt. "Aren't they on there?"

He grimaced.

Pickens shook his head. "Y'all are hilarious." He already put his hat back on as we'd walked to the scene, but he positioned it lower on his head. "Best be getting back to work. I'll let y'all know what we find."

"Wait," I said. "Any word on what caused the fire?"

"Right now, all I can do is guess, and that's not in anyone's best interests. Our fire inspector is here, though, and once he's got a sec, I'll hook you up. He's going to want to move on this quickly. He doesn't like anything sitting on his books for too long."

"And we appreciate that," Bishop said.

"Chief," I said, "can you tell me why you think the fire was started?"

He pointed at the victim. "Seems to me someone wanted to get y'all here for him."

"We expected that," Bishop said.

"I'm heading back to the fire now," Pickens said. "Unless you need me?"

"Nope, we're good," I said.

"Thanks, Chief," Bishop added.

I crouched down and stared at the baggie in the dead man's hand. "Looks like it was put there after the fact."

"Everything looks like it was put here after the fact," Bishop said. "Almost looks like a clean scene."

"Did you notice there's no blood on his neck or clothing either?" The victim's clothing appeared to have been recently cleaned and pressed, his boots newly shined, and his body freshly showered. It wasn't normal in random murders, so my first thought was the doer knew the victim.

"Yup."

"There should be a little blood at least."

"Looks like we got ourselves a homicide."

"And if I was to guess, our unsub knew the victim."

"Passion killing. Power killing. Money, sex, drugs. It could be anything."

I groaned and did a poor imitation of a Southern accent. "We ain't getting out of here anytime soon."

"Nope. Should have brought donuts."

I laughed. "You've got an addiction."

"I'm good with that."

Dr. Barron, the county medical examiner, huffed his way over. He wore an N95 mask fitted perfectly to his face. He lifted it away from his mouth and said, "What have we got?"

"Dead guy and a fire," I said.

"Thanks, Ryder. You're extremely helpful."

"I do my best, Doc."

He removed the mask from his head completely. "I can't wear these things. Don't know why the wife thinks it'll help stop my snoring anyway. I can taste the smoke through the thing."

That said a lot about the mask, but it probably wasn't as fitted as it appeared.

"Pickens thinks the fire was started to bring us to the body," Bishop said. "And check out the vic's hand."

Barron snapped on a pair of gloves, crouched down, and studied the man's hand. "What the?"

I stopped him before he removed the baggie. "Wait. We need photos first." I glanced around.

"She have approval to film and photograph the scene yet?" Bishop asked.

"I assume she does. It's no different than any other fire we've worked before, right? Besides, Pickens didn't say no to photographs, and I don't know why he would."

"True," Bishop said.

"Your crime techs are at the front of the property," Barron said. "Use your cell phone. I've got fifteen pounds of pork loin in my Green Egg."

Barron was a good old boy, and even though he was intelligent and professional, his Southern accent came out when he got emotional. His Green Egg and pork loin obviously made him emotional.

Barron pressed his lips together as I dug my phone out and clicked away. "Okay," I said. "Go for it."

He gently removed the baggie—with a frustrated sigh directed at me—and groaned his way up from his knees. "My knees are too old for this." He handed Bishop the baggie.

Bishop held it up for me to take more photos. When I nodded an okay, he opened the baggie. Inside was an index card folded in half. He opened it up, read it, then showed it to us.

"Seven?" I asked. "What's the number seven—oh, hell."

"This isn't the first victim," Bishop said.

"That's what I'm afraid of," I said.

"Well, heck," Barron said. "My loins are going to burn."

Normally I would have had a witty retort for that, but I was too worried we had a serial killer on our hands.

2

"Let's wait before we go there," Bishop said.

He was right. We could assume, guess, and theorize all we wanted, but determining the official call would take more than a few minutes of any of that.

"Anyone check for ID?" Barron asked.

"Not that we're aware of," Bishop replied. He appeared to want to take lead, and I was fine with that. "But if you're going to move the body, let's finish with the photos beforehand, please."

Nikki rushed over. "I'm sorry. Stupid holiday traffic has all the crazies out right now. I got here late and had to get my gear, and then I got stuck up front dealing with other tech stuff." She smiled at Dr. Barron. "Oh, hey. I saw you arrive."

"I saw you too, Nikki. The wife says you're supposed to be coming by this evening. Guess that's not happening."

"Probably not." She glanced at the victim. "Oh, my. He looks interesting." She gasped. "No disrespect intended, of course."

"I don't think you can upset him," I said.

She covered her smile with her hand. "Let me just get some photos and you can get back to your thing, Doc."

Bishop and I also snapped photos of the victim and the immediate surroundings too. Not because we didn't trust Nikki. She'd proven to be as good as, if not sometimes better than, Ashley, and we trusted her completely. We just wanted our own pictures.

"If you need me, I'll be taking photos around the entire lot," Nikki said.

"Make sure to get photos of the firemen," I said as she headed toward what was left of the stables.

"Why?"

"Have you seen them?"

"Oh." She smiled. "Gotcha."

Bishop coughed.

"Sorry," I said, and dropped my head in fake shame.

"Thanks, Nik," he hollered.

"Anytime, Detective."

"All right, then, I don't want to dry up my loins, so I best be getting on with this," Barron said. He carefully moved the body to check the left back pocket. When it came up empty, he pushed himself up, climbed over the remains, then did the same careful movement on the other side. The body fell to the left. "Well, that wasn't what I was shooting for."

I smirked as Bishop hesitantly adjusted the body upright again.

Barron found the wallet and identified the man easily from the picture on his driver's license. "Jacob Ramsey. Twenty-two. Lived local." He handed Bishop the wallet. "Both of you see what I see, right?"

"If you mean the fact that there's no blood around the wound, yes," I said. "We've noticed that."

"And the crime scene appears to have been cleaned," Bishop added.

Barron pulled up the man's pants and lowered his socks. "You're incorrect. This isn't your crime scene. This man was killed somewhere else and moved here after livor mortis set in. The markings on his ankles don't correspond with his position. He's in rigor, but I suspect the cold temperature is contributing to that." He unzipped and unbuttoned the pants, flipped the body over again, then lowered them and the victim's underwear.

Bishop and I turned around to give the deceased some respect. Besides, no one liked watching a doctor take the temperature of a body that way. Especially Bishop.

"I'm done," Barron said. "You can breathe now, Rob. We'll take your temperature later."

I busted out laughing. Bishop? Not so much.

"Temperature suggests he's been dead for a while, but the cold air creates a problem for us. I'll give you a definitive time, or as best I can once I do the autopsy." He redid the man's pants, laid him gently on the ground, and stood. "Now, if there are no other victims, send this one to the morgue when you're through here, and I'll get to it once my loins are finished. If they aren't already overdone."

"Yes, sir," Bishop said.

"I'm sure your loins are perfect," I said. Bishop chuckled. I ignored him. "When will it be done?"

"They should be done soon. We're having people over early for the holiday, and when the wife wants my loins, she gets them."

Bishop laughed again. "I think she means when will you get to the autopsy."

Barron removed his gloves and stuffed them into a small evidence bag. "The wife will want me to visit with the guests and eat before I leave, so let's say around midnight. You coming?"

"To the party?" I asked. "Don't think so. We have a lot to do here."

"I meant the autopsy," he responded. "Wife wanted to invite you two, but Bishop said he had plans, and he said you wouldn't want to go without him."

"He said that?" I glanced at my partner, then back at Barron. "I'm capable of going places without him, but I had plans tonight also. We'll be at the autopsy."

I watched Bishop's Adam's apple move up and down as he swallowed hard. Bishop hated autopsies.

∼

"Who undresses a guy to kill him, then cleans him up and dresses him again?" Bubba asked.

Bubba worked tech for the Hamby PD and was a technology genius. He said his Indian parents considered him a failure because they wanted him to be a doctor, but he couldn't even dissect a frog in high school, so medicine wasn't an option. His expertise was more along the lines of hacking into the school computer system to change his grade, and thus, a genius was born.

"Someone who has a lot of time on his hands," Bishop said.

"Or someone who wants a clean crime scene," I said.

"Thought that was a given," Bishop replied.

"Just making sure," I said. "Bubba, can you please check NCIC for any victims with a number on a piece of paper nearby?"

"You want me to be that specific?"

"Start with that and see where it takes you. We need to know if the number means anything related to body count."

"Seems obvious, if you ask me," he said.

"A jury might disagree. If you get something, let me know."

"Will do." He ran his hand through his dark hair. It fell over his eyes, and he flicked it back. "Anything else?"

"Maybe. We're working on it," I said. "One of us will let you know."

Bishop agreed with Bubba, but only after he walked away. "Whoever did this had a reason."

I snapped photos of the victim. "He's young, clean cut, dressed well."

"We don't know if those are his clothes."

"Agreed, but they fit well, so either we've got a fashion diva for a killer, or he put back on the clothes the vic was wearing when they met, and like Barron said, he killed him, then dumped him here."

Bishop rubbed his jaw. It was clean shaven for the first time in months. I had a feeling I knew why, but I wasn't about to approach the subject. He crouched down, added his regular old-man groan to the process, and checked the man's shoes. "They fit." He removed a shoe and a sock and compared the wear and tear on the bottom of the shoe to the shape of the man's foot. "And it looks like they belong to him." He replaced the items and stood. "There's no way those jeans fit over the shoes, so our unsub had to remove them first."

"Which confirms our theory that the unsub undressed the victim and then killed him. It's kind of brilliant, if you think about it." I tapped a text to Bubba. *Check for redressed victims too, please.*

Bishop nodded once, still studying the victim. "Easiest way to keep evidence from the scene."

"Right."

"So, let's play this out. This guy gets his victim. Did he bring him somewhere to kill him, or did he go to the vic?"

"I'm going with he brought him somewhere. He can control the environment that way."

Bishop nodded again. "Did the guy go willingly?"

I squatted and examined the man's wrists. "His wrists look like they were bound at some point. We'll have Nikki check for any obvious evidence before they take the body." I called for Nikki on the radio.

"Why this guy?" Bishop asked. "What about him says he deserved to be killed?"

"Cop 101. Murder is rarely random, so we know there's a reason hidden in the facts somewhere."

"That's my point. You've got a clean-cut kid with his throat slit in the middle of an abandoned equestrian farm. These are the kind of guys my daughter dates."

"Clean-cut kids can be scumbags too, Bishop."

"I know that. My point is: Is he?" He called Bubba's cell and put it on speaker. "I'll text you the vic's info. Run a search on him when you get done with the number-and-clothing-deal check, will you?"

"Will do."

He disconnected the call. "Might be drug related," Bishop said.

"Too OCD for a drug kill," I said.

"Could be a cover-up."

"Doubtful. Drug hits are usually quick and violent, not planned, executed, and then spit-shined like your shoes."

"He might owe someone money. Maybe he got mixed up in a gambling scam or something with Bitcoin?"

"What do you know about Bitcoin?"

"Not a thing. I can't even comprehend how something digital is considered cash. I just know it exists."

I laughed. "Right there with you, partner." I performed a more detailed search of the victim's remains. "He had a haircut recently." I checked under his nails. "And it looks like he gets manicures, or else he's got a clean-cuticle obsession."

"Or the doer cleaned his nails after he killed him," Bishop said. "To remove evidence."

"Or that."

"Considering the guy's clothes look washed and pressed, I'd say that's the right assumption."

I sighed. "If that's the case, someone's been watching crime shows on TV."

"Everyone watches crime shows on TV. I've been roped into watching *Castle* recently. Not a bad show, but entirely unrealistic. What police department would let an author pal around with a detective?"

"A fictional one."

"It's all about ratings."

"And advertising dollars."

Bishop watching crime dramas was something new, and it was just another point in favor of what I thought was going on with my partner. "An unsub who manscapes his victim after he kills him is a strange calling card. This isn't going to go well for us."

"Let's hope it goes better for us than it did for this guy."

"There's that."

I took more photos of the vic and the area around him while Bishop took notes.

A fireman walked over and told us the fire was out and the stables area was relatively safe for us to review. "The chief said there'll be someone who can assist you in your examination, but our fire inspector is in the process of doing his analysis, so you can follow along with him, if you'd like."

"Thanks," Bishop said. "We're almost through here."

"I'll head over," I said. "Can you get the ambulance to take the remains to the morgue?"

"No problem," he said. "I'm finishing a thought on my notes, so I'll be there in a minute. I'll get Nikki back here too."

"Works for me." I picked up the baggie with the number in it and stuffed it into an evidence bag. "This is going to be what catches our killer."

"Let's hope you're right."

3

I could see the smoldering remains from the location of the body, so I knew it was bad, but up close told a different story. "Wow."

I saw Chief Pickens nod from the corner of my eye. "Yup. The owner could have made a killing with the wood on that thing."

I turned and faced him.

"Oh. I'm sorry. I shouldn't have used that word."

I smirked. "I didn't give you a look because of that. I gave you the look because you're standing in a pile of ash talking about wood."

He laughed. "You see the price of the stuff lately? Barn and stable wood are at a premium. They call it reclaimed. I call it dollar signs."

I couldn't help but laugh. "One of your guys said we could get with the fire inspector during his walk-through?"

He pointed to a tall thin man with a hell of a gray beard hanging close to the bottom of his rib cage. "That's him over there. I thought it would be okay, but he asked to have someone else show you around first, and he'll get with you in a bit."

I'd prefer to do a walk-through with him, but their scene, their decision. "Got it. Any idea what started the fire yet?"

"One of the guys found remnants of a gas can at the back side of the stables, and since we know the fire started there, my best guess—and don't quote me on this, because it's not my job to determine it—someone emptied the thing and lit a match." He shook his head. "Such a waste."

"Do you know who the owner is?"

"Sure do. Michael Buckley. His dad left him the property about ten years ago. Kid hasn't touched it since."

I wrote down the name. "He live in town?"

He shook his head. "He's nearby, though, and is on his way now."

That was one of the things I liked about small towns. Everyone knew everyone. And even though Hamby was becoming more of a metro Atlanta suburb and losing its small-town label, it was still small compared to Chicago, and things still worked differently. A lot of those things frustrated me, too.

I noted the smoke still coming from the remains of the stables. "You sure it's safe to walk around?"

"Let me grab one of my guys to give you a tour."

"I appreciate that," I said.

He left, and I snapped photos while waiting for my tour guide.

Nikki stepped in front of me as I held up my phone and smiled. "Hey, isn't that my job?"

"You finish with the victim?"

"Didn't know I could go back."

"Bishop was supposed to tell you. He must have gotten distracted."

"I'll go now." She headed back to the victim, but turned around before leaving earshot and said, "Oh, I've got a lot from the fire. I don't think you're going to find anything. There's nothing left."

"You're probably right, but I want to take a look around anyway."

"I understand."

"Do me a favor, please?" I asked.

"You name it."

"Make sure you get photos of the vic's neck, legs, and wrists. Move the clothing. And quickly, because Bishop's getting the morgue for pickup."

"Will do."

The stables were a total loss. What was once a building had been reduced to ash. Some fires left bits and pieces of what once existed, but this fire left nothing, and it didn't make sense. Why destroy the property just to get eyes on a victim?

A fireman walked over and introduced himself. I knew several of them already, but the turnover rate for the department was high, and I didn't know them all.

"Billy Dunkart, ma'am," he said. "Chief said I should show you around?"

"Detective Ryder," I responded. "And I'd appreciate that."

He motioned for me to follow him. "We'll begin in the back where we think the fire started."

We walked to the back of the stables, making sure to keep our distance from the ashen ground. The perimeter of the remains formed a perfect outline of what once was. It would have been beautiful if it was planned. At least it was a relief to know there were no horses involved.

"We can't confirm anything at this point," Dunkart said. "But the chief mentioned he told you what we suspect. Once the investigation is complete, the inspector will let you know the results."

"Understood," I said. "What I'm most concerned about is if there's anything inside the building that might be connected to the body."

"I can't say for sure, but if you look from here, there's not a whole lot of anything left. Now we have to sift through it all before that's in writing. You ever dealt with a fire before?"

"More times than I can count."

He raised a brow. "You're not from around here, are you?"

"Nope."

He nodded. "That explains the accent. I thought you might be from New York."

"Chicago." I didn't need to ask where he was from. He had the same deep Southern drawl as my best friend, Savannah, who happened to be my chief's wife. Savannah came from Macon, Georgia, and while that wasn't the most Southern part of the state, it was old-school Southern, and people from there were easily recognizable by their dialect. "Macon?"

He smiled. "How'd you know?"

"I've learned the different Southern accents from around the state."

"Huh. Never thought there was much of a difference."

Given he thought I was from New York, it was obvious he didn't pay much attention to accents in general.

We finished walking the perimeter of the ash. He was right. There was nothing to see, but regardless, I took photos and a few notes, then thanked him.

Bishop tapped me on the shoulder. "Sorry about that."

"Get distracted?"

"Just doing my job."

"Get anything useful?"

He held up his phone and told me to look myself.

"They're hard to see," he said. "But they're there."

I saw something on the first image and enlarged it for a clearer view. "Are those rake marks?"

"Looks like it."

I scrolled. "How far is this from the body?"

"Ten feet, three inches, and they're perfectly lined, too. Whoever did this is a perfectionist."

"There weren't any tire tracks on the grass. We would have seen those."

"You're thinking like I am again," he said.

"That's not how I would have put it," I said.

He smirked. "Let me see. I'm thinking like you're thinking?"

"Now you're onto something." I handed him back his phone. "So, our killer transported the body there without a vehicle. That was my thought initially. But he knew he'd leave footprints around the area and was prepared to destroy them. Maybe he drove but parked in a secluded area close by?"

"Anything's possible, but one thing's for sure. There's a whole lot of premeditation in this murder," he said. "Our killer wanted this guy for a reason. Maybe the number in the baggie was just to stump us? Get us off track with a possible serial killer connection?"

"It's possible," I said. "But we need more on the victim to tell us where to go."

"Agreed. Looks like it's time to give a death notice."

I sighed. "I'd like to stick around until the fire inspector is finished with his inspection and see what he has to say. If he ever talks to me."

"Want me to go on my own?"

"I'd prefer you stay here."

"Good. I hate doing those things."

"Didn't think anyone liked them."

The fire inspector spent three hours examining the stable, both inside and out. Halfway through, we were brought inside with him.

His professionalism seemed an oxymoron of sorts with his stature and beard. I thought he'd have a strong accent, but he had none. He must not have been from Georgia.

"Inspector Donald Reed. Nice to meet you."

Bishop and I introduced ourselves.

"I've found something in what's left of the stables I thought you should see." He motioned for us to follow him inside.

I quickly glanced at Bishop. His eyes shot to his nice shoes, and he shrugged. So much for wearing his Sunday best, I thought. I couldn't help but wonder why he'd dressed to impress for a crime scene. It had to be for something else. Like a woman.

Could that be? Could Bishop be dating? I couldn't stop the smile from growing, and it was extremely inappropriate at a murder/fire scene, but there I was, smiling like an idiot at the thought of my partner on a date.

"You okay?" Bishop asked.

"Peachy," I said.

"You look strangely happy."

"I was just thinking about how great it will be to nip this one in the bud in a day or two. Then you could get back to whatever it is that's making you watch *Castle* and dress like you're going to church."

He blushed, but he didn't take the bait.

We walked into the ashen remains of what was probably once a stunning horse stable. I'd been in a few around the area, and I was amazed at their design and structure. Horses were almost worshipped by many of their owners, and understandably so. They were beautiful creatures. Tommy used to say they were just big dogs, and in a way, I agreed.

I'd yet to live up to my promise to Tommy, to live the life we'd decided for each other, which included horses and my ability to get on one and not fall off, but I'd get there eventually. Life got in the way of keeping that promise, but deep down I knew my dead husband would be happy that I wasn't still living in the past.

The building's frame was partially intact, and though the interior was mostly destroyed, one or two pieces of wood had dodged the flames and remained in almost perfect condition. I wasn't sure how smoke damaged wood, but I assumed its condition to me was probably just an uninformed opinion.

I pointed to the two pieces. "How come those aren't damaged?"

"They are," Reed said. "Since the fire was started at the back of the stables, the front area was the last hit. Over here"—he pointed to a burnt section on the ground—"and really, all over the ground, are remnants of hay, which ignites quickly. We were on scene nine minutes after the call came, and one minute later, we'd begun putting out the fire." He led us to the poles. "If you look"—he removed some of the damaged wood—"the wood is young and still wet. Looks like someone did some repairs recently and used wood that would burn slower. I can't say whether that was intentional or not."

"Are you saying someone carved the wood and used it, or could they buy it that way?" I asked.

"New wood can be used, but it settles differently, and there can be problems with it. Usually when we see new wood in fires, it's because someone didn't know better."

"So, whoever used this wood either wasn't worried about the potential problems or didn't know there could be issues," I said.

"Possibly not if they were planning to burn the place down at some point," he said. "I'd say they carved the wood themselves. 'Carved' being a generalized term."

"The owner hasn't touched the property in ten years," Bishop said.

"Maybe not, but someone has."

I got on the radio and asked if Michael Buckley had arrived yet.

"You can't hear him?" an officer asked over the radio.

I glanced at Bishop, then replied, "Not sure I understand."

"Buckley's outside the scene tape bitching up a storm about suing Hamby for letting his property be destroyed."

"Buckley's a dipwad," Bishop said. "Entitled and spoiled. Has been his whole life."

Reed laughed. "I've met a few of those over the years."

Bishop sighed. "I'll handle it." He shook Reed's hand. "Thank you for the information, Inspector."

"Just doing my job."

I hit Reed with a thread of questions as Bishop walked away. "Have you found any other, newer wood in here? Is there anything else that looks to have been repaired recently?"

He smiled. "I've read about you. You know your stuff. I'm impressed."

To some, the success I'd had as a detective made me a celebrity in their eyes. To others, I was just another cop. To me, I got things wrong a lot more than I got them right, but I wasn't about to admit that to anyone. At least in my field, my reputation garnered some respect, but I wasn't sure why he'd brought it up. "Thank you."

"My point is you have an intuition about criminals. Tell me why you think there would be new wood in the stables."

Okay, Teacher, I thought. *I'll give it a shot.* "To slow down the fire?"

"There you go." He walked over to the most front section of the stables. "Here's five more." He turned around and pointed to three other small sections I wouldn't have seen had he not pointed them out. "Notice how they're strategically placed throughout the stable?"

"The killer did it," I said. "To slow the fire and make sure the body was located before it could be burned." I turned to him. "But the body is about a hundred feet from the stable. Was it really at risk of being burnt?"

"Technically, yes, but there are always incidents where things are left unharmed. Fires can be like tornadoes. They have a path, but that path can go off course for various reasons."

"Like wood that is slow to burn."

He nodded.

"What do you think caused the fire?" I didn't reiterate what I'd been told before. I wanted a fresh, expert opinion.

"The gas can outside is a clear indicator, and if you look closely, you can see the path of the burn trail."

"The gas can is at the opposite end and corner of the stables in relation to the victim's body," I said.

"Which verifies to me the killer's goal was to draw attention to the victim."

"But why go through all this?"

"That, Detective, is a question for you to answer."

4

Bishop was correct. Michael Buckley was an entitled, spoiled dipwad, and he was over six feet tall to my five feet, five inches. The young man towered over me, in my reasonably flat Doc Martens, and he knew it. He also tried to use it to his advantage, which I found entertaining.

"What the hell happened here? Where were you people? Aren't you supposed to be trolling the roads for speeders and burnt-out headlight offenders? Couldn't you see what was happening before it got out of hand?"

"Mr. Buckley," I said. I hated feigning respect for the little twit. "It's my understanding you haven't touched this property in ten years. Perhaps a camera system to help protect your investment would have been wise."

Bishop coughed.

Buckley swore. "This is an unused property. I've no intention of maintaining something I've planned to sell." His eyes traveled to the beaten-down home on the lot off to our right. It was too far away to notice any details but close enough for us to see it was dilapidated.

"Understood," Bishop said. "Can you tell me where you were approximately five hours ago?"

Buckley blinked as his jaw fell open. "You...you think I did this? For what? The insurance?"

"You tell us," Bishop said.

Go, partner!

"I was at a brewery in Woodstock." He removed his wallet from his back pocket. "I even have the receipt." He stuck the receipt into my face.

He was trying to intimidate me. I took a deliberate step forward, gently removed the receipt, examined it, and then handed it back to him. "Reformation Brewery. I've heard good things about the place, but it's too far for me to drive for a few beers, then drive back home. Can anyone verify you were there?"

"Uh, my receipt is proof, lady." He waved it in my face. "My bill was six hundred bucks. You think I can hold my alcohol well enough to drink six hundred bucks of it?"

I was losing my patience. Part of me wished he would push me or something so I could toss him in a cell and watch his ego drop a few notches, but I knew Bishop would read me the riot act if I poked the bear. Besides, we had more important matters to deal with. "We're going to need a list of names, please."

"Fine," he said. "Whatever you need. I'm not stupid. I wouldn't burn my own property."

"Would you be willing to show us your emails and phone records?" Bishop asked. He was trying to annoy the kid, and I liked it.

We both knew, if necessary, we could subpoena those, but unless Buckley was a real suspect, we wouldn't. For the time being, he was our only person of interest. And it was fun to egg him on because of his frustrating attitude.

"What the hell do you need those for?"

"One can hire someone to start a fire, sir," I said. "And murder for hire is common these days."

He blinked. "Murder?" His face went immediately white and then switched to green. I knew what that meant, so I stepped away quickly. "Are you saying someone was in the stables?" He dragged his hand down his face. "I think I'm going to be sick." He bent over and tossed his cookies, or more like his alcohol, right in front of us.

Bishop didn't move quick enough and got a good splash of the nastiness, but he kept his anger tamed.

"Jesus," Buckley said. "I'm... This is... Are you sure he's dead?"

"We didn't say the sex of the victim," Bishop said.

"Gender," I whispered under my breath.

Bishop shot me a look.

"I just assumed," Buckley said. "Who is it?"

"We haven't notified the next of kin, so we can't release that information," I said.

"I would never do that. I mean, I'm a dick, yeah. Everyone knows that. But, kill someone? That's not my thing."

At least he knew himself. "What kind of insurance do you have on the property?" I asked.

His tone changed quickly. "Listen, do I need an attorney?"

I raised an eyebrow. "Do you think you need an attorney?"

He shook his head, and threw his arms in the air. "This is BS. I didn't kill anyone, and I wouldn't set my property on fire for a measly three million in insurance when I've had offers for six on it."

"We'll be in touch," I said.

"Don't leave the state," Bishop added.

"Jesus," Buckley said.

We walked away.

"Don't leave the state?" I laughed. "Tough guy."

"I like to shake the young ones up every now and then."

Bishop and I spoke with the ranking officer at the scene and asked her to close things up and report to us when finished. I contacted Chief Abernathy with an update and got clearance to give the death notice to the family. We knew we'd run the investigation and that one of us, if not both, would have to deliver the notice.

Bubba ran a check on the victim's driver's license number. The home in Hamby belonged to a Jefferson Ramsey, Jacob Ramsey's father.

"You ready?" Bishop asked.

"Ready as I'll ever be."

Bubba let us know he was still pulling information on the victim, but so far, he couldn't find anything that would subject him to such a violent death.

"Oh, and no one's filed a missing persons report on him either," he said.

I nodded. "Thanks."

Jefferson Ramsey and his wife, Emma, lived off Birmingham Highway in a new community of million-dollar farmhouse-style homes. When the style had first appeared in the area, I loved it, but it had taken over, and nearly every new home was farmhouse white, and everyone else had repainted or painted their homes white. It was like living in *The Stepford Wives*.

In the Ramseys' community, each home was also white, and there were three versions of elevation. The Ramseys' choice appeared to be the most popular. Wraparound porch, black shutters with matching double front doors. The four-car garage was detached, and a breezeway connected it to the home to protect the residents from inclement weather. Maybe it was just to look fancy. What did I know?

Bishop stopped the car just past the lot line for the next property. "I sure hope this kid wasn't an only child."

"Won't make it any easier for them if he wasn't."

"I know."

I checked my watch. "It's after nine. We've got another four hours of work tonight. Let's get this done."

Bishop shifted his vehicle into park and killed the ignition. It took him a moment to find the button. The department now required us to drive department-issued vehicles on shift, and it had been an adjustment for my partner. He liked his new-to-him ride with all the bells and whistles. It also had a button start, but it was in a different place than he was used to and his finger automatically went to the wrong spot every time. I preferred my Jeep with its old-fashioned key ignition.

We walked up the porch steps and the door opened before we got to it. A tall woman with short reddish hair dressed in a baggy gold-and-black Kennesaw State University sweatshirt and black leggings asked, "May I help you?"

I glanced at the door frame and saw the camera. She'd seen us coming.

Bishop pushed his thick jacket to the side and revealed his Hamby PD badge. "Detective Rob Bishop, ma'am." He turned toward me. "My partner, Detective Rachel Ryder. Hamby Police Department."

She hugged herself. "Okay. Is something wrong?"

"Are you Emma Ramsey?" I asked.

She nodded. "Can you tell me what's going on?"

An equally tall man with dark blond hair and a well-manscaped beard stepped outside. "Honey, what's—" He stopped when he saw us. "May we help you?"

Bishop introduced us again, then said, "We're here about your son."

Emma Ramsey immediately began to cry. "Jake? Oh my God! What's happened to my boy?"

Jefferson Ramsey wrapped his arm around his wife and looked Bishop straight in the eyes. "Please, tell us what's going on."

"There's been an incident," Bishop said. "I'm sorry to inform you that your son is deceased."

Emma Ramsey collapsed to her knees and sobbed. "Jakey! No!"

Mr. Ramsey watched his wife for a moment, seemingly in disbelief, then got down to her level and hugged her. He looked up at us. "Are you sure it's him? He's supposed to be out of town."

"His driver's license was on his person," Bishop said. "But we would still like you to make a proper identification. Understand, we know how hard that will be, but it's important."

Mrs. Ramsey sobbed harder.

Mr. Ramsey nodded. "Yes, okay. Can you give us a few minutes to gather ourselves?"

Mrs. Ramsey wiped her eyes and looked up at me. "How? Was it a car accident? I always tell him to drive separately from his friends. He swore he did. Was he responsible?"

"No," I said. "He wasn't responsible." I left out any further details. Giving too much at once to an already-upset person was a risk and could send them into a deeper emotional breakdown, and we didn't want that for her.

"Please, tell me what happened."

"Ma'am," Bishop replied. "We're still looking into it."

"Where is he?" Mr. Ramsey gathered his wife and held her up as he spoke. "We'll be there within the hour."

Bishop nodded and gave him the location. "We will meet you at the visitor sign-in desk."

"Thank you," he said. He walked his wife into their home and closed the door behind him.

Once out of earshot, Bishop said, "The next death notice is on you."

"Deal."

∼

After my husband's death, a Chicago PD psychiatrist claimed I had PSTD and that one of my triggers was hospitals. I believed PTSD was real, but I didn't think I had it. I just didn't like hospitals in general, for several reasons, but mostly one in particular. When my husband, Tommy, was murdered in front of me, his body was brought to the University of Chicago Trauma Center. I fought that because Tommy was dead, and the deceased were brought to the morgue, not to trauma centers or emergency rooms. My husband was shot in the head and was dead before his body hit the ground. There was no way to bring him back, but since Tommy was a cop, they followed procedure for deceased law enforcement officers, which was to review once more for possible signs of life, and I didn't have a say in where they took him. My anger escalated, and they admitted me for overnight stay for trauma. When the sedatives wore off, but my anger hadn't, they kept me for a three-day stint and a psychiatric review. The PTSD claim gained steam from there, but I was just grieving and dealing with how they handled my husband's remains.

I had a lot of reasons for not liking hospitals, but how that connected to my husband's murder was illogical. If I had PTSD, it would have been associated with the fact that I drew my weapon too late and didn't save Tommy. That I hesitated. That I looked to my husband to tell me what to do as the bullet entered his forehead. That I watched his eyes die as they stared at me.

Screw the hospital. That was nothing compared to my real trauma, and I'd found a way to push past that and do my job.

But no, I wasn't a fan of hospitals. I hated the smells in them the most. That odd mixture of antiseptic, illness, and death combined with the nervous, sweaty body odors of the sick and deceased's loved ones begging for hope or a miracle that would likely elude them. No matter how much the hospital staff tried to scrub the scents away, they were there, seeping from the walls and trapping themselves in my nose. I could handle the smell of death alone, say, at a crime scene. I was used to it. I just couldn't take the finality of it inside a hospital.

Bishop adjusted his safety belt around his waist. "I think I need new pants," he said.

We stood to the side of the visitor's desk, waiting for Mr. and Mrs. Ramsey.

"Too tight around the middle?"

He narrowed his eyes at me. "Too loose, wiseass."

I smirked. "Losing weight? Watching crime dramas? A generally cleaned-up appearance? I know what's going on here."

A pop of red glowed on his cheeks. "What are you talking about?"

"What's her name?"

He tried not to smile. "Whose name?"

My eyes widened. "Oh my God! I'm right! You've got a girlfriend!"

His eyes widened too. He looked around the entryway, then talked in a soft voice. "I don't have a girlfriend. I'm too old for a girl anyway."

"Okay, let me rephrase. You have a lady friend."

He flicked his head toward the entrance. "They're here."

"This is not the end of this conversation, partner."

"Sure seems like it to me."

The morgue was located in the back of the hospital in a small area off-limits to the public or anyone without a key card or code. One of Dr. Barron's assistants escorted us through and into the small room housing Jacob Ramsey's body.

His body was covered up to just below his chin. I could see the surgical tape securing it to the table to hide the damage to his neck. His parents didn't need to see that. His face was covered with a separate, folded sheet.

We left the Ramseys in the waiting room while we made sure everything was ready for them to enter.

"I've never seen anything like it," the medical assistant said. "I feel for the guy."

"Because he's dead or because his throat was slit?" Bishop asked.

She stared him straight in the eye and said, "Because his penis was cut off."

Bishop's face paled quickly. "Did you just say—"

She nodded. "The guy has no penis."

Bishop rubbed his face. "Holy Mother of God." He coughed into the side of his arm. "What in the hell is wrong with people?"

I swallowed hard. "We weren't aware of that. May we have a minute?"

She nodded, said, "I'll give you some privacy," then left the room through a back entrance.

I touched Bishop's arm. "Are you okay?"

"Better than Jacob Ramsey."

"What if this is a passion killing?"

"You think passion drives someone to cut off someone else's dong?"

"Lorena Bobbitt. Remember her?"

He sighed. "There are documentaries where experts agree she acted out of self-defense."

I raised a brow. "Do you agree with those experts?"

"It wasn't my case. I don't have an informed opinion."

"Well," I said, "I do. Let's take my law enforcement expertise out of it. Pretend I'm a married woman with a husband who I believe is, what, repeatedly raping me? I could be wrong on that, but I think she said something along those lines."

"I honestly don't remember."

"Fine, go with it. I'm struggling through this—this—situation, and instead of just grabbing, say, a convenient, nearby heavy object and smacking him in the head with it while he's asleep, I take the time to find a knife, then strategically whack off his wiener."

He flinched. "'Strategic' doesn't define 'passionate.'"

"Then you don't know a whole lot of women who enact revenge. It's a passionate thing to a lot of them."

He tilted his head. "Do you know this firsthand?"

"Not the penis-chopping thing, but I plead the Fifth about passionate revenge." I winked at him.

He sighed. "So, we've got what? A nod-to-a-psychotic-wife killing?"

"Or someone mimicking what she did, just taking it a step farther."

"More like an entire staircase farther. I don't see it." He exhaled. "I feel like Michels at autopsies. I want to throw up."

"Please don't," I said. "You'll never live it down."

"I don't see a woman doing this."

"It's possible. Look at Bobbitt. He allegedly raped her, but that's not the point. The point is this could be driven by a breakup or something."

"Jesus," he said.

"Hold it together, partner. We can't let the Ramseys know about this. The image of their kid on the autopsy table will stay with them forever already. They don't need this."

"Neither did I."

The assistant walked back in. "You two ready?"

"Almost," Bishop said.

"Not to change the subject, but the guy still smells of Old Spice."

I raised a brow. "Old Spice cologne?"

"No, the bodywash. My boyfriend uses it. I smell this stuff on the reg, and I'd recognize it anywhere. It's their Swagger line. Cedar is the most obvious scent in it, but there's something else too."

Bishop had his phone in his hand and had been swiping around on it. "Manliness."

I laughed. "Excuse me."

He showed us the information on the product. "Along with lime and cedarwood."

"Manliness," I repeated. "Nice."

"Huh," the assistant said. "I thought that was unique to my guy, but whatever."

We all chuckled.

"He's ready," she said. "Dr. Barron will perform the autopsy tomorrow morning at nine o'clock and said you're welcome to observe."

"I thought he was doing it tonight?" Bishop asked.

"That was his initial plan, but when he told that to his wife, she said if he tried to leave their party, he'd wind up on a gurney next to his victim." She smiled and showed us her perfectly straight and white teeth. "She's a trip."

"She's scary," Bishop said.

The assistant rechecked the long sheet, tucked it in in a few spots, and then we gave her the go-ahead.

We gathered the Ramseys and escorted them in, then gave them a moment to let what was about to happen sink in.

"When you're ready," Bishop said.

The mother cried, but Mr. Ramsey nodded. "We're ready."

The assistant carefully lifted the sheet from Jacob Ramsey's head. Mrs. Ramsey glanced at her son, turned to her husband, and sobbed into his chest. The assistant looked to Mr. Ramsey, who nodded calmly, though tears pooled in his eyes. She covered their son's face again.

Mr. Ramsey looked at us. "It's him."

Mrs. Ramsey cried harder. He wrapped his arms around her, and she sobbed into his embrace. My heart broke for them. Jacob Ramsey was young. He had his entire life ahead of him. Everything he could have done wasn't only lost to him. It was lost to them, too. Marriage, a family, successes, even failures. All gone in the blink of an eye. Their lives would never be the same. We escorted them into the waiting area. Mr. Ramsey asked what happened next.

"The medical examiner will perform an autopsy to determine cause of death," Bishop said. He couldn't finish. Mrs. Ramsey interrupted him.

"What happened? Where did you find him? I told him those boys were bad news. He'd just started that job! They did this, didn't they? They killed my boy!"

5

Grieving parents are hard to interview, but it was necessary, and we needed to hit the ground running to find the killer. Explaining that when they've just seen their dead child's body, however, was practically impossible.

Mr. Ramsey attempted to calm his wife, but it wasn't working. Her emotions kicked into high gear. She screamed and wailed so loudly, a hospital administrator, along with a doctor and two security guards, came to the room. I was sure the assistant notified them somehow.

"Ma'am," the doctor said. "Why don't we have a look at you?" He tried to take her hand, but she ripped it from his grip.

"I don't need to be looked at! My son is dead! Why couldn't you save him?"

Mr. Ramsey's efforts to calm her were useless. After thirty minutes of escalating emotions and screams, he finally agreed to a sedative, and she was put into a room for overnight observation. I understood her pain, and I hoped she didn't get stuck in the psych ward for three days too.

Bishop and I weren't pleased. A Valium-stoned, sleepy mother who'd claimed someone was responsible for her child's death wasn't helpful when most needed. We stood outside her room and waited until we had the approval to go in.

"Just the husband," the doctor said. "That woman needs her rest."

"Understood," Bishop said.

I didn't make any promises I couldn't keep.

The doctor let us in, and Mr. Ramsey moved from his sleeping wife's bedside toward us. "She's heavily sedated but will be fine, according to the doctor. Though I'm not sure she'll ever be fine again."

"These things take time," I said. "I'm sorry."

"Thank you."

"Mr. Ramsey, your wife accused someone of killing your son. Do you know who she was talking about?" Bishop asked.

He sighed. "I can only assume she's referring to his fraternity brothers. She was never happy about him joining a fraternity in college. She felt the boys involved were bad news."

"Bad news comes in all shapes and sizes," I said.

"Agreed," he said. "But it was Jacob's decision. He paid for it on his own, so we didn't have a say in the matter."

"Did you approve of him joining?" I asked.

"The Greek system has its benefits, and I thought those could help him in his future endeavors. I said they could override the negatives, but Emma didn't agree."

"But Jacob did," Bishop said.

He nodded.

"What fraternity?" I asked.

I wrote down the name, but not aware of the system in general, it didn't ring a bell. In college, I was what we referred to as a GDI. A God Damn Independent. I didn't pay attention to the Greek system, though I'd been approached by guys involved many times.

"Mr. Ramsey, you mentioned your son was supposed to be out of town. Can you tell us about that?" Bishop asked.

"Sure, yeah. He, uh... He was supposed to go to Tybee Island with some friends. They left yesterday."

"When did you see Jacob last?" I asked.

"The morning before yesterday. He said goodbye as he left for the trip."

"Who went on the trip?"

"Uh, I'm not sure. My wife usually kept tabs on the details."

"Do you know any of your son's friends?" I asked.

He thought about it for a moment, then said, "There are a few who used to come around. High school friends, but they fell along the wayside during college. His fraternity brothers are all semi-local, but I've been working so much, and he just moved back home about a month ago." He pursed his lips for a moment. "The one name I do remember is Stephen." He scrunched his face, then shook his head. "I'm sorry. I don't know his last name. Like I said, my wife is usually the one who keeps tabs on these kinds of things."

"Understood," I said. I gave him my card.

"Do you know of any recent conflicts your son has had? Maybe a problem at work, or with someone local?"

"Jake is a smart, charming young man. He's not the kind of guy who creates problems. I feel like we've done a good job raising him in that respect. What happened to my son?"

"We are waiting on the autopsy results to get that information," Bishop said.

"But you think someone did this to him or you wouldn't be asking me questions."

"At the moment, we're investigating this as a possible murder, but as I said, we can't say for sure until the coroner makes his decision."

"How was he killed?"

Bishop's eyes shifted to mine. He could have given the details, but they would figure them out eventually. "We're still waiting to find out."

It was likely that would come back to haunt him, but cops didn't care about that kind of thing. We said what we said to victims' families with their best interest in mind. Nothing except bringing back their son would satisfy them, and we couldn't do the impossible.

"Please let me know when your wife is able to talk. The sooner we find out who he was with, the sooner we can find out what happened," I said.

He rubbed his hands together. "Please, I know you know how my son died. I'm not naive. I saw the tape on the cover. I need to know."

Bishop exhaled. "Sir, your son's neck was slit." He didn't give him the rest of the details, and I thought that was smart.

The man gasped. "We can't tell Emma that. She won't be able to handle it. Do you know how long he—"

"We'll know more after the autopsy," Bishop said.

"And that's got to be done because this is a possible murder, correct?"

Bishop nodded. "It's important to learning the truth about your boy and who did this to him."

He stared off at nothing but nodded. "I understand. But please, don't tell my wife about it. She's very fragile."

"I can't guarantee it won't come up at some point, but we can stay quiet about it for now."

"When is the autopsy?"

"Tomorrow morning."

"Will you be there?"

Bishop let out a deep breath. He hated autopsies. "Yes."

"Okay, that makes it feel a little better, then. Thank you."

We said our goodbyes and left him alone with his sleeping wife. Bishop lit up a cigarette once we stepped into the hospital's parking lot. Hospitals had a special parking area for law and fire safety enforcement, and there were several vehicles from Alpharetta, Roswell, and Hamby parked near us.

He leaned against our vehicle and took a drag from his cigarette. "Can you imagine?"

"No."

He stared at the hospital as he spoke. "Did you and Tommy plan on having kids?"

"Yes and no."

He flicked the ash from his cigarette and took another drag. It was the most I'd seen him puff from one in months. "What's that mean?"

"I had a miscarriage six months before he was killed."

"I didn't know."

"Most people don't. Just Lenny and Garcia. We hadn't even told our parents."

"That must have been hard."

"It was. Tommy took it harder than me. It wasn't a planned pregnancy, and I wasn't sure I was ready, but Tommy was the day we got married."

"You'd make a great mom."

I smiled. "I don't think it's in the cards."

"You know, sometimes I think it's better not to bring kids into this world."

"Your daughter might disagree."

"Oh, trust me, I love her, and I don't know what I'd do without her, but knowing what I know now, and seeing the craziness going on in this world, I'm thinking maybe she shouldn't have kids. Why bring them into this kind of mess?"

Bishop was losing hope in society, and it made me sad. He was always the hopeful, things-will-work-out guy. I was the negative, hope-for-the-best-but-plan-for-the-worst partner. It felt like things were switching. "You'll make a fantastic grandfather."

"Well, she's too young and still single, so I don't have to worry too much about it just yet." He let the rest of his cigarette drop to the ground, then stomped on it with his shoe. "Let's go. Like you said, it's going to be a late night."

~

Bishop and I listened carefully as Bubba spoke. "He's not a criminal. No current girlfriend. Was living in an apartment in Kennesaw but moved out about a month ago."

"That part we knew," Bishop said.

"If he's had any juvie convictions, he's fulfilled his requirements for them. There's nothing on his record," Bubba said.

"Nothing we can find legally," I mumbled.

Bishop narrowed his eyes my direction. "I know. You know a guy."

I shrugged.

Bubba smirked. "You know two guys."

I raised an eyebrow. "We do?"

"I mean, I can do what your guy in Chicago does; I just can't do it on department computers."

I nodded. "It's late. Maybe you should go home and get some rest." I added a wink and a smile.

"Ryder," Bishop said. He used his dad voice on me.

"I'm just saying." I smiled, then looked at Bubba again. "Find anything on the number?"

"Not yet, but I'm still looking. I got distracted, and I'll get back to that, but I have more to share." He pulled up Jacob Ramsey's TikTok.

I nudged Bishop's shoulder. "This is called TikTok. It's a social media platform like *the Instagram*, but it's video heavy."

Bishop rolled his eyes. A while back he'd referred to Instagram as *the Instagram*. He'd said the same thing for YouTube. I'd teased him about it since.

"The TikTok," he said. He smiled at Bubba. "Am I right?"

"Not at all," Bubba said. "Anyway, there are a lot of videos of him at parties, and if you pay attention, there are a few of the same girls in all of them." He pulled up a few examples showing girls with drinks in hand, hanging on Jacob Ramsey. Some were dressed in costumes, others dressed like small-time hookers, though I figured that was more of a fashion statement than a career choice.

"Why is it necessary to post this crap?" Bishop asked.

"This generation is all about themselves," Bubba said. "Current speaker excluded, obviously."

"Obviously," I said, and I meant it. Bubba wasn't like other young adults his age. I found it hilarious that his family thought he'd failed at life by working in forensic technology instead of going to medical school. Bubba was born and raised in America by Hindu parents from Mumbai with a mile-long list of medical credentials and awards attached to their names. He still lived at home with his parents, grandparents, three sisters, and two brothers. His mother was a badass in my book. She had six kids and worked full time through it all. Each of their children either were or were planning on going to medical school. Bubba called himself the black sheep. He once said it was because blood makes him want to throw up, but he'd overcome that working with the department. He was a tech genius, his skills improving by the nanosecond, and I believed it was his calling. But to think he'd do something that might slide under the rule of law was shocking.

"So," he continued, "there are fourteen recent—and by recent, I mean within the last three months—videos of him partying. But if you go back a year, which, based on the timeline of the videos, is prior to his graduation, there's a girl in those videos who suddenly disappears a few months ago." He swiped through his touch-screen laptop. "Look."

He showed us several videos that included a pretty blond girl who liked to wear crop tops all year long. I wasn't about to show that kind of skin at my age, even though it was still decent.

"Can you tag people on TikTok?" I asked.

"Not in the way you can on other platforms, but you can mention them in the comments, and then people can click on the person's name and go to their profile."

"Is she mentioned in any of the videos?"

"Not so far, but there's two years' worth of videos to go through. Though my guess is she's not tagged. He only mentions people in comments with nicknames, and those are all guys."

"What about the Instagram?" Bishop asked.

"He's got an account, but he hasn't posted on it in two years."

"Facebook?" he asked.

"Facebook is the senior citizen's social media network for people over fifty. People my age have accounts, but they haven't updated them since middle school."

I busted out laughing. "Ouch."

Bubba shrugged as he smiled at Bishop. "No disrespect intended, sir."

"I'm not on social media, so why would I be offended?"

"Because you're over fifty, and he just called you a senior citizen," I said through laughter.

Bubba's voice went up an octave. "I didn't mean he—"

Bishop waved him off. "I get it. She's just trying to get under my skin."

"Too bad it's not working," I said, then went back to the important part of the conversation. "What makes you think something was up with this girl? Maybe she moved or dropped out of school, or maybe they were dating and broke up."

"Just a hunch, really. But if you look at the last video she's in…" He clicked on a video. "You can tell something's up. Look at her expression and watch how she flinches when he touches her."

"Interesting," Bishop said. "Are there any videos of other girls flinching when he touches them?"

"Still looking, but so far, no."

"We need her name," I said. "It might mean something, especially given what we learned at the morgue."

"What did you learn?" he asked.

"The victim's penis is missing," I said.

Bubba's eyes widened, and his face turned white as a ghost. "Excuse me?" He looked to Bishop for support.

"It's true," Bishop said.

"Killer could be a pissed off ex-girlfriend," I said.

"This is exactly why I don't date," Bubba replied.

"Smart decision," I said. "Can we get her name?"

"I'll work on it," he said.

"Maybe you should work on it at home," I said. My eyes flitted to Bishop. "What do you think?"

"I think that's a great idea. And I don't think we can do anything other than write up our reports tonight. We need to be well rested to hit the ground running tomorrow."

6

Kyle was on the couch staring at his computer when I got home. I wasn't surprised to see him because his car was in my driveway, but I was surprised he'd come back to my place after work instead of going to his in the city.

"Hey," I said. I hung my coat in the closet, removed my weapon, cleared the chamber, and dropped the clip into my free hand. I set the gun on my small dining room table, then removed the one from my right leg. Since I wasn't wearing the boots I used to wear, I'd taken to clipping the weapon onto a leg strap I'd purchased at a gun store in Cumming. It worked well, but it was an adjustment to feel the weapon in that location. "Not that I'm upset, but why are you here?" I checked my watch. "And it's after two. Why aren't you asleep?"

Kyle and I had begun dating a while back, and after some stops and starts, a whole lot of baby steps, and multiple internal negotiations on my part, things finally progressed to a comfortable groove. Being a widow is complicated, but loving a dead man and letting that love haunt you for years is hard to stop, especially when you subconsciously feel responsible for his death. I didn't pull the trigger the night Tommy died, and I eliminated the person who did, but I couldn't save my husband, and the guilt of hesitating so I could read his lips would haunt me forever.

Kyle understood that, and that's where the baby steps came in. The Marine in him gave him great patience in reaching his goal, and then he finally did. We weren't living together, but we were exclusive, and he'd even used the word "love" a few times in the recent past. I was pretty sure I felt the same, but I hadn't been able to say the word yet. Lenny told me I was Fonzie from *Happy Days*. I was familiar with the show, but it wasn't something popular for my generation, so I had to google what he meant. I didn't know what caused Fonzie's inner turmoil or adversity to love, but mine was guilt through and through.

"I'm working on a report," he said. "We finished our key investigation, and it looks like we'll get indictments on four of the arrests too."

"Oh, that's fantastic. Congratulations!"

He closed his laptop. "Technology makes my job a hell of a lot easier."

"How do you mean? Other than the obvious, that is."

"A University of North Georgia campus patrol unit spotted two men sitting in a vehicle outside of one of the dorms. It was there for almost an hour, so he went to check it out. When he pulled up behind it, the people inside took off. He searched the vehicle and found a drone. Our guys were able to track it and determined it had dropped packages at three separate Georgia college dorms in the last fifteen hours. It took some work, but we were able to locate the people who retrieved the packages. We also found the vehicle owner and he gave up the person in the vehicle with him, so we made our arrests."

"Wow. That's crazy. Did they tell you where they got the drugs?"

"Sure did, so we ended up with close to two million in drugs. It's a solid bust."

"Good for you."

"Yes and no. We got the arrests, but these drone deliveries are taking over, and we're only getting them because of luck. We need to find a way to get to them before they make the drops."

"You'll figure it out. Like you said, technology helps."

"It's not technology that's the problem. It's the feds and what they'll let us do."

I understood that completely, at least on a local level. "I'm sorry."

"Such is life. Anyway, I thought I'd come by and see what's up with your case."

"You heard?"

He nodded. "I stopped at the station on my way here. Jimmy told me." He patted the empty spot on the couch next to him. "Have a seat."

"I need a water first. Want anything?"

"Nope, I'm good."

I grabbed a blackberry Hint bottled water from my fridge and fell onto the couch beside him. A beer would have hit the spot, but I wasn't going to get into that habit. It wasn't worth the risk of overindulgence when working a case. I glanced at my betta fish, Louie, who was sound asleep. Maybe. It was hard to tell, but at least he wasn't floating belly-up at the top of his bowl.

My previous fish had died a few months before. Kyle found him floating lifelessly in his bowl. He'd called me and prepared me for the worst, and it wasn't easy. He'd been my confidant, my friend, and the one living creature that accepted me for who I was. I placed him in a box and buried him just outside the front door under a small shrub.

Two days later I purchased Louie. We'd begun to bond, but he hadn't reached Herman level, though I knew he would eventually. "You feed the child?"

"Yes, ma'am."

I didn't like being called "ma'am," but the way Kyle said it was cute. "Thank you." I sighed after taking a swig of my drink. "Who starts a fire to draw attention to a murder victim?"

"Someone who wants to know their work's been found."

"Right. Did Jimmy tell you what we found with the victim?"

"The number in the baggie? Yes. What's your theory?"

"First thought was a serial killer, but Bubba hasn't found anything in NCIC that matches." I added, "Yet."

"That's a good sign."

"It is, but why the number?"

"What was the number?"

"Seven."

"Damn."

"That was our reaction. Doesn't make sense. The number means something, and the obvious meaning would be a serial killer, but then we'd have six other victims, and we can't find any."

"Yet."

"Yet. And that's not the only thing," I added.

"You found something else?"

I shook my head. "Something else is missing. An important *thing*." I emphasized the word "thing," hoping he'd catch my meaning.

"'Thing,' as in…?" He left the rest of that question to assumption.

"Unfortunately, yes."

"His dick is missing? Did you find it?"

"I hate that expression, but yes. His penis was apparently removed, but we don't know when or why yet. We were just told. So, no. We didn't find it. And as far as I know, it wasn't left at the scene."

"So, you didn't see his…" He rubbed his hand over the top of his short hair. "Jesus, that poor kid."

"It definitely makes a statement."

"You're the first person I know who's had a victim Bobbitted."

I grinned at the reference, but I knew that was how law enforcement referred to that kind of situation. "Bishop was a little disturbed."

"I can imagine."

Kyle was up and out with me early the next morning. I followed him out of my community, but we went in opposite directions. I grabbed two dozen donuts and a six-pack of bagels with assorted cream cheeses from Dunkin', ordered two large coffees for me and Bishop, and headed straight to the department. I pulled in just ahead of my partner.

I walked over to his vehicle and handed him his coffee. "Liquid energy."

"God, do I need it."

I tilted my head and examined him. "You look like you've been run over by a truck. Are you sick?"

He coughed into his sleeve. "I think I'm coming down with the winter ick." He climbed out of his car and clicked the key fob to lock it.

"The winter ick?"

He nodded. "You know, the cold everyone gets during the winter?"

We headed inside. "You mean a winter cold?"

"Isn't that what I said?"

"You called it the winter ick. Never heard that phrase before."

"What do you call it, then?"

"A cold."

He muttered, "You kids lack creativity."

I laughed. "You ready for today?"

"I'm ready to get this thing closed quickly."

Nikki and Bubba were in the investigation room when we got there. I checked my watch. It was seven fifteen. They were dedicated during an investigation, and I appreciated that, but they weren't sitting there that early without reason.

"What'd you find?" I asked.

Bubba spoke first. "Nothing on the number or the penis connection. I looked through everything I could find. Old newspapers, true crime show listings, *America's Most Wanted* summaries, police reports, you name it. If there's been other crimes with a victim tally or just a number associated with it, it's not been made public or shared in NCIC. Oh, and so far, I can't connect the girl to a name, but I'll get there eventually."

"Appreciate it," Bishop said with a mouthful of chocolate-frosted donut.

"First off, I did not find a penis anywhere on the stable property. Thank God for that. We've been cleared to go to the home on the property, but honestly, I hope we don't find one there either," Nikki said. "I'd like to go and have a look, but I wanted to see if either or both of you wanted to go also."

"We have the autopsy this morning, but we're free after," I said.

"I can always skip the autopsy and go with Nikki," Bishop said. "Especially given what we know we're going to see."

I smiled. "You want to do that?"

"Saves time."

I snickered. Bishop's hate for autopsies intensified when it included a lopped-off penis. "Point made, chicken. Let's plan to meet back here after, then."

"Sounds good," Bishop said. He smiled at Nikki. "When can you be ready?"

She grabbed the two donuts and said, "Now."

Bishop gave Nikki a nod.

"Yes, sir," she said, and walked out with him.

I hollered, "Wuss," as he walked out the door.

Bubba just stared at me. "I've been thinking about the missing body part. What do you think it means?"

"I have no idea." I stood. "I'm heading to the autopsy. Keep checking on the girl. Let me know what you find."

"Will do."

I grabbed Detective Michels on my way toward the door. "Got an autopsy to attend, and I need another set of eyes. Bishop's working another angle on the case. You free?"

"If I say no, will it get me out of it?"

"Nope."

He shrugged. "Perk of the job, watching dead people get cut up like cattle."

"Wait until you see this one."

"What's that mean?"

"Nothing," I said, and smiled as he grabbed his things.

7

Dr. Barron was revved up and raring to go when we arrived. "This one is interesting," he said. "Had I known he came with missing parts, I could have used that to get out of the big party last night." He removed the sheet from the victim. "Though I did make some good meat."

Michels's face turned green. "What's—Ryder?" He turned to me, and his nostrils flared. "You brought me because of that, didn't you? Jesus, Mary, and Joseph." He made the sign of the cross over his chest. I had no idea he was Catholic. "I never thought I'd see missing body parts in Hamby, Georgia."

"It's fascinating, really," Barron said. "I've not seen anything like this happen in this part of the state, at least not under my watch or something I'd advised on."

I liked the doctor. He didn't let something like a chopped-off body part stop him. I'd seen many missing body parts in my time. Granted, they were legs, arms, and most often heads, and I got that it was upsetting to a man, but I'd thought missing the *other* head might be worse. Apparently, it wasn't.

Michels coughed. His face turned even more green, and he bent down with his hands on his knees. "I'm going to barf."

Barron turned around, grabbed a garbage basket, and slid it under

Michels's face. "Hit the bucket, please. I don't want to have to postpone the autopsy while they clean up after you."

He was so empathetic.

Michels gagged and heaved into the basket. I felt awful. He'd eventually adjust, and he'd been a detective awhile now, but in a town the size of Hamby, that kind of stuff was rare, so he'd only been to four autopsies. One could say he was still green. Literally and figuratively.

He finished, and Barron handed him a cloth. "Need some water? There's some in the fridge."

Michels's eyes widened. "The body fridge? I'll pass."

Barron laughed. "Not that one. The one behind me."

"Oh, yeah. I'll take one." He walked over and took a water, opened it, then slammed it down like he was at the bar doing shots. "Thanks. I think I'm ready."

"'Bout time," I said, smiling.

"You'll pay for this," he said jokingly.

Barron determined the cause of death to be the slit throat, which wasn't exactly news to any of us, but what he found interesting was the type of knife used. Once he completed the autopsy, he reviewed his findings with us.

"Appears to be a double-edged knife, and it looks like it's been recently sharpened."

"What makes that interesting?" I asked. "And how can you tell it was recently sharpened?"

"There are remnants of stainless steel in the victim's neck. Most knives are made from stainless, carbon, or tool steel. The stainless ones are more expensive. Knife used on Mr. Ramsey has a nonserrated blade, so if I had to guess, given the depth and size of the incision, it's a hunting knife, but I can't say for sure."

"There are thousands of hunting knives," Michels said. "We'll never be able to find the brand with just that."

He was right. "Was the same knife used on his penis?" I asked.

Both men flinched.

"It appears so." Barron looked at Michels. "The important thing to know here is your victim was dead when his penis was removed."

"Thank God for that," Michels said.

"Because that would have been worse than having your throat slit?" I asked.

"You can't understand," Michels said.

I smirked. "Valid point."

"The markings on his wrists and ankles are indicative to binding, and if you look at the sampling of material I recovered from his skin, you'll see it's yellow. I'd guess it's your standard polypropylene twist rope available at stores like Home Depot. His mouth was also taped shut using your everyday duct tape."

Michels inhaled and exhaled loudly. "Great."

I agreed. "All of those are a dime a dozen. We need something solid to go with."

"The only solid thing I can give you is the lack of substantial evidence to convict." He replaced the sheet over the victim and stepped toward the sink as he removed his gloves. "There's nothing on this man's body we can use to identify his killer."

"We need something, Doc," I said.

"There is one thing that could help, but the likelihood is slim to none it will."

"What's that?" Michels asked.

"Seems our young victim had crabs."

Michels coughed again. "That wasn't what I was expecting."

"It's possible your killer was exposed."

"And what do we do if we find him? Get a subpoena to check his pubic hair?" I asked.

"My job is to provide medical information, not determine legal procedure," Barron said. "And thank God for that." He chuckled. "What's most interesting about this is the killer profile, in my medical opinion, is clear. Your killer has a type-A personality. They left no evidence to identify themselves, and what minuscule evidence they might have left would be hard to pin on a particular suspect. The rope is an excellent example. You've got a tough job ahead of you. If you want my opinion, I'd look further into the number. Someone who pays this much attention to not leaving evidence doesn't leave a number for no reason."

"That much I know," I said. "There's a lot of deliberate actions in this case."

Michels cussed me out as we left the morgue. "Why do I let you do this stuff to me? Someone cut off the victim's penis. Who does that?" He adjusted his pants. "I'm having phantom knife pains for the poor guy."

"It wasn't a random killing," I said, more to myself.

"Even a new recruit would think that."

Bishop and Nikki were still at the property when we returned to the station.

Bubba found me in the investigation room, staring at the nearly blank whiteboard. "I have something," he said.

"Tell."

"Jessica Lyman."

"Is that the girl in the video?"

He shook his head. "But she's in videos with her on her own account." He waved a piece of paper at me. "And I have an address."

My eyes widened. "You're the best!" I snatched the paper from him. "When Bishop gets back, let him know where I am, will you?"

"Yes, ma'am—but wait. Did you see the victim's... His...you know?"

"You mean his penis? No, it's not there, remember?"

"I mean, did you see where it was?"

"Yes, but Barron kept it safely hidden after a quick view so Michels wouldn't throw up all over his exam room."

He laughed. "Man, that would have been hilarious."

"Not to Barron." I held up the paper. "Thanks for this."

"No problem."

Jessica Lyman lived in South Forsyth County just north of Hamby off Exit 13 on State Route 400. From the looks of the gated community, I suspected she still lived with her parents or she hadn't updated her driver's license. I hoped it wasn't the latter.

I pulled up to the gate and flashed my badge. "Detective Rachel Ryder." I let the security man see my badge. "Hamby PD. I'm looking for the Lyman home." I gave him the address.

"Do they know you're coming?"

"No, but this is regarding a criminal investigation."

He blinked. "Oh, okay." He held up a finger. "Just a sec."

I waited as he talked to the other security guard in the small building. When he returned, the second guard joined him.

"Ma'am," the other guy said, "I'm afraid we can't let you into the community uninvited. We're going to have to contact the Lymans."

"That's fine."

He nodded and said, "Just a moment," then walked back to the other side of the building again.

The first guard smiled uncomfortably. "Something bad happen?"

"I'm not at liberty to discuss an active investigation."

"Oh, yeah, I get that. I know how the system works."

I eyed him suspiciously.

He noticed. "No, I'm not saying I've been in the system or anything. I know people who have, and I get how it works."

"Probably smart to stay away from those people, then," I said.

"Yes, ma'am. I am. I do. I'm working on me."

I smiled. "Good."

The other man returned and handed me a visitor's pass. "Up on the right, about six houses down."

The gate opened as I stuck the pass in my window. I gave the men a wave and drove to the Lyman home.

A tall man with graying hair dressed in slacks and a sweater waited outside on the front step. I parked my department vehicle and walked to him.

"Mr. Lyman," I said. "Detective Rachel Ryder with the Hamby PD. I'm here for Jessica Lyman. I'm assuming she's your daughter?"

"What is this regarding?" he asked.

"An active investigation in Hamby, sir. I'm not at liberty to discuss the details."

"Does she need an attorney?"

As always, the wealthy immediately went to that. "No. I'm just here to ask her some informational questions. She's not a part of the investigation."

He nodded once. "Just a moment." He walked inside and left me standing on his front porch. It was chilly, but the porch was covered, so the light mist wouldn't destroy my hair.

He returned with his daughter. Jessica looked different than she did in the videos. Her blond hair was shorter, and she'd lost weight. My first thought was illness, but it could have been anything.

I introduced myself. "I'd like to ask you a few questions about some videos on TikTok."

She glanced up at her father. He didn't budge. "Dad, it's okay. I can talk to the detective by myself."

He stared at her and then walked back inside.

She shrugged. "I'm his only daughter. He's a little overprotective at times."

"Nothing wrong with that," I said. My dad wasn't overprotective, but Lenny was, and I understood the value in that. I showed her one of the videos. "Can you tell me who this girl is?"

She watched it twice. "That's Emily. Why?" Her eyes widened. "Is she okay?"

"To the best of my knowledge, yes. Do you know her last name?"

"Uh, I think it's Bryant or Brian or something like that. I'm not sure. I don't know her that well."

"She's in several videos with you. You weren't friends?"

"We knew each other through other people, but we didn't hang out together on our own. She was in another sorority. One of my sisters was friends with her."

I assumed she meant sorority sister. "Which sister?"

"Kate Higgins."

"Do you have her contact information?"

She removed her phone from her pocket. "Right here."

"May I take a photo of it?"

"Sure. Anything else?"

I snapped the photo. "Did you know Jacob Ramsey?"

Her happy face morphed into a grimace. "Did he finally get busted? Dude's a douche. He deserves to rot in jail."

I raised an eyebrow. "What makes you say that?"

"You're not here because he sexually assaulted a girl?"

"No."

"Well, you should be, because he has no boundaries, and he gets forceful with every girl he meets. He's known to have a reputation of forcing himself on girls in bars and at parties."

"Did he do that with you?"

She laughed. "I have three older brothers. If the dude tried, my brothers would have taken care of him before I could have mutilated his junk."

Interesting thing to say, I thought. "Do you know any of the girls he's hit on?"

"All you have to do is walk up to a girl on campus and he's hit on her."

"What about this Emily in the photo?"

Her eyes lit up. "Oh, right. She dated him for like a year, then something happened, and they broke up, then she accused him of rape, and I think every girl she knew believed her. I can't believe I didn't remember that."

"Accused him of rape? Did she go to the police?"

"I'm not sure. I just remember the rumor, and honestly, I don't really know the details. He made fun of her, though. That, I remember. If it did happen, I don't think she did anything about it, because I just saw his TikTok the other night and he was out partying."

Not anymore. "Thank you, Jessica. I appreciate it."

"No problem. I hope he does some serious jail time. He's a real jerk."

"Fate has a way of working things out."

"I hope so." She smiled, then walked back inside.

I got in my car, pulled out of the driveway and down the street, then called Bishop. "Where are you?"

"At the home on the property still. What's up?"

"You going to be there awhile?"

"Another hour, maybe?"

"I'll head that way."

Before driving over, I sent Bubba a text and asked him to pull up what he could on an Emily Bryant.

I coughed into my jacket. "How can you breathe in here?" I examined the dust-filled home through squinted eyes as I breathed through the sleeve of my leather jacket. "I'm struggling and I just got here." I dug through my bag for a mask, then slipped it on.

"You get used to it," Nikki said.

Whoever lived in the place last left without their belongings, and wildlife, mostly raccoons, mice, and rats, had moved in. The couch, a throwback to the early-2000s Tuscan design era, was shredded in sections, and the stuffing had been made into creature nests in the corners of the main room. It smelled like feces, urine, and decaying animals. None of the smells bothered me, but the rot and dust in the home were too much for my lungs.

Bishop was already masked up and gave me grief. "I thought you didn't have a problem with this kind of thing."

"I don't emotionally, but I have a physical problem with dust and decaying remains infiltrating my respiratory system."

Nikki moved the couch to the side and three rats scurried out.

One headed straight for Bishop. He jumped a few feet in the air. "Jesus!"

I laughed until another one scampered out and headed straight toward me. "A rat!" I screamed as I jumped to the side and pointed at the thing. "There!"

Bishop busted out laughing. The laugh turned into a small coughing fit, and when he finally gathered it together, he smiled at me and then laughed some more. "My tough partner is afraid of rats. That's hilarious."

"Shut it, partner. I heard you call for Jesus to return and saw you jump like a girl."

Nikki interrupted our sophomoric discussion. "Uh, guys." She held up a knife covered in something red and dry. "Could this be our murder weapon?"

8

"I think it's blood," she said. "But I have to run some tests to be sure." She placed it into an evidence bag and zipped it shut.

"Wait," I said. "May I see it?"

I slipped on a pair of gloves and examined the knife. Single blade. "It's not the murder weapon, but I think we should tag it just in case."

"How do you know?" Bishop asked.

"Double-edged knife, according to Barron."

Bishop nodded.

"I'm on it," Nikki said. She removed another evidence bag from her kit, slipped off her gloves, and placed them in there. She wrote something on the bag and put on another pair after setting it inside her kit also. "I've got the rest of this room to examine and then I'll head back."

"You've searched the rest of the home already?" I asked.

She nodded.

Bishop said, "Haven't found anything to show the victim was killed here." He began walking away and flicked his finger for me to follow. Then he turned around and said to Nikki, "Don't forget what we found in the bedroom."

"Just call when I can go in there," she said.

He nodded. "And thanks for the good work. We'll be back at the department in a bit."

"No problem. I'll get right on what I've got, but first I want to try and find some prints around the couch."

"Good luck," I said. The couch sat on a beat-up rug, and I had no clue where she'd find any prints.

"I need it," she said.

Bishop walked me into one of the bedrooms. There were two twin bed frames, one box spring, but no mattresses.

"The other two rooms don't have this much furniture or anything that could be related to our investigation, but this room does have something interesting." He walked over to the bed frame and lifted something up from behind the box spring. His hands were gloved, so I knew that meant something.

"Gross," I said. "Someone had a kink for sure." I shook my head. I'd never understood the concept of being cuffed to the bed for sexual pleasure, but, hey, just because I didn't get it, didn't mean it wasn't exciting to someone else.

"Nikki's bringing them in. I just wanted to see your reaction."

"Why?"

He shrugged. "During our first investigation you seemed to know a lot about sex games."

"From an investigational perspective," I said.

"Right. I'm just saying."

I yelled for Nikki. "Please come and take the handcuffs before Bishop says something he's going to regret."

He dropped the cuffs and they clinked when they hit the bottom of the bed frame. He laughed and then his tone turned serious. "Are you sure it's not the knife?"

"Ninety-nine percent."

"We needed that. We're running out of time."

"I know."

"It's squirrel blood," Nikki said. "I'm sorry."

I leaned back in my chair at my desk. "I wasn't expecting a miracle."

"I know. I just told Bishop and he said the same thing." She tried to smile, but her mouth didn't quite make it. "I'm looking through everything, and we should have the fire report today, right? Maybe that will give us something."

"Right."

My department phone rang, and Nikki waved goodbye as she left my cubby. I answered on the second ring. "Ryder."

"Inspector Reed is here," the front desk receptionist said. "Should I send him back?"

"Send him to the conference room near you, and I'll grab Bishop."

"Sounds good," she said, and disconnected the call.

I knocked on Bishop's partial wall. "Reed's here. Conference room one."

He stood and stretched.

Reed was dressed in black slacks and a green-and-red holiday-themed sweater with a button-down shirt underneath. The style didn't fit his vibe, but I gave him points for being brave enough to wear the sweater in public.

He must have caught me staring at him. "My wife's sister knitted it. I want to stay married."

I smiled. "You're a devoted husband, sir."

"You have no idea."

"Thank God I'm divorced and my ex-wife doesn't have a sister," Bishop said.

Reed laughed. "Now," he said as he pulled a file out of his hard old-school briefcase with the little flip locks. My grandfather used to bring one like it over when he'd stop by after work. "I've got some interesting information from my investigation." He handed us each a file folder. "Are you familiar with geometry?"

"In a general sense," Bishop said. "But I haven't used it since junior high."

I opened my folder and read through his summary on the first two pages. It was complicated and detailed and well above my comprehension level. "Sir, can you dumb this down for us? I'm not sure we're as smart as you."

He smiled and removed a computer-generated graph printed on a clear sheet. He laid that over an aerial view of the fire and crime scene map. "Our drone was able to capture the scene of the fire just after we arrived. I measured the distance and direction from the location of your victim to the location of the start of the fire, which, in case you have any doubt, was started intentionally. And if you see"—he swiveled the papers in our direction—"there is a straight angle from the location of the start of the fire to the victim." He added a second clear paper to the first two. "And if you spread out the view to include just outside of the two areas mentioned, you'll see whoever set this fire created other vertical angles—" He stopped himself. "Let me rephrase. Our suspected arsonist and murderer intentionally created a straight-angled line between the victim and point of flame."

"So, our guy's a math teacher?" Bishop asked. I wasn't sure if he was serious or not.

"I can't tell you that," Reed said. "All I can tell you is the measurement is likely deliberate due to its accuracy."

"Which means our doer is type A," I said. "Barron said the same thing."

"That narrows our suspect down a few million," Reed said.

Bishop jotted down some notes. "We already know the killer is organized, but this is a little extreme."

"I've never seen anything like it," Reed said. "But other than creating distance to guard the integrity of the victim's remains, I can't say what the reason would be in relation to the fire."

"I think that's the point," I said. "The killer started the fire to bring attention to the victim. He wanted the victim found exactly the way he left him, and to do that, he needed the fire far enough away to give us all time to get on scene." I tapped my pencil on the table. "Is there anything to show the fire was started by someone with knowledge of fire department procedure?"

He tilted his head to the right. "Are you accusing a fireman of this?"

"Just searching for facts. No disrespect intended."

"Understood, and I can't say for sure, but other than the angle of the point of fire and victim, this looks like a first-timer job."

"Why?" Bishop asked.

"Serial arsonists are rare, but those we've been able to study show patterns of skills above those who start fires for independent reasons. Serial arsonists typically don't leave easily locatable evidence such as gas cans."

"Like the one at the stables," I said.

"Yes."

"Could that have been a mistake?" Bishop asked.

"It's possible, but given the appearance of the victim, it appears you've got a serious murder investigation with a side of fire," Reed said. "I'm here to offer any input, and our department is available to assist in any way necessary."

Bishop and I escorted Reed out then headed straight to the department's kitchen. He popped a Keurig pod into one of the coffee pots while I did the same in another one.

"That was interesting," I said.

"The geometry reference was odd. Reed's clearly a smart guy, but I didn't realize he was that smart. I haven't thought about angles since my ex-wife wanted me to build her a bookcase for our bedroom."

"Did you do it?"

"Build the bookcase?" He shook his head. "I bought one at Rooms to Go."

I smiled. "That's my partner."

He added too many sugars to his small cup of coffee. "We have nothing."

"That's not true," I said. I hadn't told Bishop about my interview with Jessica Lyman. "Let's get Bubba into the investigation room."

Bubba met us there with a smile plastered on his face. "How much do you love me?" He dropped a small stack of papers in front of Bishop and me.

"I wouldn't say 'love' is the right word," Bishop said.

"I would," I said as I spread the papers out across the table. "This is fantastic!" Bubba had worked his magic and located both Kate Higgins and Emily Bryant, even though we didn't have a solid last name for her. And more than that, he'd gone through social media and found the gem we needed. "Can we verify this is about Ramsey?"

He nodded. "The comments say it all."

I read through the comments with Bishop over my shoulder.

"Damn, this kid was a piece of work," Bishop said.

"More like a serial rapist," I said. "But they're comments, not evidence."

"Just so you know, these aren't still online," Bubba said.

"Then how did you get them?" I asked.

"A cell phone is a valuable piece of technology, and it never forgets what it sees."

"Looks like we're going to see Emily Bryant," I said.

Bishop stood. "I'll drive."

I jumped out of my chair. "Why do you always get to drive?"

Bubba laughed as we walked out of the room.

"Because I get closer to God every time you get behind the wheel."

"I thought believers were good with that?"

According to Bubba's research, Emily Bryant lived at home with her mother and uncle in Alpharetta. Bishop took a back route to their home, driving down Highway 9 toward Old Milton Parkway. He turned left onto Old Milton and then took roads I'd yet to discover in my few years living in Georgia.

"I don't recognize this," I said.

"It's pretty new. When they built the amphitheater, they updated the infrastructure in the area. I've driven around here a time or two and have figured out what goes where."

"I'm still salty that this state has no grid system for their streets. In Chicago and most of the surrounding suburbs, everything is a grid. Even if you get lost, you can figure out where to go with that knowledge." I paused, then added, "And with the Never Eat Soggy Waffles theory, too."

Bishop lifted an eyebrow as he shifted his eyes toward me and then back to the road. "The *what* theory?"

"Never Eat Soggy Waffles. Didn't you learn that in elementary school?"

"We didn't make food in elementary school."

"It's not making food. Never Eat Soggy Waffles is a mnemonic something or other. You know, the thing you learn to remember something. It means north, east, south, and west. We were taught the lake is east, Indiana is south, Wisconsin is north, and the nomad's land is west; so as long as you knew where the lake was, you could easily figure out your direction by Never Eat Soggy Waffles."

"Our educational system is a wreck. And the nomad's land?"

I smiled. "The western suburbs. When I was a kid, there was nothing out there. It's all built up now, but before, it was just farmland."

"You Midwesterners do things different out there."

"I can say the same about you Southerners."

He parked the car on the curb in front of Emily Bryant's home. "You got lead?"

"Yup. This needs a woman's sensitive touch."

"Sensitive?" He laughed. "That's the last thing anyone would say about you."

"Shut it, partner."

A man with a largely receding hairline and a sorry excuse for a mustache answered the door. "Yeah?" He eyed Bishop with disinterest, then focused all his attention on me. "What can I do for you, ma'am?" He hiked up his sweatpants and pulled his extra-large Atlanta Falcons sweatshirt down over them.

Bishop and I showed him our badges at the same time.

"I'm Detective Ryder with the Hamby Police Department, and this is my partner, Detective Bishop. Is Emily Bryant home?"

He bit his bottom lip. "Hamby Police? This is Alpharetta."

"We're here regarding an investigation, sir. Is Miss Bryant home?" I asked.

"Uh, no. She's at work."

"Are you Chip Stuart, her uncle?"

He nodded. "What's this about? Is my niece in trouble?"

"No, sir. We just have a few questions for her." I glanced through the door and into the entryway. "When will she be home?"

"Don't know. If she doesn't go out after, she's home by six, otherwise, maybe eight or so, I guess."

"Where does she work?"

He gave me the name of a law firm where Emily Bryant worked as a legal assistant to a paralegal. "She works late when they've got an active case."

I nodded. "Thank you."

As I turned to leave, he asked, "May I ask what investigation this is for?"

"Unfortunately, we can't share that right now. Please let Emily know we'd like to talk to her."

Bishop flipped around and handed him one of his cards. "Have a nice day, sir."

I exhaled as Bishop hit the button to start the ignition. As I clipped my seat belt together, he groaned. "You get the same feeling I got?" I asked.

"If you think we need to check the basement for skeletons, then yes."

"Really? I was thinking more along the lines of checking the basement for preteen girls locked in a room."

He pulled away from the curb. "I'm not sure which of those is worse."

"I'll text Bubba and see what he can get on the guy."

"You don't think he's involved, do you?"

"Everyone's a suspect until they're not."

"That wasn't my question."

"Are you asking what my gut's telling me?"

"Yup."

I closed my eyes for a moment and thought about it. "Did you look inside the house?"

"Just got a cursory scan, nothing too telling."

"Did you see the dining room table?"

"Yeah. It had all the craft stuff on it."

"The numbers we found with the vic are vinyl stickers, and I'm pretty sure they can be found in any craft store."

He pressed his lips together and said, "They probably have them at Home Depot or Lowes too. I'm not sure a table full of craft supplies is enough to get a warrant. And besides, my ex-wife used to make crafts. She had a group of friends who went on retreats and to craft supply shows too. I'd bet ninety percent of the women in Fulton County have craft supplies at home."

"But do ninety percent of the men?"

"He lives with a woman and her daughter."

"Right," I said. "Doesn't mean the craft stuff doesn't belong to him." I dropped the subject for the time being, but it continued to ferment in the back of my head.

"We'll look into it," he said.

I suspected he saw the wheels of my brain turning.

～

Emily Bryant had left the office for a doctor appointment. The receptionist said she wouldn't return until after hours, and at that time there would be nobody at the front of the office. She'd made it clear that if we returned after office hours, there was no way anyone would hear us at the locked door because their offices were too far from it.

"Should we go back after hours anyway?" Bishop asked.

"Absolutely. Let's get back to the department and see if Bubba's found anything."

"On which assignment?"

"Yes," I said.

He laughed.

～

"Still nothing?" I asked Bubba.

We met Bubba in the parking lot of the department. He had a Kroger shopping bag in one hand and a liter of Dr Pepper in the other.

"Nothing," he said.

A red late-model Ford F-150 pulled into a visitor's spot in the parking lot. The man stepped out of the vehicle dressed in a pair of dark blue jeans, a button-down collared shirt, and a sports coat. He had cop written all over him.

He sauntered over and introduced himself. We must have looked like law enforcement too. "Good afternoon. I'm Detective William Johnson, Birmingham PD." He showed us his credentials. "You can call me Detective or Bill."

We introduced ourselves, and I asked what we could do for him.

"You two working the dead kid?"

I tilted my head to the right. "May I ask how you know about our deceased victim?"

"Our medical examiner knows your medical examiner. They talk."

"About active investigations?" I asked.

"If y'all don't mind, I'd like to discuss this privately."

We escorted him into our conference room as Bubba went to the kitchen.

"Four years ago," Detective Johnson said, "we had a male victim, twenty-three years old, found deceased outside an abandoned chicken farm on the south side of town."

"Deceased males are almost a dime a dozen," I said.

"Correct. But my deceased male was stripped prior to his death, then bathed and redressed. For starters."

That got our attention.

"Go on," Bishop said.

"James Ryan Johnson," he said. "Twenty-three, just finished college and started a job. He was found shot in the head near an abandoned chicken farm." He leaned toward us from across the conference table. And he had the number three in a bag in his hand."

"Did you say three?" I asked.

He nodded.

"Damn. Our guy is seven," Bishop said.

9

"And he wasn't my first," Johnson said.

Bishop and I made eye contact.

"How many?" Bishop asked.

"Three total. Each with a corresponding number."

"How long between each killing?" I asked.

"It varied. On average, about five days."

"Can you give us a moment, please?"

"Yes, ma'am."

Bishop followed me out.

"What in the ever-loving hell is Barron doing giving information about an active investigation to another ME?" I asked.

Bishop narrowed his eyes at me. "Keep it to a whisper, Ryder. The entire department can hear you."

"I don't care," I said. I threw my arms up. "Who else has he told? Did he give it to the *Hamby Herald*?"

Chief Jimmy Abernathy race-walked over. "What's going on? I can hear you in my office."

Bishop gave him a quick rundown.

"Holy hell."

"That's all you've got to say?" I asked. "Barron's giving out investigation information on an active case. We haven't even said anything to the media. Don't you think that's a problem?"

"Without knowing the circumstances, yes. How did you find this out?"

"We have the detective from Birmingham in the conference room," Bishop said.

My nostrils flared. "This is completely outside Barron's job description, and it can destroy our investigation."

"Hold on," Jimmy said. "Don't pitch a fit until we have all the details."

I wasn't pitching anything. I was mad and for good reason. If there was one thing I hated about the South, it was the stupid sayings. And I hated them most when they were used on me.

Jimmy spoke softly. "Let's just go back into the conference room and find out what we can. Then we'll get in touch with Barron and see what he has to say. Okay?"

"Fine," I said. Bishop responded, but I couldn't hear him through my frustration.

Bishop introduced Detective Johnson to Jimmy, and they discussed the situation.

Jimmy was polite but to the point. "Detective, we appreciate you coming out here today, but I must say, I have some concerns. It's not standard operating procedure for anyone involved with our investigation to discuss it with people outside of our department. Can you explain how your ME came to discuss your victim with ours?"

Johnson nodded. "You'll have to get the particulars from them, but what I do know is they went to college, then medical school together, and have been friends for years. It's my understanding they spoke recently, and Dr. Pratt, my ME, mentioned a series of cold cases from three years ago, and they matched up, in part, to your current investigation. I'm assuming it was good timing or what I'd call fate."

Jimmy grabbed the landline, hit the speaker phone, and called Barron. "Dr. Barron," he said in a professional voice. "It's Chief Abernathy. I have a Detective Johnson from the Birmingham PD here regarding our investigation into the Ramsey killing. It's my understanding you talked about this with the ME for his department. I'm curious as to why you didn't contact me."

"I did," Barron said. "I left you three messages over the course of the last five or so hours and have been waiting for your return call. I also left two other messages, one for Detective Ryder and the other for Detective Bishop. I haven't heard from them yet either."

I glanced at my phone. I had six voicemails I'd yet to check. I gave Jimmy a nod. Bishop checked his and nodded also. Jimmy removed his phone from his pocket and showed the voicemail notice to us, then said, "Cell voicemail. I'm sorry, Mike." His tone turned casual. "We've been working this case hard and haven't had a chance to check our private lines."

"Understood," Barron said. "I didn't bring it up to my friend. He's getting ready to retire, and he'd been going over cold cases he'd worked on. That one stumped him, so he gave me a call to discuss it. Given the number connection, I thought it pertinent to tell him what happened here. If I was out of line, my apologies."

"Just get with me first next time, please," Jimmy said. "Got to go." He disconnected the call.

Jimmy smiled at the Birmingham detective. "Our apologies."

"None necessary. I believe we have a mutual suspect, and I'd like to assist on the investigation," Johnson said.

"Can you brief us on your cases?" I asked.

Johnson handed us each a file from his briefcase and began telling us the basics. "Daniel Travis, twenty-two, college graduate. Just started a job with a supply chain company. He was found shot in the head outside an abandoned building off Fifth Avenue South. He was the first victim. The number was found in his left hand. Second was Justin Turner, twenty-three, college graduate. He hadn't yet found a job. His body was discovered in a new subdivision outside of a home in progress. Same MO as the other. And then, as I mentioned before, James Ryan Johnson," he said. "Twenty-three, just finished college and started a job. He was found shot in the head outside an abandoned chicken farm. Again, same MO, different location."

"And the numbers were in order?" Bishop asked.

He nodded.

Jimmy rubbed the bridge of his nose. "Damn."

I exhaled. "This was three years ago?"

"Yes, ma'am."

"And did you have any suspects?"

"No, ma'am. We had nothing. Still that way, unfortunately. The scenes were left clean, which, as I'm sure y'all know, requires some effort when it's a public location."

"Except for the chicken farm," Bishop added.

The detective gave him a questioning look.

"The chicken farm isn't a public place," Bishop said.

"Correct, but it was still left clean. The area surrounding the victim was raked in a calculated manner, as if the person was intent on keeping the lines straight."

Same, I thought. "What about persons of interest?"

Johnson shook his head.

"Outside of their murders and the scene, did you have anything to connect the victims?"

"No. They weren't connected on social media, didn't go to the same university, didn't have the same friends. They didn't have the same basic backgrounds either."

"If you don't mind," I said, "I'd like to have our tech expert do a little research. He's the best in the business."

"Anything to find our killer," he said.

I called Bubba into the conference room. Detective Johnson gave him the details of each case, and Bishop loaned him the file Johnson brought.

"Cool," Bubba said. "Give me some time, and I'll see what I can come up with."

Jimmy gave the go-ahead to work with the detective, but made it clear we were to work our investigation first and allow him to assist if necessary.

We explained what we'd learned about Ramsey and his possible sexual battery or rape of Emily Bryant.

"Our tech department didn't find anything that might suggest our victims were involved in something like that," Johnson said. "But that doesn't mean they weren't."

"If there's anything, Bubba will find it," I said.

We had yet to tell him about the missing body part. It was our golden ticket. If he brought it up, then we'd know he wasn't messing with us. If he didn't, then we could assume it was possible the murders weren't related, or it was a copycat who didn't have all the information or added their own slant on the murders, or that he was full of BS. We'd tell him eventually, just not yet.

"Excuse me for a moment," I said. I left the room and asked one of the slick sleeves in the pit to find me a clean whiteboard and bring it to the investigation room. When I stepped back into the room, Bishop and Johnson were in deep discussion.

"They were all the same?" Bishop asked.

Johnson nodded. "Down to every detail outside of location. Even the way the fire started was the same."

I sat beside Bishop again. "I've asked for another whiteboard. If we need an additional one that's fine, but I'd like you"—I gave a nod toward Johnson—"to write the specifics about each victim's death and the scene. We need to make the connection. If this is a serial killer, the first thing we need to do is look to every similarity in each murder and determine what is different."

Bishop agreed. "You're looking for a copycat, aren't you?"

"Yes." Johnson watched me carefully, but when I didn't say anything, he looked away. Something in his eyes told me he didn't believe it was a copycat. "You disagree?"

"It's not that I disagree. It's that we have four victims with the same circumstances surrounding their deaths, and you don't think it's the same guy, yet statistics show most deaths related to serial killers are done by the actual serial killer and not copycats."

"Have you ever heard of the copycat effect?" I asked.

"Yes, but I don't think we can—"

I interrupted him. "The effect is a largely underexplored theory in criminology and just like those who have taken the time to study it, I believe it can, and does, largely influence psychopaths." Johnson narrowed his eyes at me, but I continued. "Your last murder was three years ago and, in another state—"

It was his turn to interrupt me. "And my numbers were one, two, and three. So it stands to reason, ma'am, that if yours start with seven, then we're missing four, five, and six."

"Or they haven't been discovered," Bishop added.

Johnson had all but confirmed my copycat theory. "That's my point."

"But it doesn't show a copycat," he quickly added.

"Not yet," I said. "This could be some organized killer moving from state to state, murdering young men, and it's very likely that it is. My point is that we must consider all options. And the copycat theory is the definitive option for consideration whether we believe it's possible or not."

"Doesn't work for me," Johnson said.

I exhaled. "Were there any special circumstances you're leaving out of your crime scenes?"

"Such as?"

"Symbols, markings; maybe the killer took souvenirs from the victims?"

He raised an eyebrow. "Not that I'm aware of."

"Then clearly our medical examiner didn't give your medical examiner all the details."

"Such as?" he asked.

I went for it. Bishop wouldn't be pleased, but it was important to establish the need to consider all possible theories. Also, I didn't like the guy much, and I wasn't excited about sharing my investigation with him. "Such as, our victim's penis was cut off." I took great joy in watching him cringe as the realization of that kind of trauma hit home.

"That wasn't the case with my victims."

"Lucky for them," Bishop said.

"Definitely," Johnson said.

"So, either we've got the same killer who's leveled up, or a copycat who's added his own personal touch," I said.

"I can understand where you're coming from now," Johnson said. "Why didn't you tell me this before?"

"A good poker player doesn't reveal their winning cards until they have to," I said.

Johnson didn't have a response to that.

The patrol officer knocked on the door. Bishop helped him set up the whiteboard. I smiled and said thank you and asked if he could bring us one more just in case. I felt we'd need it.

"Yes ma'am," he said.

"Ma'am," Johnson said. "I've been doing this for twenty-five years, and while I can appreciate your experience in a big city like Chicago, this is not my first rodeo. I've been working these murders since day one, and your case is the first one to come across my line of sight that's even remotely similar."

Because my medical examiner had a big mouth, I thought. And that wasn't all I'd thought. Bishop's eyes shifted toward me, and I felt the side of his knee connect with mine. It was a warning, but I didn't care. I straightened my posture and then stiffened my shoulders. "Detective Johnson, I respect that you've done your homework on me. And since you have, let me ask you this. How many homicides have you worked? And how many of those homicides did you close? And of the ones you closed, how many of those killers were found guilty? Because I'm going to guess your twenty-five years of experience in the moderately sized town of Birmingham, Alabama"—I stressed the name of his state—"were a hell of a lot less than my experience in Chicago in half the time."

Bishop coughed. "How about we circle back to our goal here?" He slid a fresh dry-erase marker across the table to the detective. "If you wouldn't mind following our lead on our whiteboards. While you're doing that, I'd like to speak with Detective Ryder in the hall, please."

He practically dragged me out the door. His nostrils flared, and his face turned the color of blood. "Are you kidding me right now? Is that how you want this to go?"

I angled my head to the side and kept my voice low. I didn't want the chief coming back and getting in my face. "Careful, Rob. I don't want you stroking out in the middle of an investigation." He glared at me, and his nostrils flared even more. "Yes, Bishop. This is how I want this to go. If this backwoods, Buford T Justice–like dick is going to throw that bullshit *women are inferior to men* crap at me, you can bet I'm going to fight back."

Bishop rolled his eyes. "How many years is it going to take you to let this stuff go?"

"It would be nice to not get that kind of pushback because I have a vagina."

"Ever think it might be your people skills and not your body parts that are the problem?"

The officer returned with the additional whiteboard. He was smiling until he saw my face. "Everything okay, ma'am?"

"Yes. Thank you. Would you mind putting it in the room next to the other one?"

"Sure thing, ma'am."

I exhaled. "Fine. I'll do my best to ignore his stupidity, but just do me a favor. Have my back when he talks smack like that next time, please?"

"Will do."

"Thank you."

Johnson detailed the specifics of his three investigations, which, by the way, were as cold as a restaurant freezer. Admittedly, his cases were more like ours than I'd thought. The main difference was that his victims were shot and weren't missing any body parts.

"All three bullets were shot from the same weapon, a twenty-two using a suppressor," Johnson said. "We have the bullets. Hollow points."

"Experienced shooters know hollow points are deadlier than other bullets," Bishop said. "So, your guy is either an experienced shooter—"

"Or he didn't know the difference," I said. "Where was the shot?"

"Right eye on all three victims."

"Experienced," Bishop and I said at the same time.

My partner smiled at me. We both knew an eye shot was an almost guaranteed kill shot because it wasn't stopped by the skull. I studied Johnson's whiteboard. "Everything about these murders is calculated, well planned, and executed with attention to detail. If we go by the numbers, yours are the first victims."

"Yes," Johnson said.

"What about location of the actual murders?" Bishop asked.

"Unfortunately, we don't have the locations. We also have nothing on the victims or their clothing to show they were killed at the same location."

"Their clothing was clean, like our vic's," I said.

"Washed, dried, and pressed," Johnson said.

"Ditto," Bishop said. "Whoever did this wanted us to know he was smart enough to pull it off."

"Everything this guy did was to show us he believes he's smarter than us," I said.

Johnson's tone was considerate. "How many serial killer cases have you worked?" He directed his question to me.

"In Chicago, law enforcement defines 'serial killer' slightly different. We can have a gang member shoot five guys in a night, killing them all, and technically that's a serial killer. But in Chicago, we call it a mass shooter." I'd effectively answered the question without answering the question.

"That's a mass shooter here too," Bishop said.

"Same in Alabama," Johnson said.

Bubba rushed in. "I've got it!" His eyes were filled with excitement. "The connection. It's the girls."

"Do you mean the same girls?" Bishop asked.

Bubba shook his head. "No, I mean it's some form of sexual aggression toward girls. Each of your three guys"—he looked at Johnson—"all have accusations of assault, aggression, or date rape during college. Three different women." He handed us each a stack of papers. "Daniel Travis, Justin Turner, and James Ryan Johnson each have their own page. Daniel Travis has accusations from five years ago; Justin Turner, five and a half years ago; and James Ryan Johnson, four years and two months to the day. I've printed out copies of the information from social media. However, Johnson is the only victim who is outright accused."

"So, the first two are like our female assault victim?" Bishop asked.

"With respect to the fact that the accusations were alluded to, yes, but these social media posts are pretty obvious."

"Obvious doesn't do well in court," Johnson said.

"Reasonable doubt," Bubba said.

I wanted to give him a high five. "Do you have the contact information for the girls?"

"I knew you would ask for that. I have all but the Travis victim." He handed us each another paper with the addresses of the first two girls typed on them. "I'll continue looking for the Travis girl. Best I can tell, she's not in any photos, and if she is, she wasn't tagged or referred to by name."

"This is excellent work," Johnson said. "I can't believe you were able to make these connections so quickly."

"Bubba is a genius when it comes to technology," Bishop said.

Bubba blushed. "Thanks, though I wouldn't say 'genius.' Highly skilled in manipulating technology to the degree that I could easily hack into the government, maybe, but not yet a genius."

We all laughed.

"While Bubba continues to scour social media, I'd like to go to Jacob Ramsey's work and see what we can find out there."

"Meaning?" Johnson asked.

"Meaning if he was the scumbag I think he was."

"Oh," Bubba said. "I checked into the uncle. Nothing on him."

"Nothing at all?" I asked.

"Nope. Not even a parking ticket. In fact, he hasn't had a license in almost seven years."

"Thanks."

"No prob," Bubba said. "I'll get back in touch when I find what I'm looking for."

As he left the room, Johnson asked, "Can he really hack into the government?"

"Probably," I said.

"Damn."

10

To say Jacob Ramsey wasn't well liked at work was an understatement. Granted, he was in sales, and sales reps needed egos to succeed, and according to the four women at his office, he had the biggest ego their side of the Mason–Dixon line.

Nobody in Chicago ever thought about the Mason–Dixon line.

"Is Mr. Ramsey, okay?" the receptionist asked. "No, wait. He's been arrested, hasn't he? It's about time."

"I'm afraid there's been a situation," I said. Surprisingly, the media hadn't picked up the murder, and we didn't want too much going through the grapevine. "And we're working to determine what happened. Any insight into his time here would be appreciated."

"Jacob was the kind of guy you didn't want to look in the eye," the receptionist said. "And I hate talking ill of people behind their backs, but I have to speak my truth."

"Can you expand on that truth?" Bishop asked.

The woman looked to be in her mid-forties, and from the ragged and rough dark circles under her eyes, been around the block multiple times. "I mean, if you gave him an inch, he'd take a mile. He was a flirt, but in the sleazy, don't-trust-him kind of way." She looked up at me from the reception desk. "You're an attractive woman like me. You know what I'm saying."

I smiled. "I do, but my partner needs to be educated."

"Well," she continued, "Jacob—and that's what he preferred to be called. Not Jake. He said that was only for his close friends and family." She rolled her eyes. "Anyway, if you gave him any indication that you might find him attractive, something as simple as eye contact, he took that to mean you wanted to sleep with him."

Bishop's lip twitched. "With all due respect, ma'am, wasn't Ramsey younger than you?"

Oh boy. Dig that hole deep enough to toss yourself into it, partner.

"Age wasn't a detractor."

Bishop opened his mouth, but no words came out, so I saved him. "He liked MILFs."

"He liked women," she said. "But contrary to what you might think, this MILF wasn't an option."

"Did he ever date anyone in the office?" Johnson asked.

"Honey, Jacob Ramsey didn't *date* women. He slept with them."

"Did he sleep with anyone in the office?" he asked.

"Sir, with all due respect, that is not a question I can answer." She tapped on the company phone. "Sara, would you mind coming and speaking to these wonderful detectives about Mr. Ramsey?" She paused. "Yes, ma'am, at the reception desk." She paused again while Sara spoke, then said, "It's not my place, Sara." She hung up the phone. "Sara from Human Resources will be with you in a moment." She guided us toward the sitting area.

I stayed behind. "Miss—"

"It's Tiffani, with an *I*." She flicked her head toward the male detectives. "You got yourself an interesting group there. That one in the outdated sports coat? He's a winner."

"He's not mine," I whispered. "He's from Birmingham."

"I should have known. I'm a Georgia fan. Anyone from the state of Alabama is an archnemesis." She chuckled. "Ultimately it all comes back to college football."

"Understood," I said. "Tiffani, between us, do you know of anyone Ramsey might have had some kind of relationship with?"

"You mean did he dip the breadstick into the gravy before supper?"

"Yes," I said smiling.

"Well," she said, "between us, I didn't just call Sara up here because she's from HR."

"Thank you," I said. "You're good people, Tiffani with an *I*."

"You know it, sweetie!"

Sara Stanford was an attractive woman who'd either gone with the recent trend to color her hair gray or went gray young. I estimated her age to be around thirty-two based on the appearance of small veins on her hands and a slight eleven forming at the bridge of her nose. I was good at age-guessing. So good, my former peers in Chicago used to test me and make bets on the odds. I made a few detectives a lot of beer money.

"Please join me in the conference room," she said.

As we followed behind her, I caught a glimpse of Johnson checking out her ass. I felt an odd sense of relief when I looked to see if my partner was doing the same thing and saw he wasn't.

"Ms. Stanford, I'm sure you are aware of the situation with Jacob Ramsey," I said.

She nodded. "Of course, I would never wish anyone dead, but I can't say he didn't have it coming."

Bishop removed his spiral notepad from his jacket pocket. "Can you elaborate?"

"Jacob Ramsey had a reputation of being aggressive with the ladies, and that created a lot of issues for us given today's work environment."

"Were women reporting him to HR?" I asked.

She nodded. "But unfortunately, I'm not at liberty to share their private information."

"Can you say how many women?" I asked.

"Three in his month with us."

My eyes widened. "And in a general sense, were they women that went on dates with the victim or something else?"

"It's my understanding it was both for one, and the others just something else. Keep in mind, these are the three women who reported him. There were likely others."

I nodded, then asked the two male detectives to step outside. Johnson looked at me like I'd lost my mind. "Detective," I said. "I feel this is a conversation that would serve us better if it was just between the women."

Bishop took lead leaving the room. After the door closed, I shifted back to Sara Stanford, and with a calm, understanding tone, said, "Which of the three were you?"

She exhaled and kept her posture rigid. "Contrary to office rumors, which I'm sure the receptionist mentioned, and though he was very persuasive, I refused to go out with him."

"And how did he take that?"

"Not very well. He began harassing me. Leaving me voicemails on my personal cell phone telling me how he was so great in bed, and he'd always wanted to..." She paused. "Fuck an older woman."

"May I ask how he got your personal cell phone number?"

"It's in the company directory. Or it was. When we realized he'd done something similar to two previous employees, he was fired."

I blinked. "Jacob Ramsey was fired? When?"

"Four days ago."

That was news to me. "Ms. Stanford, about the other women, would you—"

She shook her head before I even finished. "I don't think that's appropriate."

"We can subpoena the information." That was a slight exaggeration since we had no reason to at that point, but she didn't need to know that.

"I don't want us becoming suspects in an investigation. What's happened?"

"I'm not at liberty to say, but it's better to be looked at as a person of interest rather than be investigated as a suspect."

"That makes sense," she said. "But what will happen to the women? To me?"

I asked her where she was the day we estimated Jacob Ramsey was murdered.

"I just can't believe he's dead. Are you sure it's him?"

"We have a positive ID."

"I was at work, at least during the day. That night I had a spin class at Lifetime Fitness, which I will be on record for taking and arriving and leaving the gym, and then after, I went to the grocery store, then stopped and got Chinese takeout and went home. I have my receipts, if you'd like to see them."

Stanford didn't strike me as the kind of person to commit murder, but I had to be sure. "The receipts would be great, as would the location of the gym."

"I don't wish death on anyone, but when someone acts the way Ramsey has, something bad is bound to happen."

I released a breath without realizing I was even holding it. I was worried she was going to say something like *He was bound to have his penis cut off.* I was relieved she didn't. I liked her and didn't want to arrest her even if she'd meant it as a joke.

"Can I say something off the record?" she asked.

"Nothing is off the record in a police investigation," I responded.

"Very well, but I'm going to say it anyway. If Jacob Ramsey is dead, which I'm assuming he is, I want you to find out what happened. He stalked and taunted me, and it was horrible. If someone killed him, I want to thank them. They deserve a medal."

I wasn't sure his parents would agree. "Ms. Stanford, do you think any of the other women at the office wish ill on Ramsey? Ill enough to seek revenge?"

She blinked and hesitated before speaking. "No. Ramsey liked to hit on the easily intimidated women. I think it gave him power."

"You don't strike me as someone who's easily intimidated."

"I'm not in law enforcement, but I am in human resources, and you can't be weak in my job. But I think I was different because I was a challenge and older. I must have been a notch on his bedpost he'd yet to achieve."

"Understood," I said.

She nodded. "I'll get my receipts and their information, though I ask that you keep that private, and meet you back at the reception desk."

"Thank you."

The reception desk was two feet from the conference room, which killed my opportunity to sneak to any cubicles and talk with anyone else.

"What's going on?" Bishop asked.

"She's getting me the contact info for the women."

"How'd you do that?"

I smiled. "Women's magic."

Sara Stanford walked out of the conference room with a small envelope. "None of them work here anymore, but I wouldn't have allowed you to try and talk to them here anyway. We don't like our work environment disrupted."

"Thank you," I said. I handed her my card. "If you think of anything or have additional information, please call me."

"Will do."

Johnson climbed into the back of Bishop's vehicle. "Doesn't make sense to me that a woman feels uncomfortable talking to law enforcement about a crime committed against her."

My jaw tightened, and I counted to five before speaking. I used to count to ten, which didn't help, and from the thoughts brewing in my head, I was confident five wouldn't help either, but I gave it a shot anyway. "It wasn't about being uncomfortable talking to law enforcement. It's because you're male." I rolled my eyes, but not because he was an idiot, which he was, but because I took the high road and didn't tell him that.

"We don't have any female cops on our force."

"Maybe that's why no girls have come forward about your victims," I said.

Bishop shifted his eyes my direction. It was a warning. If I was smart, I'd have taken it.

"I don't see why that should matter, us being men," Johnson said. "If you want us to catch the guy who's hurt you, you need to be honest with us."

"Male cops always have a shroud of doubt about a sexual battery or rape victim's claims," I said. "It's not rocket science. You doubt them; they become afraid to tell their story."

"The law states a suspect is innocent until proven guilty," he said.

Was he really going down that route? Was this guy from colonial times? Had he skipped learning about women's rights? "Of course suspects are innocent until proven guilty. That's not the point." I shook my head. It wasn't worth telling him the point because he wouldn't learn from it anyway.

"Then what's the point?" he asked.

Well, since he asked... "Retelling such a horrific and intimate crime is emotionally taxing. For starters, women immediately feel it's their fault, which is traumatic on its own. Often, the trauma of the event impairs their ability to recall details. Studies show eighty-five percent of rape victims had trouble recalling the events of an attack or couldn't give a chorological account of it. In many cases some did report it but showed no emotion at all or even smiled and laughed as they recounted the crime as a way of protecting their emotions and dealing with the trauma."

"What studies?" he asked.

I watched Bishop roll his eyes. "My partner is a researcher. She likes to know facts."

"It's important to the job," I said.

"Maybe where you come from," Johnson said. "But in my town, we look at the individual, not some studies funded by companies that want specific results."

I clenched my fists, but before I had a chance to speak, Bishop did. "How about we table the rest of this conversation until we find our killer?"

"I agree. That's what I'm here to do," Johnson said.

My cell phone rang. The caller ID showed the department. I answered with "Ryder."

"I've found some things I think you might want to see," Bubba said.

"We're on our way back now."

11

We rushed back and met Bubba in the investigation room.

"So, all the murder victims were in fraternities, not just Ramsey. Personally, I was a GDI, but I never cared much about the Greek system," Bubba said.

"What's a GDI?" Bishop asked.

"God Damn Independent," Bubba said. "It's kind of a play on words. You know, the Greek system uses Greek letters, so those of us who didn't join used English letters, and..." He stopped when he realized Bishop didn't care about the extended details. "Anyway, each of the six victims were in fraternities."

"The same one?" I asked.

He shook his head. "But they all held officer positions in each of their chapters."

I jotted that down.

"Are you suggesting the murders have some relationship to the college Greek system?" Johnson asked.

"I'm just looking for patterns, sir."

Johnson's lips formed a thin straight line. Bubba's excitement warped into nervousness. "Uh, and I also learned each victim went to college with a scholarship, but none of the scholarships were the same."

"Which helps us how?" Johnson asked.

I wanted to punch him in the balls. "He's developing a profile of the victims," I said. He really got on my nerves. "It helps us determine possible suspects."

Johnson's words were full of disdain. "I understand that. What I don't understand is why he isn't looking for similarities instead of differences."

"I am, but that research finds both." Bubba hopped on his toes. "They were all athletic and had no siblings."

"Did they play the same sport?" Bishop asked.

"It's split between two. Some played lacrosse; the others played baseball. No sports scholarships. Only club teams on the college level."

"I'm assuming they played prior to college?" I asked.

He nodded. "Not on the same teams, but yes, each played their respective sport from elementary school up." He handed us each a piece of paper. "I've looked into each team and am currently running a program to see if any of the teams ever played against each other."

"For what reason?" Johnson asked.

Bubba stumbled over his words so much that Bishop spoke over him. "To establish a connection."

"I understand," Johnson said.

"Anything on Travis's alleged female victim?" I asked.

"Yes, ma'am." He gave us all another paper. "Claire Baker, and contrary to what I said before, she's in several photos, but she has different hair in each of them, so I didn't catch it at first."

"So, we have all the women's contact information now," I said.

He nodded.

I gathered all my papers into my case file. "I'm going to make some calls. If I can get anything from even half of the victims, it'll help push things forward."

"I'd like to send a detective from my department to talk to our girls," Johnson said.

"I think that's a good idea," Bishop said.

"It is, but I'd like to call them first. If we send a guy out, he might scare them off. I can get the initial info and tell them someone will be coming out for a more formal interview." I looked directly at Johnson. "Would you like to head back to Birmingham and handle the interviews yourself?"

"I think that's a great idea," he said.

Thank God. "Good. Then it's settled. Once I have their stories straight, I'll be in touch."

I still couldn't speak with all of the male victim's alleged female victims, but Claire Baker answered her phone on the second ring.

"Ms. Baker, this is Detective Rachel Ryder with the Hamby Georgia Police Department. We're investigating a string of murders, one which includes your alleged assailant, Daniel Travis."

She was extremely clear and to the point for a young woman. "You mean my rapist. And how do you know about that?"

"We have a talented forensic technology team."

"None of my friends knew." She paused, then exhaled. "At least not for sure."

"There were accusations on social media."

"And they were correct, but I never told them directly. Why are you calling me?"

"We're investigating all avenues regarding the murders."

"So, you're saying I'm a suspect?" She laughed. "I didn't kill Dan, though I celebrated when I found out someone else did. Why isn't someone from Birmingham calling me?"

"I believe you'll be contacted by Detective William Johnson from the Birmingham PD, but we are working together to find Mr. Travis's killer."

"I don't understand why you'd want to find his killer. Dan was a rapist. He deserved what he got."

"I can understand how you would feel that way, but murder is a crime, and his killer may be involved in other crimes. We have a murder here in Georgia that aligns with three murders in Alabama, and one of those is your alleged assailant."

"You've said 'alleged' twice. He wasn't alleged. He *raped* me. The only reason it wasn't worse was because I kneed him in the balls. Otherwise, I don't know what else he would have done to me."

"I understand. Did you go to the hospital after the incident?"

"After the rape, you mean? No."

"May I ask why not?"

"Because I was afraid and ashamed. It doesn't matter how many people say to go to the hospital, or how many ads you see online about rape, in that moment, it's still impossible to do what they say."

"The hospital has ways of proving rape. They could have helped you."

"Maybe, but I was embarrassed that I'd let it happen. I blamed myself, and I knew Dan would get away with it. I was in college. I was young and stupid, and I'd been drinking. They would've tested my blood alcohol level and blamed me."

"You said you didn't tell any of your friends. What about a priest or someone from your church?"

"I'm agnostic, but I did tell my father."

That was surprising. Most rape victims didn't tell family, at least not in the beginning, and often, when they did, they told a female. "What about your mother?"

"She's deceased."

"I'm sorry for your loss."

"I was three. I've moved past it."

"Did your father encourage you to go to the police?"

"No. He knew I wanted to move on."

"Was he upset about that?"

"What do you think? He wanted to kill Dan, but he didn't. My father would never do that."

"Do you know any other women Mr. Travis might have had relations with?"

"I didn't have relations with him, and Alabama's a big school. I'm sure I wasn't the only girl he raped."

"I'd like to talk to your father. Can you tell me how to reach him?"

"Should be easy. He's in Atlanta on business." She gave me his cell number.

I asked her where she was the night of Daniel Travis's murder. She said she was at work and that it could be verified. I took the information and checked. Though she was obviously still angry, and her personality appeared to be type A, she didn't come off as the killer anyway.

Her father was a different story.

I contacted Scott Baker on his cell, explained why I wanted to speak with him, and asked that we meet. He had one meeting left and said we could meet where he was staying in Alpharetta.

Bishop and I headed to Alpharetta to meet with Scott Baker. He walked into the independent coffee shop, and I immediately knew it was him. Bishop knew also, but he cheated and checked his photo on his driver's license when he searched for any police record.

Scott Baker's record was clean.

I approached him while he ordered a coffee. He was tall, probably close to six feet four, well dressed in a dark suit with a crisp white shirt underneath. His hair was that perfect mix of salt and pepper, the kind of color women drooled over. He appeared distinguished and calm, and clearly type A.

He sat across from us at the small table in the corner of the café. "I spoke with my daughter. You don't think she has anything to do with Daniel Travis's death? And if you do, isn't that something the Birmingham police should handle?"

"We are investigating murders that might be connected to Daniel Travis's," I said.

He nodded. "I heard about them on the news. My daughter hasn't left the state in over a year. She couldn't possibly be involved in those."

"We aren't looking at your daughter as a suspect."

"Had you ever met Daniel Travis?" Bishop asked.

"No, and he's lucky. Had I met him after he raped my daughter, I would —" He stopped himself. "No, I did not."

Bishop asked him where he was the night Travis was murdered.

"You can't possibly think I—" He shook his head and his posture stiffened. "Perhaps I should contact my attorney."

"You're not under arrest," I said. "We're simply gathering information."

"I was home. I'd been out of town for a few days and worked from home that day. I can verify my trip."

"Was your daughter home with you?"

"I believe she was at work."

"When did she come home?" I asked.

"I don't know. She's got two jobs. I'm not sure which one she works at what time. I don't have to micromanage my daughter, Detective."

"Why didn't you encourage your daughter to go to the police?" Bishop asked.

"Do you have a daughter, Detective Bishop?"

Bishop nodded once.

"How easy is it for you to convince her to do anything?"

"I would take her to the police myself."

"Likely because you are law enforcement," he said. "But unfortunately, I am not. I have raised my daughter alone since she was three. We have a very close relationship. She was adamant about keeping the incident to herself, and I respect that decision. I didn't like it, but I promised her I would do as she wished."

"How long have you been in town?" I asked.

"Four days, and before you ask, I was in my hotel room by seven o'clock each evening. I can verify where I was with receipts."

"Did you attend any dinners?" I asked.

"I prefer keeping my nights free even when I travel."

Free to murder?

"Can anyone verify you were in your hotel room?"

"If you're asking if I had any guests, no, I didn't."

He provided us with the hotel information.

We asked him a few more questions to see if his answers would change, but they didn't.

Prior to leaving, he leaned toward us and whispered under gritted teeth, "Travis raped my daughter. If you think I'm sorry that son of a bitch is dead, you're wrong. I'm just sorry it wasn't me that took him out."

We waited until he left the coffee shop's parking lot to make sure he wasn't going to his hotel. Bishop looked at me from the driver's seat. "Nice ride."

Baker drove a late-model Infiniti sports car. I didn't know the specific model, but I knew an Infiniti when I saw one. "I don't like that guy, and I'm with you, and he doesn't have a verifiable alibi for either murder."

"Seems pretty detail oriented to me. Just like our killer."

I agreed. "Did you see his fingernails? He gets manicures."

Bishop grimaced. "I don't understand why guys do that."

"Maybe to get DNA off their fingers? The way he said he was happy Travis is dead was calculated and cold."

"We need to spend some time on this guy."

"Hotel first," I said.

He drove to the Marriott on Windward Parkway. The staff wouldn't give us any personal information or even confirm Mr. Baker was a guest. The manager also wouldn't show us any video footage without a subpoena. Bishop explained the information could be vital to an important investigation, and since the cameras were in plain view, guests gave up their rights to privacy on them, but it didn't matter.

The manager either thought he was supporting his client or he was hiding something. "We're happy to get a subpoena to view your cameras, and if we find anything related to any crimes, we will make sure those are handled appropriately," I said. I smiled, then we turned around and left.

"Useless," Bishop said. "And we won't get a subpoena, not anytime before this goes to trial, but I think we're onto something here. Baker's got motive and he's been in town. He's our key person of interest."

"Let's keep that under the belt for the time being," I said. "We don't want that getting out to the papers."

"That means Jimmy will have to keep it from the mayor."

"I don't see a problem with that," I said, and then I yawned. I was exhausted.

Bubba and I did some research on Scott Baker.

"He's clean," Bubba said.

"A clean record doesn't mean he's innocent. It could mean he's just not been caught yet."

"If this is the guy it could be huge. We could catch a serial killer."

"We need a hell of a lot of evidence to prove he's the guy."

"If he is, you'll find it," Bubba said.

He had more confidence in me than I did. Something about Baker struck me as off, and he did check several of the profile boxes, but internally, my gut wasn't feeling him as the one. My head, however, disagreed. "Whoever's doing this is good. We may not find anything."

"I did some research. Right now, other than our guy, there are nine serial killers still at large in the US. And did you know that at any time there are somewhere between twenty-five to fifty active serial killers out there? That's crazy. I read about one still on the loose, Jeff Davis. His victims had a lot more in common than ours. That's why I keep looking for something to connect our victims."

"All it takes is one connection, and it could be a connection only the killer sees." I glanced at my cell phone. "Have you heard from Michels?" I'd asked Michels to do a little research on Johnson. I realized it was out of line, but the guy appeared from nowhere, granted, with a solid reason, but I didn't like him, and that meant I didn't trust him.

"Not yet." He looked at his watch. "Dang, I didn't realize it was so late." He yawned and it made me yawn too. "I'll stay for another thirty minutes or so and see what I can find, but I've got to get some rest."

"Right there with you."

I needed five minutes to decompress. The case weighed heavily on my shoulders, and nothing was going the way it should have. Time was passing, and if we didn't find a suspect soon, we'd be out of luck.

Bishop walked into my cubicle. "Hey. You okay?"

I lifted my head off my arms resting on my desk. "I'm tired and cranky and hangry."

"That's a recipe for disaster."

"Be thankful Detective Johnson's gone and you're not him."

He sat across from me. "You really don't like that guy."

"How'd you guess?"

He laughed. "The whole department can tell. I'm not really a fan either, but we've got to work with him."

"I know, but I don't have to like it or him."

"True." He crooked his neck from one side to the other and it made a popping sound. "Ah, that feels better." He smiled. "It's late. Let's get some dinner and toss ideas around."

"We've been tossing ideas at each other all day and it's not helping, but dinner sounds perfect."

"Duke's?"

I nodded. "I could use a burger."

"Duke's it is."

We took separate cars, our personal vehicles, this time. I called Kyle on the way.

"Find your guy yet?" he asked.

"Not even close."

"You will. You're the best there is."

"That's sweet. Highly exaggerated, but sweet."

"So, you think the doer is the same as the one in Birmingham?"

"Did you talk to Jimmy again?"

"He called me and warned me you might be in a bad place."

"Because we have a possible serial killer or copycat?"

"Because you think the detective from Alabama is an asshole."

"He is, and in my defense, Bishop isn't a fan either."

He laughed. "No judgment on my end."

"He's a backward cop who's never heard of the women's rights movement."

"I'm sure he's heard of it. He probably just doesn't care about it."

"Then he's a bigger asshole."

"You going home? I can come out."

"I'm going to eat with Bishop. I'm hangry."

"Poor Bishop."

"Seriously. Then I'll probably head home and get some sleep. We've got our night shift detectives reading through everything related to the case, including the autopsy reports. If they find something, they'll call us in, but we need sleep." I paused, and then said, "Oh, did Jimmy tell you the Birmingham victims still had all their body parts?"

"He did, and I can admit I felt some relief for them."

I laughed. "I bet!"

"Does that say 'copycat' to you?"

"That's the direction I'm heading, and I'm going to discuss it with Bishop at dinner, but we have an alleged sexual assault victim from Alabama whose father is a person of interest."

"That's a good thing."

"Like Bishop said, he checks a lot of the boxes for your average highly intelligent serial killer, but even so, something's not right. I'm not feeling it."

"You think he's intelligent?"

"Maybe that's a bad word choice. I think he's detailed-oriented and a perfectionist, which many serial killers are."

"You'll figure it out."

I yawned. "Hopefully before someone else dies."

Bishop got us a private booth in the back of the restaurant. The staff knew when Hamby PD sat in the back booth, their conversation was serious, and they didn't bug us more than necessary.

"I'll take a Duke's burger with pepper jack cheese and the works," I said. "Oh, and may I have extra pickles and tater tots instead of fries?"

"Sure thing," the server said.

Bishop ordered his food and then smiled at me when the server left. "Did you know you only eat tater tots when you say you're hangry?"

"Really?"

He nodded. "Been your partner for a few years now. If anyone would know, it would be me."

"Speaking of partners knowing their partners, regarding your girlfriend..." It was the perfect time to bring it up. We both needed something lighthearted, and I was nosy.

He sipped his beer then tilted his left ear toward me. "What's that? I thought I heard girlfriend, but I'm entirely too old for one of those."

"Even though you've denied it, you're dating someone."

He choked on another sip.

I pointed to him. "I knew it!" I leaned back in the seat and crossed my arms over my chest. "I demand details."

He played dumb. "What makes you think I'm dating someone?"

I eyed him and used his words against him. "Been your partner for a few years now. If anyone would know, it would be me."

"Well played."

"So?"

"So, yes. There is a woman, not a girl. It's nothing serious. We're just getting to know each other. Or we were until we got this case."

"Murder puts a damper on the sex life, doesn't it?"

He blushed. "I'm not having sex with her. I'm spending time with her."

"Oh, okay. Whatever you want to call it is fine with me. Why didn't you tell me?"

"I was planning to, but the fire and the murder took precedence."

"Don't lie to me."

"I'm not lying to you. We're just spending time together. I wouldn't exactly call that dating."

"It's one and the same, and you've been doing it for at least a month."

The side of his mouth twitched. "What makes you think that?"

"Because you've shaved almost every day. You never do that."

The side of his mouth twitched again. He sighed. "I have spent time with her over the last month, yes, but that's it. We aren't going steady or anything like that."

I smacked my hand onto the table, then yelled, "I knew it!" and half the restaurant stared at me. I lowered my voice. "Again, why didn't you tell me? And FYI, nobody goes steady. That went out when CDs were invented."

He shrugged, then leaned toward me and kept his voice low. "I just didn't want to jinx it, you know? Besides, I gave you so much crap about Olsen, I didn't want you getting retribution."

"I would never do that."

He dipped his head and rolled his eyes. "Right."

"Okay, fine. I'm definitely going to do that, but I'm happy for you. You deserve to be happy." My smile faded, and my tone turned serious. "You are happy, aren't you?"

"I'm cautiously optimistic."

Bishop's wife cheated on him. It happened before I'd come to Hamby, but from what I'd learned, it had hit him hard. According to Jimmy, his relationship with his daughter suffered for a bit, but it was back on track and had been for a while. His ex-wife rarely came up in conversation, but I suspected he was lonely and very likely afraid to get back in the dating game. I was glad he'd finally decided to give it a shot.

"I'll take that," I said.

The food arrived. I slathered ketchup and mustard on my burger and dove in like I hadn't eaten in years. And it felt like that. "This is so good."

He stared at my face. "You've got a little mustard right here." He pointed to the corner of my mouth and handed me a napkin. "I can't take you anywhere, can I?"

I spoke with a full mouth. "Tell me about her. What's her name? How old is she? Where does she live? What does she do? How did you meet her? Does she know you have a female partner? A younger, attractive female partner, that is."

"I had no idea you were this nosy."

"I'm a detective. It comes with the territory. Now spill it."

"Maybe we should be talking about our possible suspect instead?"

I sighed. "I need to distract myself from the case for a little bit. It's overwhelming, and my brain is stuck. I need a distraction, and this is perfect."

"Her name is Catherine Jensen. She's forty-six." His eyes kind of glazed over as he spoke. "She lives in Cumming."

The name rang a bell, but I couldn't place it. "And?"

"And what?"

"And what about the rest of my questions? Seriously, if you don't want me to hound you endlessly for details, because you know I will, then tell me now."

"Even if I tell you everything, you'll hound me endlessly for details."

I'd just finished chewing and swallowed before speaking. "That's true, but still, tell me what I want to know."

He took a bite of his chicken breast and held up a finger. He was stalling, so I kicked him under the table. "Ouch, that hurt. You're wearing heavy boots."

"Then you'd better start talking. Those aren't my only means of extracting information from someone."

He smiled. "She's a schoolteacher."

"You met her when you were pretend coaching, didn't you?" We'd worked a joint provisional task force with the DEA and Kyle a while back. Bishop worked undercover as a history teacher and football coach, and he had the time of his life. I played the role of a school counselor, under extreme duress, but I got through it without too many scrapes and cuts. Aside from the tragedy of multiple kids dying from drug overdosing, Bishop thrived in his undercover position. It took me a second, but I got there. "Catherine? I mean, Mrs. Jensen, the European history teacher?"

He smiled, a big, toothy, full-faced smile. "That's the one."

"I loved her! And she's hot." I popped a tater tot into my mouth. "You're definitely dating up, dude."

"Gee, thanks." He laughed. "Now that we're done spilling the tea about my personal life, can we talk about the investigation, please?"

My mouth dropped open, and I stared at my partner in disbelief. "Did you really just say 'spilling the tea'?"

"Catherine is well versed in today's slang."

"I bet you're learning a lot from her."

He furrowed his brow. "The investigation, Ryder."

I popped another tot into my mouth. "I was edging closer to copycat, but now, I'm not so sure, and Baker? I don't know. It doesn't feel right."

"Explain the copycat change first." He took a forkful of lemon and balsamic Brussels sprouts and stuffed it into his mouth.

"I'm still working through it, but I think the biggest thing for me is the first three victims were shot in the head, and our guy had his throat sliced. And then of course, there's the penis issue."

He cringed. "I'd call that leveling up his game."

"That's my point. Serial killers change their MO all the time. Look at Bundy. Initially, he broke into women's homes, but he progressed to luring them to his vehicle to abduct them."

"And then he switched back to breaking and entering."

"He was desperate by then, so it doesn't have to be a copycat. It can be the same killer just changing his MO."

"True, but it could be that the copycat doesn't know all the details, or just decided to personalize the murder for shits and giggles," Bishop said.

"I wouldn't call lopping off someone's thing an act of shits and giggles."

He shuddered. "Point taken. Now, what about Baker? You liked him for it before. What's changed?"

"I don't know. I mean, he fits the general profile, but my gut tells me it's not him. We need that hotel tape."

"I agree. I made a few calls while you were talking to Bubba. I think we can get a subpoena for it, but not right away. DA's office says we need something concrete first. They don't want to mess this up. They want every *t* crossed and every *i* dotted when we bring someone in."

"What makes you think we'll get the subpoena, then?"

"Because I'm confident we'll get something on Baker that says it's him."

"Feels like a long shot at the moment."

"Keep the faith."

I leaned toward him. "I'm going to say something, and it's really hard for me to admit, so don't be a jerk."

"Well, when you put it that way, it'll be hard for me not to be."

I narrowed my eyes at him.

"I'm kidding. What is it?"

"I think we need to bring in a professional to help us with this."

"We are the professionals."

"I mean a criminal profiler. I know just enough about serial killers to be dangerous, and I'm guessing you either know about the same or less, but our chauvinist detective from Alabama knows even less than every civilian in this place right now combined. We need someone to help us profile our killer or killers, or we may never find him. Them. Her." I wiped my face with my napkin and sighed. "I don't think we have any other option here."

"Is that what's bothering you? Are you worried you won't be able to catch the killer?"

"Yes, I'm worried we won't be able to catch the killer, at least not before they kill again, and based on what we know about the first three numbers, we're going to have another killing."

"Do you know any profilers?"

"In Chicago, sure. Out here? Nope."

"Let's get the chief on the phone."

"How about we go to his place? I could use a dose of baby right about now, and then I need to go home and go to bed."

"It's after ten. You think the baby is still awake?"

"Savannah said she doesn't sleep more than an hour at a time."

"Poor kid."

"Poor Savannah," I said.

"Then a dose of baby is dessert." He ate the last of his meal while I finished mine.

Jimmy and Savannah had a baby girl. After five months of bed rest that drove everyone crazy, Scarlet came out perfectly a while back, and Savannah was only a little worse for wear. In a shocking and amazing turn of events, they made me her godmother. By definition, a godmother promised to care for that child in the unlikely event that something happened to its parents.

The closest I'd ever gotten to taking care of another living creature was Herman, and he upped and died on me. What did that say about me? Granted, he lived a heck of a lot longer than a betta fish should, but that was irrelevant. Herman never required much maintenance, and I didn't think my skills at feeding him once or twice a day and changing his water every week would qualify me for godparenting, but I gladly accepted the assignment.

And then proceeded to panic and read every book I could find on raising a daughter. Kyle thought it was hilarious and adorable, and Bishop didn't stop laughing for a month. Every time I asked him a question about diapers, colic, having the sex talk with a teenager, if that was even the proper age anymore, and if private schools were the best option, he'd roll his eyes. I just wanted to be prepared. I'd learned life was fleeting and could change in the blink of an eye.

Savannah met us at the door with a chunky, blond, blue-eyed little terror screaming her head off. "Here," she said, and handed me Scarlet. "Take this hot mess. I need a break."

I took the hot mess and made ridiculous cooing noises that resembled a sick animal. She wailed louder. I looked to my partner for help. "Help me, please."

He stretched out his arms. "Give me that sweet girl."

Bishop was a freaking wizard with babies. "There, now, sweet Scarlet." He rocked her and moved his hips back and forth.

"You're hired," Savannah said. "You're a master at this."

We followed her into the family room as Scarlet's cries softened to coos.

"He's hired," Jimmy said from the couch. He looked as exhausted as I felt.

Savannah plopped down beside him. "He's never leaving."

I laughed. Poor Sav. She was exhausted too. My Southern belle best friend who'd won beauty pageants, cotillion awards, and a host of other things normally put on her makeup and did her hair whether she'd planned to leave home or not, but not lately. I'm not sure she'd taken a shower every day since the baby arrived. Her hair was a tangled mess wrapped in a bun on the top of her head. She wore Jimmy's sweats and a bulky University of Georgia sweatshirt with baby-made stains all over it. Her nails hadn't seen a salon in months, and the dark circles under her eyes weren't intentional. Savannah was, as she'd said, a hot mess, but even so, I thought she was a boss. I thought that about every mother, though.

"I'm so exhausted, and oh my God, I'm dying for buffalo wings," she said. "I'll give you my life savings if you have buffalo wings."

"We do not," I said.

She leaned her head onto Jimmy's shoulder. "Useless detectives."

"Shh," Jimmy said. "One of them is holding our no-longer-crying hellion."

"Good point," she said. She closed her eyes. "I'm just going to enjoy the calm for a moment or two. Carry on."

"What's up?" Jimmy asked. "Tell me you're here because you caught our killer."

"We're here to tell you we caught our killer," I said.

He sat up. "Are you serious?"

Savannah fell behind him on the couch. "Why'd you move?"

I cringed. "No, but you told me to tell you it, so I did."

Savannah groaned. "And I was so comfortable."

I sat across from them in the chair while Bishop walked around the room rocking Scarlet. "If this is the same killer from Birmingham, we've got another two, maybe three days before they strike again."

"Bishop said you have a possible suspect. One of the fathers of an alleged assault victim in Birmingham?"

"She's not feeling it," Bishop said. He kissed Scarlet's forehead. "She's a silly girl, isn't she, Miss Scarlet?"

"He can't verify where he's been, and he claims he was at the hotel during the times of the fires, but the hotel won't give us the security tapes to verify his statement."

"I contacted the DA," Bishop said. "They don't seem all that interested to help without more to go on."

"It's a video tape," Jimmy said. "And if he's not on it, it's evidence to prove he's lying, which puts us in a possible right direction."

"I think she'll come around," Bishop said.

"We don't have time for that," I said. "We need to get this guy before he kills again."

"Hold on." He pulled out his cell phone and made a call. "District Attorney, it's James Abernathy, Hamby Chief of Police. I understand you're asking for more evidence before allowing a subpoena for—" He glanced at me.

"Windward Marriott."

"Video tape access from the Windward Marriott. My detectives have— Yes, ma'am. As I was saying, my detectives have a viable person of— No, ma'am." He paused. "If we are in fact dealing with a serial killer, then we've got one to two days before another murder. If word were to get out that we didn't move on this— Thank you, ma'am." He disconnected the call. "She'll have it to you in the morning."

I breathed a sigh of relief. "That's great, but we still need help. We need to get ahead of the game, and we don't have anything to get us there. Especially if the video tape ends up a dead end."

"What kind of help are you talking about?"

"A criminal profiler."

He rubbed his jaw. "They don't come cheap."

"I know."

"The mayor's on my ass about this already. He wanted the killer caught last night."

"We're detectives, not miracle workers," I said.

"Does he know we're dealing with a possible serial killer?" Bishop asked.

Jimmy shook his head. "I don't want that getting out to anyone."

"Even the mayor?" I asked.

"He's buddies with Jason Stiles now, like every mayor this town's had. We tell him we've got a possible serial killer, Stiles will find out. This doesn't need to be made public. We don't need that kind of chaos in town."

Jason Stiles was a reporter for the *Hamby Herald*, and a royal pain in the ass. The less he knew, the better off we all were. "Understood, but like I told Bishop, I don't think we can get this guy without help."

"You sure it's not a copycat?" Jimmy asked.

"I'm not sure of anything, and that's why we need help. We need to at least have a profile of the killer, something, anything, really, to help us define a suspect."

"I'm with her," Bishop said. He went back to rocking and walking and cooing softly at the baby.

"What's your gut tell you?"

"That Baker isn't our guy, but I can't tell you why." I rubbed my neck. "I'm exhausted. Bishop's exhausted. Bubba and I had a yawning competition an hour ago. We need someone with serial-killer-personality knowledge to look at this."

"Okay." He walked past Bishop and Scarlet, stopping for a moment to admire the child he'd made, then walked into the kitchen with his phone in hand.

While Jimmy talked with his contact, and Savannah snored on the couch—she would have been horrified to know that—Bishop and I competed for Scarlet's attention.

"It's my turn," I said.

He twisted away from me. "No. You'll make her cry like before."

So territorial. "Rob Bishop, I'm that child's godmother, and I demand you give me her now," I whispered, but I was sincere.

"No. She's finally asleep."

I laughed. "You're going to be such a good grandpa."

His eyes widened. "Like I said before, I'm not sure I want my girl having a baby in this world. Besides, I'm not ready for that." He carefully placed Scarlet in my ready arms. "Here, be gentle."

"I am being gentle."

"Don't wake her up. Don't even move. If you make her cry, you're on your own."

"Savannah's sleeping. I'm more worried about waking her up." Scarlet smelled glorious, like a freshly bathed baby, a hint of gentle soapy cleanliness and baby powder. To date, Louie never smelled, but his water did if it needed a cleaning, and it wasn't at all pleasant. There were a lot of differences between Scarlet and Louie, and they stressed me out just thinking about them. "Scarlet, sweetie," I whispered. "You're the prettiest little baby chunk in the world." And she was. I froze, worried talking directly to her would wake her. "Oh, thank God, she's still asleep."

"Praise God, and thank you, Jesus," Savannah said. She'd obviously woken up. "Don't move. She's a light sleeper."

My cell phone rang in my pocket and woke the beast. Scarlet's eyes pushed open and narrowed, and her mouth went from peaceful to pursed, and then fully opened when the raging began. I rushed her to Savannah. "Sorry, police business."

"I hate all of you," Savannah said.

"We love you too," I said, and answered my phone. "Ryder."

"This is Emily Bryant. I understand you want to talk to me?"

12

We met Emily Bryant at the police station. It was well past eleven, and we were exhausted, but when duty called, it was our job to answer. At least neither of us had baby barf on our clothing.

Emily looked different than she did online. She'd dyed her hair dark, cut it into a pixie, and wore almost no makeup. She dressed in clothing too big for her small frame. I assumed she did it to hide, not for comfort. Rape and sexual assault victims often did that.

"Please, have a seat," I said. We'd gone to a conference room. Bishop wasn't with us. He'd chosen to stay and listen in and watch from Bubba's tech room. We connected through my earpiece in case he had input.

She sat in the seat closest to the door. I noticed she wore her watch on her left wrist, so I assumed she was right-handed, and sat on her dominant side. I kept our chairs at a reasonable distance, but close enough that we could keep our voices down. Talking calmly and softly with a female alleged or real sexual assault victim eased their stress, and I needed her comfortable enough to talk. Sitting too close made them feel trapped and ready to bolt.

"Miss Bryant, there's been an incident—"

"I know Jake is dead."

There were few ways Bryant could know that. "How did you know?"

"His mother." She looked me straight in the eyes, and with intent, said, "I didn't kill him."

"That's good to know," I said. "But we're not to that question just yet." I offered her a small smile. "I'd like to talk to you about what happened between the two of you. Can you do that?" She was timid and insecure, and I didn't want to scare her off by using trigger words like "assault" or "rape."

"Nothing really happened. We went out for about a year and then we broke up."

"You dated him for that long?"

"Yes, ma'am. Isn't that why you wanted to talk to me?"

I moved forward with my questions without answering hers. "How did the relationship end?"

She stared off toward the back wall, and as her body stiffened, I knew her allegations were true. "You know, don't you?"

"I know something happened, but I don't know the details," I said.

Her bottom lip quivered. "He raped me, and then the next day it was like I was invisible."

"Did you report it to the police?"

She shook her head. "Why bother? We were dating when it happened. They wouldn't believe me."

It would have been a tough sell, but if she'd have had a rape exam, she'd have a better chance at being believed. "Emily, please know that when this happens, the first thing you should do is go to the hospital. They can perform an exam that will ensure the police understand what happened to you."

"You don't understand. I let him, but only at first. When he got aggressive, I wanted it to end."

"Did you tell him to stop?"

She nodded meekly. "We were dating. We had sex before. It wasn't like it was the first time and he forced it on me, at least not the normal things."

"Then it's rape whether you're dating or not." I paused to let that sink in. "Did he hurt you?"

"Yes, but I don't want to talk about it. Why am I here? Am I a suspect?"

"Tell me about the next day."

"That's when he broke up with me."

"What happened?"

"We were in the arboretum at school. I was with my friends, and he was sitting across the room with another girl. He was laughing and touching her knee. She was leaning into him and flirting. I watched them." She began to cry. I retrieved a box of tissues from the credenza in the room and handed it to her. "Thank you," she said. "Anyway, I watched them, and they kissed. When the girl left, I went over to him. By the time I made it across the room, a few of his friends were with him. I told him I saw what he'd done, and that after what happened the night before, he was a piece of trash."

"Good for you," I said.

She continued. "But he didn't care. He just laughed. He said I wanted exactly what he'd given me, and that's when he decided I wasn't good enough for him. He said he liked more of a challenge. And he told me that in front of all his friends. He said I was a bad—you know, and they all laughed. And then, it was like I didn't exist."

"That must have been hard."

She sucked back a sob. "He's an asshole." She spoke of him in present tense, a clear sign she wasn't the killer. Killers typically spoke of their victims in past tense.

"When did his mother call you?"

"This morning on my way to work."

"Were you two close?"

"Not really. She was upset, and I think she was on something because she slurred her words. Besides, she knew we dated for a year, so…"

"Did she know what happened with you two?"

She snickered. "Jake's a mama's boy. He doesn't do anything wrong, and it's not like she would have believed me if I'd told her."

"Do you know any other girls he may have done this to?"

"There were always rumors and social media posts about him with other girls, so I'm pretty sure he cheated on me all the time. Whether he raped someone else, I don't know, and I don't want to know."

"What did he do when you were around?"

"Hit on girls. It's like he was trying to make me angry, you know? Like he wanted to make me look stupid."

"Did that make you angry enough to kill him?"

"You think I did it?"

"I'm running an investigation, and it's my responsibility to ask questions like this."

Tears fell down her cheeks. "I was at my part-time job." She raised her hand and covered her face. "I haven't told anyone about it, but you can ask my boss. He'll confirm."

"Where's your part-time job?"

"Los Tequilas in Alpharetta. I'm a bartender. I was at work until two a.m." I tilted my head, but before I could say anything, she said, "I'm trying to save money to buy a townhouse or condo in downtown Alpharetta. I'm working my ass off, and I'm exhausted. I can't live at home anymore. It's too complicated."

"You live with your mother and uncle?"

She nodded.

"Where's your father?"

She shrugged. "I haven't seen him since I was a kid, and I don't care if I see him again."

"You said home is complicated. Can you explain?"

"My uncle is weird. He's got a medical condition, but he was weird before that. Always watching stupid shows my grandparents like on TV. Reads a lot, and he just sits around being, you know, weird. He makes me uncomfortable."

"And your mother?"

"She's gone through a lot. It's just hard to be around her. That's why I want to move. I don't like living there. It doesn't feel like home."

"Do you know of anyone that might want to hurt Jacob?"

She shook her head. "The guys liked him. He even did well in school. Mr. Charmer. Always sucking up to the professors. His parents are rich. He could do whatever he wanted."

I closed my notepad. "Emily, I'd like to leave the door open for us to talk further if need be." I stood.

She stood then too, and said, "Okay. But to be honest, I'm not upset he's dead, and if I had the guts, I would have killed him myself."

Bishop sat in the kitchen with a bottled water in his hand, his head leaned back, and his mouth wide open. The guy was tits up, as Lenny always said. I pushed his chin up to close his mouth, and he woke up.

He shook his head and gathered his senses. "Sorry, power nap."

It was really late. We all needed to go home and get some rest. "I'm jealous."

"So, what happened? You think she did it?"

"You didn't listen like you said?"

"I did, but I couldn't stay awake." He checked his watch. "It's late. I've barely had any sleep. I'm tired. Tell me, what happened?"

"She said he raped her." I grabbed a bottled water from the fridge and sat down next to him. "But no, I don't think she's the one. Though she did tell me if she had the balls, she would have done it herself."

"Damn." Bishop shook his head. "I'm just glad this didn't happen to my daughter. I'd be in prison."

"I have no doubt."

"So, we're at the same point we were before we talked to her."

I nodded.

"We need to put something out in the media on this." Bishop rubbed his eyes.

Maybe we do a call out for..." He pushed the chair back and stood. The chair legs scratched the tile floor, making me cringe.

"We don't make that call, and Jimmy doesn't want this on the news, remember? He doesn't want anyone knowing we've got a possible serial killer."

"If we don't do something, someone else will die, and then everyone will know."

"Then what are we supposed to say? *Dear public, there is a possible serial killer or copycat on the loose. If you have sexually assaulted or raped a young woman and you're a recent college graduate, then you better protect yourself?*"

"That's the part I'm stuck on." He yawned and stretched his back. "I need some real sleep. We've got our night team on this too, so let's get home and meet back here first thing in the morning."

"Works for me," I said.

Our cell phones rang as we headed out of the kitchen. We looked at them at the same time and saw our chief on FaceTime. When we answered, the look on his face told me everything we needed to know.

"We've got our next victim," he said.

13

Johnson stood next to the body.

I wasn't happy he was there. "What are you doing here? I thought you went back to Birmingham."

"I understand you only spoke with one of the alleged assault victims. I have a peer making contact for interviews. I was planning to leave for there in the morning. I rushed over when I heard about this."

"You never went to Alabama? Detective Johnson, I'm lead on this investigation, and I gave you an...a direct assignment to go back to Birmingham and interview the alleged assault victims. Now you're telling me you never left? Where have you been?"

"Let me be clear, Detective. I do not report to you, and you do not have the authority to direct me to do anything. When I learned you were only able to speak to one alleged assault victim, I made an executive decision to have a peer contact the women involved with my victims and schedule meetings for this morning. I don't owe you any explanation other than that."

"Do what you want, but when we catch this guy, and we will, don't think you'll be getting any credit." I stared down at the victim. "Damn," I said to Bishop. "We can't keep this hidden."

Except for the location, the scene was like the previous one. Young man, throat sliced, cleaned, and left to rest near a tree on the outskirts of the back of the polo fields. Neither Bishop nor I checked his pants to see if something was missing. I would have, but Bishop asked me not to. He wanted to leave that to Barron. The fields hadn't been used in years, and were for sale, but last I'd heard, no one was biting.

Jimmy walked up as I spoke. "No, we can't. Mayor's already on his way, and he's planning a news conference. He wants the world to know there's a serial killer on the loose, and he's determined to successfully take him out," Jimmy said.

"You're kidding, right?" I asked.

"Do I look like I'm kidding?"

"How does he know we're considering a serial killer?"

"Stiles is here. He heard two officers talking and called him. He's given Stiles the go-ahead to write it up."

"He can't say we've got a serial killer on the loose. The town will freak," Bishop said. "And the mayor can't either."

"No need to worry about the mayor," I said with sarcasm. "Because he's going to take him out."

Jimmy stared down at the victim. "Anyone check his area?"

Area. Nice word choice. "Not yet."

"Just giving the victim some privacy," Bishop said.

"Bishop asked me to wait until Barron got here," I said.

"You don't understand," Bishop said. "You don't have a penis."

"No, but at least I've got balls."

The fire inspector heard that exchange and laughed. He stood next to me. "Evening, folks. Sorry to have to meet this way again."

"Right," I said.

Jimmy shook Reed's hand. "Sorry you had to get up and deal with this, Don."

Detective Johnson walked around the victim and studied him carefully. He was in his own little world, and as long as he didn't bug me or disrupt our investigation, I didn't care what he did.

"Not your fault," Reed said. Once the fire's completely out, which should be in a matter of minutes, I'll proceed with my investigation, but from the looks of where the fire originated, and the remains of the gas can on scene, it appears it's a duplicate of what we saw the other night." He scratched his chin and moved his expertly coiffed beard slightly to the right. He adjusted it quickly. Clearly, he'd done that before. "Should we expect another one of these soon?"

I sighed. Bishop pressed his lips together, and Jimmy exhaled.

"I had three fires with murders in Alabama," Johnson said. "Each fire was started in a similar way. We're looking at a multistate serial killer, and given his calling card, the numbers in bags, we could be looking at his eighth murder."

"I'll take that as a yes," Reed said. "Do me a favor, let me be a part of the media frenzy when this blows up, will you? I'd like to make sure the fire part is handled properly."

"Of course," Jimmy said. "I think the mayor's planning a conference first thing in the morning."

"Oh hell. He shouldn't be the one doing that, not without our final report. I'll have a talk with him." Reed gave us a nod and walked away.

"He definitely shouldn't be doing that," Bishop said. "What happened to Stiles reporting it?"

"He's going to. This is step two in the mayor's plan to catch a killer."

"First of all—" I said.

Jimmy held up his hand. "I know."

I changed direction. "I really like Reed. He's not from around here."

Bishop smiled. "He's from Blue Ridge."

My eyes widened. "Really? He doesn't have an accent, and he seems so..." I stopped myself before I insulted my partner and the chief.

"Not all Southerners have an accent, Detective," Johnson said.

"Understood," I said with disdain.

"He's one of the guys that worked hard to get rid of his accent," Jimmy said. "Told me once it was a hinderance to people taking him seriously, especially in college."

"I can see that. In Chicago, if someone has a Southern accent, my first thought is the guy is stupid." I said that as I looked directly at Johnson, even though he didn't have much of an accent.

"That's why you treated us the way you did when you first came on board?" Bishop asked with a smile.

"You're an asshole."

Johnson laughed under his breath.

I ignored him again. "Love you too, Bishop."

Jimmy laughed, then his tone changed when he glanced down at the victim again. "Wallet was in his back pocket. Jameson Talbot, twenty-three."

"Damn," Bishop said. "That's not good."

"Why? Is it important?" I asked.

"His dad is the CEO of Talbot Property Investors. They're the company building ninety-nine percent of the condos here and in Alpharetta."

Jimmy rubbed the back of his neck. "The mayor's going to shit himself with this."

"Is he en route?" I asked. "The mayor, I mean."

He nodded. "We need Barron on this, stat."

"I'm here now," Barron said. He stepped toward us from the direction of the parking lot of the fields. "Looks like we've got the same MO on our hands." He glanced at the young man's hand. "Number eight, I presume?"

Jimmy nodded.

The thought hit me like a brick. "Chief, can we tag and bag the number? I'd like to get prints run on it ASAP even though we're not going to find any."

"And then what?"

"Then Bishop and I are going on a crafting excursion."

Jimmy furrowed his brow. "I'm not sure I understand."

"She wants to see if the stickers came from a local store."

"Like a Michaels or something?" Jimmy asked.

I nodded. "Or even a Home Depot."

"You do realize these things can be found just about anywhere," Bishop said. "Even Dollar General or Dollar Tree. You're sending us on a wild goose chase."

"Not really," I said. "But maybe we can find out who makes them. Once we have that, we might be able to figure out where they came from. I know it's a long shot, but it's about all we've got right now."

"Can't Bubba get that for us?" Jimmy asked.

"Yes, with a lot of time and effort, and we can get it quicker just by talking to a store employee. These people are master crafters, and they know what they've got in their stores." *Or most of them, anyway*, I thought.

"I checked into the numbers three years ago," Johnson said. "You won't find anything. They're standard vinyl numbers found all over. There's no definitive marking that shows the manufacturing, and there are at least a hundred similar styles. Two of my three had slight differences. If this is the same guy, and I'm sure it is, he's using numbers from different stores to screw with us."

"I'd like to check anyway."

"Don't spend too much time on it," Jimmy said. "It doesn't matter where the numbers came from. Johnson's right. The things can be purchased all over the world. We'll never track them down."

"Understood," I said.

Barron had been examining the area around the victim, checked his pocket for a wallet and then his driver's license. "Jameson Talbot. Poor kid." He patted Bishop on the back. "Looks like you got your second one a little early."

"It appears so," Jimmy said. "Which means our guy is either feeling the pressure or leveling up his game."

"Well, let's get down to it and see what we can decipher from this poor young man." Barron crouched down and began his routine. After his brief examination, he pronounced the victim dead, then proceeded to take his body temperature. "If I had to guess, which you know I don't like doing, I'd say within the past twelve hours."

"He's leveling up his game," Jimmy said. He tapped a number into his cell phone as he stepped away.

"He's stressed," Bishop said.

"Just a bit," I added.

Barron unzipped Talbot's jeans and checked what Bishop begged to put off earlier. "Victim's penis has been removed and the area of detachment cauterized."

I watched Bishop's Adam's apple move as he swallowed.

He zipped up the victim's pants and continued upward. "Neck wound cleaned in same fashion as previous victim," he said.

I realized then he was recording himself while talking to us.

"You think the killer wants to get this done and move on to the next state?" Bishop asked.

"That goes against his MO from Birmingham, but if it's a copycat, you could be right."

"Doesn't have to be a copycat to move faster," Johnson said.

"But why?" Bishop asked. "He can't think we haven't moved the dial on this? Stiles didn't report the first one with the fire. If he didn't report about the murder, why would the killer decide to speed up his plan?"

"He might know something we don't," Johnson said. "He could be watching us."

As much as I hated to say it, Johnson was right. "That's a good point."

Bishop eyed me suspiciously.

"Listen, serial killers like attention, and we didn't give him any with the first murder. He wants notoriety, and the best way to get it is to come back hard and fast. We can't force the media to ignore the murders now."

Jimmy's cell phone beeped. He glanced at the screen and said, "The help you requested is here. I'll be right back." He walked away and passed Nikki as she ran toward us.

"I found a note," she said. She held out an envelope. "And..." She went to hand it to me, then stopped and said, "You need gloves. All of you."

We put on our latex gloves.

Nikki handed the note to me. "It..." she said through quick breaths. "I found it on your vehicle. I know I shouldn't have opened it, but I just had this feeling, and I—oh, I wore gloves, obviously."

"It's okay," I said as I opened the envelope and read the note. I looked up at Bishop. "Johnson's right. He's moving faster because the bastard's watching us."

14

Bishop read the typed note.

My dearest Detective Ryder,

Perhaps I should call you Rachel? After all, I've learned so much about you, I feel as if I know you. You must know how exhilarating it is to have a formidable investigator working alongside me in bringing these vile sexual deviants to judgment. These young women must have justice for the wrongs imposed onto them, and I am optimistic you will continue to be quite the assistant. But I cannot ignore the lack of information released to the public. You must know that kind of deceitful behavior only angers people such as myself. I have an important job to do, and I will receive recognition for my work.

Let me be clear. We are working together. Do not work against me. You will not succeed. The board is mine, Detective, and you are simply one of my pawns.

Bishop's brows furrowed. "He thinks this is a game?"

Barron pushed himself from the ground. "Sounds like the man's got some issues with women."

"This can't be the same guy," Johnson added. "My victim's body parts were intact, and I didn't receive a note. I think we've got an ill-informed copycat on our hands."

"Maybe you just don't like him alluding to your lack of investigation skills," I mumbled.

Bishop tapped his foot against mine. Hard.

"Oh, did I say that out loud?"

"I'm sorry if you have a problem with me, ma'am," Johnson said. "But I'm simply doing my job, and just because I do my job differently than you doesn't mean I'm less of an investigator."

"Tell that to our killer," I said.

"Ryder, enough," Bishop said.

He was right. I was tired and annoyed, and I wasn't in the mood for sparring with the guy. "My apologies," I mumbled. I wasn't sorry about what I said. I was sorry about the timing of it, which did have a lot to do with my exhaustion.

"Understood," Bishop said.

Barron smirked.

Jimmy returned with a tall, classily dressed blond woman by his side. She walked right up to me. "Detective Ryder, I've heard many great things about you." She shook my hand. "Dr. Stella Calloway. It's a pleasure to meet you."

I stood a little dumbfounded but replied with, "Nice to meet you."

Jimmy took over the conversation. "Dr. Calloway is a criminal profiler, and the best there is in the Southeast. She's on loan to us from the University of Georgia to help with our investigation."

Jimmy made the rest of the introductions, then said, "I've requested copies of everything on the case for Dr. Calloway, and I'd like her to be a part of the scene investigation."

"Yes, Chief," Bishop said.

"I'm not here to change the way you investigate," Calloway said. "Just to observe and offer my professional analysis by first addressing the scene, then learning the particulars of the case and working with each of you to determine an assessment of the killer's profile."

I showed her the note. "How about you start with this? He just left it on my vehicle. He's looking at himself as a justice warrior against sexual deviants—his words—and believes he's bringing them to justice."

"Along with the help of his formidable ally Detective Rachel Ryder," Bishop said.

Nikki handed Calloway a pair of gloves. She slipped them over her manicured hands and long, painted nails, read the note, and then handed it back to me. "Based on my experience, serial killers only communicate with police when they believe they won't be caught. Many think they're untouchable, even invincible. Sounds like your guy is one of those."

"So, are you saying our killer doesn't think Ryder is a formidable ally, then? Is he being sarcastic in that?" Johnson asked. "Because I never received a note during my investigations."

I caught Bishop's eye and rolled mine to show him my annoyance. He shrugged.

"I'm only suggesting our killer is confident in his ability to follow through with his plan without risk of being caught."

Jimmy smiled at Johnson. "I'd like you to examine the scene also, and when you're finished, if you'd discuss your investigations with Dr. Calloway, we can move forward from there."

Calloway smiled. "I believe within the next several hours we can come together with a general profile of our killer."

Several hours was a long time. Bishop shot me a glance. The scene investigation would take at least three hours, if not more. Working with her meant no sleep. I pounded out a quick text to Kyle to let him know the situation. He wasn't planning on coming over, but if by chance he changed his mind, I wanted him to know I wouldn't be there.

Barron gave permission for the body to remain in its current state while we shared the case details with Calloway. Before we began, I asked him to provide her with the medical details.

"Dr. Calloway, pleasure to meet you." He shook her hand.

"You too, Dr. Barron."

"This unfortunate circumstance for our victim is much like our first murder. Victim is a twenty-three-year-old male and has been dead somewhere between twelve and twenty-four hours. I'll have a better estimate once I've completed the autopsy. His throat was slit, and based on the appearance of the wound, I suspect the knife is the same or like the one that killed the first victim. The wound itself is straight and carefully executed. I ran tests for drugs on our first victim to determine if the victim was unconscious prior to death. There were no drugs in his system, so I feel confident the victim was conscious upon death like our first victim."

Barron hadn't told us he'd tested Ramsey's blood for drugs, though it was standard operating procedure. I remembered it was in the autopsy report; it was a nonissue to the investigation.

"The victim was undressed prior to his murder, though I'm not quite sure how, given he wasn't sedated. Our killer would have to be stronger than the young man. The victim was tortured extensively, then murdered, and his penis removed after death. Once complete, he was bathed and cleaned meticulously, and then redressed in his clothing that appears to have been dry-cleaned or pressed prior to wearing, though I can't say if that was after being abducted or before."

"Did you say his penis was removed?" she asked. She didn't flinch or have any expression on her face. It was impressive.

Barron exhaled. "Yes, ma'am. After it was removed, the wound was cauterized. However, the cauterization does not appear to be a professional job, which leads me to believe the killer is not trained in any surgical procedure."

"Which rules out a medical professional," Johnson said.

"The condition of the clothes is what stumps me," I said. I wanted to draw the attention away from Johnson. "Which strikes me as odd, because if they were the same clothes the victim's had on prior to their deaths, having them cleaned and pressed or doing it himself is risky."

"My victims' were also cleaned and dressed again," Johnson said.

She nodded. "I understand our killer is using a number system." She crouched down and examined the plastic baggie with the number eight on a piece of paper inside. "So, he wants us to assume this is our eighth murder?" She stood and spoke directly to me. "The first was seven?"

"For us, yes. However, Detective Johnson had one, two, and three."

"And do we know where the in-betweens are?"

"Nope," I said.

"We can't even guarantee there are in-betweens," Bishop said.

"Interesting." She moved to the other side of the victim and examined his wound. "Clean. Efficient. Just like Dr. Barron said." She studied the victim's clothing. "Again, as Dr. Barron said, everything is orderly and in place, all classic signs of a determined, intentional murder."

"Yes," I said.

"Correct," Bishop added.

"And yours?" she asked Johnson.

"Similar clothing situation, and my victims were bathed, however they were shot in the head, specifically the eye, and their body was intact."

"Justice killings are typically well planned, calculated, and executed with care." She stepped back from the victim and looked down at him. "It's clear this killer is announcing his murders through scene preparation. It's a ritual for him. Cleaning and prepping the victim. Maintaining a clean scene. Your killer is orderly. He doesn't like dysfunction or messiness." She studied the grass around the victim's body. "I'm assuming there were no footprints?"

"The scene was raked," I said. "I believe the killer lays out the body, cleans up his tracks, and then starts the fire."

"I agree. Were the other scenes similar?"

The three of us nodded.

"Very well. What about the fire? Can you tell me how it was started?"

We all looked toward the fields to the smoldering small administrative building.

I said, "The fire is to draw us to the victim's remains. The victim is killed somewhere else and transported here. Once he sets up and cleans the scene, he then starts a fire with a simple can of gas at the farthest point from the body. He doesn't want the fire to damage the victim. The fire inspector doesn't believe the intention is to burn the building down but to announce his victim's location."

"We can head over to the building and see if the inspector has anything yet," Bishop said.

Nikki had been busy taking photographs but followed us as we headed that direction. "This time the can was left inside the building. Last time it was left outside."

"I wonder why the difference," Johnson said.

"I can't take the can until after the inspector clears the scene but only if he doesn't take it himself."

"Which he will," I said.

"Probably, but the odds of us finding anything on it are slim anyway, and it'll come to me eventually."

"Agreed. Have you been able to access anything inside the building yet?"

"No, ma'am."

We walked over to the scene and spoke with Inspector Reed.

"Your tech girl tell you about the gas can?" he asked.

"Yes, sir," Bishop said. "She said we'll be able to look at it soon."

"Eventually. In the meantime, I can give you a rundown on what we've got here so far, but until I'm done with my inspection, and more specifically, until the fire is completely out, I can't give you any affirmatives."

"We know," I said.

"Good. The fire scene is comparable to the first fire. A standard can, purchasable at any local auto parts store or even your neighborhood Ace Hardware. Fire set on the opposite side of the building, in this case, the offices for the polo fields. As with the previous one, the building wasn't doused in gas. The gas was spread over one area. What's different about this is this building is cement, and there is little wood to burn. Our guy had to pile wood up against it and break into the building to access flammable materials inside."

"That seems like a lot of extra work," Bishop said.

"We rushed him by not giving him credit," I said.

"It is extra work, but as you know, there are very few abandoned or closed properties in Hamby. Most of the land's been sold and any buildings on those properties are already in process of demolition or already demolished. I find comfort in knowing your killer will be hard pressed to find another location," Reed said.

"I believe the killer's already found his next location. He's too meticulous to not have researched and determined his drop spots," I said. "He would have planned it all out in advance."

"I agree," Bishop said.

"I think she's probably right," Johnson added. "Unless, of course, he's changed his calling card, and given he's changed his work up from his Birmingham murders, we should consider he's desperate and not thinking clearly."

Calloway added, "Thank you for all the information. It's helpful, and I believe now there is no need for me to view the internal area of the building tonight. I'd like to head back to the station to review notes. The chief said he'd have my files ready there."

Investigator Reed looked at her like he didn't know who the hell she was. I jumped in and introduced them.

"Nice to meet you," Reed said.

"I'd like to stay and check out the fire damage," I said.

"Me too," Johnson said.

Bishop glared at me, and I shrugged. The dark purple bags under his eyes were bigger than a few hours before. He was exhausted.

"I'm fine going on my own," Calloway said. "I'll need a few hours to review the materials and develop a general profile. We can meet and fill in the blanks for a more detailed workup in the morning. My goal is to have a full workup by tomorrow afternoon."

We gave her our cell phone numbers one at a time. She called each of us to secure the number in her phone. "Okay, then, if you learn something that might impact my analysis, please contact me." She nodded and then walked away.

Johnson coughed. "That's a ballbreaker right there."

I rolled my eyes. "Nice."

Reed raised his eyebrow. "She's certainly intense."

"I'm sure she has to be," I said. "Her head probably goes to dark places."

"I have no doubt," Reed said. "It'll be a while before we can get inside. Most of the fire is out, but I'm concerned about the chemicals."

"We'll stick around," Bishop said.

"Very well," Reed said.

Two hours later things still weren't clear, so we made the decision to go home and rest. Johnson said he'd book a hotel in Alpharetta off Windward Parkway, and I wondered if it was the Marriott, but I didn't ask. He didn't know about Baker, and I wasn't willing to give him the information just then. I wanted more before I threw out accusations to other departments. I didn't bother saying goodbye to him.

"He's not that bad," Bishop said as we headed to our vehicles. "And we need him."

"You're allowed your opinion."

"I'm allowed my— What's your problem with the guy? He's cleaned up his act toward you. Maybe you need to cut him some slack."

"It's not about how he's treated me anymore. It's his personality. I just don't like him."

"Okay, then."

We reached our vehicles.

"I called night shift and asked them to give the death notification to the parents. We can head over to their house in the morning," I said.

"I know. I called to do the same, but you beat me to it."

"I don't think I could have stomached it tonight," I said.

"There's not been any missing persons report filed on the man, so let's let the parents have their last night of sleep in a while."

"Agreed. I'll see you tomorrow," I said.

"It already is tomorrow."

"Then see you in a few hours."

15

Bishop eyed the food on the department's kitchen table. He shot a questioning look toward Kyle. "You bring that?"

"Figured you all could use a decent meal."

Bishop walked over and scooped a breakfast burrito onto a paper plate, tossed some salsa on top, dropped a dollop of sour cream on top of that, then stacked two sliced pickled jalapeño over his creation. "If you weren't involved with my partner, I'd marry you myself."

"Thanks, but you're not my type," Kyle said.

I laughed. "When are you leaving?" I asked Kyle.

"I'm heading out from here," he said. "If things go as we expect, I won't be gone long. Time enough for you to catch your killer, get some rest, and be back to normal again."

Bishop laughed. "You think she's normal?" Most of the sour cream from his burrito was on his chin.

I flipped my partner the bird and pointed to the glop of sour cream becoming one with his stubble. "You've got stuff on your chin."

He took a napkin off the table and wiped the sides of his mouth, then went back to eating the burrito.

Kyle leaned against the kitchen counter. I adjusted the collar on his shirt. "How dangerous is this one?"

"No more dangerous than your job."

"Great." I wasn't handing out parking tickets or directing traffic, and neither was Kyle.

He smiled. "The life of a law enforcement officer."

"Can you tell me anything about it?"

He shook his head. "But I can tell you I won't be at risk."

He knew I had anxiety associated with his job. It was my issue, not his. If anything, I had PTSD when the people I cared about risked their lives and I couldn't do anything to help. I felt I'd earned that PTSD when a Chicago gang member held his gun to my husband's head and shot him. It didn't matter that as Tommy fell to the ground, I shot and killed his killer. The PTSD wasn't because I'd killed the man. It was because I'd hesitated. Had I not, Tommy wouldn't have died.

"I'll text you to keep you posted," Kyle said.

"Thank you." I walked him out of the kitchen.

As we left, Bishop yelled, "Thanks for the grub, and good luck!"

I'd gone home a few hours before to sleep, but I ended up tossing and turning for a few hours and creating my own mental profile on our killer. When I finally did doze off, I woke up late and took off for work without a shower or fresh clothes. I felt and looked like trash. Kyle brought me a change of clothing, a fresh pair of intimates, clean jeans, and a black T-shirt. After we finished eating. I took a shower in the department locker room. I relished in the feeling of a clean body dressed in clean clothes. With my job, I never took the little things for granted.

We met back in the investigation room. Johnson was in there waiting.

"When are you going to interview the women?"

"It's more important to hear what Dr. Calloway has to say about our killer. It might help with my investigation at home."

"Great," I said with absolutely no excitement.

Calloway didn't look the worse for wear. I'd wrapped my hair up into a ponytail, then twisted it into a bun at the base of my neck. My face was scrubbed to a shiny polish, but I'd chosen not to apply any makeup even though Kyle tossed some in with my things. I barely wore more than a bit of mascara and a swiping of blush anyway. I just didn't see the point in a predominantly male environment.

Calloway, on the other hand, looked like she just walked off a fashion show runway. Admittedly, I was envious of her looks, but not in a snotty middle-school-girl way. Her perfectly coiffed hair, makeup that gave the look of not having any on, and her well-pressed, fashion-forward clothes had all the men in the department gawking. I didn't want men drooling over me; I just wanted to be able to pull off that look as effortlessly as she did. Even if I had stunning natural beauty like her, I didn't have the patience to pull myself together that meticulously. Jeans and a T-shirt with a pair of Doc Martens or another comfortable boot were the best I could do.

Savannah hated my uncomplicated style. Even pregnant, she'd dressed like she was headed straight to a social event. She'd get along well with Calloway, and I was glad they hadn't met because Savannah would pester me again about my lack of fashion. A while back, she tried to up my appearance game and ordered me clothes through one of those clothing subscription boxes. I wore them through my counseling gig, but they hadn't left my closet since.

"Did you get any sleep?" I asked.

"I'm a power napper. I slept for an hour in the specialist's room here, then showered and got back to it."

She was damn impressive.

"I've completed the profile in my standard and easy-to-read format. Some profilers have other formats," Calloway said. "But I prefer a simple Excel spreadsheet with notes. I've added color-coding to connect suggested links to personality traits and mental disorders." She handed us each a blue file folder. "You'll find the spreadsheet located in the file. I've also emailed a copy of it to each of you. I'd like to review this now in relation to the notes."

She drew two columns on the whiteboard. On top of the left side, she wrote personality traits, and next to it, on the other side, she added potential physical characteristics.

"I believe we all would agree our killer has a type-A personality with controlling tendencies. If you look at the third column on the sheet, you'll notice things I noted from our conversation." She made eye contact with me. "Detective Ryder pointed out something about herself that, fortunately for us, relates to the killer."

Bishop's eyes shifted toward me. I held up my hands because I had no idea where she was going.

"Our detective is type A," she said.

Bishop laughed.

The door opened and Michels walked in. "Sorry I'm late." He smiled at Calloway. "Detective Michels, ma'am."

"Dr. Calloway."

I eyed Michels and whispered, "Anything?"

He shook his head. "I'll fill you in later."

"As I was saying," Calloway said, "the detective is type A, and things need to be neat and in order for her to feel as though she has control of a situation."

"We know that from her investigative techniques," Bishop said.

I gave him a death stare. "Can we stick to the investigation, please?"

He cringed.

"The crime scenes tell me our unsub is like the detective," she said. She wrote down *Type A* under *Personality* on the whiteboard. "He likes things done his way, pays attention to detail, and leaves little room for error. The raking of the dirt, the cleanliness of the wound. Those are signs of attention to detail. I'm not saying our suspect cares about his victims. He doesn't. He's admitted these are justice killings. I also believe our suspect is a victim of abuse himself or is closely related to someone who's been abused, though I won't pinpoint it strictly as sexual abuse. If pressed to pick one, I'd say he was personally abused."

Johnson raised his hand like a schoolboy.

She smiled. "Yes, Detective Johnson?"

"I'm unsure what about his personality says he was abused."

"Statistics show many who have been abused in some way as a child tend to carry on the abuse as they age." She jotted down abused on the whiteboard. "And given his personality type, he fits the classic victim profile."

"Which is?" Michels asked.

"Type-A personalities tend to want control and order because they don't or didn't have it in an important area or time in their lives."

Everyone in the room turned and stared at me.

"You make more sense now," Bishop said.

"Bite me," I replied with a smile. I spoke to Calloway. "Since everyone is assuming our killer and I share detailed personality traits, I think it's important to know I wasn't abused in any way growing up. Type A doesn't guarantee an abusive past or an abusive personality. Controlling, yeah, I'll give you that, but not necessarily abusive. And to that, if he was sexually abused in the past, wouldn't his targets be male sex offenders who abused other males?"

"I see your point, however, statistics show many serial killers have been abused in one way or another. Of course, not all type-A personalities are serial killers, thus we can assume not all have been abused either.

"I'd like to add that our killer has a temper. He's easily agitated, lacks patience when it comes to other people, and is a perfectionist. If somebody does something wrong or doesn't follow the path he believes should be taken, he can and will lose his temper."

Bishop shot me a look. I shrugged.

"For example, consider the reaction when a cashier in a grocery store bags items. When he's in this situation, and their way is not what he considers appropriate or the right way, his anger builds. And it continues to build until it explodes. The explosion, mind you, can be intense, yes, but it's not necessarily inflicted on the person who angered him or a trigger for murder, and it might not happen anywhere near the time of the event. It could be a slow-building, comprehensive anger. But his everyday functionality is disturbed by his temper, and eventually, it will explode."

"There are a few people in this room who can relate to that," Bishop said.

"A temper isn't necessarily a bad thing," Calloway said. "Tempers help balance our emotions, and they help to express our feelings. Society, however, set a limit on tempers. We call those limits laws. Our killer doesn't believe in laws." She jotted down *anti–law abiding* on the whiteboard. "He believes he is above the law, and he believes his temper is controlled, but it's not. The grocery store example is a perfect example of how he would react."

"So," Michels said, "our guy is every man after a hard day of work when his wife sends him out to the store."

"I think what she means is he can handle the big things in life, but not the small things." I looked up at Calloway and smiled.

She pointed her finger at me. "That's exactly it. He spent years hiding his abuse and his feelings about it, but those feelings must come out. Instead of dealing with them in an appropriate way, or dealing with his abuser, he takes his anger out on people in his everyday life or people he deems are not worthy of participating in society. People who he sees as evil. Our suspect is incapable of close relationships. He keeps people at a distance. If he has family, he's either no longer associated with them or his relationships are filtered. By 'filtered,' I mean he only lets them see what he wants them to see."

"He's a sociopath," I said.

"In layman's terms, yes. A medical diagnosis would likely say he suffers from antisocial personality disorder and narcissistic personality disorder. These two diagnoses are often intertwined. Any kind of abuse, but primarily abuse of a sexual nature, often leads to sociopathic tendencies, and my educated guess, because that's all profiling really is, is that your killer is suffering from years of abuse decaying his mind to the point that he feels nothing except the exhilaration of justice served when his victims die."

"That doesn't sound like Baker," I whispered to Bishop.

"I agree."

"The guy sounds crazy," Michels said.

"That's one way of putting it," Calloway said. "But don't let him fool you. You could meet this man in the aisle at the grocery store and he would be charming, even eloquent, though I suspect his condescending attitude will show itself rather quickly. Since he believes he's smarter than everyone else, he'll show off his intelligence, smile, and greet you like you're his best friend, but with a hint of disdain in his tone. That's what sociopaths do and that's how they gain access to their victims. Ted Bundy is a perfect example. He was charismatic, attractive, intelligent, and didn't blink an eye when he killed his victims."

"Are you saying our guy is attractive?" Bishop asked.

"In a general sense, beauty is in the eyes of the beholder," Calloway said. "But overall, your killer will likely have features commonly considered attractive by the public. A decent, athletic physique, pleasant eyes, a nice smile. Things that will allow others to feel comfortable around him." She wrote the physical traits down on the whiteboard. "Again, it's quite possible your killer is an anomaly, but it would be surprising."

I was conflicted again. All of that could easily fit Baker. "We're looking for a relatively attractive male, neatly dressed, reasonably athletic build, who's charming and pays attention to detail," I said. "That's about ninety percent of this town and probably a good portion of Birmingham."

"You haven't spent much time in Alabama, have you?" Bishop asked.

Johnson laughed. "That's obvious."

"I'm not suggesting your killer lives in Hamby or Alabama. In fact, I don't believe he does," Calloway said. "It's probable he's grouping his victims by location intentionally. He's determined the location of his crimes based on extensive research, not distance from his home."

I nodded. "Any suggestions on the connecting element?"

"I'll need more before I can determine possibilities."

"Our tech department has done comprehensive research on our first victim, which is how we came up with the alleged sexual assault. We then compared that to the victims in Birmingham and further validated our theory. I'm going to assume we'll find an alleged assault victim by this one also," I said. "In the meantime, we can look for other similarities, but I don't think we'll find more than we have."

"I'd appreciate that," Calloway said. "We can chart personality traits through social media history, relationships, jobs, education, sporting activities. There is something connecting these victims outside of the sexual abuse accusations. Our killer is finding victims and grouping them together for convenience of killing, but there is a reason he's chosen these specific victims."

"Can you discuss anything about the location of the murders?" Bishop asked.

"Our suspect, as meticulous as he is, has planned the murders down to the most minute of details. He is educated, and likely holds an executive level job, though that's not always the case. He makes good money, or he's saved money and no longer works. His money is likely being used to rent a facility to execute his justice killings. Perhaps he owns a business or has access to a warehouse. Either way, the location is out of the way and wouldn't be the first place in which people would assume something tragic would occur."

"We need those locations," Johnson said.

"Bubba may be able to find recently rented warehouses," Bishop said.

"I'll continue working the profile," Calloway said. "Once you have more information, I'll add it, and if we're lucky, we'll have a solid description of our killer. Please keep in mind the information I've provided is not definitive. Though it's based on research and interviews of serial killers, people continue to stump data. Your killer could be the exact opposite of my description."

She left the room without another word. Michels, Bishop, Johnson, and I stared silently at the whiteboard.

"She's a smart woman," Michels said.

"She's got a doctorate in psychology. That's a lot of work," I said.

"And she's gorgeous. What a package," he said.

I lifted my head and rolled my eyes. "Nice."

Michels shrugged. "I'm just saying the truth."

"So, basically we've got another Bundy but in Hamby," Bishop said. He rubbed his jaw. "This town is going to flip."

I agreed. "And so will the mayor." I looked to Michels. "Can we chat alone?"

"Sure thing," he said and followed me to the conference room.

I closed the door behind us. "You didn't find anything?"

"Nothing. He's got an exemplary record. His close rate is over seventy percent, and his chief says everyone in the department loves him."

"Everyone loves him? Really?"

"There was a drive-by shooting in Birmingham last year. Remember that?"

"The one where the six-month-old died?"

"Yeah. Guess who found the shooter."

I blew out a breath. "Fine. So, he's a decent detective. Thanks, Michels. I appreciate it."

"Anytime."

Bishop knocked on the door as he opened it. "Let's go. We've a death notice to give."

"Good luck," Michels said.

We walked out of the room and Johnson was standing in the hall. "I'd like to go along," he said.

"Why?" I asked.

"Hearing what the victim's family says might coincide with something from my investigation."

"Suit yourself," I said.

Two hours later we'd returned to the department emotionally drained. Death was horrible, and violent death, even worse. We made arrangements for Johnson to take the couple to the morgue for identification purposes.

"I can't believe you let him do that," Bishop said.

"It gets him out of our investigation. He can do some basic questioning and let us know what he gets, but we'll meet with them also. I don't trust him to get the facts straight, but I think he'll be okay standing on the sidelines while Barron tells them about their son."

Bubba was ecstatic to figure out Talbot's possible sexual assault victim in fifteen minutes, but he admitted most of the work was already done for him. "A lot of shade's thrown on the internet, and this guy got it from all angles. He hit on Abby Meyer, some cheerleader from Georgia State, then dragged her into a room and was getting started. He didn't finish the job, but if there's another girl out there, she's nowhere on social media."

"Good work," I said. "I'm in awe of your abilities."

"Guess you can say you know a guy here in Georgia too."

"I guess I can."

Around noon, the mayor held a ridiculously off-base press conference on the town hall steps that sent the department into crisis-control mode. My stomach performed a gymnastics routine just listening to his garbage.

"My excellent law enforcement officers have been working nonstop to find a suspect, and I am pleased to announce they have moved forward.

While I cannot name the suspect himself, rest assured my team is working hard to bring him in."

Bishop and I stood in the back of the small crowd. He leaned in and whispered, "Great job on that suspect, partner."

"We are excellent and swift, aren't we?" The mayor was right. We had been working nonstop, but we didn't have a clue who the suspect was, nor were we even sure it was a male. "Calloway didn't say it outright, but this suspect could be a female. Yet here's our worthless mayor babbling on and on about an imaginary male suspect."

The mayor rambled on as I only partially listened.

"He only got elected because he promised free soda machines in the school cafeteria," Bishop said.

"What?"

He chuckled. "My high school student council president got elected solely on that pitch. The mayor reminds me of him."

"Ah, you mean during the time before electricity."

He sighed. "Close to then."

"And with that, I can tell you with one hundred percent certainty, we will not see another young man murdered. Not in my town, and not on my watch," the mayor said.

The few reporters there immediately shouted out questions. One strong male voice rose above the rest. "Sir, what is your opinion regarding the serial killer theory?"

"Shit," Bishop said.

"Copy that."

We didn't even bother listening to his answer. Once the words "serial" and "killer" were brought into play, we automatically went into crisis mode, and we both knew Jimmy's head would explode once he left the mayor's side. We needed to be prepared.

Inside the building the department staff was already moving in crisis mode.

"I can't believe this shit," a patrol officer said.

"The damn dicks don't even have a suspect," another said.

I glanced at Bishop. "We're not too popular at the moment, are we?"

"Popularity doesn't catch killers."

We made it through the pit without any questions from the patrol team, but before Bishop and I went to our respective cubbies to prepare, we talked about getting in touch with Abby Meyer.

"Should we go there now? In the middle of this?" I asked.

"I hate for word to get out and damage her interview."

"Then we need to do it quickly," I said. "Bubba gave me her work and home addresses. Work first."

"Sounds like a plan."

We put on our protective vests. It was standard operating procedure when all hands were on deck, even though we were heading out on a call. Just the mention of a serial killer brought out the crazies, and the entire department would work overtime to keep things calm. Jimmy charged over as we stood outside our cubbies putting together our plan. His forehead was sweaty, his cheeks were red, and the veins in his neck stood out like a whore in church. The volcano building in his gut threatened to burst right in front of our eyes.

"Mother freaking—son of a—dammit!"

I tilted my head and glanced at Bishop. We watched Jimmy carefully.

He pumped his fist. "I gave up swearing because of the baby."

"How's that working out for you?" Bishop asked. Bishop had big balls. I was all for keeping it light during a heavy investigation, but Jimmy looked like he could stroke out any minute, and joking didn't seem appropriate.

"We don't have time for all y'all to be off this investigation and monitoring a bunch of civilians freaking out because the mayor dropped the serial killer bomb. I need you and Michels working this until it's solved. Do you understand?" He was looking right at me.

"I understand."

"Yes, sir," Bishop said.

He shook his head. "Hold on. Change that. Forget Michels for now. I need him to organize the patrol with their captains and keep the city calm. The phones are already ringing off the hook. We've had twelve 911 calls claiming the killer is a neighbor, a store owner, and, get this: Santa Claus. Michels got a good head on his shoulders. He can handle keeping everyone on task and out of any conflict.

"But I don't know what to do. I've got seven reporters standing in my office right now waiting for a statement. What the hell am I supposed to tell them? Why, yes, we do have a serial killer, and by the way, based on our knowledge, he's going to kill again?"

I sighed. "The mayor did this because he has faith in us, faith in you." That was likely BS, but I needed to say something to calm him. "Let's just focus on the end game. For now, that means damage control on your part while Bishop and I find the killer."

His ripened face paled back to a light pink. "Calloway give you a good profile? Do you think you can get this guy before the third murder?"

"We established a basic profile," Bishop said. "But there's a lot about him that could be attributed to anyone. Before the news conference, our plan was to sit down with Bubba and develop a strategy to figure out what links the victims, but he gave us the name of the alleged victim for Talbot, so we want to get to her before the shit really hits the fan."

"Calloway thinks connecting the victims via commonality will lead us to the killer. I think we need to start with the female assault victims and starting with Talbot's victim kills two birds at once," I said. "It's quick and allows us to gain more facts instead of assumptions based on social media. There might be something other than the assaults that connects them, but I honestly think whatever it is, we won't find it. But if by chance we do, it could help us find the killer."

"Agree," Bishop said.

Jimmy nodded. "Okay, okay. Let's move forward." His cell phone rang. "I need to get to those reporters." He turned around and headed toward the heart of the pit.

Abby Meyer worked for a clothing boutique in Alpharetta. She was tiny, probably not a pound over one hundred and fifteen, with long black hair, blue eyes, and a well-inked tattoo of a butterfly on her lower neck.

"He didn't rape me," she said.

"You're going to hear the news soon, but Jameson Talbot was found deceased," Bishop said.

Her mouth fell open. Tears formed in her eyes, but she quickly wiped them away. "What happened?"

"We're not at liberty to discuss that," Bishop said.

I asked where she was during the time of the murder, though I was sure she wasn't involved. Talbot had at least sixty pounds on her. There was no way she'd be able to touch him.

"You don't think I did it, do you?"

"Abby, we just have to ask the question."

"I was home with my son."

My eyes widened. She had a kid? "You have a son?"

She nodded. "Howard Meyer. He's two months old, and no, before you ask, Jameson isn't his father."

I checked her ring finger. Bare.

Bishop asked, "Can you tell us what happened between you and Mr. Talbot?"

"Sure. We were at a football game afterparty. Jameson didn't play, obviously. He was drunk, he said he needed to talk to me privately, and I was stupid enough to go with him to a bedroom. The next thing I knew, he was falling on me and trying to get my skirt off. Thankfully, I'd left the door open. He was too drunk to realize, and I screamed loud enough for two of the football players down the hall to hear. They came in, beat the shit out of Jameson, and got me home safely."

"And you didn't go to the police?" I asked.

"Like I said, he didn't rape me, and besides, he got what he deserved. The guys were defense." She smiled.

We asked her a few more questions, but we didn't get much from her. She asked again how he died, but we again refused to give her the details. She'd know soon enough.

Bishop and I headed to the investigation room. I pounded out a text to Bubba and asked him to meet us there. With his generation it was easier to text than call. They had some mental adverse reaction or trigger when speaking on the phone too much. I wasn't thrilled with human interaction at times either, but it was my job.

Johnson stopped us on our way. "That was brutal, but they didn't have anything to share outside of what my victims' parents shared."

"Did you ask if they were aware of any sexual assault accusations?" Bishop asked.

He nodded. "Nothing."

"Figures," I said.

"So," Johnson said. "Looks like you've got a storm brewing out there."

"You think?" I asked.

"Anything I can do?"

"Yeah, help us find the killer," I said, and pushed past him.

He followed us.

Bubba sat with a laptop in front of him with his head close to the screen. He looked up and smiled when the door opened. "Give me a sec, I think I'm heading toward something."

After just a minute, Bubba pounded his fist on the table. "Got it!" He turned his laptop toward us. "Each of the dude victims was in Mastermind. It's a club through their university." He walked over to our side of the table and clicked on the past members' link. The list was alphabetical by college, and Bubba was able to pull up each of the five names.

I raised an eyebrow. "That feels too easy."

"It doesn't have to be complicated," Bishop said. "It just has to be a connection." He tapped on the laptop keyboard and was instantly frustrated. "These keys are so small." He looked up at Bubba standing over us. "Can you find who's responsible for this program?"

Bubba pulled the laptop closer and hit the keys so fast, I held my breath. The *click, click, click* sound pumped my heart rate up a notch too. "Bubba, you've got some crazy fast fingers."

He smiled as he typed. "The organization was started by Ron Howard."

Bishop laughed. "As in Ron Howard from *Happy Days*?"

"*Happy Days*? I don't know what that means," Bubba said.

Bishop exhaled. "Jesus, I'm old."

"Yes, you are." I couldn't help but laugh. "Bubba wasn't born when *Happy Days* was popular, and by the way, I think I was a toddler when they stopped filming." I laughed again just because Bishop looked like he was going to hop right into his coffin and croak due to old age. I spoke to Bubba. "Did you watch *Arrested Development*?"

He nodded. "Was he in that?"

"He was the narrator. Back in the seventies, when he was a teenager, he was in *Happy Days*. I'm sure your parents watched it. They're close to Bishop's age, right?"

"About that, I think, yeah, but they were in India in the eighties."

"Then I'm not sure they'd know what he's talking about. The show had a character named Fonzie, but he called himself the Fonz. Sound at all familiar?" If someone had asked me to bet on that, I'd bet against him knowing.

"Oh yeah! My dad had this Halloween costume back when I was a kid. It was this hideous black leather jacket, a pair of jeans two inches too short, and a white T-shirt. He did his hair in this retro style. A..." He struggled to find the right word. "Pompom or something like that."

"Pompadour," Bishop said.

"Yeah, that's it. It was really embarrassing having to troll for candy with him, but he said he was cool. He said everyone knew the Fonz."

"Then he must have seen the show at some point," I said.

"It was a cool show," Bishop said.

"Groovy," I said with a smile.

Johnson had been quiet the whole time and finally laughed.

Maybe he wasn't so bad after all. Maybe.

Bubba dug deep into Ron Howard's profile on the site for the Mastermind program. He pulled up a picture of an older gentleman with a white beard and a tuft of white hair on the top of his head as well as some scrappy nubs of white hair along the sides. "Is this your guy?"

"Nope," Bishop said.

"Definitely not. Richie Cunningham would be horrified to be compared to that guy," Johnson said.

Bubba read off his profile while we all judged the older man's appearance in relationship to our killings. He definitely didn't look like he was physically capable of killing a mouse, let alone a strong, younger man.

Bishop leaned back in the chair and exhaled. "Doesn't sound or look like our killer."

"I don't think so either," I said. "But we can't rule him out."

"Doesn't seem to fit the profile," Johnson said. "Though Dr. Calloway did say it wasn't definitive."

"Agreed, but I don't want to waste a trip to Montgomery, Alabama, to talk to him unless we have something more than a minor connection," Bishop said.

I adjusted the bun on the back of my neck. "Michels is busy taming the lions, but maybe Jimmy will let him go?"

"If we find our killer, the lions will tame themselves," Johnson said.

"In a perfect world," I said. "What're the odds Jimmy will give us Michels for this?"

"He's already been working the investigation with us. He only pulled him off because the mayor's a dumbass, but this is important. He'll let him go. He'll realize it's the only way to know if he's our guy. That is, if you spin it right," Bishop said.

I nodded my agreement.

Bishop gave Johnson a nod. "Or you could do it."

"I'd need to get approval. I've only been approved for coming here."

"But everyone at your department loves you," I said.

His face went slack, and then he said, "You've checked on me."

I smiled. "Guilty, but you'd do the same."

"I assume so," he said.

"We'll see if Michels can do it," I said. The truth was I didn't want Johnson having control over a possible suspect. He'd yet to talk to the victims in Birmingham nor had he reported back about their interviews with his peer. Michels was still green under the collar, but I trusted him and that made all the difference. "Hey, how are the alleged assault victim interviews going?"

"My partner is on the last one. He'll report back with them in a few hours."

"So, he's already talked to two?" Bishop asked. "Did he have anything to say?"

"Nothing we didn't already assume, but he's writing it up and sending it over. If need be, I'll head back and dig deeper with each victim."

Bishop nodded, then asked Bubba, "What about the people who ran the program at each school? Anything on them?"

"None were the same guy," he said. "And two are dead."

"And the rest?" Bishop asked.

"Still teaching at their colleges, and it's all in class."

"We'll look at their information just in case," I said. "Can you check NCIC for all of them?"

The landline in the room buzzed. "Detective Ryder? I have a Scott Baker on the phone for you. Line one."

I made eye contact with Bishop and hit the speaker button. "Detective Ryder."

"Scott Baker here, Detective."

"What can I do for you?"

"I'm calling to follow up with the status of your investigation. I'll be leaving Alpharetta today, and I wanted to make sure you were informed of my schedule."

"We didn't ask you not to leave town."

"I felt it was somewhat implied. Have you gained a suspect?"

Gained a suspect? What an interesting way to phrase it. "I'm not at liberty to discuss the details of an active investigation, Mr. Baker."

"Understood, though, I assume I'll hear from you again if you choose to include me on your suspect list. When you do find Daniel Travis's killer, thank him for me." He disconnected the call.

"Who was that?" Johnson asked.

"The father of your alleged assault victim of Travis," I said.

"He's in Georgia? Why wasn't I informed?"

"Slipped our minds?"

He looked to Bishop who threw me under the bus without even flinching. "It was her choice, and I let her make it."

He let me make it.

"I'll be speaking to your chief about that."

"Sounds like a plan," I said. I looked back to Bubba. "Anything?"

He pulled up Ron Howard. "Nothing." He pulled up the next, then the next, and so on. All had nothing except a parking ticket on one guy's record.

"This isn't going anywhere," Bishop said.

"We'll at least contact them," I said. "You two continue to work on this, and I'll go trapeze through the jungle of lion tamers to find Jimmy." I stood. "Wish me luck."

∽

Jimmy had thirty seconds to listen to my pitch.

"We found a connection at a university in Alabama," I said. "One man handles the organization from the top, and I'd like to send Michels to interview him."

"Why not Johnson? Alabama's his turf."

"He says he'll need approval from his chief. We don't have time for that."

"I need Michels here." Jimmy exhaled. "Do you think this guy's a suspect?"

Maybe, maybe not. "Everybody's a suspect until we catch the killer."

"Understood. Can't you or Bishop go?"

"We can, but we'd rather not spend ten hours wasted if he's not the guy. If Michels gets anything from him, we'll handle it."

He rubbed the top of his head. "Okay, he's yours, but he needs to be back tonight."

"I'll text you both the information. Thanks."

I returned to the investigation room to see Bishop at the whiteboard drawing what I could only assume was an oddly shaped home without windows. There were some squiggly lines which could have been windows, but they were very narrow, and I couldn't quite determine what they were. "What are you trying to do, show off your lack of architectural skill? If so, you've completely succeeded."

"I'm working on a chart of everything our victims had in common. Did Jimmy approve Michels going?"

"Yes, but about this chart… First of all, do you mean our murder victims or their sexual assault victims? And how the hell is that a chart? Are those squiggly lines supposed to be lines separating the names?"

"What squiggly lines?"

I walked over and pointed at the squiggly lines. "These."

Bubba laughed. "Those are the female victims' names."

"Oh, for the love of Mike." I swiped the dry eraser back and forth until his chart disappeared. "You must have missed the part of elementary school where they taught writing."

Bubba read me off each of the female victims' names. I wrote them neatly on the board on a top line and then separated them into columns. "What do we have?"

Bubba scoured through his notes. He held up a hand, and then said, "There aren't many similar factors. They're not the same size. They don't look to be the same weight. Each has a different hairstyle, although most of them are on the blonder side. One in Alabama is Asian, so she's an anomaly to the rest. Not all of them were in sororities. Two were majored in business, two in communications, and the other in journalism and sociology. Interesting combo. So, they would never even have shared similar classes except their core ones, obviously. And those you can find at any university."

"I appreciate the assessment, but I need it broken down by alleged victim."

He reiterated the information victim by victim.

"Did you compare classes for the male victims?" I asked.

"All different also."

"Okay. What about social activities for the girls?"

"Like I said, they weren't all in sororities, so it's really hard to say. I didn't see any real club activity for any of them."

"The guys were all in that Mastermind group," I said. "So, it stands to reason that the girls might've been in some collective group too."

"I'll check, though I don't know why we're looking into them."

"It's a crapshoot, but it's worth the gamble if we get a hit."

"Like the fact that they've all been sexually assaulted?" Bubba asked.

"Aside from that," I said.

"Can you just check, please?" Bishop asked.

He typed ferociously on his laptop again. "I created a formula for extracting information from their files."

"Files?" Bishop asked.

"You know—classes, clubs, sports. College stuff."

"College records, as in transcripts?"

"Not exactly. But I can access information for clubs and teachers. I put in the formula I need, and my laptop retrieves what I'm looking for." He smiled. "It's not illegal, but if you'd like, I can perform an illegal dip into their transcripts." He sighed. "But you have a guy in Chicago for that."

"Yes, I *know* a guy." I accentuated the word know because that was the Chicago phrase. *I know a guy.*

He smiled bigger. "'Know.' Got it."

"We need personality traits, hobbies, something that connects these girls," Bishop said.

"Hobbies I might be able to pull off, but personality traits, that's above my pay grade."

"What we need," I said, "is something that connects these girls to our killer. Why he chose to avenge their assaults. Maybe we can establish their personality by their social media posts."

Bubba nodded. "We can sure try or at least infer. Hold on." He'd kept my heart rate in the fat burning zone with his fast typing.

"I'm working on a quick program to retrieve what we want." More typing, and then, "Ah. And…" He paused. "I just dumped the information into a file." It took all of two minutes. "Like this information?" He opened the file.

Bishop and I scanned the screen.

Michels walked in. "Guess I'm going on a field trip, so thank you for saving me from that special kind of hell. The town is losing their minds over the mayor's press conference."

"You should see that happen in a big city like Chicago," I said.

"I'll pass. Address?"

"Oh, I was supposed to text the info. Sorry about that."

As Bubba jotted the information down, we filled Michels in on Ron Howard.

"Sunday, Monday, Happy Days," he sang when Bishop said the man's name.

"That's what I'm talking about," Bishop said. He attempted to high-five Michels, but Michels just stood there confused. "Forget it," Bishop said.

"How do you know that show?" Bubba asked.

"It's on TV Land, dude. It's hilarious and oddly wholesome, which, after a day here, everyone needs."

He left with intel and an address, promising to update us ASAP.

We went back to the information on the female victims.

"They all liked their college football team," Bishop said. He removed a pair of glasses from his interior jacket pocket and placed them on his head. "It's amazing how much better I can see with these things."

I rolled my eyes. "You really need to keep those things on a chain or something. I don't want to be in a shoot-out where you hit me instead of the target."

"Sometimes I like to pretend you are the target."

Bubba chuckled. "They all went to a Brad Paisley concert in Alpharetta."

"Interesting. All of them? When was the concert?"

He gave me the date.

"Maybe our killer likes country music?" Bishop asked.

"But how would he make the connection?" I shook my head. "We're heading down the wrong path. The connection isn't with the female victims. It's the males. Our guy found out about their assaults, either by scouring through social media, running a program or whatever like Bubba, or good old-fashioned stalking."

"If he ran a program on his computer, that's traceable," Bubba said. "If he's smart, he's not putting anything online from his personal computer."

"Which means he'd use a public one in a library or one of those internet cafés," Bishop said.

"And that could be anywhere," I said. "But it's the men, and it's not just their alleged sexual assaults. He had to know them in some way. We're missing something," I said.

Johnson leaned back in his chair and crossed his arms over his chest. "Now you see why I couldn't find him three years ago."

"At least we've found the alleged assault victims," I said. I let the rest of my intended dig hang in the air.

"I agree with Detective Ryder," he said. "We're going down a rabbit hole. The women are not connected to the killer outside of their alleged assaults, and practically every college-aged girl likes country music. That connection is invalid."

"What makes you say that?" Bishop asked.

"About country music?" Johnson asked.

"No, about agreeing with Ryder's thoughts."

"Your partner isn't the only one with intuition." His cell phone rang. He left the room to take a call and we didn't see him again for a few hours.

∽

"We got the subpoena," Jimmy said.

I glanced at Bishop. He smiled. "A little schmoozing goes a long way."

"I don't care what either of you did," Jimmy said. "We just need something or nothing that is on those videos, do you understand?"

"We'll do our best," I said.

Bishop and I headed out wondering how we could magically not make Scott Baker appear on video. The hotel manager wasn't thrilled about the subpoena, but he didn't have a choice, other than giving us access to the videos then or bringing them into the department himself. He chose to show us instead.

We went through each video for each day Baker was registered at the hotel, and unfortunately, the videos verified his statement. He wasn't our guy, and we were back to nothing. We didn't talk on the way back to the department. When we got there, things were a hundred percent worse than when we'd left.

The media reported the serial killer link on the internet, in the print papers, and on the news, and it quickly went viral. The town wasn't the only place up in arms, the national media was too, which sent Jimmy flying into stroke territory again. He was angry, and he took it out on us because he couldn't take it out on the mayor.

"It's on CNN and Fox News. Almost the same reporting too, and those two networks have polar-opposite reporting, but apparently not when it comes to a serial killer in my town," he said. He paced a loop around the investigation table. "We need to find that killer before he hits again. Do you hear me?"

"Yes, sir," Bishop said. His eyes shifted to mine.

Jimmy was close to losing it. A young baby, a big-mouthed, controlling mayor on his butt, and a double murder were enough to make anyone lose it, but he needed to keep it together. All eyes were on us and this case, and if we didn't catch the killer soon, we'd all be out of a job.

So, I took an alternative route. "Put me on the news. I'll draw out the killer. Force him to communicate with me again."

Jimmy stopped dead in his tracks. "What?" He shook his head. "No way. You're the last person I'd put on TV."

Gee, thanks. "The guy left me a note. He's courting me. Let me talk to him directly. Trust me, it'll distract him. If we can do that, we'll have a better chance of catching him."

"Or put him on high alert," Jimmy said.

I couldn't argue that.

Bishop nodded. "She's right. Our guy feels a connection to her. Let her talk to him directly."

Jimmy rubbed the top of his head and sighed. "The mayor will have my ass for this."

"Don't tell him," I said.

"If you're on the news, he'll find out."

"You won't be there with me. Plausible deniability," I said.

"Doesn't matter. Shit rolls down."

"I promise you we'll get a reaction from the killer. I can make that happen, and then you can take all the credit with the mayor."

"You know I don't care about credit, Rachel."

"I know, but you still can."

"Can you guarantee he won't kill again as a reaction?"

"No."

"This isn't a good idea."

"It's all we've got right now. Seriously, we have nothing. No DNA, no bloody crime scene, no witnesses, and no idea who the killer is. We need to cause a reaction, not be the reactors."

"She's right, chief," Bishop said.

"Thank you," I said. "You still have reporters here?" I asked Jimmy.

"A few in the reception area. They're waiting to talk to someone, but I've been putting them off."

"Then let's have a chat."

"Right now? No," he said. He shook his head. "You need to be prepped.

You need to approach this cautiously. Let me get Calloway. She can tell you how to talk to him."

"I know how to talk to him," I said. "Jimmy, come on. You've got to trust me. I can do this."

"I can't lose my job. I've got a kid to put through college, and Savannah's already talking about popping out another one." He exhaled. "Damn, that's a lot of college tuition."

I smiled. "I've got this. I promise."

"It's okay." He took a deep breath and let it out. "I'll handle it."

"No," Bishop said. "She's right. Plausible deniability, and Chief, you're on edge. We can't afford having you crack on camera."

"Fine, but if this works against us, you're off the case."

I nodded even though I didn't believe him.

I took a moment to prepare myself, fixed my hair, and checked to make sure my clothes weren't on inside out. I didn't think they were, but I had rushed to get dressed and I'd been distracted by a serial killer, and I didn't want to appear desperate or unprepared.

I met the guys by the front desk. There were three reporters in the lobby on the other side of the glass partition, one woman and two men.

"You can't say we don't have a suspect," Jimmy said. "You need to talk about the investigation as if we've got something or the mayor will look bad, and that will be the end of our careers. Let the killer think it."

Again, it wasn't my first rodeo. I'd given information to the press before, and in doing so, talked to a suspect via the news. "I've got this, Chief, but you two"—I glanced through the partition—"need to stand to the side. Make them think you walked away. If they see you and you're not out here, they're going to wonder. We don't need questions about that. I'm just going to chat with our lovely front desk officer, read through a paper or two, then walk out there. They'll ask me something, and we'll go from there."

Jimmy exhaled. "Don't screw this up."

"Never," I said. "Now go."

He and Bishop made a big deal about walking away, but they were only out of the reception area's line of sight. I clicked the speaker to hear what they were discussing before going out there as I pretended to read some papers.

"That's the detective handling the investigation," one of the men said.

"Detective Ryder," a woman reporter said. "She's the one that killed her husband's killer."

"That's her?" the other man asked. "That's who we need to interview."

I turned off the speaker. "I'm quite popular," I said to the front desk officer. "When I get out there click the button back for the chief, okay?"

"Will do, ma'am."

"Here goes nothing." I gave a small nod to Bishop and Jimmy and then opened the door into the main lobby.

They charged after me as if I was the prey, and they were the wolves.

"Detective Rachel Ryder?" the female asked. "What's the name of the suspect, and when will you arrest him?"

I held up my hands. "Whoa, can we settle down for a minute? I'm happy to take questions, but..." I stepped back two steps to give myself space. "I can't have all of you in my face to answer them."

The three of them stepped back a quarter of an inch tops.

I gathered my composure and looked at the woman. "Which station are you from?"

"ABC."

"Name?"

"Sandra O'Brien. I'm an investigative news reporter. Can you please provide any updated information on the serial killer?"

"I can tell you this. Our killer is possibly connected to killings in another state, however we have no concrete information to verify if it's the same person at this time." I let that sink in, but before they could ask another question, I spoke again. "There were three killings three years ago in Alabama. Detective Johnson with the Birmingham Police Department has been investigating those killings and was able to make a connection between his victims and the MO of the killer and ours. However, there are differences."

One of the men spoke. "Can you describe the differences?"

"I can't reveal details on an active investigation, but based on our information, it appears we may have a different killer than our counterparts in Alabama." I held up my hand as they stepped forward, and they stopped.

The woman spoke again. "But a serial killer is defined by the number of murders they've committed, and we've had two here, which falls under that definition. So, would you say our killer is a serial killer?"

"Can you prove one person killed both individuals?" That shut her up. "I believe Detective Johnson may have a serial killer, and we may or may not share the same killer. You could also note the killings in Birmingham have stopped. Are you familiar with the BTK killer?"

All three nodded.

Sandra spoke again. "Are you saying this is a copycat of the BTK killer?"

"No, I'm saying there are similarities, but our killer isn't that smart. He wants attention and notoriety, but we shouldn't be talking about him. We should be talking about the victims. The victims and their families deserve justice. We are not a pawn in this chess match, the killer is, and we will bring justice for them."

"How do you think—"

I stopped the man before he could continue with his question. "At this time that's all I have to say. Rest assured, when we find this killer, and we will find him, you all will be the first to know."

They spouted out questions as I walked back through the locked door into the reception desk area. I headed straight to Bishop and Jimmy.

"Game on," Bishop said.

16

It didn't take long for the news to get out. The local ABC station ran it as a special report, and their national program picked it up too. Within two hours the mayor was in Jimmy's office losing it, and the entire department heard.

Bishop sat across from me in my cubby as we tapped our fingers on stacks of dozens of file folders as we reviewed each investigation record for all five murders again looking for anything we'd missed.

My cell dinged, and I read the text to Bishop. "That was Jimmy. He needs me in his office, stat."

"Need me to support you?"

"Yes, please."

The mayor wore a pair of khaki pants, dress shoes, and a buttoned collar shirt with a plaid sweater vest. Very retro and not appropriate for his physique. The ugly sweater vest begged for attention to his growing belly. I glanced at Bishop when I saw it. He caught my look and raised his eyebrows. We'd been partners long enough he knew what I was thinking.

The mayor wasn't up for niceties and jumped on me immediately after I said hello. "What the hell is wrong with you? Speaking to the press without coming to me first? Out of line, Ryder, way out of line."

"Mr. Mayor," Jimmy said. "As I said, it was my idea."

I stood my ground. "It was my idea, and it was the right thing to do."

The mayor huffed. I half expected him to beat on his chest and chant, *Me Tarzan, you Jane.* "Any conversations with the media should be handled by me."

I dug my heels into the floor. "You're wrong, sir, and let me tell you why." Bishop and Jimmy kept silent, possibly out of respect, but likely out of fear. I made sure to choose the rest of my words carefully. "The killer left a note for me." I pointed to my chest. "He feels a connection to me. I need to be the one communicating with him and the most effective way to do it is through the media. I'm sorry if it upset you, but my priority is catching this guy before we have another victim. I had to convince both Chief Abernathy and Detective Bishop to go along with it. I took advantage of an opportunity and went for it."

He pulled his sweater down over his belly. "All that did was rile up the media and freak out the community. You all but verified we've got a serial killer roaming around town looking for his next victim."

Bishop stepped forward. "With all due respect, sir, the city was already freaking out and living in fear of a serial killer because of your recent press conference."

Day-um. Bishop was a boss! I watched Jimmy's jaw drop.

"Unfortunately, he's right," I said. "Our department's managing chaos right now out in the community guaranteeing the citizens we'll stop the serial killer. Had the term not been used, our police resources could be used to catch the killer instead of managing a scared population. I agree with you. What I said might have added additional stress in town, but it will help draw out the killer and that's what we need to do to catch him."

The mayor pressed his lips together, then said, "I didn't directly say we have a serial killer."

"In my experience you don't have to be definitive when using the term for the city to go into panic mode." But yeah, basically you did.

"This isn't in Chicago, Detective. We do things differently in Hamby."

I squeezed my hands into fists. When I first moved to town, the then mayor and the chief despised me, and the rest of my work peers didn't respect me. I was talked down to, called *girl* and *missy*, told I was too emotional and that I should be barefoot and pregnant, cooking dinner for my husband. Eventually word got out that I'd killed the gang member who'd shot my husband, then hunted down and put away the politician who hired him. That garnered me a little respect, but the leg draggers needed more. Which they got, by means of me catching the town's most unexpected killer and taking down a corrupt government in the process. With the help of my partner, of course.

Over the years, my time with the department, things changed. New mayors, a new chief, and a partner with whom I'd become close. I would not fall back into the idiocy of when I first arrived in town, letting old-school men treat me like I was inferior. I wasn't a feminist, at least not in the current sense, but I wasn't submissive either, and I would make sure that was known if necessary. I wasn't about to step back in time and/or prove myself all over again. "I am well aware of the fact that this isn't Chicago, sir. No Chicago mayor would get in front of the media and use the words 'serial killer' as a political maneuver." That was entirely untrue, but it felt great to say.

Jimmy immediately bolted from his side of the desk and over to me. "May I talk to you outside, Detective?" He didn't give me an opportunity to answer, instead just pulled me from the office. He closed the door behind me. His face was red again. I had to bite my lip from saying something snarky. It most definitely wasn't the time for that.

"What the hell are you thinking?"

"I'm thinking about finding a serial killer."

He ran his hand over the top of his short hair. "You can't continue to piss people off and expect them to respect you. The mayor can fire you. He doesn't need me to do it. And you're my best detective. I need you, and I need you on this case. So keep your damn mouth shut. Am I being clear?"

"Clear as a bell, Chief."

He glared at me. I kept my eyes focused on his and waited until he looked away. The stare-down, much like one between a dog and a human, was a means of control and power. Whoever looked away first submitted the power to the other. I was lead on the investigation. Yes, Jimmy was the chief, and he had the final say, but until I was off lead, I would do what had to be done.

He looked away and stormed back into his office.

Bishop worked a miracle and had the mayor calmed down, but he still narrowed his eyes at me and grunted something impolite as he walked out of Jimmy's office and closed the door behind him.

"Wow, what'd you say to him?" I asked.

"I have a way of calming people down, especially people angry with you."

"And I appreciate that."

"I assured the mayor we did the right thing, but that if we had to do something like that again, we would get his approval first. I also said we didn't have time to fret about the process because all theories indicated we would have another murder in a matter of days, and we needed to get to work."

Jimmy opened the door and nodded to Bishop. "Good job. Now get back out there."

Bishop read me the riot act after we returned to our cubicles, but before I had a chance to defend myself, our investigation took a turn.

∽

The front desk officer called me up, saying I had a kid waiting in the reception area.

I'd never seen the kid before. He was eighteen years old at most and wore a pair of blue jeans hanging down below his waist with a large oversized and dirty gray sweatshirt. His hair hung just to his shoulders and was so ratty, my mother would have said he couldn't get a comb through it. He smelled like he hadn't showered in days. He'd picked his face so much, the scars had scars. I assumed if I ran his fingerprints, we would find several arrests for meth use and petty crimes.

"Detective Ryder. What can I do for you?"

He handed me a legal-sized envelope. "This is for you."

I took his envelope and acted like it meant nothing, but asked, "Is this from you?" Though I knew it wasn't.

"No, ma'am. I was paid to deliver it to you personally."

My eyes shifted to the ceiling and the camera in the room. "I need you to come in back with me for just a moment."

"I..." He bounced on his heels. "I gotta run. I got stuff to do."

I grabbed his shoulder and flipped him back around as he turned toward the door. "Now, listen carefully. If you choose to walk out that door"—I pointed to the exit—"I'll follow you and arrest you for accessory to murder."

His eyes bulged. "All I did was take the dude's envelope and fifty bucks and do what he said. I didn't accessorize no crime."

"You want to leave that to a judge to decide?"

He blinked repeatedly.

"I just need some information on the person that gave you this envelope. But if you want, I can run your prints, and I bet I'll find a bunch of failure to appears, shoplifting, and from the way you've picked at your face, meth arrests. It'll just get ugly from there. Is that what you want?"

He shook his head. "I didn't murder nobody."

"This way." I moved him in front of me with my hand lightly pressed into his back to direct him toward the interrogation room. I left the kid sitting there while Bishop, Jimmy, and I opened the envelope.

"He saw the news," I said. "The killer saw the interview."

Jimmy leaned over the table and stared at the crossword puzzle. What the hell does this mean?"

"The BTK killer," I said. "I mentioned him to the reporters on purpose. The BTK killer thought he was smarter than the cops, just like this guy, and he gave them clues. That's what our killer is doing. This puzzle is a clue."

"These are justice killings," Bishop said. "Why would he give us a clue if he's not finished?"

"Because he doesn't think we're smart enough to catch him, and it makes him feel good to be smarter, to brag about what he's doing, how he's winning," I said.

"Jesus."

"It's a step in the right direction," I said.

"I suck at crossword puzzles," Jimmy said.

"Me too," Bishop said.

"I bet there's someone here that's smart enough to do this." I called Bubba on his cell. "You like crosswords?"

"Define 'like.' My parents made me do them as a kid. They thought it would develop my brain faster. I'm good at them, but I wouldn't say I like them."

"The killer gave us one."

"Investigation room?"

"Yup."

"On my way."

Bishop slammed his hands on the table. "This asshole is screwing with us."

Johnson walked in and handed us each a bag from Wendy's. I was surprised and appreciative. "Wow, thanks."

"What's going on?" He glanced down at the puzzle. "Is that what I think it is?"

"Yup," I said.

"Interesting. I was meeting with Dr. Calloway. She believes our guy will kill again in the next twenty-four hours. I thought it was too early, but if he sent this, then I'm inclined to agree with her."

I stared down at the crossword puzzle. "Maybe that's what he's trying to tell us with this thing."

"Has anyone figured it out?"

"The words, yes, but what they mean, not even close. We're smarter than he thinks we are, though. We can figure it out." I ran my fingers along the words. "This is a simple design, which tells me he's not as smart as he thinks he is."

Bishop agreed. "Or he was in a hurry because you pissed him off and made him look bad in front of the entire nation."

"I didn't make him look bad."

"We're dealing with a narcissistic sociopath. His reality is different from ours."

"Point taken."

"And maybe he didn't have enough time to think cleverly because of his anger. He wanted to get this to us to prove his intelligence."

"I think this was a calculated move on his part," Johnson said.

"I agree," Jimmy said.

"Calloway even said he couldn't hold his anger. I'm the grocery clerk and this note is his way of yelling at me."

"You're probably right," Johnson said. "Seven, swiftly, nineteen, and sesame. What could those words possibly mean?"

"Could it be an address?" Bubba asked. He'd brought his computer with him and quickly got online. "Let me see what I can find."

As he tapped away, we all continued to toss around ideas, but we couldn't come up with anything that fit.

The front desk called Jimmy. "We have an issue, and we need you to handle it."

We all wished him luck.

"There's nothing in Hamby with any of these words as street names or companies, but there are several street numbers with nineteen and seven in them."

"How many is several?" Bishop asked.

"At least four hundred, but I'd have to go through them all to count and be sure."

"We don't have time for that," I said. "What about swiftly? The words don't have to mean what they say. Nineteen and seven could be numbers, but they could be, I don't know, part of a longitude or latitude reference."

Bishop shook his head. "That doesn't make sense to me. Why would he give us only partial longitudes or latitudes? These are justice killings. He wants us to find the bodies."

"I know," I said. "But he doesn't want us to find them until he's ready."

Calloway walked in. "Your chief has a tough one on his hands."

"What's going on?" Bishop asked.

"A seventy-two-year-old man thought walking around Hamby with a loaded shotgun was the appropriate way to ward off potential serial killers. The man waved the gun at residents in the shopping district and threatened to kill anyone who got close to him. A few citizens tackled him to the ground, and in the process, the gun went off and shot through a public mailbox outside the post office. He was brought in. He doesn't have a carry license, but he's threatening to sue based on the Second Amendment."

Fear always wreaked havoc on the human mind.

"Poor Jimmy. He's already got enough on his plate," I said.

"Wait a minute," Bubba said. "I think I found something!" He slid his computer around to face us. "Swift construction is building a new strip mall off Providence Road."

"That's right!" Bishop said. "This was a big deal. City council pushed it through because of the revenue it could bring to town."

"Isn't there a storage facility going up behind it? One the whole community pushed back on?" I asked.

"Yes," Bishop said.

Bubba walked around the table and typed something into the computer. "I pulled up the architectural committee's plan design from the meeting notes for city council. Look at this." He pointed to the drawing on his screen. "There are one hundred and ninety-seven storage units. Nineteen and seven."

"Seven, swiftly, and nineteen," I said. "That fits, but what about sesame?"

"Let me do a search," Bubba said.

Bishop and I paced opposite directions in the small investigation room. With all the cases we'd had over the years since the room was completed, we'd yet to put holes in the carpet, but they'd happen eventually.

"You expected this, correct?" Calloway asked. "That's why you held the interview. To draw him out."

"Yes," I said.

"This was a mistake. You've managed to anger him."

I pointed to the crossword puzzle. "He gave us a clue. It could be about the next murder. Maybe he wants to be caught."

"No, he wants you to look stupid. Those words will have nothing to do with the next murder."

"I guess we'll have to see," I said.

"Very well. I'll be around if you need me." She left the room.

I flipped off the door as it shut. "She's got attitude."

"And she's not the only one," Bishop said.

Johnson laughed.

"Shut up," I said. I was angry because I was worried she was right.

"I can't find anything," Bubba said.

"I think that's his objective." I walked back over to the crossword puzzle and calmed down. "All of these easily come together. But sesame makes no sense." I looked straight at Johnson. "Does any of this make sense to you?"

"I'm afraid not. The only thing I know about sesame is Chinese food and bagels."

"That's not helpful," I said.

"I didn't say it was."

"He's trying to trip us up." I said. "His next victim is going to be at that Swiftly construction site somewhere around the storage center. Which means that building is going up in flames soon."

Bubba looked up at me from his laptop. "Aren't storage buildings made from metal and concrete? Would they burn in a fire?"

"Yes," Bishop said. "People think their things are safer there because metal doesn't burn, but that's not true. Depending on how long the fire burns, the heat it produces can cause damage to the metal, misshaping and melting it, and allow the concrete to crack, which creates permanent structural damage, and the fire will eventually get to their belongings."

I checked my watch. It had been several hours since my news appearance. "We need to get to that facility. And we need the fire department with us. I've seen those storage facilities come down in fires. The fires start and take off inside before anybody knows, and by the time they figure it out, it's already too late."

"But our guy doesn't start fires on the inside," Bishop said.

"Doesn't matter. We need people there just in case."

"Let's go," Bishop said. "We can call Hamby fire en route."

As we walked out, I turned to Johnson. "Can you get in touch with Michels and see where he is with Ron Howard?"

He checked his watch. "Yes, ma'am."

Providence Road had been predominantly residential for years. When Hamby branched off from Alpharetta long before I moved to town, the city plan included a commitment to keep that area of town residential, but new government, more residents, and a stronger need for retail and medical facilities, not to mention the possible revenue for the city, changed that. It was probably the thing that ticked off the residents the most, but under the guise for the greater good, City Council made it happen.

Hamby fire got to the location about three minutes before us.

"There's nothing," one of the firemen said. "We've checked everything."

I tipped my head back and pressed my palm into my forehead. "Shit." I exhaled, inhaled deeply, and then exhaled again. "You looked on just the outside, right?"

"Yes, ma'am."

"Son of a bitch," Bishop said. "He sent us on a wild goose chase."

He was probably right, but I wasn't ready to admit it. "Let's just have a look ourselves."

I smiled at the firemen. "Can you guys stick around for a while? I want to make sure things are completely clear before you all leave."

He nodded. "Yes, ma'am."

"Thank you."

Bishop and I headed to the back of the facility where we expected the fire would have started. The fireman was right. There was nothing.

"Given what this guy has done," I said, "this is the perfect setting. Behind the building there's a bunch of trees. The houses are so far back that they can't see through those trees, so he could drop the body here and no one would ever know until the fire started." I took a deep breath. I'd taken a lot of deep breaths through the investigation. "What if he was going to use this location but decided against it because of my fifteen minutes of fame?"

"How do you mean?" Bishop asked.

"His options in town for fires and victim staging together are limited. Think about it, this guy doesn't want to hurt anyone else. He only wants to hurt his victims, and there just aren't that many places where it's safe to do that."

"I'm not sure I agree. Setting the fires hurts people in their wallets."

"I think that's different. He's not physically hurting them. Maybe he justifies the financial hit that way?"

"So, you're saying your talk with the reporters upset him enough to change his plan and lead us astray like Calloway mentioned."

"I am, but that could mean he's getting desperate."

"Or intentionally putting us off track so he can prove he's smarter than us like Calloway said. What's to stop him from misdirecting us while he's dumping a body and starting a fire somewhere else as we speak?"

Bishop was right and I had to admit that too. "At least Calloway didn't call that."

"Not funny, partner. We need to put the fire department on high alert. Right now."

Chief Pickens was at the location and talking to Johnson when we found him. "Detectives," he said. "No fire is good news, correct?"

"Maybe not," Bishop said. "We're concerned he's misled us intentionally, and we need everyone on high alert."

"The fire department is always on high alert," Pickens said.

"Appreciate it," Bishop said.

We did one more walk through of the grounds but found nothing.

Nikki arrived as we were heading back to the car. "I'm so sorry. Let's just say I was otherwise engaged."

Bishop raised an eyebrow, and I coughed.

"Not that kind of engagement," she said. I thought it was great that the assumption didn't make her uncomfortable.

"Anyway," she said. "What's going on? Bubba said there was no body. Is that true?"

Word made the rounds quickly in the department.

Bishop nodded. "You know about the note? The crossword puzzle?"

She nodded. "Bubba called me and filled me in on everything." She looked at me and smiled. "You looking to be discovered for a reality TV show or something?"

I laughed. "Yes, that's my goal."

She laughed too.

"Can you do a detailed search around here and see if you find anything that could relate to our other crime scenes?" I asked.

"Yes ma'am," she said. "Though, from what I gather, the fire department has been all over the scene, so if there was anything, it might have been trampled by now."

"Understood," Bishop said. "Just go ahead and do what you can."

She nodded. "I'll do my best."

Bubba caught us as we walked back into the department. "Are you psychic?" He looked at me.

I pointed to my chest and raised my eyebrows. "Me?" I shook my head. "I'd be retired and living in Jamaica on my lottery winnings if that was the case. What's up?"

"Johnson's partner arrived with the three female assault victims like ten minutes after you two left."

"That's surprising," I mumbled under my breath. "I guess Johnson has some street cred after all."

"You might want to work on your whispering technique," Bishop said.

I shrugged. "Why bother? Effort never helped before." I pointed at Bubba and then hitched my thumb behind me. "Investigation room?"

He nodded. "I'll be in in five."

Detective Edward Anderson sat across from the three female sexual assault victims at the conference table. Johnson walked in and introduced us.

Two of the girls looked worse for wear, but the other one looked like nothing had phased her. I suspected that was Claire Baker. She'd put up a front if only because she'd talked to me already.

"Detective Anderson," Bishop said. He made eye contact with each of the women. "Ladies, thank you for coming."

We sat down and grabbed the files we'd left on the table earlier. I tapped Bishop's foot with mine. It was a sign that I wanted to be the one to get the ball rolling.

"Ladies, I'm assuming Detectives Johnson and Anderson explained why you're here today. Since your attackers were murdered three years ago, we've had two additional murders, both over the past few days, and both here in Hamby. I believe when our department contacted you recently, you were informed of this."

They all nodded.

"And I spoke to Claire." I made eye contact with the young woman I thought was her. "I'm assuming that's you?"

"Yes."

I smiled. "Now, based on the information we've gathered, we believe without a doubt our killer is the same person who killed your attackers."

Claire spoke up. "Good for him. I'm glad to see he's wiping the world clean of that filth. I'm just sorry I didn't think of it first."

Women said that kind of thing out of fear. "I suspect a lot of women feel that way, and while I don't disagree with wanting revenge for someone who's hurt you, justice killings are not the route to take. Whether those killings are committed by an outsider or one of the victims." I took a deep breath. Someone might have said that's exactly what I did when Tommy was murdered, and in a way, it was, but if I hadn't pulled the trigger, he would have turned his gun on me. "We can't have a serial killer seeking justice for crimes committed against women."

"Why not?" She asked. "I researched you. I know you killed your husband's killer. What's the difference? What makes you above the law? And besides, it saves tax dollars, clears up our court system and the prisons, and it stops the bastards from hurting other women. It's the perfect solution to the issue."

Admittedly, she had a point, but regardless, the actions were against the law, and it was the law that determined justice. "My situation is not similar, Ms. Baker, and there are legal ways to get the same outcome you're seeking. Let me ask you this. How many people did you tell about your attack?"

She looked down at the table before she spoke. "I told you, just my father." She looked back up at me.

"How would you feel to know your father was a suspect?"

"He's not. He already told me you questioned him. If he was, he'd be in jail."

"Not exactly," I lied. "And tell me again why you didn't go to the hospital or tell the police?" I intentionally pushed her buttons. I needed them all to understand the seriousness of the situation and to speak honestly.

"Let's just say I had a reputation for being someone who liked to have a good time. So why would I go tell anybody else when I know that that's what the cops would be told?"

Bishop took over. "We've asked you here today to discuss the similarities between your attackers."

"Is that because you have no suspects?" the second victim asked.

Bishop checked the files Johnson had waiting for us. "You're Ms. Wilson, correct?"

"Yes."

"It's because we're attempting to establish a pattern in these killings," Bishop said. "While we believe they are connected, we need evidence to support that so when the case goes to court, the prosecuting attorney has what's necessary for a guilty verdict."

Bishop had a way of talking to younger women. His tone, his inflection, even his body language all made them more comfortable than I had. I needed to remember that.

"My rapist didn't look like theirs," the last girl said.

I checked my file. Beth Finn.

"I watched the news and I paid attention; they were very different," she said.

"May I ask why?" I asked.

"It was just strange you know, three murders near fires. I couldn't help but wonder if they were somehow connected. Everyone thought it. It was all over the news."

Johnson leaned forward. "We didn't reveal much with respect to details on the killings, but the media did report their association with the fires obviously."

She shrugged. "I would have made it anyway, I think. Three guys, about the same age, killed in a close time frame. Even without the fires, they felt connected somehow."

I nodded. "That makes sense. Did the media say anything else that led you to that connection?"

"No, but Detective Johnson made me feel like a suspect."

"Miss Finn, I'm afraid everyone is a person of interest until we can clear them."

"So you lied to me on the phone," Claire Baker said. "You said the police would have believed us if we'd gone to them."

"I said they may have, yes, but that's different than what we're talking about. Being raped and being accused of murder are two separate issues."

"We are victims," she said

"I understand. It's simply a process of elimination. If someone is a victim of an awful crime and the person who committed that crime against them is murdered, the first person law enforcement wants to rule out is their victim. I can't speak for Detective Johnson, but I suspect he wasn't accusing you of the crime. He was looking to remove you from the suspect list."

Johnson gave me a slight nod. "Detective Ryder is right," he said. "Our interviews were simply to gather information about your circumstances surrounding the victim."

All three women nodded.

"Detective Johnson, if you wouldn't mind talking further with the women, Bishop and I have a situation we need to attend to." I didn't believe we'd get anything from the women, but I felt Johnson and Anderson could work through the details. Bishop and I had a killer to catch, and I didn't want us wasting time on interviewing the women.

Johnson agreed.

We sat in Jimmy's office filling him in on what we'd learned.

"So, basically, you got nothing from the women?"

We both nodded.

"Why did you leave Anderson and Johnson with them?" Jimmy pointed to me. "You, especially. They might say things to you they won't say to the men."

"There's nothing for them to say. I assessed the situation, and I don't believe they can offer us anything to pull our victims together. Our killer made a connection in his mind, and I don't think it's something we can connect through the murder victims or their victims. At least not anything more than we've already determined. Whatever our killer sees as a connection is in his head."

"And we need Calloway to help us with that," Bishop said.

"Yes," I said. "My mind can go to very dark places, but—"

Bishop interrupted me with, "Ain't that the truth."

I narrowed my eyes at him. "As dark as I can get, I'm not at our killer's level, he's a sociopath. And I don't have the training Calloway does."

"I see some similarities," Bishop said.

"Shut it, partner."

We all laughed. If we didn't lighten the mood every now and then, we risked going to the darkness within the case, and we might never return.

Thirty minutes later, Calloway was back in the investigation room handing each of us copies of an updated twenty-page report further analyzing our suspect.

"As you'll see in my updated report, I've put together a detailed psychological profile of our suspect. Everything we discussed is in it, and I've also added additional information. I think it's important to discuss a few points I've outlined in my introduction as I believe they're important to the investigation. You'll find the introduction on page two."

I scanned the introduction quickly. "You think the killer is a Black man?"

"We can't rule it out. Based on the definition of a serial killing over a mass murder or mass shooting, we must go with what the facts show, and the facts show that in recent years, the number of serial killings committed by Black people has increased from twenty percent to fifty percent."

"Try telling the media that," Bishop said. "They'll call you a racist."

"And I'll show them the facts," Calloway said.

I liked her more and more.

"They're not looking at the true definition of the term. I accept two or more killings across separate events as serial killings, though some experts will say only one can define a serial killing."

"Wait a minute," Bishop said. "Isn't serial, by definition, plural?"

"I would say yes," she said. "And in accordance with that definition, two is plural."

"Who would be considered a serial killer under that definition? The only one I can think of is Wayne Williams," Bishop asked.

"Yes, and that's an excellent question," she said. "More recent names that come to mind are Chester Turner, Derek Todd Lee, who, by the way, was convicted of two murders."

"Except those two examples don't fit our killer," I said. "Their victims were women, and, if I'm correct, sexually assaulted."

"I'm simply pointing out that we can't discount the possibility that our killer is Black."

"Understood," I said.

"Serial murderers often come from working class or lower-middle class environments, which contributes to their generalized feeling of inadequacy."

"So, you think our guy is broke? Isn't that a contradiction of what you said before?"

"I'm saying our killer suffered from some kind of financial insecurity as a child, and that even though he may have found a way out of that, he's internalized those feelings from his childhood, and his expression of that comes through in the execution of his plan."

"Let me get this straight," I said. "You believe the killer shows confidence, but is insecure, has money now, but didn't before."

"Exactly," she said.

"That doesn't make a damn bit of sense," Bishop said.

"Actually, it does," I said. "Our guy struggled with instability, and the only way out of it was to control his environment. So maybe our guy struggled with someone related to his murders, prior to the killings, obviously, and his way of fixing that is to seek justice for them."

"That's a stretch," Bishop said.

"Not really," Calloway said. "He believes these are justice killings, and in that sense, they are, but they're also a power move on his part, hence the reason he sent the notes to Detective Ryder. He feels the need to prove his intelligence, his abilities, and to show control and power."

"But you think he's desperate?" I asked.

"I think those insecurities are tapping him on the shoulder and pushing him to react. What he initially thought was control—sending the first note, then the crossword puzzle, and bringing you to a fake scene. But, really, they are acts of desperation because he feels you know something about him he doesn't know you know."

Bishop nodded. "I get it. He's desperate because his doubts are telling him he's not really in control."

"When in fact," she said, "he is."

"Not for long," I said.

"I'll give you each some time to read the report, but based on the change in the killer's process, I believe his murders, or desires for those murders, are escalating, and we should expect another soon."

"Define 'soon,'" I said.

She checked her watch. "Within the next twenty-four hours."

"What makes you think that?"

"Everything I just said. His insecurities are telling him to move fast and move on because we are gaining speed in the investigation."

Bishop exhaled. "Jesus, this guy is nuts."

"In layman's terms, yes," she said. "If you have any questions, let me know. I'm going to meet with the mayor and then I'll be back in a temporary office for assistance when needed."

"Good luck with the mayor," Bishop said.

"Thank you."

Her report was excellent. It read like a thesis for a master's degree with footnotes and a bibliography to link to studies and books supporting her theories.

Michels walked in and let out an exasperated sigh. "Howard isn't our guy."

"Explain," Bishop said.

"Aside from the fact that I was able to confirm his alibi for each murder, he has a limp and walks with a cane. The man has absolutely no muscle to be able to do any of what our killer's done." He saw the twenty-page report on the table. "What's that?"

"Calloway's final profile of the killer. Doesn't include anything about a limp or a cane," I said.

He scanned through the pages. "Damn, Calloway's smart."

"Did you think otherwise?"

"I guess I just thought the psychoanalyzing stuff was psychobabble, but this all reads like the real deal."

"Psychology plays a big part in the why, and the how, too, of criminal activity. Look at the Oklahoma bomber or Jeffrey Dahmer."

"That dude had some serious issues."

"A few, maybe," I said.

Bishop's cell phone rang. He checked the caller ID then excused himself from the room. I went back to work and jotted notes from the report.

"He's been doing that a lot," Michels said.

"Doing what?" I knew what he was talking about, but I played dumb.

"Taking private phone calls. Is he interviewing for another department or something?"

"Or something."

We'd taken a two-hour break that allowed me to go home, feed Louie, grab a quick meal, and shower. I raced through it all, sat on my couch, and tried to call Kyle. Surprisingly, he answered.

"We're finishing up. It went faster than we expected."

"That's great. Did you get the bad guy?"

"Not me personally, but yes, and it's bad guys. Seven of them in LaGrange. We busted them with twenty pounds of packaged ecstasy, over six thousand pills, and twelve weapons. We had one guy injured, but he'll be treated and released. All in all, it was a good bust. How's things with your investigation?"

"We're still where we were before. We brought in the victim's victims from Alabama, but they had nothing to add. Even Johnson, who wasn't pleased we'd called them in since he'd already interviewed them, said none of them were involved."

"Hard to see a woman committing those kinds of crimes."

"Lorena Bobbitt."

"Jesus, that girl changed men forever. Are you saying you think the doer is a woman?"

"I'm not saying it isn't, but it doesn't matter anyway because right now we have nothing that really points to either sex or any specific race. We have nothing, and Jimmy's losing his mind because the mayor is on him."

"Anything I can do?"

"Go home and get sleep. You can always come by the station tomorrow. I'm sure Jimmy can put you to work." DEA agents would usually work a case and then get a few days' break, and Jimmy wasn't opposed to taking advantage of Kyle's expert skills if offered.

"If it gets my eyes on you, I'm there."

I smiled. "I do kind of miss those eyes on me."

"I hope that's not all."

"Definitely not."

We disconnected, and I laid my head back and closed my eyes for just a moment. The next thing I knew, my cell phone rang and woke me out of a deep sleep.

"Ryder," I said with a sleepy voice.

"Swiftly has another building going up at the Cherokee County line, and it's burning now," Bishop said. "I'm en route."

I jumped off the couch and grabbed my boots. "Is there a body?"

"Yes."

17

The Swiftly construction site wasn't far from the one we'd found earlier. I chastised myself for not knowing they'd secured multiple contracts in Hamby. When I arrived on scene, a small gathering of rubberneckers and a larger crowd of reporters had already crowded the gravel construction parking lot. I pulled up next to Bishop's vehicle, grabbed my things, and jogged toward the scene.

A reporter and cameraman stepped into my path. "Detective Ryder," the reporter said.

I rushed past, saying, "No comment."

The reporter shouted from behind, "Is this the serial killer, the fire starter?"

Great. Multiple nicknames for the killer had come out already and that guy had just added "fire starter" to the mix. All that mattered to the media was advertising dollars, and the best way to get it was through fear. Give the killer multiple names covering different bases, and fear intensified. I didn't bother with an answer.

Bishop stood over the body. "That's three."

"At least it's the last one," I said.

He looked at me. "We don't know that for a fact. All we know is we've got three numbers on three victims. We don't know what happened between Johnson's victims and ours. For all we know, the killer can be marking them out of order just to mess with us, or maybe the numbers don't mean anything at all."

"Or maybe they're not accurate," I said. I stared down at the victim. The scene and the body were the same as our other victims. The deceased was reasonably attractive, cleaned and prepped after the murder, with a slit stretching across the width of his neck. I hadn't looked, but I suspected his penis had been cut off also. I slipped on a pair of latex gloves and picked up the number. As I stood, I said, "Maybe that's the point. Maybe the numbers are meant as a distraction."

"Meaning what?" Bishop asked.

"Meaning they don't mean what we think, and it's possible they don't have any bearing on what the killer's doing." I held the baggie with a number in my hand. "What if the numbers are his way of telling us he thinks he's smarter than we are? What if he's not desperate like Calloway says? What if he's playing us?"

Bishop looked at me. "That doesn't make sense."

"It only has to make sense to him, and it's police work 101. The obvious is usually the answer, but in this case, it wasn't. Maybe this guy's studied law enforcement?"

"We never considered the coroner connection," Bishop said.

"That was a major error on my part. I should have considered that." I crouched down and examined the victim's slit neck. "This guy might not be lying here if I had."

"We're partners. It was an error on both of our parts, and it was an understandable error. You need to stop carrying the load of the investigation on your own."

"It seems awfully convenient, the Birmingham coroner and Barron talking at just the right moment."

"Yes. We should have questioned that earlier. That's on us," Bishop said. "Had we, we could have stopped the second killing, among other things, but even Jimmy didn't consider it. We trust Barron, and we all trusted his reference for the other coroner."

I tapped out a text to Jimmy explaining our theory and asking how he wanted it handled. "We'll see what the chief says."

The chief was apparently a few feet behind us. "One of us should have caught that. I'll handle it. I don't think it's him, but I'll check and get back to you. Now, what do we have here?" He glanced down at the victim. "Another family that will never be the same."

The fire inspector walked over. "We're looking at the same guy, only the fire was started inside the building this time. Went up fast that way, but given its size, it would have taken some time to burn. Your killer might have gambled on that, though. Something to consider."

"When can Nikki check the scene?" I asked.

"About an hour or two. I'll let her walk through with me."

"We'd appreciate that," Jimmy said.

After the fire department put out the fire, Bishop, Michels, Jimmy, and I stood away from the lagging reporters and discussed what we knew, which wasn't much.

"Why isn't Detective Johnson here?" Michels asked.

"He drove one of the girls back to Alabama," Bishop said. "He thought they should at least keep one separated if this ever goes to trial."

"Probably smart," Michels said.

I exhaled. "He's not as bad as I thought, but he's still behind the times when it comes to working with women."

"Some men never adjust to that," Jimmy said.

"Who's serving the death notice?" Michels asked. "I'd rather not. Those things suck the life out of me."

I pressed my lips together and made a popping sound with them. "Great choice of words, Detective."

"My bad."

"I'm doing this one. The victim is Austin Chastain. His family is a big deal in the area; I need to be the one to deliver the news." He shook his head. "I hate to think of it this way, but it's probably good for business. The public needs to know I'm actively working the investigation."

"When was the last time you did one?" I asked.

"A while ago. I should be doing more of the daily work to stay in the loop."

"It's too bad we can't tell them we have a suspect," Bishop said.

"We need to change that," Jimmy said. "We've got three murders and no suspect. Baker's cleared. We need to start over, and while we're doing that, we'll have Bubba look into Chastain and check his history. See if there's a connection between any of the female or male victims."

"He won't find any," I said. "That's not how this guy works. That much we know. All he'll find is an alleged sexual assault with a victim that never went to the hospital or the cops. That's what the girls have in common."

Bishop agreed. "He's too smart for that. The assaults are the only connection, but we have no idea how this guy found out about them."

"Maybe he's like Bubba?" Michels asked. "Maybe he's a tech guru and made the connections the same way Bubba did."

"I don't know enough about social media to know if he can access people on it without knowing them," I said.

"Sure he can, at least on most of them, and if the people are public, it's easy," Michels said.

Jimmy put his hands on his hips, bent down his head, and muttered repetitive f-bombs. We waited until he finished. Finally, he said, "Find him," then he walked away.

The three of us stared at each other.

Bishop's face reddened. "What the hell does he think we're doing?"

"You heard him," I said. "We need to start over. And that means go back to our first victim."

"I'll get with Bubba once we're back at the department and see if he can explain how the killer could find the victims on social media," Michels said.

∼

We headed to Waffle House. It was late, we needed coffee, and theirs was better than anything we could get at the station. Even though we had multiple Keurigs, something about police department coffee just made the stuff bad. I figured it was cursed.

The place was packed. Several of the customers were young enough to likely just come from a night out and were eating some pre-hangover food. The others were men who had a reason they didn't want to go home. If we got a squad there, we'd have at least two DUIs leave the lot. It smelled like fried food including mostly potatoes and bacon. I caught a hint of eggs, but the smell didn't make me want them. The only eggs I liked were the ones Kyle made.

"Let's talk about the scenes," I suggested.

"What about them? They're all the same," Michels said.

"Except they're not. One was a barn, another the polo fields, and the recent one, a construction site."

"And?" Bishop asked.

"And can we relate those scenes together in any way other than the fires and victims?"

"The barn was abandoned and a private lot," Michels said.

"Right, and the polo fields weren't in use anymore," Bishop said. "And they were on the market."

"And this one is a construction site that's obviously not in use and isn't on the market," I added.

"Did we find out who owns the property?" Michels asked.

Bishop nodded. "Bubba's first job. Private investment company out of Indianapolis. According to documents filed with the city, they're building an office building. Nothing to do with barns or polo. I don't see any connections to the properties, other than the obvious, that is."

The server refilled our cups. Michels glanced at Bishop. "You want something?"

"I could eat."

Bishop looked at me. "You?"

"Nope. I'm good."

"The regular it is," Bishop said to Michels.

Michels smiled at the server. "Mark, quarter cheese deluxe on two, make one a double plate."

What? How did he do that? I was in awe.

"You got it," the server said. She walked over to the kitchen and called out the order exactly as Michels said.

Still in awe, I blinked as I asked, "How did you do that, and what did you order?"

They laughed.

"I ordered a quarter cheese with lettuce, tomatoes, and onions, a deluxe, for me, and for Bishop, the same but with a large hash brown. I worked here in high school."

I pointed to the table. "Here, here?"

He shook his head. "Across the street."

When I considered Georgia as my new residence, I'd read there was a Waffle House on practically every corner, and that wasn't a lie. There were at least four in a mile radius from our location, and one was directly across the street.

"It's the Waffle House way, a specialized training every employee has to go through. Even the president of the company understands the menu. I could recite it in my sleep."

"Crazy," I said.

Bishop directed us back to our investigation. "Worrying about some unclear connection is a waste of time. Like Jimmy said, we start over. Reinterview everyone."

I dropped my chin. That was the last thing I wanted to do, but Bishop was right. We'd start with our first victim and move forward.

"I'll take the most recent victim," Bishop said. "Jimmy's probably already given the death notice, so I can start the interviewing process. Once Bubba has the girl, and we know there will be a girl, I'll interview her."

"Don't you think I should do that?" I asked.

"If I need you, I'll call."

"Then I'll take our first victim," I said. I smiled at Michels. "Looks like you've got the middle guy, and we need an interview with his victim."

"The middle child is always the last anyone thinks about. Trust me, I know that personally."

I played an imaginary violin with my thumb and index finger. "Poor guy. It must be hard, being you."

Their food arrived, and as he lifted the burger to his smiling face, he said, "Not at the moment."

While they ate what I thought gave Bishop high cholesterol, I stared out the window and went over the case in my head. "Hey, is that...?" I pointed to a dark-colored Infiniti sports car. As it passed, I caught the Alabama plate. "Son of a bitch!" I jumped from my seat and raced out to my vehicle. Bishop and Michels caught up as I climbed into the driver's seat. "It's Baker!"

18

I pulled Baker over a mile down the street.

He acted surprised, but I knew it was bull. "Detective Ryder, what a surprise to see you out and about. How's the case going?"

"License and registration, please."

He smirked. "Have you been demoted to plain clothes traffic stop officer because you can't find a serial killer?"

Bishop walked up before I had a chance to say anything. "Mr. Baker, it was our understanding you were returning home to Alabama, yet here you are in Hamby, and conveniently driving through the parking lot of the restaurant where we were having dinner. How about you tell me what's going on?"

"Nothing's going on. I decided to stay in town in case I needed to answer any more questions."

Michels had been examining the car. He walked over and pulled us aside. "This vehicle was at the crime scene earlier. I walked past it."

"Are you sure it's the same one?" Bishop asked.

"There's a scrape on the back right bumper. I noticed it on scene. It's the same vehicle."

I stared at Bishop. "He's on the tape."

"We need to bring him in," Bishop said.

We stuffed him in an interrogation room and developed a plan down the hall.

"He's mine," I said. "If this is our guy, he's playing with me on purpose."

"Don't tell him we saw the videotapes," Bishop said. "He doesn't need to know that."

"Agree."

We walked into the room. Michels made sure to tape it from Bubba's office since Bubba wasn't there.

"Mr. Baker, your daughter was here earlier. Did you know that?" I asked.

"I am aware."

"She reminds me of you," I said.

"Thank you."

I walked from one side of the room to the other while Baker watched. "You know, that simmering temper, just under the boiling point, waiting to explode at just the right moment."

His stone-cold expression flashed with worry for just a moment.

"Let me tell you what I think is going on here, and you can tell me if I'm right." I took a gamble and made up a reason I thought would set his temper off. "Your daughter comes home the night she's raped. You threaten to kill Travis, but Claire begs you not to. Of course, she needs you. You're the only family she's got. But she's like you, that temper, the desire to be perfect. It was evident when she was here earlier. And her anger simmers. She watches Travis go on with his life, flirting with other girls, probably even raping them. She watches, and she can't take it, but she can't just kill him. She knows that even though she didn't tell anyone what happened, people talk. She knows someone knew something. So, instead of killing him, she searches social media, looking at photos and videos, checking for a guy she thinks is like Travis. Someone who would take advantage of a woman, even rape her. She finds two, and she studies them. She studies their social media, studies their lives. She gets to know them, and she decides killing them along with Travis is a win-win. She'll kill her rapist, and she'll take eyes off her with the other kills. Their sexually aggressive history is really just gravy, but it keeps her a victim."

His face hardened into a scowl, and the vein through his forehead swelled.

"Then, you start doing more business in this area. Now Claire's got the itch. She got away with three murders, and she feels like justice was served. But she can't stop the itch. That's what happens to serial killers, they get an itch that can only be—"

He slammed his hands on the table and stood, pushing the chair backward and to the ground. "My daughter isn't a killer!"

Bishop had walked over to him and got in his face. "Sit."

Baker sat.

"How do you know?" I asked. "We think you're protecting her. That you found out, and that's why you're here, hanging out at our crime scenes and following us." The only problem with that theory was we all knew she was en route to Birmingham, so I needed to change lanes. "Or, better yet, maybe you figured it out. You figured out what she did in Alabama. Maybe she told you, and since you're her only family, you couldn't bear to lose each other, so you told her you'd fix it. You had her find another three victims, this time conveniently located here, where you'd be for business, and you'll take any possible scent from her."

"I didn't kill anyone."

I slammed my hands down on the table. "Then why the hell are you at our crime scenes?"

"I told you, I want to thank the person who killed Travis, and when he's caught, I'm going to offer to pay his attorney fees."

I laughed. "You expect me to believe that?" I looked at Bishop. "You hearing this? He thinks we're idiots, doesn't he?"

Bishop smirked. "Just like our killer."

"Right." I smiled at Baker. "Tell us what's really going on. We may be able to reduce your sentence, or perhaps your daughter's. Maybe the death penalty will come off the table."

"I'm telling you the truth. My daughter and I are innocent. I listened at that murder tonight. This killer is detailed. If I killed Travis, I would have just shot him in the head. I wouldn't waste my time on the rest of this shit. I'm not afraid to go to prison."

"Oh..." I snickered. "You'd be a catch in prison, trust me."

Bishop laughed.

"Mr. Baker, it's interesting you say you'd shoot someone in the head. That's how the first three victims were killed."

His face went white. He already knew that, so making that comment struck me as truthful and straight emotion. "I didn't kill him. My daughter didn't kill him. I swear, I just wanted to pay for the guy's attorney. Check my suitcase. I've got ten thousand in cash for a retainer. It's all I could get from the bank today. I can get another ten every day until I've got enough."

I glanced at Bishop and flicked my head toward the door. We stepped outside.

"I believe him," Bishop said. "The guy stinks of sweat. He's nervous."

I tilted my chin down and nodded. "I believe him too."

We let Baker go with a stern warning to get the hell out of town and said if we saw him again, we'd arrest him on disturbing a crime scene, among other things. He left with his tail between his legs.

It was still early, so the three of us headed home for showers.

Bishop went to meet with the family of the recent victim, Austin Chastain. Since he had a history in town, he was the best choice for a well-known resident. Michels's plan was to head straight to Jameson Talbot's parents' house and then to his alleged victim. She would be tough for him. I came into the office before heading to the Ramseys' and updated the investigation files, stuffed copies in everyone's mail slots, then, after eight o'clock, headed out to talk to the Ramseys' again.

They weren't excited to see me. Mrs. Ramsey was sullen and depressed, which was completely understandable, and Mr. Ramsey was thoroughly ticked off that we had yet to catch his son's killer.

Had it been possible, Mr. Ramsey would have shot daggers from his eyes into mine. "You've got a serial killer on the loose. A serial killer!" He shook his head. "Why the hell was my son a victim of a serial killer, and why haven't you caught the guy?"

I deserved every bit of his anger. I'd failed to find even a person of interest since his son's body was found. Logically, I knew it wasn't my fault, but emotionally, I took the heat for the entire team. I took it personally. I had the skills, and the knowledge to close the case, and I hadn't made it happen. "Mr. Ramsey, we're doing everything we can to find your son's killer. In fact, that's why I'm here."

Mrs. Ramsey looked up at me with hope-filled eyes. "Do you have a suspect? Do you know who killed my son?"

I shook my head. "We're still working the investigation, and I promise you we are doing everything we can." I was repeating myself, but that happened a lot when dealing with a victim's family. "I would like to talk with you again about your son." I was on their front porch, and they were inside. "May I come in?"

Mr. Ramsey moved himself and his wife to the side and pushed the door open. "Fine."

I followed them into the sitting area off from the kitchen. The couple sat on the couch while I sat across from them on an ottoman.

"We have determined that each of our three victims were involved in relationships that..." I paused. I needed to say it the right way. Trying to sweeten the news about their son would only make it harder when the truth came out. "I'm sorry to inform you, but your son has been accused of sexual assault." I didn't give them time to respond. "And because of that, we need to dig deeper into the few days before his murder."

Mr. Ramsey clenched his fists while Mrs. Ramsey cried.

"I've heard the rumors," Mr. Ramsey said. "My son was a good-looking, smart, outgoing young man. Of course women were attracted to him. But I raised him to be honorable and respectful with everyone, including women."

Thanks for the inclusion, I thought. I nodded once. "Mr. Ramsey, I am not personally accusing your son of anything. I'm simply stating what we've uncovered. I need to know if you know of any incidences of aggressive behavior with women in the recent past."

Mr. Ramsey stood. "I want you to leave!"

Mrs. Ramsey grabbed her husband's arm while still sitting on the couch. "Sit down, honey. She's trying to find the person who murdered our son."

Mr. Ramsey looked down at his wife, and his anger faded. As he sat, he caught my eye and said, "I wasn't involved in his personal relationships to a degree that would provide me such information, but my wife might know something."

My eyes shifted to Mrs. Ramsey.

She exhaled. "Jake never told me anything outright, but I believe this may have happened in the past, and recently, as you asked."

I took out my notepad. "Can you tell me what you know?" I waited for her to mention Emily Bryant, but given she mentioned Jacob's recent past, I knew she would give me another name.

"He'd gone out with his friends one night a few weeks ago, like he always did. I couldn't sleep that night, so I was up watching TV when he came home. He seemed disheveled, his clothes kind of wrinkled, like he had just dressed again in a hurry. His hair was a mess, which wasn't common for Jake, and he had scratch marks on his face. I thought he'd been in a fight, or at least that's what I told myself. I asked him, and he said yes, that he'd been in an altercation." She swallowed back a sob. "I knew it was probably a girl, but I just didn't want to go there. That's my son, and I couldn't imagine him being aggressive toward the girl."

"Did he ever tell you anything else?"

She shook her head. "But I overheard him on his phone. He was laughing about a girl he'd met at a bar. Laughing about how—" She sobbed. "I'm sorry, this is so hard." She blew her nose into a tissue.

"Take all the time you need."

She took several deep breaths and exhaled the last one with a sigh. "He said she deserved it."

"Did he say the girl's name?"

She shook her head. "But he was talking to his friend Tanner. I have his phone number."

"May I have that, please?"

She stood. "Let me get that for you."

While she stepped away, I offered Mr. Ramsey a half smile. "This is no reflection on you. Please remember that."

He dragged his fingers down his chin. "I... I don't understand. I didn't raise him like that. I love my wife and respect my wife. He didn't grow up seeing disrespect or aggression toward women."

Mrs. Ramsey returned before I had a chance to say anything, and I was grateful for that. I wasn't sure what I could say to help a grieving father wrap his head around the truth about his dead child.

"I don't know when they talked last," she said. "But I know that he and Tanner kept in touch."

"Is Tanner local?"

"He's in Atlanta. Midtown, I think. I don't have the address."

"It's okay, I can find it." I stood. "I know this is hard. I can't imagine what you're going through, but I can promise you my team and I will find the person responsible for your son's murder."

"Thank you."

"Mrs. Ramsey, you contacted Emily Bryant after your son was murdered."

She nodded. "I thought she should know."

"Because they dated?"

"Yes."

"Miss Bryant has accused your son of raping her."

"They were dating," Mr. Ramsey said.

"No means no, Mr. Ramsey, and if a man doesn't take that seriously, that constitutes rape whether you're dating—" I looked at Mrs. Ramsey. "Or married."

"I was worried something like that happened," she said. "Their breakup was so unexpected, and Jacob wouldn't tell me anything about it. I'd tried to contact Emily, but she wanted nothing to do with me. I couldn't help but assume."

"Why didn't you tell me any of this?" her husband asked.

"I was afraid of how you'd react."

Before they got into an argument, I stepped in and redirected the conversation. "As I said, we're doing everything we can to find your son's killer. In the meantime, if you think of anything else, please let me know."

Mrs. Ramsey cried again, and Mr. Ramsey walked me out.

"You find the person who murdered our son. My wife needs closure. We both need closure."

I drove down the street and pulled off onto the side of the road to run Tanner's name in the system. There was one Tanner McCluskey in Atlanta. He had no arrests and no speeding tickets. At least there was that. I dialed his number on my cell as I drove to Emily Bryant's office. The call went straight to voicemail. "Tanner McCluskey, this is Detective Rachel Ryder with the Hamby Police Department. I'm the lead detective investigating the murder of your friend Jacob Ramsey. I have a few questions for you. I'd appreciate a call back at this number as soon as possible."

Emily Bryant wasn't at work and hadn't been since the day before. She'd called in sick, so I drove out to her house. She wasn't home either, but her uncle was, and he didn't appear to care about seeing my face again. Something was different, though I couldn't put my finger on what. He wore weather-inappropriate clothing, an extra-large Braves jersey and a pair of knee-length cargo shorts. Savannah would have cringed at the outfit and then given the guy an education in how to dress to attract women. As if the guy ever had a shot at getting a woman. I laughed internally at the thought of that.

He bit into a piece of white bread. "You find the killer?"

"Do you know where I can find Emily?"

He shrugged. "Last I knew she was taking a day or two off, but I haven't seen her since yesterday, so I can't be sure."

I glanced inside and saw the craft supplies still spread out on the table. "May I come in?"

"For what?"

"I have some questions regarding our investigation."

He took a step back and hesitated before saying, "Sure." He stuffed the rest of the slice of bread into his mouth and walked me into the family room.

The home was a downgrade from the Ramseys', but other than the mess, nothing to complain about. My type-A personality kicked in, and I had to stop myself from telling him to clean the place. "Can you tell me how Emily has been since Jacob Ramsey was murdered?"

"You mean like her emotional state?"

I smiled. "Have you noticed any changes in her behavior or attitude lately?"

"I don't know, I guess she's been fine. Why?"

My eyes traveled back to the crafts on the table. He saw me staring that direction and turned around and looked.

"Think I told you my sister does that stuff. She never cleans it up either. I want to hire a housekeeper, but she says we don't have the money and we all should contribute to keeping the home clean."

"My mother always told us it was a privilege to live in our home and we were responsible for its maintenance."

"Your mother dead?"

"No."

He smiled. "I read about you the other day. You come from Chicago, and you're the cop that watched her husband get shot and then murdered the guy that shot him."

I didn't bother with correcting his poor word choice. "Yes. Now, regarding your niece, have you noticed any mood swings, seen her cry, or, as I said, has she been acting different?"

"What was it like?"

I blinked. "I'm sorry?"

"Shooting that guy. What was it like?"

"How about we talk about your niece, Mr. Stuart?"

"Yeah, we will, but real quick, how many guys have you shot? Probably a lot, right? You've been at this a while."

"I'd like to keep the conversation focused on Emily." I glanced at the dining room table again. "May I have a glass of water?"

He exhaled. "Sure."

I got up with him and followed him toward the kitchen. The dining room was just outside the kitchen with a large walk-through so he could see me standing near the dining room table. I studied the things on the table and focused specifically on the numbers stacked in a pile on the side. I didn't touch anything but made note of their average size.

"My sister tells me that stuff costs a lot of money. She never has time to do anything with it, so if she stopped buying it, we could probably afford the housekeeper." He handed me the water.

"Thank you."

I followed him back to the family room.

"I've been thinking about it, and I think maybe you're right. Emily has kind of changed a little since that guy got killed. She's more, I don't know, sad than relieved, I guess. I mean, yeah, I know they dated, but he dumped her a while ago, so I don't know why she would be so upset. She got over him pretty quick after he dumped her."

The guy had the emotional maturity of a five-year-old. "Sometimes breakups are hard. Tell me more about her behaviors."

He shrugged. "Not much to say. She's always been moody. As for him being killed, maybe she felt he got what he deserved, even though she still missed him, I guess."

"Did you ever meet Jacob Ramsey?"

He nodded. "Couple times. Didn't seem like that great of a catch, and if I were a serial killer, I wouldn't see anything special to pick him." He glanced at my waist and pointed to my weapon. "What kind of gun is that? I got a Glock. I go to Riverbend to shoot. You ever been there?"

"This is a standard-issue police weapon." I stood. "Thank you for your time. When your niece returns home, can you ask her to call me?"

"Don't you have her cell?"

"Yes, and I've already left her a message."

"Then I guess she'll call you back if she feels like it."

"Mr. Stuart, where were you the night Jacob Ramsey was murdered?"

He laughed. "My butt was right on that couch watching TV. I don't like going out at night."

"Was anyone home with you?"

"Nope, but that's normal. My sister stays out late all the time. Sometimes she doesn't even come home, and Emily, I don't think she likes living here a whole lot. She comes and goes, but mostly, she's gone. I think she's trying to get her own place. She had a Realtor leave some information for her the other day."

He didn't seem at all concerned about my question. "So, there's no one that can verify you were home the night Jacob Ramsey was murdered?"

"Nope, not a soul." He tried to smile, but it was more a sneer at first, then it morphed into a fake smile. "I don't get out much what with my condition and all."

"Condition?"

He pointed to the side of his head. "Brain damage."

"You have brain damage?"

"According to the doctors, yup."

He struck me as maybe borderline on the spectrum, but not anything close to someone with brain damage. I felt he was more socially awkward than anything.

"That's why I don't get out much."

"I understand." I was going to ask for details, but I decided to hold off. "Please ask Emily to call me when you see her."

"If I see her, you mean."

He watched me as I pulled out of the driveway. Something about the guy unsettled me, and it put me on high alert. It occurred to me that his medical condition could be the reason he left me feeling unsettled.

It was almost eleven by the time I got back to the police station. I'd stopped at Emily Bryant's second job and was told she'd taken a few days off. No one seemed to know where she'd gone. I tried her cell again, but the call went straight to voicemail.

Uncle Chip was weird, Emily wasn't anywhere to be found, and her mother was MIA. We'd yet to talk to her. It was time to hunt her down, so I got Bubba on that.

Bishop met me in the kitchen and leaned against the counter. "Have I told you how much I hate talking to the parents of dead children?"

"Unfortunately, too many times. Did you learn anything?"

He grabbed a bottled water from the refrigerator and drank half of it before responding. "The mother was aware of an incident, and she asked why that would have to do with his murder by a serial killer."

"What did you tell her?"

"The truth. What was I supposed to say?"

"The truth as in everything?"

He pressed his lips together and blew out a breath. "No, the truth as in limited information that would get her to talk."

"Austin Chastain, who, as you know, is of the Alpharetta Chastains, a historically prominent family for Georgia, which is a very big deal, was accused of sexually assaulting a miss—" He checked his notes. "Marissa Wentworth. It happened six months ago, at a bar in Atlanta. She claimed the altercation took place shortly before two a.m. and the bartender called the bouncers to remove him from the building."

"And the mother knew all this how?"

"Because the next day Marissa Wentworth's father came to pay Chastain a visit."

19

The next morning, we brought Niles Wentworth in for questioning, completely bypassing his daughter based on what Bubba found on his record. Niles Wentworth had two arrests for assault over twenty-five years before, but the charges for each were dropped. For our purpose, they represented a personality trait and a pattern, and it was something we needed to explore. My guess was the guy cleaned up his act when he got married, but when his daughter was attacked, he reverted to his pre-marriage behaviors. The plan was to put Wentworth on edge, let his anxiety and fear, maybe even his anger, build up enough that we'd get him to confess, if, in fact, he was the killer. So, to do that, we let him sit and stew in his fear in an investigation room.

Bishop and I hung back in his cubby tossing around questions for our person of interest.

"I'm not sure Wentworth's our guy," Bishop said. "Two arrests with dropped charges twenty-five years ago doesn't quite upgrade him to a serial killer."

"No, but we need to question him regardless."

"That's a given. My issue is the why. If he killed to get justice for his daughter, that's one thing, but he doesn't look like the type that would kill others. You saw him. He's just your everyday fatherly type. A little dad belly, a receding hairline. Just doesn't say 'serial killer.'"

"I agree, but everyone is a—"

"I know. Everyone's a suspect until they're not. I graduated from the academy a long time before you, remember? I think I've got this stuff down."

"A really, really long time before me." He flipped me the bird, so I blew him a kiss. "By the way, where's Johnson? He should be back from Birmingham already."

"Maybe he got another case. I don't know. I just know he's staying there for a bit. Said he'll be back, though."

"All the better," I said. "He didn't contribute much to the investigation. Did you see his report from his interview with the girls from Birmingham? He got nothing."

"I thought he was growing on you."

I folded my arms over my chest and grimaced. "Not really. I just cut him some slack."

"Seemed like a good detective."

"He wasn't bad, but he just didn't bring anything to the table. I didn't want us finding the killer then him taking any credit."

"Rachel, we all want this guy caught. It's not a competition."

"I didn't say it was."

"You didn't have to." He checked his watch. "It's been thirty minutes. I think we've given Wentworth enough time."

"Let's do this."

Niles Wentworth drummed his fingers on the table. "Can somebody please tell me why I'm here? I have a business to run. I don't have time for this."

I pulled out my chair and sat while Bishop leaned against the wall behind me. "Mr. Wentworth, are you aware there was a murder recently? Someone you know, too," I said.

He looked down at the table. When he looked back up his eyes were cold and hard. "Yes, I'm aware. How could I not be? It was all over the news and on the first page of the AJC."

I had to admit, his composure was stellar. I didn't expect that after sitting alone for thirty minutes in the investigation room. "How did you know the victim, Mr. Wentworth?"

"You obviously know the answer to that, or I wouldn't be here. But if you think I killed him, you're wrong. Though had I felt confident I wouldn't be caught, I probably would've done it myself. I'm not upset the bastard's dead." He leaned back in his chair. "It's about time he paid for his crimes."

So much for regular-looking dad type. The man had a temper simmering under his dad clothes, the little belly, and the receding hairline. Something he'd kept from his earlier days.

"I had a friend who was sexually assaulted in high school by this rich kid from Highland Park." It wasn't true, but for the sake of our interrogation, I went with it. "Oh, Highland Park is a city in Illinois, just outside of Chicago, which is where I'm from. This friend didn't tell the police or even her friends. She was too embarrassed, felt like it was her fault. But she told her parents. Her mother wanted her to go to the police. And she should have. She had a solid case against the guy. People saw them together at a party. They saw the guy being aggressive toward her. But my friend said it wouldn't matter. They'd call it flirting, and she didn't want to be vilified in the community. The guy apparently came from a family with a lot of money and power, and she was a Chicago girl on a scholarship to a small Catholic high school in the city.

"Her father was enraged. His little girl had been attacked and no one was doing anything about it. He didn't want her dragged through the mud in court, so he took justice upon himself. Two days after the attack, the rich kid was found with a gunshot through the forehead at the Highland Park train station. Three days later, the father was arrested for first-degree murder. He's serving a life sentence in a maximum security prison." I shook my head. "Not only was my friend sexually assaulted, but her family and her life were torn apart because her father couldn't curb his temper." I tilted my head to the side. "I understand you have a temper, too, Mr. Wentworth." I handed him a copy of his arrest record.

He scanned the paper and tossed it back across the table. "These were bar fights from over twenty years ago. They mean nothing."

"They mean you've let your anger get the best of you before. I'm not sure of the circumstances surrounding those assaults, but I imagine they're nothing compared to your daughter being sexually assaulted. What's to say you didn't let that anger get the best of you this time?"

"First of all, she wasn't assaulted. He didn't get the chance because the bartenders threw him out. And I'm telling you I didn't let my anger get the best of me." His face reddened. He glanced up at Bishop. "Do I need an attorney?"

Bishop smiled. "We're just asking some questions. Calling an attorney would put us on offense, and we're pretty good at getting the goal."

He leaned back in the chair and sighed. "Listen, I can prove where I've been over the last forty-eight hours, and it wasn't killing Austin Chastain."

"Where have you been?" Bishop asked.

"Where's my phone? You took that and my wallet without my approval. Get me those, and I can show you proof."

"Mr. Wentworth, it's our policy to hold all phones of Hamby Police Department visitors."

"My phone has my calendar, and it can show you that I was in Knoxville on business the last two days."

"Anybody can use a calendar, Mr. Wentworth," Bishop said. "It doesn't mean they followed that schedule."

"Maybe so, but I did. I was in client meetings. After the meetings, we had dinner, and then we went to a bar. I was entertaining them, so I have receipts in my wallet, photos on my cell phone, and contact information for my clients. This was a business trip, and everything is documented." He leaned forward and smiled at me. "Like I said, I'm not upset the bastard is dead. After what he tried to do to my daughter, the guy who killed him deserves a medal. And I guarantee the fathers of the other victims would agree with me. Have you questioned them?"

He didn't have to be a genius to figure out the rest of the men would be upset. "We're handling our investigation," I said as I stood. "One moment, please."

I walked out of the room to retrieve the bag holding his cell phone and wallet and brought them to Mr. Wentworth. I tossed the bag on the table. "Show us."

Wentworth documented his trip accordingly and provided cell phone numbers for his business associates.

"These are my clients," he said. "If your contacting them damages my business or even my relationships with them in any way, I'll sue you for libel."

Bishop smiled and opened the door. "Thank you for your time."

"Mr. Wentworth," I said.

He turned around as he walked out of the interrogation room. "What?"

"Don't go on any more trips until you hear from us."

"I'm getting an attorney."

"You do that. Have a nice day," I said.

I waited outside of the interrogation room while Bishop saw Wentworth out.

When he returned, he said, "I take it back. He's not a regular dad. That guy I don't like."

"We have that in common."

"Did you see his suit?"

I nodded. "Looked like a suit to me."

Bishop rolled his eyes. "I know good suit material when I see it, and that thing wasn't cheap. The guy's got money. He could easily have paid somebody to do this."

I smiled. "You really don't like the guy, huh?"

"Maybe he wanted the men dead, but he doesn't like to get his hands dirty. You saw how quick he was to prove his whereabouts. Doesn't that raise the little hairs on the back of your neck?"

"Maybe a little."

The entire team gathered in the investigation room for a brainstorming session.

Michels filled us in on his conversation with Jameson Talbot's family. "His dad is a tool. All the money that guy has, he earned off screwing other people."

"That's not entirely true," Bishop said.

"I did some research. He's got five civil suits against him right now, and he's settled out of court for eleven others. Eleven. He wouldn't talk to me. Just told me to find the killer. His mother was a train wreck, and I'm pretty sure she's snorting coke. One minute she was crying, the next she swore people were coming for her. Her eyes were dilated, and her husband had to shove her back into the house. I think he was afraid I'd bring her in. He probably drugs her to keep her under his control."

"So," I said, "tell us how you really feel."

"Like I said, the guy's a tool. He doesn't give a damn about his son, that's for sure."

"What makes you say that?" Bishop asked.

"Just a feeling." He looked at me. "You're not the only one who's got a good gut."

"What about his alleged victim?" I asked.

"Abby was adamant she didn't want to answer any more questions. She said she's already told us what we needed to know, and she just wanted to move on. She wouldn't even unlatch the chain lock on her door."

"She doesn't want to have to deal with the emotions she's still not dealt with," I said. "Makes sense if you think about it. Did you confirm where she was on the nights of the murders?"

"That much I did, but only because I explained if she didn't have alibis for her time, I'd get a warrant and bring her in."

"Nice technique," I said. "Thanks for the update."

"Sure thing. Sorry I didn't have anything more."

"None of us do, and we need something," I said. "It's been too long to go without suspects. The wolves are circling, and if we don't catch this guy, we'll all be out of work. The case is too high profile to grow cold."

"Hell, we don't even have any real persons of interest," Bishop said. "I'd take that as a win right now."

Michels spoke first. "We might have a suspect if we could find the locations of the murders. This guy's got a leg up on us, and without that information, he'll stay on top."

"Regarding the crime scene locations, I've scoured through everything related to the case," Bubba said. "And the bad news is I can't find anything on social media or online that might lead us to them. I even looked at the social media accounts for every person in the background of our victim's social media photos." He sighed. "Do you know how long that took? Forty-five people. I looked at the social media history of forty-five people, and I found nothing."

Nikki slid us each a photograph. "I've been doing a little investigating myself and I found something interesting. I'm pretty sure it means nothing, but I thought it was worth showing, just in case y'all had a thought."

I glanced at the photo. "Jacob Ramsey's shoes?"

She nodded. "Each of the victims had the same brand of shoes. Even the victims in Birmingham."

"When did you discover this?" Bishop asked.

"I just finished the research about an hour ago. I didn't want to say anything until I had something to show, but I'll be honest, it's not much." She handed us each an additional five papers. "It's the same brand, though each victim was wearing a different color."

"How did we miss this?" Bishop asked.

"I can probably answer that," she said. "These aren't popular in your age group, but they're popular in mine. My brother has four pairs of these in different colors. I'm not saying this is a reason the killer picked these victims, because obviously that's a stretch, but maybe he worked at a shoe store where the victims shopped? Or maybe he bought them himself and replaced them for the shoes they had on?"

I glanced at Michels. "Can you get someone to call the parents of the victims?"

"Sure. Why?"

"Have them describe the clothes and find out if the parents recognize them. Wait, talk to the mothers. They'll know before the fathers."

"I'm on it," he said and left the room.

"Nikki, this is great work. Have you pulled the shoes from evidence and examined them again?"

She shook her head. "I reviewed the photos, but as I put in my original report, the fingerprints weren't retrievable. And honestly, they're shoes. Based on everything else at each scene, I knew we wouldn't find any clear prints, but I think I dropped the ball without realizing it. I contacted Dr. Barron for the victims' prints, something I should have asked for right away. I think I assumed any partial prints I'd find would match the victims', but that's not the case."

"Are you saying the victims didn't touch their shoes?" I asked.

"I'm saying it's highly unlikely, and I'm sure the prints were muddled or wiped to make them hard to see, but it's possible in theory, though I'm not sure it would be considered verifiable evidence in court."

"That's okay," I said. "This is good. This means we can hit up where the shoes are sold."

Nikki spoke again. "Like I said, these are popular shoes. They're available everywhere and online. There's no way to tell where they were purchased. The barcode is on the box, not the shoe."

The barcode could pull up where they were bought, but not who bought them.

Bishop swore under his breath. "Are you sure you can't pull even a partial?"

"Yes, sir. I'm sure."

"And you found nothing else?" he asked.

She shook her head. "No, I haven't, but I thought it was important to note just in case."

"Chew on that a little longer," I said. "If you think of something, let us know." I glanced at Bubba. "I know you've had a lot on your plate, and most of it's been from me. Can you provide an update on what you said a few minutes ago?"

"I did find something, but after further review, it doesn't fit."

"What?" Bishop asked.

Michels returned to the room. "Someone's on it."

"Have them ask about the shoes, too." I flicked my head toward Nikki. "Can you tell him the brand?"

She filled him in, and he sent a text to whomever he'd asked to make the calls.

"Sorry, Bubba. As I was saying, do you have any update?"

"As I said, I've reviewed everything for a connection or something to lead us to a suspect, but I've found nothing. The Mastermind group was a complete bust, and I'm sorry for that. I went back and searched through the fraternity information and tried to piece together some kind of common history there." He laughed. "Those dudes party their asses off, but that's about the only thing the frats have in common. I even went back and ran the sexual assault victims' family members through NCIC. I figured since we'd done it for a few already, I should do them all. Everyone was clear except for Bryant's mother. She has a prostitution arrest and a fraudulent check charge."

"How long ago was the prostitution charge?"

"Three years ago, but the charges were dropped."

I nodded. "Her brother said she claimed to not have the money to hire a housekeeper, so maybe they're having financial problems?"

"Not a motive for murder," Bishop said.

"Agreed, but the woman's been MIA since this started. I think we need to find her."

"There's more," Bubba said. "She just got out of alcohol rehab two weeks ago, and she lost her job right before she went in. I contacted the rehab facility, but they claimed talking was a HIPAA violation. I called back and talked to the receptionist. You know, tried to charm information out of her."

"That never works for me," Michels said.

"Didn't work for me either. But..." He smiled. "The night-shift receptionist was very chatty. She told me the program is six weeks, and if the patients progress, they can choose to stay longer and do one of their entering-back-into-normal-life half-day programs."

"Did you find out how long Bryant lasted?"

His smile stretched across his face. "Not directly. She told me she'd left three weeks ago, so this morning I contacted her employer, who said she hasn't been employed with the company in four weeks. A little math and assumption on my part says she didn't make it the full six weeks."

"Chip Stuart says he hasn't seen her in a while. Maybe she's out on a bender?" I asked.

"Or maybe she's dead," Michels said.

"Thanks for that, Mr. Positive," I said. I smiled at Bubba. "You did fantastic, and I appreciate the effort. I just don't think an alcoholic woman would seek justice for her daughter or anyone else. Alcoholics focus primarily on the alcohol. It's a coping mechanism to deal with the stuff they handle emotionally. Our killer is too detailed and strategic to be an alcoholic."

"I'm with Michels. If we find the original crime scenes, we'll be able to find our killer," Bubba said.

"But that'll take a miracle," Michels said. "As for my victim's assault victim, there's nothing new to report on her. Her story stayed the same."

I tapped a pencil on the table, then looked at the whiteboards and studied them carefully. "Since Baker is out of the picture, we have one possible person of interest. He tries to come off as weak and dumber than a rock, but I'm thinking that might be an act." I turned to Bishop. "Chip Stuart."

Bishop shook his head. "I don't see it. He might be weird, but he's not type A, and I don't think he's acting when it comes to his intelligence level."

"Is that common?" Nikki asked.

"No," Bishop said.

"But," I said, "serial killers have been known to fake psychosis and rehabilitation. Look at Edmund Kemper. He convinced psychiatrists he was rehabilitated, and they released him from prison. His mother even testified he wasn't a danger to anyone, and he ended up murdering her too."

"That sucks for the mom," Michels said.

"No doubt," Nikki said.

"Is that the co-ed killer dude? I read about him," Bubba said.

"You read about him? How many hours do you have in a day?" Bishop asked.

"I'm not big on sleep."

"Yes," I said. "It's the co-ed killer."

"But he wasn't pretending to be stupid," Michels said.

"But he was pretending something, and that's not uncommon for serial killers. Listen, we have nothing. All I'm saying is Stuart's a viable person of interest, I didn't say suspect, and I think we need to move on him. If for no other reason than to eliminate him as an option."

"You want to interview him again?" Bishop asked.

"Not yet." I picked my phone up off the table and called Emily Bryant. That time, she answered.

20

Emily Bryant arrived at the department an hour later.

"I'll help," Bishop said.

"No, I'll handle it. I think she'll have more to say without a man present."

"Got it."

She stood in the reception area with her arms crossed over her chest and a scowl on her face. "I really don't have time for this. I've been off work for a few days, and I need to get caught up."

"We won't be long. Thank you for stopping by. Let's go to the conference room." I smiled as we walked down the hall. "How's your mother doing?"

She didn't answer.

Emily refused to sit in the chair I offered. "Why are you bothering me? Can't you just let me live my life?"

I kept my tone casual, hoping that would help her lighten up. "Have a seat, please."

She took the seat that time, and I spoke again. "I'm not doing anything to stop you from living your life, but I am trying to find a serial killer. You do know how important that is to the safety of Hamby, right?" A little guilt went a long way. She refused to look at me, instead choosing to stare at the wall. "And because you were attacked by one of the victims, you might know something that you don't realize you know. I also have some questions about someone in your life." She finally made eye contact, but the anger in her eyes was still there. "Would you be willing to answer some questions?"

"I already told you I don't know anything, and why are you asking about my mother? You can't think she's a serial killer. She can barely function on a regular day."

"There's a saying in my line of work, and it's always relative, but especially so in investigations like this. *Everyone is a suspect until they're not.* Unfortunately, that includes everyone who's been negatively impacted by the victim."

"I'm the victim," Emily said. She jabbed her thumb into her chest several times. "Me! And you're treating me, and now my mother, like suspects."

"I'll be honest, I don't think you killed these men, and I don't think your mother did either. But I have questions, and I need answers. It's the only way to close this investigation and catch our killer. Do you understand that?"

She nodded.

"Good. So, how about we get to these questions?"

She narrowed her eyes at me. "Fine."

"I understand your mother was recently released from rehab. Have you seen her?"

"My mother is taking some time away. She needs to do that, and I understand."

"Do you know where she is?"

"Not specifically, just somewhere in north Georgia. I think she's staying with a friend."

"Emily, I need to get in touch with your mother. Can you help me do that?"

"She's fragile right now. She can't be worrying about this. She's got to take care of herself."

"I understand, and I'll be sensitive to her situation. I just have some questions for her."

"But you said you don't think she did it?"

"That doesn't mean I don't have to speak with her. It's the only way to remove her from the list."

"Fine."

I slid a piece of paper over to her and she wrote down a phone number.

"That's her cell. She'll answer even if she doesn't know the number."

"Thank you. How long has your uncle lived with you?"

She shrugged. "A long time. Since my parents' divorce, so maybe fifteen years?"

"Does he work?"

"He's on disability. He was in a car accident seven years ago. He's got a TBI."

"Traumatic brain injuries are tough. Has it impacted his personal life too?"

"Not really, and he can work, but he qualifies for disability, so he chooses not to. He went through rehab at that place in Atlanta."

"The Shepherd Center?"

"Yeah, that's it. When they released him, they said he was able to go back to work."

"But he's still getting disability payments?"

She nodded. "I don't know how that stuff works."

"What does he do all day?"

"Is he a suspect?"

Something in her expression changed. She was less angry and more interested. She even relaxed her shoulders and leaned toward me. "Like I said, I'm just asking questions."

"I don't know. My uncle is strange, and it's not because of the accident. He's always been weird. I think my mom felt sorry for him, and that's why she let him move in with us, but neither of us really want him there. He makes things uncomfortable."

"How so?"

"He's just awkward. He's always asking questions about my life, what I'm doing, who I'm going out with. He's not my father." She shuddered. "Thank God."

"Has he met any of your friends?"

"He did when I was in high school, but he creeped them out, so I stopped bringing them around."

"What about Jacob? Did he meet him?"

She nodded. "It was the holiday break. We were going out, so he came to get me, but I was running late. My uncle started talking to him about some true crime show he was watching. Jake said it made him really uncomfortable, but I think he would have been anyway because he knows I don't like my uncle."

"Has he made you uncomfortable lately?"

"I haven't been around much. I do know he goes out a lot, but I don't know what he does. When he's home, he just sits on the couch and watches TV. He likes all the weird crime shows like *Criminal Minds*. My uncle is weird. He always has been, but since the accident, it's worse. Still, I don't think he's capable of killing anyone."

"Your uncle goes out often?"

"Like, all the time lately. I mean, he's been basically trapped in the house for years now, so it makes sense. I'd be nuts too if I sat around all the time."

"But he's never mentioned where he's going?"

She shook her head. "I don't usually ask, but I did once, and he said he joined a church group."

"Did he say what church?"

"No, and I didn't ask."

"Thank you." I stood. "I know this has been frustrating, but I appreciate you coming in." I headed toward the door and opened it. "I'll see you out."

"Wait," she said. She sprung from her seat. "I just remembered. I think my uncle was out the night Jake was murdered."

"Chip Stuart wasn't home the night we found Ramsey."

Bishop pressed his lips together and nodded. "Interesting."

"That's good for us," Michels said.

"Also, she confirmed he suffered a TBI seven years ago. He's on disability now, so he's got a lot of free time, and Emily said he's always been weird, but since the accident, he's worse. Oh, and he claims to have joined a church group."

"A church group?" Bishop asked.

"That was his answer the one time she asked where he was going."

"Did she say what church?"

"She didn't ask, and he didn't tell."

"That could mean something, but with respect to the weird factor, most people aren't the same after a traumatic brain injury. I'm not saying they're weird, they're just not the same, and that's to be expected."

"True, but the ones that are lucky to be able to return to their mostly normal lives usually have few symptoms. According to Emily, Chip Stuart didn't return to his normal life even though the Shepherd Center cleared him to."

"Weird isn't a symptom," Michels said. "Recovery is relative to the injury and the person."

"Yes, which is exactly why I think we need someone on the guy." I smiled at Michels. "You up for a little surveillance duty?"

He pressed his lips together. "Seriously? Can't we get one of the slick sleeves to do it?"

I smiled. "Our patrol is busy with the extra calls coming in because we have a serial killer on the loose. Besides, we need somebody good on Chip Stuart, and that's you."

"I always get the shit jobs." Michels said. "But at least you said I'm good."

"You are." I laughed and then I grabbed a twenty from my wallet, smiling as I touched the soft, worn leather. Tommy got me a men's wallet years ago because I'd hated my bulky women's one and complained about it. Sometimes, I'd switch to his old wallet, but mostly I stuck with the one he got me. I handed Michels the twenty. "Dinner's on me."

He snatched the bill from my hands. "Yes, it is."

"You know the drill," I said. "Where he goes, what time he goes, and anything and everything in between."

"I'm on it."

Bishop laughed after Michels left. "Sucks to be the new guy, doesn't it?"

"Hey, at least he's not stuck busting defiant teenagers breaking into sports park concession stands."

Bishop smiled and laughed at the mention of one of our first investigations together. "I'd take those defiant kids and their candy-stealing over a serial killer any day."

"Ditto."

His cell phone dinged. He glanced at the message and smiled, then tapped out a response. The smile didn't leave his face until he was finished. He stuffed the phone back into his pocket. He caught the big grin on my face. "What?"

"Rob has a girlfriend," I whispered.

He blushed. "I don't have time for a relationship right now."

"You make time for the things that matter."

"How's that working for you and Kyle?"

"Actually, we kind of have a rhythm now. We don't see each other every day, but honestly, I think that would suffocate us."

"I think you're wrong. If he could, he'd spend every day with you."

I pursed my lips and then said, "What makes you say that?"

"I see how he looks at you, Ryder. The guy's in love."

My stomach flipped. "He is not." My cell phone dinged with Savannah's text sound. "Oh, look at this, an important text. Sorry, we'll chat later!" I rushed off as I read the message.

I'm in your cubby with a very big and very demanding baby. Come say hi.

I jogged to my cubby and smiled when I saw the cutest little chunky monkey in the world. Savannah had her dressed in a red-and-white tulle-and-lace dress that looked like a better version of my prom dress, but obviously a different color, a white sweater, and a little white hat. She looked adorable. "Oh my gosh!" I stuck my arms out. "Let me hold that baby."

Savannah willingly gave her to me with a slight groan as she lifted her at head level. "Have you ever done Santa pictures with a baby?"

I booped Scarlet's nose and gave her a kiss on the forehead. "Is that a serious question?"

"I'm sure you've passed by them in the mall."

I giggled. "Now, that I have, and it's part of the reason I'm childless."

"I kid you not, every child there, except my sweet Scarlet, of course, was pitching a fit the size of Texas. Those poor elves were as useless as gum on a heel trying to calm them. I tipped the poor girls fifty bucks, that's how sorry I felt for them."

"But Scarlet didn't cry?"

"Not at all. Believe me, I was as surprised as the elves, and I think that pitiful Santa was run ragged. He was just so sweet to Scarlet, though. She tugged on his beard, and he pretended to cry, so she placed her little hand on his face and smiled."

"Wow, she's already manipulating the men and she's not even a year old."

"She's a true Southern belle, my girl."

I handed her belle back. "I'm going to want one of those photos."

"Of course. The town's a hot mess, and I feel so bad for him. When are you going to catch this guy?"

"Soon."

"Soon? So, you don't have any suspects, do you? Goodness, this city is going to implode if he's not caught."

"What makes you think we don't have any suspects?"

"For starters, I live with the chief, and I have very skilled ways of making him talk, but also, I can tell by your appearance. When was the last time you washed your hair?"

"I'm pleading the Fifth." I honestly couldn't remember, but I knew it wasn't too far into the past.

"You haven't slept much either. Those dark circles under your eyes are getting bigger."

I rolled my eyes. "Did you come here to pick on my personal appearance, because if so, it'll get you nowhere." My tone wasn't serious, and she could tell.

"I love you anyway."

Scarlet cooed, so we cooed back. Babies reduced adults to high-pitched-babbling softies, but the time with Scarlet was worth it. When she yawned, Savannah said, "That's my sign. Time to drive this little one around so she'll sleep."

"Sounds like a plan." I kissed Scarlet's forehead again. "Be good to Mama, little one."

I watched them walk through the pit, Savannah stopping to let officers baby talk to Scarlet. While I did, I felt something inside me twitch, and I wondered if one day, I'd be in her shoes, or if it was too late.

Bishop leaned against the partial wall of my cubby. "There's something we failed to consider."

"I'm sure we've failed to consider a lot of things. This is probably the hardest case I've ever had, and I suspect that's true for you too."

"Yup." He sat in the chair in front of my desk. "We need to address the fact that our killer may have already moved on. He's committed three murders, just like in Birmingham. If his pattern hasn't changed, then we're going to end up with three cold cases just like Johnson."

"I've been thinking that too, but remember, things are different here. That connection he feels may make him stick around longer."

"And commit another murder?"

I shrugged. "I hope not, but he considers us worthy of his actions, so..."

"If this guy is as smart as Calloway says, then like we said before, he could be switching things up to mess with us. And that could mean he's already the hell out of Dodge. The Alabama murders happened three years ago. We have no idea where the next three murders were committed or if they even happened. For all we know, the guy went cold for three years."

"I think we're right about the numbers meaning nothing."

"What else could it be? We can't find anything even like our murders in the system, and we haven't had one single law enforcement inquiry since the media went national. If there had been murders with even the slightest similarity, a department would have contacted us."

I rubbed my neck and felt the heat rising from my gut. I wasn't prone to anxiety, but occasionally it crept in, especially when I was stuck with an investigation. "I don't know what to do."

"Neither do I."

21

When a detective can't move forward with an investigation, the natural thing to do was to go back to square one and go back twenty times if that was what it took to catch a break. I'd lost count on how many times I'd personally started over, but we'd spent twelve more hours doing it again.

We kept our heads down into our notes, redid the whiteboards with more details, and consumed three Domino's pizzas. Michels came in about halfway through, having set up the detail with two slick sleeves looking for overtime duty. I fully expected that. One officer couldn't do a twenty-four-hour detail like that for several reasons, but mostly because sitting in a vehicle for that long was impossible. Sitting in a vehicle for six hours like Michels had was nearly impossible. I knew guys who wound up with a serious case of hemorrhoids from that.

"Stuart is boring as hell," he said. He glanced at the whiteboards. "You've been busy. Come up with anything?"

"Not really," Bishop said. "But we're not giving up."

"Did he leave at all?" I asked.

"Nope."

He sighed. "It's possible. He came out to get the mail. I was two houses down on the other side of the street watching through my mirrors. He saw my vehicle, but he went back inside. I stayed put, and sure enough, about five minutes later, he was back out messing around in his yard. That's when I brought in another guy."

"We need to bring him in," I said.

"On what?" Bishop asked. "Suspicion of busting a cop on detail?"

"Can't pull a guy in for walking around his yard," Michels said.

"Obviously not," I said. "But I screwed up. We should have gone back to Stuart when Emily Bryant told me he wasn't home when she got home the night of Ramsey's murder."

"It was the right decision," Bishop said.

Michels agreed. "If he's the guy, bringing him in would just alert him to our suspicion."

"And surveillance wouldn't?"

"It's less threatening, and he doesn't know if it's a guarantee we're watching him. We could be waiting for Emily. As far as he knows, we haven't had any other contact with her."

"That's a good point," Bishop said. "Either way, if he's the guy, we'll know soon enough. Every time we've pushed the killer, he's reacted. If he feels threatened now, he'll react again."

"If he's the killer," Michels said.

"When you originally questioned him, he said he was home, right?" Bishop asked me.

"Yes."

"Do you think it's possible she's the one lying?"

I blinked. "Do you think she's trying to frame her uncle for Ramsey's murder?"

"I'm just playing devil's advocate. It wouldn't be the first time a woman committed murder and framed someone else."

I pushed my chair back from the table so hard it dropped to the ground. It was an accident, but the unintended effect didn't go unnoticed. "If she could defend herself and was capable of murder, she would have sliced his neck and chopped off his dick that night. And the dates don't match up. The Alabama victims happened before her attack. She's not our killer, Bishop."

"Then how is her uncle? If he's seeking justice for his niece, what about the Birmingham murders? Like you said, the dates don't match up."

Damn it. "Then maybe we're back to the copycat theory. It's the only thing that makes sense, and it would explain the notes and the leveling-up with mutilation."

"You think Stuart is smart enough to send those notes?" Bishop asked.

Michels leaned back in his chair and stuffed a bite of cold pizza into his mouth. Bishop and I stared at him. "Don't look at me; I'm just here for the fight."

"We're not fighting," Bishop said.

"We're discussing," I added.

"Em-hmm."

"I think I was right before. A smart person can appear dumb if it fits his needs."

"But Stuart isn't anything like Calloway's profile, and she's good. She knows her stuff."

"That doesn't mean she's right," I said. "We're bringing him in." I looked at Bishop. "I could be wrong, but my gut is telling me we need to move on him."

Michels grabbed another piece of pizza. "I'm going with Ryder on this. I trust her gut more than I trust my mother."

"Then bring him in," Bishop said. It was clear by his tense neck, he'd said it under duress.

Chip Stuart came to the police station willingly—a little too willingly for my liking. We set him up in an interrogation room and let him marinate in his aloneness for an hour while we gathered every bit of information we could to throw at him. The information was slim from a suspect standpoint, but we weren't opposed to throwing out some misinformation and seeing if it stuck.

Bishop was bad cop and I was good cop. Most of the time I was the bad cop because I enjoyed it, and Bishop said if I got my bitchiness out with a suspect, I'd be less of one to him. I didn't take the joke personally. He was right, I could be a serious bitch, but not usually to him. Sometimes.

We'd let Stuart stew in his fear without even a glass of water. Depriving someone of something to do with their hands when they were nervous was a common interrogation technique with a high success rate of putting a suspect on edge.

I took a seat across from Stuart, smiled, then glanced at the empty table and shook my head. "You don't have any water?" I turned to Bishop, who stayed standing on my left side. "Why didn't anybody get this guy something to drink?"

Bishop rolled his eyes. "You think this loser deserves anything?"

I let out an exaggerated sigh. "He came in for this interview willingly, Detective. The least we could do is give him something to drink." I glanced back at Stuart. "Mr. Stuart, would you like a glass of water or a cup of coffee? I'll be honest, the coffee here isn't the best, but it's better than nothing."

"I'm fine," he said. His eyes were bigger than when I talked to him last. He stared up at Bishop. "I'm not a killer. Is that why you asked me here? Because you think I killed someone?"

"Yes," Bishop said.

"No. We just want to ask you a few questions about the night Jacob Ramsey was killed. I think we have a miscommunication issue." I spoke through gritted teeth with a hint of impatience and anger in my tone. "Right, Detective?"

"I didn't kill anyone! I suffered a traumatic brain injury a few years ago. I can't work. I can't do much of anything, and I definitely can't kill someone."

"I understand," I said. "We spoke with your niece, and she explained you have a TBI."

"Doesn't stop him from being a killer," Bishop said.

"The news is saying a serial killer is responsible." He looked up at Bishop again. "You think I'm a serial killer?"

"I follow the evidence," Bishop said.

Don't go too far, partner.

Stuart twisted his hands into a ball. "Evidence? What kind of evidence could you have on me? I barely even leave the house."

Bishop walked around to Stuart's side of the table, leaned toward his left ear, and whispered, "We have enough evidence for the death penalty."

Too far. Bishop wasn't accustomed to playing bad cop and hadn't paced his anger well. I needed to calm both men down. "Mr. Stewart, may I call you Chip?"

Chip nodded once.

"You're not under arrest. We simply brought you here because we have some questions. We've come across some information that contradicts something you told me."

"Among other things," Bishop said under his breath.

I smiled at Stuart again. "You'll have to forgive my partner. It's been a long few twenty-four-hour days and it's tough on someone his age."

"I want an attorney."

"You're not under arrest," I said. "We're just trying to clear up some discrepancies."

"I still want an attorney."

"You don't have the right to an attorney, asshole," Bishop said.

Nice play. To the point and intimidating. He was back on bad-cop track.

"He's right," I said. "I know you said you watch a lot of crime dramas. Unfortunately, those shows are fiction. They're not a true representation of how our justice system works. We're just having a conversation. If you insist on an attorney and refuse to speak to us, we're going to have to assume you're doing so because you're guilty. Do you understand?"

He nodded. "But you can hold me here for, what, seventy-two hours?"

"No. We can only hold you for forty-eight hours with a warrant for your arrest, and as I've said, you're not under arrest."

He took a deep breath and exhaled loudly. "Okay, fine. Get on with your questions, then." He rubbed his head. "I get a headache when I'm stressed. It's from the TBI."

He hadn't mentioned the TBI in our previous conversation. I found it interesting he'd brought it up when he felt threatened. That convinced me of his guilt even more. "When we spoke before, you said you were at home watching TV the night Jacob Ramsey was killed, but we've recently learned you weren't home. Now, I'm sure it's just a matter of mixed dates, probably something that happens a lot with you because of your TBI, but we need confirmation."

"Stop being soft on the guy, Ryder," Bishop said. He leaned down and put his hands on the table. "We know you weren't home the night Ramsey was murdered. Where were you?"

I watched Stuart closely. His face paled, and his pupils dilated. Dilated pupils were a key indicator of lying. Lying caused the brain to work harder, and that impacted the body in physical ways.

"I told you, I was home."

"What did you watch on TV that night?"

"What I always do. *Major Crimes* and *Criminal Minds*."

"Just those two shows?"

"A few episodes of each."

"What time did you go to bed?"

"I guess around midnight."

"Why don't you tell me about the episodes?"

"All of them?"

I nodded.

Stuart gave a brief description of a few of each series then stopped. "You know, I've watched so many of them. I can't remember what was on when."

"Don't worry," Bishop said. "We'll check."

"Mr. Stuart, do you own a vehicle?"

He shook his head. "I'm cleared to drive, but I'm not comfortable getting behind the wheel. I have episodes."

"What do you mean by 'episodes'?" I asked.

"Sometimes I zone out and time passes, but I wasn't really there when it passed."

"How much time passes during these zone-outs?" I asked.

"It depends. Sometimes a few minutes. Sometimes an hour or two."

He was setting himself up for a defense if necessary. The guy wasn't as dumb as he seemed.

"That must be troubling," I said. "What about your sister? Does she own a car?" Thanks to Bubba, I already knew the answer, but I wanted to see if Stuart would continue to lie.

"Yeah, it's a beater, though."

"Chip, have you ever been to Birmingham?"

"Alabama?" He shook his head. "Not that I know of. Maybe as a kid, but I don't really know."

I asked him where he was on the nights of the three murders there.

"Those were three years ago? I mean, I was probably home on the couch doing what I always do, watching TV. If you think I drove to Alabama and killed those boys, how would I get there?"

"Bus," Bishop said.

"Nope."

Bishop had moved to the corner of the room and stood with his arms crossed over his chest. I looked over to him and asked, "Anything else?"

"I have several questions," Bishop said.

"Okay, then," I said. I turned back to Stuart. "My partner has a few questions, and then we can get you on your way, okay?"

"Fine."

Bishop walked over to the table and stood next to me. "Where were you the night Jameson Talbot and Austin Chastain were murdered?"

"Home watching TV like I am every night. I'm telling you, I don't go out. I don't like being around people with my condition." He didn't bother saying what shows. He was annoyed, which was what we wanted. "I think I'm done answering questions."

Since we had no legal right to hold him, we had to let him go. But I was more convinced than ever he was our guy. He lied. He played dumb, and he acted like his TBI was debilitating, though he'd not once mentioned it before I had. He tried to take advantage of the opportunity.

Bishop and I met in Jimmy's office about fifteen minutes later.

"He's not our guy," Bishop said.

"What?" I'd just finished a phone call with Bubba asking him to check the show schedule for the night of Ramsey's murder. "He lied about being home that night."

"I'm sorry, I just don't see it. The guy might be a little off, but that's probably the TBI. I don't think he's smart enough to pull off three, maybe even six murders, and I don't know why he would. He reads lazy SOB taking the government system for granted, but he doesn't read 'serial killer.'"

"You're wrong."

"Doesn't matter if he's wrong," Jimmy said. "What matters is you don't have any evidence to support your theory. Listen, I trust your gut, but a gut feeling doesn't bring this guy to court. We need evidence. Get me that, and we'll arrest him."

I stormed out of Jimmy's office angry because the chief was right, but frustrated because I was too. My gut had been wrong a few times, yes, but it wasn't wrong about Stuart. I knew he was our guy. I just needed to prove it.

22

The tension between my partner and me was thick, so we avoided each other for several hours. I reread Calloway's profile on the killer and searched my notes for anything that remotely matched Stuart.

I highlighted four very specific sentences of her twenty-page document and went straight to Jimmy's office. "Look, even Calloway's report connects Stuart's personality to the case." I handed him the document. "I've highlighted four key sentences in yellow."

Jimmy flipped through the pages. "Fascination with crime?"

"Stuart is a crime-show buff, and he asked me a lot of questions about my gun. Plus, he claims to have a Glock, though if he does, it's not registered."

"My mother is a crime-show buff, and she's always asking me questions about my work. And she owns a Ruger. Is she a serial killer too?"

He deflated my excitement, though I'd known my argument was weak to start. "He manipulates. Calloway said that would be a key personality trait. He pulled out his TBI card when he felt threatened. Played stupid up, but when he came in tonight, there were signs it's an act."

"My wife can manipulate the hell out of me, and sometimes, especially when she was pregnant, she has mood swings. That doesn't make her a serial killer either." He handed the report back to me. "Listen, I know how you get when you can't solve a case, and I know you want this guy. You'll get him. It's a tough case. We're all under a lot of pressure, and I know you and Bishop have been here too much. Go home. Get some rest. Nothing's going to change before tomorrow. I need you focused and prepared to move forward, without any problems with your partner." He raised his eyebrows. "Am I clear?"

"I don't want to go home. I'm close, Jimmy. I can feel it."

"Then you'll still be close tomorrow." He got on his phone and rang Bishop's extension.

"Yes, Chief?" He said on speaker.

"I'm here with your partner. The entire department can feel the tension between you two."

"Understood," Bishop said. "I'll change that."

"Ditto," I said.

"Good," Jimmy said. "Listen, Bishop, I'm kicking you both out for twelve hours. Either of you come back before then, and you're off the case. Am I clear?"

"Twelve—"

He interrupted me. "Am I clear?"

"Clear," Bishop said.

"Fine," I said and walked out.

I made a quick private call to a judge I'd become friends with over the past few years. He was from Lincoln Park in Chicago and an avid Cubs fan. It didn't take much for us to bond. Also, he was Polish, like Lenny, and I knew how to talk the talk when it came to Polish men.

"Judge Nowak, Rachel Ryder. I know it's late, and I apologize for calling, but I need help. I need a court order to get access to some financial records."

"Is this for the serial killer investigation?"

"Yes, sir."

"You have a suspect?"

"I have a solid person of interest, and a strong gut, but I need some financial information to see if I'm right."

"Does the chief know you're asking for a court order?"

"No, sir."

"Dammit, Ryder, you do this to me every time."

"I've got a lead on a signed Walter Payton jersey."

"Bribery is illegal, you know."

"It's just information on a jersey I know you'd like."

He sighed. "I hate when you do this to me. I'll get it, but I'm going to notify the chief. You prepared for the backlash?"

"I relish in backlash."

"I'll have it to you within the hour."

"Thank you, oh, and go, Bears."

"They came and went. They suck this season."

"They suck most seasons," I said.

"Gone are the days of Payton and Jimmy McMahon."

"I'm with you on that."

Before leaving, I tapped out a text to Bubba. *Can you run Chip Stuart's DMV records for me? I need to know what kind of vehicle he had and when he sold it. Also, please run Emily Bryant's mother if you didn't when you got her arrests. Find out her vehicle info. And if you can, find any credit cards for them and let me know if anything like gas was purchased in Alabama or on the way there during those murders. I know it's late. I don't need it until the morning.* I hit send.

Do you have a court order? I can only get so much from the banks and credit card companies, and I think I've worn out my welcome.

Court order will be here within an hour. I'll send it to you when I get it.

My pleasure, he texted back.

Bishop met me outside our cubbies and apologized. "I know how important this case is to you."

"You don't have anything to apologize for. Well, other than being a first class a-hole, but I'm used to that."

He smiled. "That's something I'll never apologize for."

"I figured."

I arrived home to Kyle snoozing on my couch. His slight snore made me chuckle.

"Hey," he said when my kiss to his forehead woke him. "What time is it?"

"I'm afraid to check. I thought you were coming to the station?"

"I was, but I got pulled into a meeting. I texted you."

"You did?" I removed my phone from my pocket. "Oh, you did. Sorry, long day."

He sat up, and I fell onto the couch beside him. "I'm exhausted."

"I bet. How 'bout I get the shower started for you? And I can make you something to eat, if you'd like?"

"I still don't have food."

He smiled. "Yes, you do. I went shopping."

"You're amazing."

"So, I've heard."

My eyes widened and darted to his. "From whom?"

"You, for starters, but my mother's said it since I was a baby."

I laughed. "I can start my shower. Did you buy any sliced ham?"

"A half pound, and all the other things you like on a sandwich, including that bread from Atlanta Bread you love so much."

"Oh my God, that bread!"

"Get in the shower, and I'll get it ready."

I stood and dragged myself into my bedroom. The thought of the bright bathroom light over the shower glaring down on me sounded awful, so I switched it off and left the bedroom light on instead.

Five minutes later, as I closed my eyes and let the water stream down my face, Kyle opened the shower door and stepped inside.

I sent the court order to Bubba before falling asleep the night before and asked him to keep it on the down-low until I could discuss it with the team. Then I texted Savannah early the next morning. *Hey, is Jimmy still home?*

Yes, she texted back.

Can you make him stick around? I'd like to come by and see the baby, and I want to talk to him.

Sure. I'll make him change the hellion. It takes him an hour. Not a joke either.

I laughed. Jimmy couldn't get the diaper thing down no matter how hard he tried. Savannah said his first effort cost them a box of diapers, and the baby hadn't moved while he made his several attempts. The man was the chief of police. He could shoot someone without even a blink, but he couldn't change his kid's diaper without stressing out. Savannah said it was because God had a sense of humor. I thought it was funny even though I didn't believe in God. I couldn't imagine a superior being allowing the world to suffer as it had. I knew what the Bible said. My Catholic education taught me all the details, and I could easily recite them to prove it, but I no longer believed them. Cops tend to go one way or the other. Either their faith strengthens or they lose it.

I lost mine when Tommy died.

I watched Kyle slip into a pair of freshly pressed tan pants. They fit like a koozie fit a beer can: snug and perfect. I shook my head to stop staring. "What's your plan for the day?"

"You don't know?" He pulled a crisp white undershirt over his broad shoulders.

"Apparently not." I finished wrapping my hair into a ponytail band. Normally, I'd wear it in a bun at the lowest point of my head, but it felt like a good day to switch it up.

"Jimmy officially asked me to consult on the case, and since I've got a few days off, I figured I'd do it."

I slipped a knife into the side of my Doc Martens. My gun wouldn't fit into the side, so I improvised. The gun went in the back of my jeans instead. It wasn't my department-issued weapon. It was one of my several personally owned ones, and my favorite. My Sig Sauer. "Then it's not a few days off."

"It's a few days off from my kind of work."

"True. Would you like to stop by Jimmy's before heading to the department? I'm going to see the baby."

"Didn't you say you saw her yesterday?"

"I'm addicted. What can I say?"

He smiled and checked his watch. "Isn't Jimmy at the office?"

"Savannah asked him to change Scarlet's diaper."

He laughed. "Then we have time to make breakfast, eat, get the car washed, and head over."

"There's a lot of truth to that, but I'd still like a little time with my goddaughter."

His smile stretched across his face. "I could use a dose of baby myself."

Thirty minutes later, coffee and bagels in hand, we arrived at Jimmy and Savannah's.

Jimmy was all smiles. "I did it, and it only took forty-five minutes!" He held up Scarlet, and the diaper slipped halfway down her chunky thighs. "Son of a baseball!"

Savannah laughed. "Bless your sweet heart." She took the baby from her husband and went to fix the diaper.

Kyle whispered in my ear. "Son of a baseball?"

"He's trying not to swear because of the baby."

"Then he needs a new career."

"I know, right?" I smiled at Jimmy. "She'll be in them a few years. You'll get it."

"Maybe," Kyle said.

"I get it now," Jimmy said. "Sav had me change the baby to stall me from leaving. And you're not supposed to be working right now."

"I'm not," I said. "I'm here to see Scarlet."

"Right. This is about your call to Nowak and the court order he got you, isn't it?"

Nowak followed through with his promise to call Jimmy. I'd expected it but wished he hadn't. "Yes and no." I exhaled. "Bubba's checking Chip Stuart's financial records."

"Like I said, get some evidence, and we'll move forward."

"That's what I'm trying to do. I have a plan, just let me see it through."

Jimmy sat on the couch. "Spill it."

"If we go on what he's done in Alabama, and the murders here, we have a pattern, right?"

He nodded.

Savannah walked in with Scarlet. "Oh, y'all are talking work."

As she turned to leave, Kyle held out his arms. "May I hold her?"

"In the kitchen. I don't want her exposed to the job."

"I agree," Kyle said. He carried the baby into the kitchen.

I watched him as he walked. He was at complete ease with Scarlet. He'd make a great father, but men wait longer, liked to be older before having kids. Women were on a clock they couldn't control. "Anyway," I continued. "The pattern changed after I spoke to the media."

"Where are you going with this?"

"I think I can get him to switch up his pattern again."

He shook his head. "No. You're not talking to the media again. You saw how the mayor flipped his sh—stuff. I let you do that again; we'll both get pink slips."

"We can get his approval first. If we tell the mayor why we're doing it, then we have a good chance of catching Chip in the act."

"How is that?"

"We keep eyes on him."

He rubbed his chin. "Rach, we have nothing connecting this guy to any of the murders, especially the ones in Alabama. I sent Johnson Stuart's photo and asked him to show it to the victims' families as well as the victims' victims, and none of them have ever seen Stuart. I just don't think he's our guy."

"If you'll let me—"

He cut me off. "What do you want to say to the media?"

"I don't know yet, but it'll be something that makes him angry. Trust me, it'll work."

"We don't even know if the killer's still in town. He killed his three victims. He could be long gone by now, and he could go cold for God knows how long."

"He's taunted me with the notes. He'll do something else. Whether he's here or not, he'll see the interview. Please, just give me this. If it doesn't draw him out, then I'll stop pushing Stuart. I promise."

He sighed. "You really think this is the guy? Have you even checked on where he was the nights of the Alabama murders?"

I'd received the information from Bubba after pulling out of Dunkin' that morning. Stuart had made three random cash deposits of one thousand dollars each over a four-week span three months prior to the killings in Hamby. "He claims he was home watching TV, but it was three years ago, and we can't verify that."

"Did you have Bubba check his bank and credit card records?"

"Yes. There's nothing on a vehicle or his sister's vehicle either."

"Then he's not our guy."

"The deposits are worth looking into, and he could have borrowed or even stolen a vehicle."

"Fine. Look into the deposits and find me a vehicle, and we'll get you with the media."

"I can do that."

Savannah walked out of the kitchen. "Are y'all finished with the work talk? Baby Scarlet wants to see her auntie Rachel." She walked over with the baby in hand and gave her to me.

I took her more cautiously than I did my weapon. "Hey, sweet girl." I snuggled her close to my body. "I'm always afraid I'm going to drop her."

"Don't toss her in the air, and I think you'll be fine. Just relax."

Scarlet cooed and smiled and then a loud sound released from her diaper and vibrated into my hand. "Oh," I said smiling. A second later the smell hit. "Oh, wow!" I stretched out my arms and handed the baby back to her mother. "She's all yours."

Savannah laughed. As she held the baby, she said, "She gets the stankiness from her daddy. Mama is too sweet to produce that kind of foul odor." She smiled. "Be right back."

"Actually, we have to go," I said.

"Then y'all better come back quick, because before you know it, this little one will be heading off to school."

"We'll be back before that. Promise," I said.

Jimmy checked his watch. "Thought you weren't supposed to be back at work yet?"

"When have I ever listened to authority?"

He shook his head. "See you there in a bit."

I stopped at Bubba's office and thanked him for the late-night and early-morning work.

"Not a problem. By the way, do you know how hard it was to get the information from the bank manager? Woman was ready to beat me over the phone."

"I'm sorry about that. I'll get her an apology and take ownership soon."

"It's all right," he said. "She got to the bank and found the cleaning people having sex in her office. She said she appreciated the request, or she wouldn't have known about that."

"Probably was better off not knowing," I said.

"She said she made them disinfect the desk before she fired them."

I laughed out loud. "Thanks for the information."

"Anything else?"

I'd read the order, and Nowak gave me a lot of room for requesting more information, but nothing on tapping the suspect's phone line, and I didn't want to ask for something else without solid evidence. "Just keep doing what you're doing," I said.

My cell phone rang. I checked the caller ID, but I didn't recognize the number.

23

"I'll be right there," I said. "What are you calling from?" I asked. I headed out to the reception area.

"Oh, it's my personal cell," Michels said.

"I thought I had that number already."

"You have my personal cell for work people. This is for civilians."

"Why have two?"

"I try to keep my personal life detached from my professional life."

"How's that working out for you?"

"Does calling you from my personal life cell phone say anything to that?"

I laughed. "Be right there."

There was a woman waiting at the reception desk. Michels talked with her briefly, but she'd demanded to speak to just me. "Detective Ryder. What can I do for you?"

"I'd like to ask you a few questions about the serial killer."

"Are you with the media?"

"AJC. Do you have a few minutes?"

"I'm sorry," I said. "No comment."

"Detective Ryder, I've done my research. I can't find any killings similar to this other than in Alabama. I'd like to know if you think the killer is done, or if he's moving on."

I raised an eyebrow. "What do you mean you've done your research?"

"I know about the numbers," she said.

I maintained my reserve. "Come with me, please." I showed her to an empty interrogation room and asked her to wait there, then headed to see if Bishop had arrived yet. He hadn't, and neither had Jimmy.

"Shit, shit, shit," I said out loud.

I quickly grabbed Bubba and asked him to set up recording my conversation.

"Sure thing," he said. "It's all set up. Just have to hit record."

I closed the door to the investigation room behind me and sat in front of the woman. "May I have your name, please?"

"Jessica Walters. No relation to Barbara."

"Tell me about these numbers, Ms. Walters."

"We don't have to play this game, Detective. I know the first three murders were one, two, and three, and I know yours were seven, eight, and nine. I've searched everywhere for four, five, and six, and I can't find them anywhere. Can you tell me why?"

"How did you find out about the numbers? We never said anything to the public."

She opened her leather folio, removed an envelope, and slid it across the table. "Your killer contacted me."

"He contacted you?" I used a tissue to open the note.

Detective Ryder isn't giving you all the information. I've left a number with each victim. One, two, and three were in Birmingham, Alabama. Seven, eight, and nine in Hamby, Georgia. Why hasn't the detective said anything? Because she's not smart enough to find the other three.

"Where did you get this?"

"It was on my car when I left for work."

"Where was your car?"

"In my driveway."

"Do you have a Ring or any other recording system?"

"The battery is dead."

"How long was your vehicle in the driveway?"

"From about nine o'clock last night until about seven the following morning."

"May I have your address, please?"

She wrote down her address and handed me the paper. "I asked the neighbors if they saw anything, but none of them have."

"We'll get Detective Michels and his team on them also." I glanced at the video camera and gave it a slight nod. Bubba would make sure Michels did as I'd requested. "Tell me about your research."

"Not much to tell. I was able to verify there were three numbers with the victims in Birmingham, Alabama, but that's about it."

"Who verified that?"

"Detective William Johnson."

"And did he tell you our victims had numbers?"

"He wouldn't verify, but he did say the next three numbers haven't been located. It didn't take much to figure out the rest."

"I'll need to keep the note."

"I understand, but please, can you tell me anything about the killer?"

Jimmy said I couldn't get on TV, but he didn't say I couldn't get in the newspaper. I knew there wasn't much of a difference, but men are usually literal, so I went with it. Besides, the killer contacted this reporter for a reason, and I knew he was waiting for my response, and I needed to give him one. "The numbers are correct. It is our belief the killer is playing with us, that the in-between numbers are not associated with any victims. The killer isn't as smart as he wants us to believe. As a matter of fact, we have known from the beginning the three missing numbers were empty threats."

"Did you follow up to determine that was the case?"

"To the best of our ability, yes."

"Do you think the killer will strike again?"

"I won't make any assumptions, but I can say I expect this investigation to be finished quickly." Jimmy would have my ass if I'd said it would be closed soon, so I altered the words to cover myself.

"So, you have a suspect?"

"No comment," I said.

"Detective, what do you think is causing this killer to kill?"

Bingo! Just what I'd waited for. Something to knock the killer off his high horse. I couldn't release the information on the sexual assaults and attacks, but I could dart around the subject. "He believes he's doing the right thing, but what he fails to see is he's lowering himself to a level much lower than his victims." I stood. "Thank you for your time."

"I'd like to use the note in my article."

"I'm afraid that's not possible."

"I have a photo of it on my phone, and it was delivered to me, so technically, it's my note."

"No, it's part of an investigation."

"But I can write about the note, correct?"

I didn't want to answer that. There was a fine line between giving approval and talking with a reporter. The interview had been on record, and I'd said things I knew Jimmy would lose his mind about, but it was the best way to get under the killer's skin, and that's what I wanted. "I'll walk you out."

"You what?" Jimmy's face matched the red on his shirt. "I told you no interviews!"

"You said no TV interviews."

His nostrils flared. "It's the same damn thing, Ryder, and you know it." He planted his legs firmly on the floor and placed his hands on his waist. "I've got the mayor up my ass already, and you go and do this?" He stepped forward, then back, and then finally stood still and dropped repeated f-bombs.

"I know you're angry, but—"

"Really? How can you tell?"

I exhaled. "What I did was necessary. The killer's watching us carefully, and that interview will make him angry enough to stick around, or if he's already left, come back. We need him here if we want to catch him, Jimmy. Tell that to the mayor."

He stepped closer to me, getting into my personal space, which he knew I hated. He stared at me with cold, hard eyes. "Find the damn killer."

Before he had a chance to say anything else, his assistant buzzed in on his office line. "Chief, there's a reporter at the front desk."

"We're not doing any interviews," he said tersely.

"She's not here for an interview. She's here to see Detective Ryder about a personal matter."

"I'll send her up," he said. He steeled his eyes on me. "Nothing on the record, you hear me? Nothing."

"Got it."

The woman was visibly upset. She was sweating, her hands were shaking, and she had nothing with her other than her purse. No notepad, no recorder, no cameraperson. "I... I'm... I think my son is missing, and I think the serial killer has him."

24

We'd received at least a thousand calls from nervous parents about their young adult son disappearing. Most said they hadn't seen the child in a few days, that their calls or texts weren't being acknowledged, but none of them turned out to be missing. "What's your name?"

"Stephanie Miller. My son is Brian Miller, and he's twenty-three. I've been working on a hate crime trial in Atlanta, and I haven't been home in two days, so I can't say for sure when he went missing, but he's not answering my calls, and I'm worried."

"Did you file a missing persons report?"

"No. It's my experience those are a waste of time. Unless the person is disabled or a senior citizen, the police don't actively search for missing persons, especially men my son's age."

Given that she said that to a cop, I wondered why she came to me, but I waited to ask until I gathered more information. "Does he live with you?"

She shook her head. "He lives with friends in a rental in Alpharetta. And before you ask, yes, I contacted them both, or tried, that is. One's been gone for a week on a cruise with his parents, and the other is in Tennessee doing some work for his uncle, so obviously neither have seen him."

"Have they had contact with him?"

"I can only say for sure about the one in Tennessee, and he hasn't."

"Alpharetta isn't our jurisdiction, but I'll see if I can get someone there to help you. Can you wait here a moment?"

"I want you on this."

I turned back around. "Again, Alpharetta isn't our jurisdiction."

"I don't care. I know the killer's contacted you, so I want you on it."

We hadn't made any of the notes public, but reporters were sometimes given information off the record. "Where did you hear that?"

"Detective Ryder, I'm a well-known investigative crime reporter in Atlanta. I'm privy to confidential information from across the state. Sometimes I know things even the police don't."

"What other confidential information do you know?" I asked.

"I know that these are likely justice killings, and that each victim has, in the least, sexually assaulted a woman."

"Can you tell me where you learned that?" I asked.

"Will you help me?"

"I'll do what I can, but Alpharetta has to take the lead. If we have reason to believe your son was abducted by the killer, the case will come to us."

She looked me straight in the eyes. "Detective Edward Anderson, Birmingham Police Department."

Dammit.

"Detective, I believe my son has sexually assaulted one woman, if not more. Please, I don't want anything to happen to him."

"Okay, as I said, I'm required to contact the Alpharetta PD, so let me do that, and we'll go from there."

I stepped back behind the glass and made a call.

"Did you get anything on the neighbors' alarm systems? I asked Michels.

"Nope. All claimed they don't pay for the taping service, but part of me thinks they don't want to get involved."

"Damn, we could have used at least one." He checked his watch. "Let me get to Alpharetta to find that kid."

"Keep us posted. If you find any link to our killer, we're coming in."

"Got it."

Michels took two of our patrol to work directly with the Alpharetta PD and Stephanie Miller to locate her son while Bishop and I met with Calloway again.

"This doesn't seem right," Calloway said. "It's not what I expected from this killer, given his first three murders in Alabama."

"He went off plan because of me," I said.

"Agreed," Bishop said. "The question is, where's the victim? And will Ryder's recent interview have an impact on what happens to him?"

"It's hard to say whether he'll kill again locally. His initial killings are a good foundation of what to expect in general, but given the notes and the antagonistic nature of Detective Ryder—"

I crossed my arms and clenched my jaw. "I don't have an antagonistic nature."

Bishop laughed out loud. "Right. And I'm Tom Brady."

Calloway chuckled. "You two have a very strong connection, probably one of the best I've seen between partners in a long time."

"He can be a major a-hole," I said.

"Ditto," Bishop said.

I blew him a kiss.

"As I was saying," Calloway said. "If we factor in the communication efforts of Detective Ryder, our killer has gone off plan. If I were to guess, he's enjoying your repartee, and he'll want to continue it."

"So, he'll stick around and kill again," Bishop said.

"Maybe he wasn't planning to go anywhere in the first place," I said.

"We all know this isn't written in stone. There are many factors that can impact character and personality traits, and to label everyone the same is impossible and bad for the investigation. My point is, while serial killers tend to have very specific motivations, that doesn't mean they won't change, or that they won't expand. And our killer seems to be adding motivations outside of his search for justice."

She reviewed the summary she'd put together. "And based on the information at hand, I'll reiterate that his additional motivation is his connection to Detective Ryder."

"We are not connected," I said.

"To him, you are. He feels he's established a relationship with you, that he's bonded with you. I expect, once that article is published, you'll receive another message from him."

"Could a traumatic brain injury cause contradictions in his behaviors?" I asked.

"It's possible," she said. "May I ask why you're asking?"

"I have a person of interest who suffered a TBI in an accident seven years ago. I've talked to him a few times, and we've had him in for questioning. His personality fluctuates. Sometimes he seems almost immature and childlike, and other times he appears calculated and smart."

"That's interesting," she said. "Is this the uncle of the first assault victim in Hamby?"

Bishop nodded. "But we have no solid evidence that he's our guy."

Calloway looked directly at me. "But you think he is?"

"Yes."

She looked to Bishop. "And you disagree?"

He rubbed his bottom lip. "We don't have anything to tie him to the murders."

I jumped in. "I was able to access Stuart's financial information. Three months prior to the killings he made three separate cash deposits of one thousand dollars each. Three killings, three thousand dollars."

She raised an eyebrow. "Are you suggesting someone paid him to kill these boys?"

"I'm saying he made three separate cash deposits three months before the Hamby murders. Other than those deposits, he's only had disability checks deposited. Where did that money come from, and what did he do to get it?"

"A thousand bucks a person for these kinds of murders?" Bishop shook his head. "I don't see it. And why would he deposit blood money into his account?"

"A person with a damaged brain from a traumatic accident," I said, "doesn't always act like we'd expect, which is exactly what our killer is doing. One puzzle. Two pieces that fit together."

Calloway smiled. "You'd be surprised at what people can do."

"Not me," I said.

Bishop waved his hand. "Ditto."

"Then you're saying it's possible he's the guy?" I asked him.

"We don't have any solid evidence. And like the chief said, we need it if we're going to get anywhere with him."

"I know that, but we can't find evidence if we don't look for it."

Calloway smiled at Bishop. "She has a point."

He exhaled. "Following slim circumstantial evidence like him being gone the night of the murder, with nothing concrete on where he was the nights of the other murders and a small amount of money deposited into his account, is barely enough to grow from."

Calloway stood up and walked over to the first whiteboard next to the table. She studied the information I'd added on Chip Stuart and shook her head as she turned around. "TBI studies show some types of TBIs can cause violent behaviors, but I've not yet seen anything to the degree of this killer. And I must agree with Detective Bishop. These killings are too detailed and too violent for such a small payment, though I will preface that with a term we use as a scapegoat in forensic psychology. Anything's possible."

"Great," I said.

"What about purchases?" Bishop asked. "Did Stuart make any major purchases or even hit up a Lowes for murder supplies?"

"No, but that doesn't mean he didn't get those items another way."

"I think he's worth another interview in the near future," Calloway said. "And I would like to be the one asking the questions."

Bishop leaned back in his chair and cracked the knuckles on his right hand. Cops often did that to draw attention to themselves and even intimidate a suspect, but in that moment, he was just frustrated.

"Instead of interviewing a suspect sans evidence"—he looked at me—"wouldn't our time be better spent looking for the locations of each murder?"

That tipped me over the edge. We had a person of interest, granted, with slim evidence, but it was more evidence than anything else we had on anyone else. "Maybe, just maybe, if we follow this guy for more than a day, we'll find what we need. Because right now we don't have a damn thing pointing to anyone. Besides, it's virtually impossible to find the locations of the murders because we don't have shit on that either." I leaned back in my chair and took a deep breath.

Calloway and Bishop were silent for a good thirty seconds until Bishop finally said, "Feel better?"

"Not really."

"Let's bring him in soon," Calloway said. "But before we talk to him, I'd like you two to interview his former employer. We need to see if he had any personnel issues, complaints, how he handled stress, that kind of thing."

"His accident was seven years ago," I said. "The company may not have the same employees."

"Someone will know him, and people always like the attention they receive when answering questions."

Chip Stuart worked for a lumber company on the county line for Forsyth and Cherokee counties. He was employed there for five years, but prior to that, he worked for a moving company no longer in business. He was a little on the thick side, but it didn't appear that thickness was once muscle, instead it was more like the thick one got from sitting for hours on the couch blindly eating potato chips. Regardless, he worked for two companies that required strength and muscle, so he must have had some at some point.

Bishop drove, of course. "Maybe he was more active prior to his TBI, which might eliminate your theory he's the guy."

"It doesn't necessarily take strength to manipulate someone emotionally and compromise them physically."

"You think he's smart enough to do that?"

"I think he's smarter than he wants us to believe."

"That doesn't make him a killer."

"I know that."

He drove down Campground Road and past the Christian camp. The camp made me uncomfortable to look at. The buildings were old and so beat-up, when I'd first seen them, I thought it was some kind of detention housing that had closed down years before, but nope. It was still an active summer camp for teenagers, and there were even a few more just like it in the area. "No way I'd go to camp there. It's the perfect place for Jason to chase naive teens with a chainsaw."

Bishop laughed. "It was a great camp back in the day."

"You mean like a hundred years ago when the buildings were built?"

His eyes shifted toward me and gave me a slight grimace. "I went there when I was sixteen. Met Annabella Fulton there."

"Annabella Fulton? You mean of the Fulton County Fultons?" I impressed myself for saying it without laughing. Georgians were all about their history and who from founding community families was still around. Chicago, on the other hand, was about crime and political corruption. Chicagoans had their priorities.

"Yup."

"You meet her behind the bathrooms for a little something-something?"

"I was a gentleman."

"So, in other words, she didn't know you existed?"

"Pretty much."

"Ah, the perils of teenage angst. Never changes."

He turned into the lumber yard lot. "Great. I just got this car washed. This gravel is going to muck it up."

"It's winter, and it's a department vehicle. Besides, I won't even get my Jeep washed until May."

"We do things differently in the South."

"You have no idea how true that statement is." His cell phone beeped. He'd changed the standard tone to a bell, and I smiled. "That your girlfriend?"

"You're like the high school bully picking on the little guy sometimes, you know that?"

"I think it's cute how you changed her ringtone."

"My daughter suggested it. Said it would help me answer her texts faster."

"Definitely a plus for a new relationship."

"My daughter make you change yours for Kyle? Because we both know you wouldn't have thought of that yourself."

"Nope. Savannah."

"Ah, she is an expert at a lot of things." He put the car in park and climbed out and wiped a bit of dust off the side.

I just rolled my eyes and shook my head.

The lumber yard was just what one would expect. Lumber, and a lot of it. Rows and rows of cut trees in various shapes and sizes lined up in sections. I couldn't name one tree, but Bishop rattled them off like he'd just studied for a tree exam.

"That's all oak," he said, pointing to one section. "Over there is pine. Easy to come by in Georgia, but too soft for my taste."

"Soft?"

"Yeah, put anything with weight on it and you risk denting it."

"Why would you put something on a log?"

"I'm talking about furniture. Sometimes I wonder how you became a detective."

I ignored the jab. "My guess is the owner is the same as when Stuart worked here, and I doubt he's got any hard-and-fast HR policies."

"Agree," he said.

We headed toward the small trailer we assumed was the office.

A burly man with a long dark beard peppered with hints of gray and hair long enough to be pulled back into at least a six-inch ponytail sat at an old metal desk. "Help you?"

Bishop and I showed him our badges.

Bishop said, "Detectives Bishop and Ryder." He flicked his head my direction when he said my name. "Hamby Police Department. We're here to talk with you about a former employee."

"I got a lot of former employees. Pick one, and I can tell y'all about them."

"And you are?"

"Oh, Buck Patton. I own the place. Took it over from my pa twenty-some years ago."

I jotted down his name in my small notepad. "Chip Stuart is the employee we're here about."

He nodded. "Ah, the Chipper. That one was interesting. To be honest..."

he said. He took a drink from a large thermos. "Didn't think he'd last as long as he did or do the work he did either. Surprised me."

"What do you mean?" Bishop asked.

"Seemed like the Chipper wanted you to think he was something different than he was, but when it came down to it, he was a good worker."

"How so?" I asked.

"'Course he had his issues, like he wasn't that social except in the mornings. Rest of the time he kept to himself and focused on his work. Took it seriously. Always had a determined look on his face."

"What kind of work did he do for you?" Bishop asked.

"That's the reason we called him the Chipper, other than his name, 'course. He'd take the damaged wood, chop it up to pieces, and then send it through the chipper. Some of those logs weighed two hundred and three hundred pounds, and he'd drag or carry them by himself, chop them up with an ax like he was chopping the heads off chickens."

I glanced at my partner with one of my *I told you so* looks. "Did Mr. Stuart have aggressive tendencies at work?" I asked.

"Anyone using an ax for eight hours a day is getting rid of whatever aggressive they have, so I'd say a man's got to be a little on the tense side to want the job, but the Chipper, he didn't act angry or nothing like that. Matter of fact, he was a touch on the weird side."

"Weird in what way?" I asked.

"He had some weird fascination with true crime and was always talking about it when he got to work. Like I said, in the mornings. We give our guys a good fifteen minutes for a cup of coffee before hitting it hard. That extra dose of caffeine helps, you know? And he'd hog the time talking about men who'd chop up body parts and stuff them in grinders." He shook his head. "Talking about it now makes it sound a lot creepier than it did at the time. Other than that, he was all right. Hard worker and stronger than he looked. Wasn't a big guy and didn't have a lot of muscle, but he knew how to use an ax."

"Did you have any employee problems with Mr. Stuart?" I asked.

"Nope. Aside from the morning-coffee-killer babble, he'd do his work, take his lunch by himself in his car, and then do his work again. When five o'clock came, he was out fast as a whore at Sunday church. Didn't work any longer than he was supposed to. Most of the guys here work until their work is done, but the Chipper had an end time, and he stuck to it." He leaned back in his chair. It was the rolling kind with the sway back that if you sat down and didn't know the chair moved, your back would go halfway down and scare the hell out of you. "Can I ask why you're inquiring about Chipper?"

Bishop took that one. I figured he was afraid I would say we thought he was a serial killer. "Just have a case we're working on and his name came up."

"You talking about that serial killer?"

"Just an investigation," Bishop repeated.

The man nodded. "Okay, then, because the Chipper might be a weird one, but even with all that talk about chopping people up, he don't strike me as a killer."

"What makes you say that?" I asked.

"He was a rule follower. Someone broke a rule, he came right up and said something to them. Couldn't handle people messing with things, taking shortcuts, or not following procedure, but he wasn't threatening. If I had to label it, I'd say he was talking down to people, like he wanted to school them on the rules."

"How long did he work here?" Bishop asked.

Patton twisted the bottom of his beard into a tight point. "Guess about four or five years. Can't say I remember for sure."

"Why did he leave?" I asked.

Patton shrugged. "Just came in one day and said he was done."

"So, he didn't quit because of his accident?" Bishop asked.

Patton raised his eyebrow. "Don't know about no accident."

"He had a minor accident," I said. I didn't want to provide any details to sway the man to say something he didn't mean. The best way to handle interviews was to let them talk without telling them what to say. Of course, there were times we liked to nudge people in the right direction, if we felt that was where they'd end up, but we tried not to do that when it came to discussing persons of interest.

"Never knew he had an accident," he said. "He just up and quit one day. Never gave a reason."

"Did any other employers call you for references?" Bishop asked.

"Not that I remember."

Another man who looked like the guy we were talking to, only younger, interrupted our conversation. "Pa, got a snakebite over in row seven, Henry Huck again."

Patton sighed as he stood "Dammit. Don't know how the hell these snakes get out in the middle of winter, but every time they do, they bite the shit out of one of my guys." He walked toward the door. "Hate to up and leave on you like this, but my employees come first."

As we headed to the car, I saw another older man standing near a pile of wood I also couldn't name looking at us. "Hold on," I said, and jogged over to him.

Bishop followed.

"Excuse me, how long have you worked here?"

The man gave me a once-over, slowing at my breasts and sticking to them for a good five seconds. I felt the sudden desire for a steaming hot shower. He then looked at Bishop. "Y'all cops?"

"Detectives," I said.

"I can tell. I can always smell a cop." He inhaled through his nose, then spit on the ground beside me. "Smells like pig." He rolled his eyes up and down my body once again, then let them linger at my breasts.

Talk about a pig. If I took another step forward, my knee in his crotch would have him on the ground and in the fetal position in three seconds flat. Oh, how I wished I could do that sometimes. I unclipped my badge from my waist and held it up near his face. "Eyes up here."

He blinked and took a step back. "I did my time. Ain't no reason no pigs should be hounding me."

"You sound like a winner, but I'm not here for you. I'm here about a former employee. So, I'll ask again. How long have you worked here?"

"On and off, 'bout twenty years. Who you asking about? 'Cause I don't rat on my friends."

"You rat on acquaintances?" Bishop asked.

"Depends."

"Chip Stuart," I said.

His eyes widened. "The Chipper? Guy was a freak. Everyone stayed away from him. He had this thing about choppin' people up. Always talkin' about it like it was no big deal. I ain't opposed to hurting someone who deserves it, but slicin' and dicin'? That's over the line for me."

"Are you referring to his obsession with crime TV?" Bishop asked.

"It wasn't just TV. He said he read about serial killers too. I'm tellin' ya, we stayed away from him. I don't know what you think he's done, but I'd say he did it. We all knew he was gonna blow one day. Just glad it wasn't here. Man could use an ax with the best of us, and I don't know one guy here that wasn't worried he'd be the Chipper's target one day."

"He ever threaten anyone?" I asked.

"He was always gettin' on us about followin' the rules. Tellin' us what to do and how to do it like he was the boss. Got this crazy, wild-eyed look at the time, too."

"Thank you," I said.

He smiled. "Sure thing, honey. You got a card? I could use a connection like you in the police department."

"I'm sure we'll see each other again someday," I said, and walked away. I felt his eyes on me the whole time.

Once we got in the vehicle, Bishop said, "Fine. He's a person of interest."

I smiled. "Calloway's going to eat this up. Now it's time to nail his ass to the wall."

25

"Am I going to get an earful from Abernathy again?" Judge Nowak asked. He offered me and Bishop a seat across from his desk.

"He's on board," I said.

He glanced at Bishop.

"She's correct, Your Honor."

"I'm not into the formalities when the robe is off. You can call me Stan."

"Will do, sir."

"Now, what's this for?" he asked.

His assistant opened his office door. "One of the assistant DAs is here. She said it's regarding this case."

He let out a frustrated-sounding breath. "Let her in."

A young blond woman dressed in a black pantsuit strutted in. She'd pulled her long hair into a bun low on her head, just like mine. Her attempt to project confidence came off as fake, and I felt sorry for her. She was young, naive, and afraid to talk to the judge. Eventually, though, if she made it through her first year as a lawyer, she'd adjust. "Judge Nowak, the district attorney's office doesn't agree with this request for a warrant. We have reviewed the investigation and find no probable cause. It is our decision to not move forward until such probable cause is determined. It would behoove you to deny this warrant request."

Ouch, that was going to bite her in the ass.

"Miss—what is your name?"

"Samantha Harris, Your Honor."

"Miss Harris, how long have you worked with the district attorney?"

"Two months, Your Honor, but I worked with Pickens County for a year prior. I believe I am well equipped for this position."

"I'm sure you are. However, I suggest you not storm into a judge's chambers and demand they follow your instructions. I am well aware of the law. In fact, I've practiced it for several years longer than you've been alive."

"My apologies, Your Honor. I did not mean to offend, but as you know, the court does not consider the arrest or incarceration of a person lightly, and I—"

"The district attorney's standing on this issue is duly noted."

I couldn't believe she tried to repeat constitutional rights back to a judge. The impact of that would follow her professionally for a long time.

Nowak looked at me. "Detective Ryder, did you find something from the previous warrant that determines probable cause for Mr. Stuart?"

Samantha Harris's head shifted from Nowak to me. "I'm sorry, we aren't aware of any previous warrants issued against Mr. Stuart."

"We didn't share it with you," I said. I smiled at the judge. "Yes, Your Honor. We found three separate cash deposits totaling three thousand dollars prior to the murders, and Mr. Stuart is the uncle of a female alleging sexual assault by the first victim in Hamby, Jacob Ramsey. Also, we have interview statements suggesting a fascination with violent killing. The reason for the warrant is to bring Chip Stuart in for questioning and analysis by ourselves and the forensic psychologist and, if necessary, retaining him in custody for the allowed forty-eight hours to further determine evidence." I whipped my head toward Harris. "Sometimes we have to beat the information out of the suspect," I said, and I winked.

Bishop coughed.

"Over the line, Detective," Nowak said.

"Sorry, Your Honor."

He drummed his fingers on his desk then focused on something above my head. "Detectives, I have a nephew who is fascinated with Jeffrey Dahmer. I don't understand the fascination, but he reads books on him and watches documentaries about him. That, however, does not make my nephew a serial killer. My wife loves Hallmark movies, and while I might enjoy the occasional Christmas one under duress at times, I consider neither of us hopeless romantics. My point is that a fascination with something, whether that something can be like the murder, isn't a reason to suspect one of the same. I do agree that the financial information is suspect, but given the seriousness of these crimes, and the amount of money you stated he received, I'm not sure our district attorney's office can build a case on three thousand dollars, a few interviews, and a relationship to an alleged assault victim."

"Sir, Mr. Stuart lied about his whereabouts the night Jacob Ramsey was murdered," I said.

"Do you know where he was during the times of the other killings?"

"We haven't found anything to say he was or wasn't in Birmingham," I said.

"What does Stuart say?" he asked.

"That it was three years ago, and he was probably home on his couch."

"Your honor," Harris said. "Mr. Stuart has a traumatic brain injury. He hasn't been able to work in seven years, and he's had no priors. I just don't see how we can connect him to these brutal crimes."

"Miss Harris, it is the job of our detectives here to find those connections, and sometimes we must make decisions that allow them to do just that." He smiled at me and Bishop. "It sounds to me like you're trying to eliminate him as a suspect rather than pin the murders on him. Either way, I think you have enough circumstantial evidence to bring him in. My suggestion, however, is to attempt another round of questioning without a warrant. My concern is an arrest will allow your person of interest to retain an attorney and then any shot at him talking to you again will be lost. If you can't get him in voluntarily, we can issue the warrant."

"Thank you, Your Honor," Harris said. She smiled, thinking she'd won.

"Understood," I said. I wanted to say more, but I needed a connection in the courts, and there was no better connection than a judge. Besides, I liked Judge Nowak, and I didn't want to tick him off.

Nowak breathed in deeply through his nose and then expelled the air through his mouth. "Miss Harris, I'd like a moment alone with the detectives. It was a pleasure meeting you."

She smiled and left.

Nowak asked us to sit. "Tell me what makes you think this is the guy. Your evidence is slim, but I know you wouldn't come here asking for a warrant if you didn't think he did it."

My eyes met Bishop's. "My partner disagrees with me on this, but my gut tells me Stuart is good for these. But you're right, evidence is slim, and we're stuck. Having Calloway talk to him might push him to mess up, or even to act."

"You mean kill again?"

I shook my head. "No, or at least I hope not. We have had some slight communication with the killer in the form of notes—"

"To Ryder," Bishop said.

"To me, yes, and I have attempted to communicate with him through the media. In fact, I recently attempted communication, but so far, he's not taken the bait."

"You really think the psychologist can help?" Nowak asked.

"I think it's our best shot at the moment," I said. "And there's a young adult male missing from Alpharetta. His mother came to me because she thinks the killer has him."

"I'm sure any mother of a young adult male is worried right now, but that's not proof the killer has him."

"She's a reporter, and she has information about the case no one else does, specifically that the male victims have been accused of sexual assault and/or rape."

"How did she get that?" he asked.

"She didn't say, but she believes her son has assaulted a woman before."

"Have you looked into the young man?"

"The victim is in Alpharetta. We have a detective working with them, but until we have something solid to connect him to our investigation, we can't request lead."

"Understood." He turned to Bishop. "What are your thoughts on the situation?"

"I think we have nothing pointing to anyone, and if nothing else, at least we can eliminate a person of interest."

"Keep me informed."

"Will do," I said.

∼

Bishop read me the riot act in the car. "What made you think we'd get that? I went along because I'm trying to support you, but—"

"No, you went along because we have nothing on this case and the clock is ticking. Don't act like you think I'm right."

"I didn't say I thought you were right. I said I went along to support you."

I bit my bottom lip. "I have an idea."

"Oh hell. That's what always gets you in trouble."

"No, that's what always closes investigations."

"Whatever. What's the idea? And yes, I know I'm going to regret asking that."

"Let's not bring him in again—"

"But Calloway wants to talk to him."

"I know, and she will, but not right away. Let him sit. He'll think we don't have anything on him."

"We don't have anything on him."

"We have a little, and that's enough to move forward."

"A little doesn't get confessions or guilty verdicts."

"Criminals have been convicted on circumstantial evidence before."

"Jesus, Ryder. Don't go there. We aren't pushing him on what we've got."

"No, I know. I was just making a point."

"Then get to the point regarding your idea."

We pulled into the parking lot of the station. "We go to his house again."

"That's your idea."

"Trust me on this."

He started the vehicle once more and pulled out of the lot. "Usually when I trust you, someone gets shot."

I couldn't deny that.

A short, dark-haired woman answered the door. She looked like she'd spent the night with a bottle of hard liquor. Bourbon, if my nose was correct.

"Mrs. Bryant?" I asked. Both Bishop and I showed her our badges.

She squinted from the bright sun hitting her face. "Yes, and you are?" She rubbed her eyes. "Sorry, I have a migraine."

More like a hangover. "We're here to talk to your brother."

"Chip's not home. He left late last night, and I don't know when he'll be back."

Bishop's eyes met mine. "Did he say where he was going?"

"Nope, and I didn't ask. Is this about the Ramsey kid? Do you know what he did to my daughter? Why are you even investigating his death?"

"Because it's our job, ma'am," Bishop said.

"Do you think my brother has something to do with that kid's murder?"

"We just want to talk to him," I said.

"He couldn't." She shook her head and then pressed her temples with her fingers. "He's got a medical condition. A traumatic brain injury. He can't even work."

"We know," I said. "Did your brother leave with a friend?"

"No, he took a car."

"You mean like Uber?" I asked.

"No, I mean like a car he drove."

"Your car?" Bishop asked.

"I just said he's got a TBI. You think I'd let him drive my car?"

"Is your car here?" I asked.

She nodded. "It's in the garage. Do you need me to show you?"

"Yes, ma'am," Bishop said. "We'd appreciate it."

"Fine." She closed the front door. A few seconds later the garage door opened and there sat her vehicle.

"Do you have any idea what car he took?" I asked.

"All I know is there was a car parked in front of the house, and that's what he took. He gets disability, and I think he's been putting money aside for a beater, and trust me, that's what that was."

Stuart's license had expired, and we had no record of any vehicle he'd purchased. "Thank you," I said. "When he returns, please have him contact the Hamby PD. He knows my name."

"Sure," she said and closed the door. The garage door shut shortly after.

"Interesting," Bishop said. "He has a vehicle."

"Believe me now?"

"I'm getting closer."

26

Calloway stood in the kitchen of the department. "You don't have him?"

"We're holding off," I said.

"Why? My interview will help determine if he's a suspect."

"I want to try something. If it doesn't work, then we'll bring him in."

"May I ask what you're going to try?"

"You may, but I'm not ready to answer just yet."

"I think that is a mistake."

"Noted."

"Detective, if your person of interest is our killer, you mustn't do anything to agitate him. His actions are trending toward unpredictable, so we can't assume he'll react in any suspected manner. I can't support your actions without first assessing if the person of interest is a danger to the community. I do not recommend you move forward until I assess him."

I smiled. "I respect what you do, but I'm not asking for your support. I'm informing you of the status of our person of interest."

She gave me an icy stare. "I am a part of this investigation."

"And I am the lead detective. My game. My rules."

"Let's let the chief decide that."

I casually walked toward the kitchen door. "I've got some time. Is he here?"

Kyle stepped in front of the door. He handed me a fresh cup of Dunkin'. "At your service."

"Thanks," I said. I turned back toward Calloway. "You coming?"

"We'll discuss this later." She charged over and smacked her shoulder into Kyle's as she headed out the door. "Excuse me."

Kyle watched her stomp down the hallway, her heels clicking loudly and echoing in the hall. "What'd you do to her?"

"Put a feather up her butt."

He nodded once. "Sounds like fun." He smiled as he leaned against the doorframe. "You needed me for a reason, I assume?"

"Always." We headed to the investigation room.

He smiled at all the files on the table and the collection of whiteboards filling the room. "I was analyzing the file while you were gone. You've been busy."

"We all have been."

Bishop walked in with a bottled water. "How'd she drag you into this?"

"She owns a gun."

"Several," I said. "But Jimmy was the one that asked him to look at the investigation."

He shrugged at Bishop. "DEA agents are full of knowledge."

"Is that what you're calling it?" Bishop asked.

"I like to dress it up, so yeah."

"We currently have no drug issues in the state so, he's free." I smiled.

"Yes, the entire state of Georgia is now drug-free," Kyle said with a smile.

"Because of him," I added.

"That too," Kyle teased. "I'm off for three days."

"And you don't do time off well?" Bishop asked.

"Not unless I'm on a beach with a bottle of beer in my hand."

"God, that sounds great," I said. I wasn't a big beer drinker. In fact, I barely drank, but I did drop the occasional shot and consume a few libations now and then. Lying on a beach with Kyle sounded like something a beer would make even better.

"Close this case, and we'll go."

I handed him a file. "Did you read this yet?"

"I don't think so."

"Then start here. We've missed something, but I don't know what." I filled him in on what we knew and gave him the latest update on Stuart. He didn't agree or disagree with my theory.

"I'll give it all a look."

"Thanks," I said. I asked Bishop. "I have an idea. You ready?"

Bishop checked his watch. "Can it wait? I need an hour."

"For what?"

"Personal business."

My eyes widened. "He's got a date."

Kyle's eyes widened. "Is she serious?"

"It's a quick meal."

"Is it with Catherine?" I asked.

He shook his head and furrowed his brow as if I'd said something completely ridiculous. "What are you, twelve?" He walked out of the room.

"Definitely a date," Kyle said.

"Yup." I organized the rest of the files for him. "I've got something to take care of, but if you find something, text me."

"You have a date too?"

"Something like that." I smiled. "Oh, may I take your car?"

"Why do I feel like I'm going to regret it if I say yes?"

"Because you know me."

"Leave me your keys in case I need to run."

I tossed him my keys and he tossed his back.

"Be careful," he said. "With the car." He winked at me.

"Yes, sir."

I called Johnson on my way back to Chip Stuart's house. My call went to voicemail. "Johnson, it's Ryder. What happened? You fall off the face of the earth? Listen, we have more evidence against Stuart. It's skimming the bottom of the trash can, but it's something. Call me when you get this. I need you back here."

It was getting late, and my stomach growled as I passed a McDonald's. I pulled into the drive-through and grabbed two cheeseburgers, no onions, and a diet Coke. I gobbled the burgers down in a few bites and regretted not getting any fries.

I drove through Stuart's neighborhood and noted every vehicle on the street, taking photos of each one. There were a few that would qualify as beaters, so I checked the plates on them. They came back clean and with different owners. I pulled over a street away from Stuart's place, opened Kyle's bag in the trunk, and removed the Atlanta Braves baseball cap. I let my hair down, then put the hat low on my forehead and fluffed my hair. It was getting long and needed a trim.

I climbed back into Kyle's vehicle and drove to Stuart's. I passed the house, checked for lights—they were all off, then did a U-turn, and parked on the opposite side of the street, two houses down from his.

Then I waited.

Kyle texted an hour later. *Long date?*

I'm sitting outside Chip Stuart's house.

Anything interesting happening?

Nope.

You need me?

Nope. You find anything?

Not yet. Still looking. You coming back here, or should I meet you at your place?

My place. I'll be there soon.

Got it. Be safe.

I did another drive through the neighborhood and checked for cars. Three were gone, but they were all late-model, decent vehicles. Two additional cars had parked on two side streets connected to Stuart's place through only a crossroad, and the two beaters were still there. I took photos of the new vehicles, then headed back to Stuart's house for one more quick drive by.

I slowed as I passed the house next to his, noticing a light coming from Stuart's home. Chip Stuart stood on the front porch, smoking a cigarette. We made eye contact. He formed a gun with his hand and pointed it at my vehicle, then turned around and went inside.

27

"He could have done that for a number of reasons," Kyle said.

I hitched my boot up onto the wooden trunk I used for a coffee table, untied my boot, and pulled it off, then repeated it with the other foot. I wiggled my toes and sighed. "I know, but think about it. Where did he go, and with what vehicle? And why would he be outside if he didn't know I was there?"

"I can't answer those."

"Okay, what about this? His personality shifts. One minute he's acting like he's some closed-in nerd who sits in front of the TV all day, and the next he's calculated and deceptive. That's an act. He's putting on a show for his sister and niece. Not to mention all the lies he's told us already."

"I'll give you that. He's up to something, but you've brought him into the station and all but accused him of killing three, no, six men, so maybe he's pissed and reacting."

"My interview I did was published and we've gotten no response. Why didn't he react to that? It doesn't make sense."

"Have you considered it might not be Stuart?"

I looked into Kyle's eyes and then to my fish, Louie. "No." I stood up, walked over to Louie and greeted him. "Sorry I haven't been around much. I say that a lot, don't I?" I dropped a few pellets into his fish home. Louie didn't really ask for much. He wasn't the talkative type, and that worked for me. Low-maintenance pets were best for detectives.

Kyle walked into the kitchen while I moved pillows around on my leather couch and got comfortable again. He removed a small tray of cold meats, cheeses, and olives from the refrigerator. He opened a box of crackers and laid them out on the tray. He walked back to the couch and set it on the trunk. "Best I could do with limited time."

I grabbed a piece of prosciutto and mozzarella and took a bite. The salty, creamy taste and texture hit my tongue and made me groan. Prosciutto and mozzarella together were one of my favorite treats. "You hit the mark perfectly." I popped an olive into my mouth. "Calloway and I had a little spat in the kitchen tonight."

"I was there."

"Only for the back end of it. She wants to bring Stuart in for analysis."

"I think that's a good idea."

"I was all for that in the beginning, but now I'm not so sure."

"What changed?"

"Stuart's sister didn't succeed in rehab. She goes on benders, and from what I saw earlier, she's nursing some pretty serious hangovers. Emily's barely home, and that's probably because her mother's a drunk and her uncle's a freak. Stuart can put on an act for them, and while his sister's passed out and his niece is gone, he could be out doing whatever the hell he wants."

"Like murdering alleged sexual assaulters?"

"Yes."

"Then you should get him in front of Calloway. She's known for breaking cases wide open with her analysis."

"I'm close, Kyle. I can feel it."

"What you feel is him reacting to your actions. You're just pushing his buttons. You don't have anything solid to pin him to the murders." He ate an olive. "I know where you're going and why you feel the way you do, but you have to let other people take part in this investigation. You're not going to close this on your own."

"She hasn't contributed a lot yet. Everything she told us was either an educated guess or something I could have found through Google."

"Psychology is a complicated science."

"And we don't have time for complicated science. We need to do something to get this guy to react. To draw him out of hiding."

"Actions have consequences."

I rolled my eyes. "Gee, thanks for filling me in on that, Dad. I would've never known." I popped another olive into my mouth.

"How is pushing Stuart going to get you evidence of his involvement? Are you shooting for another murder? If this guy is the killer, wouldn't bringing him in and letting Calloway yank his chain have the same effect?"

I gritted my teeth. He was right, and it annoyed me.

"I'm not your enemy. I'm just trying to help you see things clearly."

I sighed.

He smiled. "You want to get him yourself. That's it, isn't it? You want to catch this guy in the act."

"Yes, I do, and I'm going to figure out a way to make that happen."

Johnson showed up at the department the next morning.

"Where've you been?" I asked.

He'd brought me a cup of coffee. "Just cream, no sugar. I think that's what you get."

"What are you, a mind reader?"

"Heard Bishop say it before I went back to Birmingham."

"Uncover anything that can break the case for us?"

"We went back and reanalyzed the scenes, but it's been so long, we couldn't find anything."

I wasn't sure why he'd do that. A crime scene can change in a matter of days, let alone a matter of years.

"We also went through all the news articles from then and now, ran everything through the system again, and got nothing. My leads are cold. We need something from your investigation that will tie the murderer to my cases."

"We'll get it."

Michels walked into the kitchen and pointed at his watch. "Clock's ticking, people."

We headed to the investigation room.

We were days into the investigation with limited information and, admittedly, a sorry excuse for a suspect. Half the department sided with Bishop, and the other half with me, on whether Stuart was our guy.

"They're taking bets," Michels said. "Odds are in Ryder's favor."

I slammed my hand on the table. "There you go!" I took the last Boston cream donut and for my snide remark, Bishop snatched it from my plate and stuffed most of it into his mouth.

"On the lips and straight to the hips, or in your case, belly," I said.

"Oh, day-um," Michels said.

Bubba laughed. "Be nice to Ryder. She's got some big balls."

"She's not as tough as she seems," Bishop said. He had cream in the cracks of his lips, so I tossed him a napkin.

"She's a smart one," Johnson said.

Jimmy walked in, set his things down, and said, "Break for fifteen. Detective Ryder, my office. Now."

Michels whispered, "Oh, day-um," very quietly. That time it didn't get a remark from Bubba.

I had to jog to keep up with Jimmy. I followed him across the pit and to his office, where he waited for me to enter, then slammed the door shut behind us.

"You're good at pissing people off, aren't you?"

I had a choice to make. I could either make a snarky comment, at which I excelled, or tuck my tail between my legs and take his verbal beating. "I hear it's one of my strong points."

His nostrils flared. "Dammit, Ryder."

I probably made the wrong choice.

"Stop wearing your ass on your shoulder when it comes to Calloway."

"My ass isn't on my shoulder."

"I'm serious. You don't have to like her to work with her. Get over it."

"I don't dislike her. I just don't see her bringing much value to the investigation." Tension balled up in my gut. "I can't believe she came to you and complained. Talk about wearing your ass on your shoulder."

"She's concerned you're going renegade on this case, and I don't disagree with her."

"I'm just doing my job."

"We need Calloway. She knows what she's doing, and she has an excellent track record. I'm overriding your decision. She's interviewing Stuart."

"Fine."

Jimmy blinked. I don't think I'd ever acquiesced that quickly, but I knew it was a battle I wouldn't win.

"'Fine'? That's it? No snide remark?"

"No, sir. Just 'fine.'"

He raised his left eyebrow and shook his head. "You're up to something."

I couldn't help but smile. "I'd like to be in the interview."

"If you promise to let her do her thing."

"I'll do my best."

"Ryder, you're excellent at what you do, but even great detectives need help sometimes."

"Yes, sir."

He furrowed his brow. "Dammit. If you do something, anything, to mess this up, I'm pulling you off the case. Understand? I've already had to beg the mayor to not pull rank. Don't mess this up, Ryder."

"Yes, sir."

He shook his head. "I mean it." He walked over to the door and opened it. "After you."

I filled the group in on what happened the night before.

Bishop's eyes widened. "Was that your idea? Why the hell didn't you tell me?"

"Because she wanted to do it alone," Michels said.

"You're going to get yourself killed one of these days."

Jimmy coughed. "Let me handle the reprimands." He looked at me. "You held surveillance on the suspect without alerting anyone on the team?"

"At least we are calling him a suspect now," I said.

Jimmy ignored that.

"Isn't this guy a little—I'm trying to find the PC way to say it..." Johnson said. "Challenged?"

"He likes to give that impression, but I think it's an act."

"Michels, what's the status on the missing kid in Alpharetta?" Jimmy asked.

"Mother's still freaking out, and we've got a BOLO on his vehicle, but that's about it." He smiled. "Good news is we haven't had another fire, so he's probably not part of this."

"I did a little searching," Bubba added. "With the Alpharetta IT guy, of course, and we found a lot on his social media to suspect him of assault. If the killer is going for four in the area, he's got the guy."

"Our killer works in threes," Johnson said. "He's not going to kill again. It's against character."

"Sometimes character changes," I said.

The door opened and Nikki walked in. She handed me a note. "It's game time."

28

The note appeared to be printed on the same paper, the kind you could find at Walmart or any office supply store, but instead of a crossword puzzle, it was an actual computer-created note.

"He's not happy," Bishop said.

"Good," I replied. "That's what we want. Make him mad, he'll make mistakes, and then we'll catch him."

The note was short and terse.

Detective Ryder,
Angering me does not give you control. It gives me power.
Actions have consequences.

Jimmy read the note out loud. "We need to get this to Calloway and get Stuart in now." He looked at me. "You shouldn't have done that interview. If someone else dies, you're off the case."

The room went silent as Jimmy charged out.

Thirty minutes later Bishop and I knocked on Chip Stuart's door.

Emily Bryant answered. "Did you find the killer?"

"Emily," I said calmly. "We're here for your uncle. Is he home?"

Her shoulders slumped. "My uncle's weird, but he's not a killer."

"Is he home?" I asked again.

Her bottom lip trembled. "He's getting ready for a doctor appointment.

I'm supposed to take him." She checked her Apple Watch. "We have to leave in ten minutes."

Her mother walked into the room. "Who the hell is ringing the—" She stopped whining when she saw us outside. "Oh. What's going on?"

"They want to talk to Uncle Chip."

"Then go get him."

"We have to leave for the doctor."

"Your uncle won't be going to the doctor today," Bishop said.

"He's under arrest?" Lisa Bryant asked.

"We have some things to discuss at the station."

"Oh hell, come in. I don't want the neighbors getting wind of this. They already think we're trash. Em, go get your uncle. I'm sure he knows they're here. We don't want him sneaking out his window."

I glanced at Bishop. "Is his room on the first floor?" I asked Lisa Bryant.

"No, but it's on the roof line, and he's done it before. This was my parents' house. He used to climb through the window to sneak out as a kid. I did it too."

Duly noted.

Legally, once invited into a home, an officer can use anything within eyesight in a case. We can't touch anything unless given approval by the owner, but we didn't need to touch anything to see what we saw.

"Ms. Bryant, your brother says you're a crafter. I see your things. I do a little crafting too," I lied. "What are you making now?"

"I was, but I haven't done it in years. Don't know why that stuff's out. Emily must have done something with it while I was in re—on vacation."

I noticed an iPad on the coffee table. "I have an iPad, but it's an old one. Which one is that?"

She shrugged. "It's Stuart's. He broke his laptop a while ago and bought this at a garage sale."

Lisa Bryant wasn't winning any sister—or mother, for that matter—of the year awards anytime soon.

Chip Stuart walked out. "Am I under arrest?" His personality was in naive, impaired mode. "I don't understand."

"You're just coming in for questioning," I said.

"Again?"

"Yes, again," Bishop said.

"I need to make a call first." He walked into the kitchen without saying another word.

"You should have brought him in yesterday," Calloway said. "He might have talked to me before he lawyered up."

"He tried to lawyer up when we brought him in before. That's what guilty people do."

"How the hell could he afford an attorney anyway?" Bishop asked. "We saw his account. His disability makes him poverty level, if even."

Johnson paced the room. "Any other known relatives?"

"Parents are dead," I said.

"He's only got the one sister," Bishop said.

"And you said he doesn't really have friends?" Johnson asked.

"Wait," I said. "What about someone at his old job? Maybe someone from there called him and gave him a heads-up about us coming there, and they offered to help? Could he be calling in a favor?"

"Owner said his employees come first. Could have meant his ex-employees too," Bishop said.

Michels took lead on that. "Text me the address. I'll go have a talk with the employees. I love this stuff."

The front desk officer buzzed on the landline. "The lawyer is ready to see you."

Jimmy gave us—well, mostly me—a strict warning: Behave or be off the case.

Bishop and I walked into the interrogation room while Jimmy, Johnson, and Calloway stayed behind the glass and listened. Calloway complained about not being in the room, but the rest of us agreed it could potentially harm our case to have a forensic psychologist in with the lawyer. Besides, once she introduced herself, the lawyer would have walked out with his client anyway.

"Detectives, my client is a disabled, low-functioning TBI sufferer who feels he's being harassed by your department."

"We're investigating a triple murder with ties to a triple murder in Birmingham. I wouldn't call that harassing."

"Is he under arrest for those crimes?" He had me and he knew it.

"No. We just have some questions for him."

He smiled. "My client has expressed his disinterest in answering any more questions."

"Mr.—I'm sorry, did you say your last name?"

"Not to you," he said. "Only to your officer up front. It's Shelby."

"Thank you. Mr. Shelby, have you advised your client that when the police want to ask questions and a person refuses, it only makes them look guilty?"

"You have no evidence to support your cause for questioning. Mr. Stuart has already answered questions, willingly, as a matter of fact. As it stands now, we are determining if legal action for harassment is appropriate."

"Very well. May I ask you a question instead?"

"That depends."

"How did Mr. Stuart pay you for your time?"

"I think we've heard enough," he said. He and Stuart stood and headed toward the door.

Jimmy opened the door as they stood. "Fire at Wills Park in Alpharetta."

Stuart turned to me, shaped his thumb and finger into a gun, and pretended to shoot.

29

Jimmy pulled us back before we even made it to our vehicle. "They didn't find a body."

Bishop and I shared a look.

"Thank God," he said.

"Just more reason to believe it's Stuart," I said. "He couldn't have started a fire and left a body while we had him."

Jimmy held the door open as we walked in. "My office now."

Calloway sat in front of Jimmy's desk, and she didn't bother turning to greet us when we walked in.

"You should have let Calloway interview him when she asked," Jimmy said. He sat at his desk and leaned toward Calloway. "We wouldn't be in the situation we're in now."

"He would've lawyered up then too, and you know it," I said. "It wasn't about the timing. He'd already paid that attorney, and he was just waiting for the call."

Calloway nodded. "I have to agree with Detective Ryder. His actions were calculated and meticulous. Both suggest type-A personalities and above-average intelligence."

"Or he has OCD," Bishop said.

"Many highly intelligent people, as well as geniuses, have OCD in some shape or form."

"We have nothing on him," Jimmy said. "And we can't move forward without any real evidence."

"We need to watch him again," I said."

"Michels already has, and so have you. He's done nothing."

"Because he knows we're watching. We need to make him think we've given up on him. If he thinks we're done, he'll take action."

"Your detective is right," Calloway said.

I was beginning to like her.

"Letting the killer think the investigation is over will cause him to act."

"What are you suggesting?" Jimmy asked.

"We can't lie to the community," Bishop said.

"I'm not suggesting we lie," Calloway said. "I'm suggesting we let things lie."

"You mean stop the investigation?" Bishop asked.

"Of course not. We just let him think it. We must be careful and not let him see us."

"It's been five days," I said. "We have nothing. The investigation is colder than Jacob Ramsey lying in that morgue. Even pretending to stop investigating will slow things down. We can't afford that kind of delay."

Calloway's cell phone rang. She glanced at the screen and said, "Excuse me for a moment," then walked out of the room.

"We can't act like we aren't investigating," I said.

"Agreed."

I bit my bottom lip as a plan developed in my brain. "When all else fails, surveillance."

Bishop sighed. "I knew you were going to say that. We've already done that twice. He's expecting that."

"I know, but he's not expecting an internet truck parked on his street with people working outside and at the neighbor's house."

"Jimmy won't approve that expense."

"I know, but I know a guy."

"I pulled a few strings and got you what you need, but Hamby's on the hook for gas," Kyle said.

We were in Jimmy's office discussing our next steps.

I looked at Calloway. "It's two birds, one stone. We give the impression we aren't investigating, but we've still got eyes on Stuart."

Jimmy looked in her direction. "Any thoughts?"

"I think it's an excellent plan, but I'd like to suggest the detectives significantly change their appearance so they're not recognized."

"That's part of the plan," Bishop said.

Jimmy nodded. "We'll cover gas, and I'll see if we've got anything in the budget to pay these guys for their time."

Kyle smiled. "They're doing it pro bono. This stuff is easy for them."

"We'll see about that," I said. I checked my watch. "You said five thirty, correct?"

Kyle nodded. "Give or take."

I stood. "Then we need to get ready."

Michels and Bishop followed me to the locker rooms, where Savannah and a gorgeous woman with long black hair and a curvaceous figure waited. Michels tripped over himself when he saw the woman. His hands hit the ground right before his head.

Bishop busted out laughing. "Suave."

I laughed too. "Nice move there, Romeo."

He swiped his hands and then dusted off his knees. The woman either didn't notice or was so used to it—that got my vote—she didn't even flinch, and she'd turned toward us at the very moment he'd laid eyes on her and went down. Michels would be grateful for that.

Savannah turned around and smiled. "Hey, y'all! Who wants to go first?"

The setup was impressive for last minute. When I texted Sav for help with our disguises, she called her stylist, and they'd moved fast. Two folding tables were brought into the locker rooms, and each had an assortment of hairpieces, makeup, and facial hairpieces among other things. They'd even brought clothes for us. I had no idea where those came from or how they got the men's measurements.

"I'll volunteer," Michels said.

Bishop chuckled. "I bet you will."

"Okay," Savannah said. "This is Ansley, my stylist. And by stylist, I mean hair, makeup, clothing, everything. She moved here from Hollywood a few years ago where she worked for a production company doing makeup and costumes. Trust me, the woman is a goddess and a genius."

We each introduced ourselves, and Ansley smiled at Michels, then eyed him carefully. "Hmm. I think you'd look great with some facial hair." She crooked her finger. "Come on over, Detective Michels, and we'll get you all prettied up."

He nearly tripped over his feet again as he ran the few steps to the chair.

Bishop cleared his throat.

Savannah walked over to me with a toothy grin plastered on her face.

My shoulders curled inward, and I stepped back, shielding myself behind Bishop.

Bishop laughed. "You can't hide from her."

"No, she can't," Savannah said. "And I've been waiting for this day since the day we met."

"Help" squeaked out of my throat without any effort from me.

Bishop moved to the side. "She's all yours."

Two hours later they let us see ourselves. We'd been sworn to secrecy regarding our appearance, and when we laid eyes on the new us, we were in awe.

"Dayum, Ryder, you look hot," Michels said. He tried to recover quickly. "—er. Hotter."

"Nice try," Bishop said. "What about me?"

We turned to him and laughed. Ansley said Bishop's aura—she was into all that stuff—felt like Santa, and she'd done a great rendition of Mr. Claus on my partner. She'd worked her magic on his face, adding bushy white eyebrows, a full though short white beard, and topped his hair with a white wig. The hair barely passed his ears and the back looked like it needed a good trim. His clothes were something you'd imagine Santa to wear in the off-season, even though it was his month. Dark jean overalls with a plaid shirt and cowboy boots. He wasn't prepped for anyone to sit on his lap, but he was a perfect fit for the community where Stuart lived.

"What am I supposed to do dressed like this?" he asked.

Kyle laughed. When he finished, he spoke. "You're going to be the new neighbor two doors down across the street. The house sold recently, and new owners moved in, but they haven't seen any of the neighbors yet. You'll be outside walking your dog and interacting with the internet company for your system." He gave me a once-over and pressed his lips together.

"Go ahead," I said. "You can laugh."

So he did. "I'm sorry, I just never expected to see you like this."

"You and me both," I said.

Savannah clapped. "I love it! This is the perfect Halloween costume for next year. I think you look great!"

I stared at myself in the mirror again. "'Great'? You call this 'great'?" I turned around and glared at my best friend. "I look like a dude!"

Bishop covered his mouth, but it didn't hide his laughter. "Not an attractive one, if that's any consolation."

I narrowed my eyes at him. "It's not."

He flinched.

Savannah wrapped her arm around my shoulder. "This was Kyle's suggestion. Talk to him about it."

I flipped around and scowled at Kyle. "You did this to me?" I gazed down at my dark work uniform, then touched my short blond mustache. "Why would you do this to me?"

Kyle's lip twitched. "Stuart's seen you several times. If he got a good look at a female Xfinity worker, he could recognize you. You can't afford that."

I hated that he was right. "You're correct, dammit."

Bishop laughed. "I think you look good. The bald look is good on you."

I whipped a hairbrush at him. It bounced off his fake belly and fell onto the floor.

"Ho, ho, ho," he said.

Michels laughed and then asked, "Can we talk about me for a sec? I mean, look at my shoulders. I'm massive."

He was, and it was hilarious. Ansley gave him broad shoulders, added some chest muscle, dressed his head with a dark black wig slicked back into a ponytail. She added a matching mustache, darker eyebrows, and a five-o'clock shadow. She created a scar over his left eye. "You look like an ex-con. It's perfect."

"My guys are ready to go," Kyle said. He smiled at me and tried not to laugh. "You ready?"

"Ready as I'll ever be."

"Let's do this," Bishop said.

"Let's catch ourselves a serial killer," Michels said. He added a grunt to the end.

30

We arrived at the neighbor's house. Three men dressed for the part dug holes in the neighbor's yard. Two other men stood at the front door waiting for Bishop to enter through the back of the house and answer. One man was marking lines through the lot, and another was writing down what he said. Three others were in two vans. There were a total of three vans, including the one we'd driven in.

"Whoa, when you said you had a few guys willing to help us, I thought you meant two or three."

"Originally it was a few guys, but word got out, and a few became ten."

I nodded. "And they all know the plan?"

"Yup."

"Okay, then, let's get this ball rolling."

Michels hopped out. "This will be awesome."

I laughed. I hoped it was awesome enough to catch Chip Stuart doing something related to the murders. I waited for him to get to his designated spot and then discussed the plan again with Kyle. "You're heading communication. I'll be managing the team outside with Michels' help, and Bishop will be the customer."

"Are you confirming or reiterating?"

"Yes."

He smiled. "This ain't our first rodeo, Rachel. We've got this."

I breathed in deeply and then exhaled slowly. "If you see any movement, you'll let me know."

"Yes, now go."

I left the vehicle and got to work.

The buzz on the street brought out two neighbors. One complained we were disrupting his cable access, which was impossible since we weren't actually doing anything, and the other wanted to know if he could switch services. I explained he'd have to go through customer service for that. I didn't want him calling customer service, so I explained they'd be having a sale in a week, and it was best to wait until then to make the call. He was so appreciative, he took my—fake—name to tell the customer service people how great I was.

We spent hours doing a whole lot of nothing, dealing with neighbors who were upset we had to work after hours, and alternating vehicles coming and going throughout the area.

It was after nine o'clock, and neither Emily nor her mother were home. The TV glowed through the front window, and I'd caught a few glimpses of Chip Stuart moving around the room.

When the TV clicked off, I got on the mic and said, "It's go time."

"Suspect is exiting through the back door," someone on the mic said. "We've got eyes on him. Heading east."

I ran to the unmarked handicapped van down the street, climbed out of my uniform, and stuffed it in the back of the van. I'd worn a pair of baggy jeans and a sweatshirt underneath the uniform. "Thank God," I said to Bishop.

He'd just jumped into the passenger seat. "I thought I was driving?"

"Not this time, partner."

"Great. We're all going to die."

I laughed.

"Suspect is driving a black late-nineties Toyota. License plate Charles, Pappa, Indigo, four, four, seven."

"Charles, Pappa, Indigo, four, four, seven," I repeated.

"Heading north on Chesterville Road."

I whipped the van to the left and jerked Bishop toward his door. "Slow down. You get too close to him and we're done."

I let my foot off the gas.

"Detective, we've got a drone on the vehicle. You can maintain adequate distance," someone said into my ear.

"They've got a drone on him?" Bishop asked. "We need more advanced equipment."

"They're ridding the world of the drugs. They need drones."

"Point made."

We drove out of Hamby and up Georgia 400 toward Dahlonega. "Where the hell is he going?" I asked.

"Don't think it's his church group," Bishop said.

"Copy that," I replied.

Stuart exited 400 heading east on Exit 17. He drove for two miles, then turned left on a side road.

Kyle spoke in our ears. "Pause follow."

"What? Why?" I asked.

"Drone went up ahead three miles. There's a warehouse with a 'for sale' sign out front. Lot is empty other than a dumpster."

Bishop responded with, "Ten-four."

I pulled off the road and parked behind a small strip mall including a bait-and-tackle store that sold homemade biscuits and gravy. I'd never understand how someone could eat breakfast in a store full of worms.

"This is the shitty part," Bishop said.

"We'll get him. We just need to be patient."

"When have you ever been patient?" he asked.

"I'm starting now. I want this guy with every fiber of my being."

"Copy that."

"We're attempting to position the drone near a window, but so far all of the windows are too stained and discolored for a visual," Kyle said.

"Wouldn't he see it anyway?" Bishop asked.

"Not this one. It's the size of a hummingbird."

"We really need that technology," Bishop whispered.

"How many drones are there?" I asked.

"Two. The one that followed, and now the one the second van sent a few minutes ago. The first one is too big and would be easily seen."

Another agent spoke. "He's on the move."

"Get someone inside that warehouse," Bishop said. "Now!"

31

I drove back to Browns Bridge Road, pulled into a gas station, and waited. When Stuart's vehicle passed, I followed three vehicles behind. He turned left two streets ahead. The road was dark, and there were only boat storage facilities located on just one side. I stayed back.

"Drone is on him," Kyle said. "Road ends less than two miles ahead."

Two minutes later, we moved.

"He's out of the vehicle. Black boat storage one mile up. It's got a red garage. He pulled up on that side and drove around to the back. A gray windowless van with no tag is parked on the right side of a windowless garage door. There are three windows back there. We've got the drone on them, but view isn't clear," Kyle said.

"Something's covering the windows, sir. I can't get a good angle," the drone operator said. "Wait, the door is— Holy shit! He's got someone with him!"

I kicked the van into drive. "Headed there now."

"He's not moving toward his vehicle. He's headed toward the gray van."

"Can you see who's with him?" I asked.

"Yes. He's naked. Has a bag over his head and is bound at the hands and feet."

I glanced at Bishop. "He's moving him?"

"He may be onto us. Stay back."

I pulled into a storage lot, shut off the lights, and waited. "If he's got his next victim, he's moving him. Keep on him. See if you can get any identifying markings off his victim."

"He's naked," Kyle said. "I'm pretty sure that's identifiable enough right now."

Bishop laughed.

"Shut it," I said.

"Yes, ma'am," Kyle said.

"No, that was for Bishop."

Bishop laughed again. I shot him a death glare, and he held up his hands in mock defense.

We watched Stuart pass and turn into the next storage facility. He pulled behind the building. I searched for the drone but couldn't see it.

"We'll send the drone in with him if we can," Kyle said.

"Ten-four," I replied.

"Stay here," Bishop said. "We don't want to scare him off."

"He's got a naked male with him. He's going to kill him. We can't just sit here and wait to see what happens."

"Drone is in—move! Move! Move!"

Bishop and I jumped out of the van and ran to the storage facility. I pushed in front of him and made it to the back entrance a few seconds before him.

"Wait for us," Kyle said.

I saw the lights before he finished that sentence. "You're here. I'm going in."

Bishop finally caught up. I carefully tried the door, but it was locked. "Shit!"

"Over there," he said. "Another door."

We sprinted to it, our guns out and ready to fire. That door was locked also. "Dammit, we need to get in there. What's the status?" I asked on the mic.

"It's a torture chamber," the drone handler replied. "I'm looking for additional entrances."

"We need in," I said. I couldn't shoot off the lock. He couldn't be alerted because we had no idea how fast he could or would act. "Get us in there now!"

"There's an open window at the front on the south side of the building. It's big enough for Detective Ryder only."

Bishop looked at me. "You can't go in there without backup."

"Like hell I can't." I headed toward the south side of the building. Bishop followed. "The drone will watch me. The handler will let you know when to enter."

We froze when we heard a man scream.

"I'm going in," I said.

"She's right," Kyle said. "We've got everyone close by. We'll all enter when it's clear."

Bishop grabbed my shoulders and looked me in the eyes. I'd never seen so much concern from him before. "Be careful."

I swallowed hard. "Will do, partner." I climbed through the window and carefully dropped to the ground. I couldn't see Stuart or his victim, but I could hear them.

Stuart was singing something that sounded like a nursery rhyme. *"One, two, three, you can't pin on me. Seven, eight, nine, I'll add to my crimes. Four, five, six, add to the mix."*

I stepped quietly behind a large boat. I still didn't have a view on the men.

"I have you in my sight," the drone handler said. "He's in the center of the storage facility. You can't miss him. Move two boats up, then three boats to your left. They're smaller. Be careful. If you make any sound, he might be able to hear, and if he looks, he'll see you. Nod once if you understand."

I was grateful for my Doc Martens. They were soft on the ground and made no noise. I nodded once.

"Acknowledgment received."

I followed the handler's directions perfectly. My breath hitched in my throat when I saw the equipment. I'd never seen anything like it. Chains with cuffs, saws, knives, knuckle-breaking hammers, a body stretcher, and a barrel filled with what I thought was water, and that was only part of it. Two large curtains hid the rest from view, but I could see them under the bottom of the curtains, and some of the items looked similar.

"We've got the building surrounded," Kyle said. "On your word."

Stuart sung his rhyme again. *"One, two, three, you can't pin on me. Seven, eight, nine, I'll add to my crimes. Four, five, six, add to the mix."* He'd tied the victim to metal cuffs on a large upright wooden board supported by ten-by-fours pushed at an angle into portable steps up to a boat. "All sinners must pay for their crimes. It is the duty of the Mastermind. Justice shall be served." He removed the bag from the victim's head.

Brian Miller. The bastard had Brian Miller. "It's Miller," I said quietly.

Stuart turned my direction. I stepped up onto the rim of another set of portable stairs on the side of the boat I hid behind.

"Detective Ryder, is that you?" Stuart asked.

I exhaled and slowly peeked around the boat. He had turned back to his victim. I kept my gun out and moved into the center of the warehouse, a few feet away from him. "Good guess, Stuart. Now turn around slowly and put your hands in the air."

Stuart turned slowly; his face distorted into a demented scowl of what I could only describe as pure evil. He held up a sharp hunting knife in his hand and smiled. "My father was a hunter. He used to take me deer hunting up in Ellijay. We'd spend hours out there, waiting and watching. I'm very good at waiting and watching."

"Put down the knife."

Brian Miller sobbed. We made eye contact. I hoped he knew he was safe, that we would keep him from anything more. His body was bruised and beaten with slices in several places, not at all Stuart's MO.

I flicked my head toward Miller. "You switched things up, but at least he's not dead."

"Yet," he said.

Just then, the entire metal-and-aluminum building shook. The rushed sound of feet hitting the ground blasted toward us, and the crowd of law enforcement soon followed.

I kept my gun aimed at Stuart. "Drop the knife, dammit!"

He watched the men aim their guns directly at him. "Call off your men, and I'll tell you everything. I'll even go willingly."

"What's there to tell? You killed six men."

"One, two, three, you can't pin on me. Seven, eight, nine, I'll add to my crimes. Four, five, six, add to the mix." He smiled.

"What does that mean? Tell me what that means!"

One, two, three, you can't pin on me. Seven, eight, nine, I'll add to my crimes. Four, five, six, add to the mix. "Are you trying to tell me you didn't kill all six victims?"

"Call off your men. I know you're a good shot, so you'll need to put down your gun. I'll gladly tell you everything. I can't wait to make it into the news. Can you imagine the notoriety, the attention? I'll never be forgotten. They'll write books about me. I'll finally have the attention I deserve instead of being invisible, being thought a headcase. Call off your men."

There was no way in hell I'd give him a chance for any of that, but I needed him to talk, and I had to figure out what to do to make that happen. "Stand down," I yelled. I narrowed my eyes at Stuart. "Drop the knife."

"It takes two, Detective Ryder. You put down your weapon, and I'll put down my knife. Your victims are mine, and if you'll put down your weapon first, I'll tell you all about them, and all about what happened to the men in Alabama."

"I know what happened. Now drop the damn knife!"

"Tit for tat," he said. His voice was calm. He smiled. "Put the gun down, Detective."

I steadied my gun at him. "It doesn't work that way, Stuart."

"Either way, I lose, don't I? If I don't put down the knife, you'll shoot me. If I do, I'll get the chair. Do you think any of that matters? I've succeeded. I've finished my assignment, and I will be forever remembered. The rest is gravy. Of course, while I'd like to continue with this man, I see it won't be that way." He twitched and suddenly the knife changed directions. Before I had a chance to react—it was less than seconds—he stabbed himself in the gut. He smiled as he twisted the knife back and forth inside him, then as he fell to the ground, said, *"One, two, three, you can't pin on me. Seven, eight, nine, I'll add to my crimes. Four, five, six, add to the mix."*

"Son of a bitch!" I rushed toward him. "I need something to stop the bleeding!"

Bishop and Kyle rushed over. Kyle ripped off his jacket and stuck it near my hands. It wasn't enough. I took off my sweatshirt and pressed it into the wound. "You son of a bitch! Why did you do this?"

His eyes rolled backward. "Lisa." He gasped and a gurgling sound escaped his throat. "I did it for—"

I turned toward Kyle. "Hold this!"

Stuart raised his right hand and grabbed my wrist. I moved closer to his face. "I'm not—"

"What about Lisa?"

"I'm not—" His throat gurgled again, and blood seeped out of his mouth. "I'm not—" His mouth froze.

"Dammit, Stuart! Don't you die on me!" I checked his pulse. Nothing. I pressed my hands onto his chest and pumped. "Don't you fucking die on me!" I pushed and pumped, checking his wrist every few pushes until Kyle pulled me off.

"Rachel, he's gone." He wiped the sweat off my face. "You can't bring him back."

I wiped my mouth. I tasted blood, but it wasn't mine.

"Someone get her some water," Kyle yelled.

"I don't need water," I said. "I need him alive!"

Bishop crouched down and placed his hand on my knee. "He's not going to tell us anything now. Come on, we've got a living victim to take care of."

32

Other than some minor knife wounds and serious bruises, Brian Miller was okay. The doctor chose to admit him but allowed us—against his better judgment—to talk with him.

I removed the wig and changed out of my bloody clothes before we did. Bishop did the same. The last thing Miller needed was a reminder of what happened in that boat storage facility.

I smiled at Stephanie Miller sitting in the seat next to her son. "Thank you," she said.

"It was a team effort." I smiled at her son. "Brian Miller," I said. "I'm Detective Rachel Ryder, and this is my partner, Rob Bishop. We'd like to talk to you about what happened. Are you up for a brief conversation?"

"You're the one that tried to save him."

"Yes."

"I recognize your eyes."

"The rest of me was undercover, but nice job on the recognition. Can you tell me what happened? How you came to be in that facility?"

"I don't know exactly. I was at…" He closed his eyes, breathed in and out, and then said, "I was at Charlie's, a bar in Atlanta. He came up to me and told me he had my mother, and if I didn't go with him, he'd kill her. I laughed it off, I mean, that doesn't happen, you know? But he showed me a picture of her in the place he'd kept me. At first, I thought the photo was fake, but it looked so real, and when he played the recording of her voice, I knew it was her."

"So, you went with him." I looked at his mother. Tears fell down her cheeks.

He nodded. "But it wasn't my mom. It wasn't anyone. He tripped me, and he knocked me out with something to the back of my head. When I woke up, I was in another building, naked, with a bag over my head. I don't know how long I was there."

"You were missing for several days, honey," his mother said. "But you're safe now."

Brian Miller finished his story.

"Did he give you any reason as to why he abducted you?" Bishop asked.

"He said something about a girl he thinks I assaulted, but I didn't, I swear."

I looked at his mother. She mouthed, *I think he did.*

I nodded once.

"He said he killed the others, and that he was going to do to me what he did to them, but worse." He paused and caught his breath. "Then he beat me."

The doctor walked in. "Time's up."

I smiled at Miller. "Thank you. We'll be in touch soon."

Even though Chip Stuart was a serial killer, there was no joy in delivering his death notice to his sister. Regardless of how she might have felt about him, he was her blood, and even serial killers had loved ones.

It was a tough meeting, because we also needed to know why Stuart said her name when I asked why he did what he did.

She cried when we told her he was dead, and she cried harder when we told her it was by his own hand. "He used to be such a good person. He was a little odd, but he always was. I just can't understand why he'd do this."

"Before he...he passed, he said your name. Do you have any idea why he'd do that?"

She gasped. "He...he said my name?" She cried even harder. "Oh my God! I can't believe he did that for me!"

We waited while she sobbed. When she finished, Bishop asked her. "Can you tell me what you mean?"

She straightened her shoulders and lifted her chin. She was trying to be brave, and I felt sorry for her. "I was raped in college. I never told anyone but my brother. He swore one day he'd take care of the person who raped me, but he was killed a year later in a drunk-driving accident."

"Did you report this to the police?"

She shook her head. "I'd gone with him willingly. I didn't think he'd be arrested. Besides, he was a football player. Who was going to believe some mousy college freshman over a football player?"

"Was that Rylan Pastore?" Bishop asked.

She nodded. "Best defense at UGA."

I glanced at Bishop. "He was a top pick for the NFL. Killed in a head-on collision two days before the draft."

"He didn't deserve that kind of success. I'm not sorry he's dead. I started drinking after he raped me." She looked straight into my eyes. "I'm in recovery now. I've been clean for twenty-four hours."

"One day at a time," Bishop said.

"Yes."

"Did your brother ever mention anything about the person who raped you again?" He asked.

"At first he did. He was angry. I've never seen him so angry, but after a while, he never mentioned it again." She buried her head into her hands. "I can't believe he did this. He killed all those men."

"Ms. Bryant, we're going to need his things. We've got officers ready to come and get them. Are you okay with being here?" Bishop asked.

"Why do you need his things?"

"We need to see if we can find anything about any of the murders. It's procedure," he said.

She nodded. "Oh, okay. I... That's fine. I need to make some calls."

Bishop requested Michels and the team. "They're on their way."

We didn't stick around.

Detectives Johnson and Anderson arrived in the early morning hours of the next day. They thanked us for working with them, and for solving their murders. Bishop was proud of me for telling them it was a team effort and not including that they weren't part of that team. Which obviously, I wanted to do. Their efforts were adequate at best, but we had a win, and really, that was all that mattered.

One, two, three, you can't pin me. Seven, eight, nine, I'll add to my crimes. Four, five, six, add to the mix. I couldn't get that out of my head.

Bishop and I sat in his cubby, winding down from the hell we'd just survived. "What do you think Stuart meant by *One, two, three, you can't pin on me. Seven, eight, nine, I'll add to my crimes. Four, five, six, add to the mix*?"

"Like Kyle said, he wanted to trip us up one last time. We can't prove those were his kills because that's not our jurisdiction. He's telling you that. You don't get to solve those in his eyes. It was his MO, Ryder. Just let it go. We got the guy and he admitted to the murders. Don't let him screw with your head."

I wasn't sure I could do that, let it go.

Bishop's department line rang. He hit the speaker button to answer. "Detective Bishop."

"Detective Bishop, this is Scott Baker."

Bishop and I made eye contact. He tilted his head to the side with a *what the hell?* expression on his face. "Baker? What do you want?"

"To commend you and the rest of the department for good work. Obviously, I would have liked to thank Mr. Stuart personally for his efforts, but I understand the logistics of the law and that it is no longer possible."

Bishop's eyes widened. "That was quick. We just—"

Baker cut him off. "I pay attention," he said, and then disconnected the call.

"What the hell was that?"

"Baker paid Stuart's attorney fees. That's got to be it."

"The man's an asshole," Bishop said.

"Can't deny that."

33

Soft jazz played as I walked into my townhome. The smell of garlic and onions kidnapped my nose and sent me straight to the kitchen.

Kyle stood in front of the stove stirring something and scooping it over two chicken breasts. "There's a glass of wine on the counter."

It was two days after everything went down. The mayor awarded the department with certificates of heroism, and the media ran with it. We'd saved the world from a serial killer, made it safe once again, he said. It was a lot of hoopla for just doing our jobs.

I sipped the wine and leaned against the counter. "That smells amazing."

"Garlic chicken with asparagus spears roasting in the oven."

"Sounds like heaven." I took another sip of wine. "Do I have time to shower? I'd like to get the department stench off me."

He lowered the heat on the stove. "Plenty of time."

"Perfect," I said, and headed toward my bedroom. I turned on the shower, flicked off the bathroom light, and undressed next to my bed. As I walked back into the bathroom, I flipped on the light on my dresser and left the bathroom door open.

As I'd hoped, Kyle walked in and closed the door behind him.

"Sweet baby Jesus, this place smells worse than Scarlet's diaper after she eats sweet potatoes." Savannah stared at the pile of horse manure on the stable floor and then gasped. She shook her head. "Is this... Are we... No. When you said a girls' day, I heard 'lunch and shopping.' I did not hear 'volunteering at a horse stable.'"

I tried to hand her a shovel and gave her a toothy grin. "It's only for two hours. After we finish here, we can go to lunch, and I'll even go shopping, though it'll be under duress."

She shook her head. "No." She pointed at the pile of horse manure and shook her head again, then looked at me with horror-filled eyes. "You do not expect me to use that..." She pointed to the shovel. "To pick up that!" She splayed her arms. "Do you see what I'm wearing? It's Kate Spade!"

I laughed. "I'm positive that came from your trust fund and not your husband's salary." I attempted to hand her the shovel again. When she wouldn't take it, I grabbed a pair of boots behind me and tossed them on the ground next to the pile. A horse neighed in the stall next to us. "Put those on so you don't ruin your shoes."

"We can't do this and go out in public." She squeezed her nostrils. "We'll need to stand in a car wash for at least an hour to get rid of the stench." She backed out of the stall and stood behind the gate.

I tried not to laugh, but the giggle betrayed me and snuck out. "I made a commitment to do this, in honor of Tommy. Come on. It's only two hours, and I promise, I'll never ask you to do it again."

"Why did you ask me in the first place? You knew how I'd feel about it."

"You're my best friend, and it's Tommy's birthday. Did you expect me to ask Kyle?"

"It's Tommy's birthday? Oh hell. You're pulling on my heartstrings."

"Is it working?"

She looked back at the horse manure, grimaced, then shook her head. "Not really."

"Sav, listen. I made a promise to him, and I haven't even begun to keep it. This is about as good as I can do for the moment, and I really didn't want to do it alone."

She sighed with great exaggeration. "Fine, but we're getting mani-pedis too, and you're getting nail tips."

I gasped. "Oh no! The dreaded tips! However will I survive?" I smiled. "I'll do that for you because you're supporting me." I opened the gate, and she walked back in. I handed her the boots. "I'll go get you a cover for your dress. Wait for me."

"As if I'd start this without you."

She had two pieces of a tissue stuck into her nostrils when I returned. I handed her the cover. "Wait, I need a picture of this."

She held the cover in front of her face. "If you ever tell anyone about this, I'll make you cut your own switch from a tree and tan your hide with it."

My eyes widened, and I tried not to laugh. Savannah wasn't in bad shape, but her strength wouldn't compare to mine. "You'd have to catch me first. And seriously, did people really do that?"

"Are you kidding? My brothers left two trees branchless in our yard because Pa made them get so many switches."

I laughed.

We spent an hour cleaning the stables, and then, as promised, we headed out for manicures and pedicures. Savannah and the nail tech tried to convince me to get tips put on my nails, but I couldn't imagine handling a suspect with them. Besides, I wasn't a tip kind of girl. I wasn't a manicure kind of girl either, but it was the least I could do to repay my friend for shoveling horse manure.

Kyle was making dinner again when I returned home. It had been six months since Chip Stuart died, and we hadn't had any other murders in Hamby. The case was complicated and tasking, and it frustrated all of us that he died before he could be tried in court, but we knew we had our guy. Catching him with the last victim and his deathbed confession were enough to close our investigation.

Michels found a secret computer during the search of Stuart's home, but it was so tightly secured, Bubba hadn't been able to access it.

He'd continued to try every chance he'd had but still hadn't had any luck.

Stuart's confession still haunted me. His last words played back in my head, and I couldn't let them go.

One, two, three, you can't pin on me. Seven, eight, nine, I'll add to my crimes. Four, five, six, add to the mix. If it meant what I thought it meant, then Stuart didn't kill the victims in Alabama, and he'd referred to that shortly before he died. Was that what he was going to tell me? Would I ever know?

"Rach? You there?"

I shook my head slightly to bring me back to reality. "I'm here. Sorry, was just thinking about something."

"It was a dead man's way of messing with you, babe. He did it from the start. Don't let it consume you."

"I'm not," I lied. "I was thinking about how strange it is that Bishop's in a serious relationship. You know how that impacts partners. She'll get jealous, insecure, and he'll ask to change. He'll get Michels, and I'll end up with some newbie or night detective I can't stand."

"She won't get jealous, and you won't have to change partners." He handed me a bowl of mixed greens with an assortment of veggies chopped up and folded in. "Put this on the table for me. They'll be here any minute." The doorbell rang as he said that. He smiled at me. "She's going to love you."

"We'll see about that." I opened the door and greeted Bishop and Catherine with a smile. Before they could walk inside, Bishop's and my cell phones rang.

EPILOGUE

One, two, three, you can pin on me. Seven, eight, nine, Stuart added to his crimes. Four, five, six, he'll add to the mix. The Mastermind has returned, and the sinners will burn.

The young woman lay on the ground as if she'd just tripped and fallen. He admired the dried blood crusting over where her neck had been slit. She was beautiful, her long blond hair lying haphazardly above her head, her makeup smeared and smudged from her crying and begging for her life. Complete imperfection, exactly as he'd wished.

He'd paid attention to every detail, followed every rule, and the Mastermind was pleased. He gently kissed her forehead, then smiled into her open eyes. She was exactly as he instructed, and it would begin again.

He set one plastic baggie inside her right hand and left the other next to her body. They would know. Someone would tell them. The chase would begin again.

As he walked away, the plastic bags on his shoes crunching against the fresh spring grass. He turned toward the girl and smiled. "It's time."

FATAL SILENCE
Rachel Ryder Book 6

"One, two, three, you can't pin on me.
Seven, eight, nine, I'll add to my crimes.
Four, five, six, add to the mix."

The riddle still haunts her.

Months after Detective Rachel Ryder exposed the madman who killed six people, she can't forget his sinister puzzle...and when the body of a young woman is found on an elite golf course with a familiar set of clues, Rachel can't escape the impossible feeling that an old enemy has risen from the grave.

Thrown headlong into an investigation that feels eerily similar yet strangely different, Rachel and her partner Rob Bishop fight to stop the past from repeating itself. But they're walking straight into a dangerous game of cat and mouse—and when someone from her team goes missing, Rachel begins to realize that she's playing right into the murderer's plan.

More innocent lives are on the line. If Rachel fails, their blood will be on her hands. Can she unearth the truth behind these seemingly copycat murders? Or is history doomed to repeat itself with devastating consequences?

Get your copy today at
severnriverbooks.com

ACKNOWLEDGMENTS

First and foremost, I'd like to thank my readers! The way you've responded to Rachel and her counterparts brings me great joy. I am so thankful for your positive comments, gentle urgings to write faster, and your wonderful emails. To know I can write something that makes people stay up late to read is a fantastic feeling!

I am grateful and blessed to have an expert team behind me. Thanks to Amber, Mo, Catherine, and the rest of the team at Severn River Publishing. They do the real work, the behind-the-scenes hard stuff that allows me to sit at my computer and make things up.

A special thank you to Major Ara Baronian with the Georgia Public Safety Training Center, for always answering my calls and texts, having the patience to muddle through my crazy questions and knowing the answers. Oh, and for never flinching when he suggests a mode of murder, and I get crazy excited at the idea.

A big thanks to Forsyth County Georgia Assistant District Attorney (and State Judge elect) James Dunn, who, minutes after meeting me, gladly gave me his cell phone number. He probably regrets that, but his answers have been helpful and important to this series.

Another big thanks to Forsyth County Georgia Fire Department Division Chief Jason Shivers for graciously answering my questions involving fires, how they're handled, and who's in charge. I hope I didn't mess it up too much!

Thanks to Lynn Shaw for being with me since book one and pushing me to not give up! And to my niece, Allison Winkse, for organizing my story histories and knowing the answers to my questions regarding what I've written in the past.

Thank you to my husband Jack, my best friend, my biggest fan, and the person I am most grateful for in my life. I would not have taken this leap if you hadn't held my hand and jumped with me.

ABOUT CAROLYN

USA Today Bestselling author Carolyn Ridder Aspenson writes cozy mysteries, thrillers, and paranormal women's fiction featuring strong female leads. Her stories shine through her dialogue, which readers have praised for being realistic and compelling.

Her first novel, *Unfinished Business,* was a Reader's Favorite and reached the top 100 books sold on Amazon. In 2021 she introduced readers to detective Rachel Ryder in *Damaging Secrets. Overkill,* the third book in the Rachel Ryder series was one of Thrillerfix's best thrillers of 2021.

Prior to publishing, she worked as a journalist in the suburbs of Atlanta where her work appeared in multiple newspapers and magazines.

Writing is only one of Carolyn's passions. She is an avid dog lover and currently babies two pit bull boxer mixes. She lives in the mountains of North Georgia as an empty nester with her husband, a cantankerous cat, and those two spoiled dogs. You can chat with Carolyn on Facebook at Carolyn Ridder Aspenson Books.

Sign up for Carolyn's reader list at
severnriverbooks.com

Printed in the United States
by Baker & Taylor Publisher Services